WHAT WAS THIS STRANGE POWER, THIS FIRE THAT BOUND HER TO THIS ARROGANT MAN?

She yearned for him, longed to be within the sound of his voice and the sight of his eyes.

CeLa remembered the tales of the heroes, the legends of men who walked with the gods and were made as they. Was it so strange that the man who had saved her life, who had given her tenderness and courage in the bitterness of her fear, should now walk in her dreams? He was the first man who had touched her woman's flesh and aroused it. Cruel he had been, but were the gods not also cruel, and for less reason?

She shivered in the heat, for she knew, without knowing how, that their futures were intertwined.

"Let him turn to me, great ones!"

She spoke the words and knew that they were heard.

THE
WINGED LION

ANNE CARSLEY

A Dell Book

Published by
Dell Publishing Co., Inc.
1 Dag Hammarskjold Plaza
New York, New York 10017

Dell ® TM 681510, Dell Publishing Co., Inc.

ISBN: 0-440-19600-0

Printed in the United States of America
First printing—November 1981

To ETHELRED
Un chevalier sans peur y sans reproche,
for all the days

THE
WINGED LION

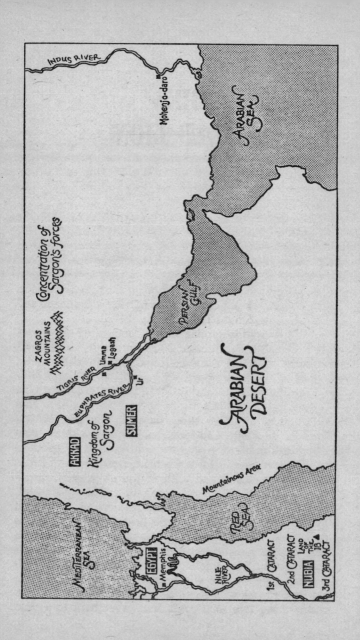

1

Perilous Path

CeLa paced up and down on the flat roof of the house as she looked toward the distant river, barely visible in the evening haze. Her green robe, faded from many washings, snapped with the speed of her movements. She frowned in concentration as she strained to see one certain face on the crowded streets below. Increasing dread made her heart hammer, and her slender fingers twisted convulsively.

Where could Nandar be? A moon and more ago, her father had announced his intention to go as a private scribe to a merchant who planned to escort his own shipment of grain far up the Euphrates. They would be paid in kind and the landlord would be satisfied for the first time in months. The ship had been due to return three days ago but the golden orb of the moon had faded and there was very little food in the house.

CeLa stood still for a moment, hearing the tuneless chant that Argi, the harelipped, mute slave girl, cheaply bought in a reckless moment, called music and, beyond her, the calls of those revelers in the streets as another night of pleasure began. It was pointless to stand here and worry, but it was impossible to banish the apprehension that grew stronger with every breath. The smell of cooking fish mingled with rotten odors as the wind rattled palm fronds in the courtyard below. The moon lifted yet higher and she turned her face to it as memory went back to a time

in her earliest youth when they were still a family
and, as such, had often taken gifts for the god as they
stood in awe at the mighty ziggurat of Nippur, city
of Enlil. She remembered the awe and the fear less
distinctly than the sense of being ringed about with
love, the warmth of human caring. Time had run
together for her since then. When she looked back on
recent years, they seemed a series of swift scenes. Bartered boat rides down the swath of the river, the
often begrudged food and drink for a day's scribing,
the bickering and haggling for lodging or a wage,
the hard work of cooking and cleaning that must be
done even before she was scarcely out of childhood,
while Nandar sought the vagueness of drink that
alone could give him peace.

The chant was grating on CeLa's nerves now as it
rose even higher. She heard her strained voice and
felt the grit on her lips as the wind rose.

"Argi! Stop that this instant. Surely there is something for you to do! Must I come and lay out your
duties again?"

Argi's sudden silence was eloquent. So was the rattle of earthen jars and the emphatic thud as one
broke on the hard floor of the eating area.

Ashamed of her outburst, CeLa lingered on the
roof rather than go down to supervise preparations
for the necessarily scant meal. She must face it. she
told herself. If some disaster had not overtaken the
ship itself, then Nandar must either have been robbed
or gone to a tavern somewhere. The little that might
come in must be spent for food even before buying
the tablets necessary to his trade when he practiced
it. Too often he bought the tablets of others, myths,
epics, legends, and read them over and over, so CeLa
had been taught in those long-gone days.

It was dark now and still very hot, for the errant
wind had died. It was growing noisier as well in this
crowded area near the river. The houses were close

together and the rooftops looked out on each other. Passers in the street could almost look through to the backs of the houses in some places. The dull mud walls were dusty, yet gave some measure of coolness.

She went down the side stairs and entered through the roughly cut doorway into the small room where Argi had set out the barley cakes and thin beer that would constitute the evening meal. They could not even afford a sweet in honor of Nandar's expected arrival. So had it been with them for the last several evenings that he had been expected. Now CeLa ignored the reproachful look Argi gave her as she moved across to the door that faced the street.

"Ho, my pretty, come out and join us! Don't be shy." A large drunken man, one of a party, stopped to call at her as she drew back.

"My husband comes from the docks. You should not linger in our doorway." The answer was as automatic as the question and taken in that spirit. CeLa had sometimes had occasion to use the dagger at her waist, but her tongue was as quick.

She heard the laughter as she jerked the hangings back and retreated to the eating area where she poured out a little thin beer in a cup, then moved to an alcove where a crude shrine was cut out. The image there was round-eyed and stubby, with crudely cut hands held together over a suggestion of a paunch. He had a subtly menacing look but the mouth had an almost human smile. Intar was the personal deity of their family who watched over them, credited with their honors and excoriated with their losses.

CeLa poured the beer before him, then bent respectfully. Was he actually there and in a mood to listen? The elder gods were capricious, why not he?

"Intar, hear me. This offering is poor indeed, but you know our circumstances better than we. Watch over Nandar, bring him safely back. That is all I ask of you. I promise that somehow there will be rich wine and sweet cakes, incense to assail your nostrils and meat cooked before you. We have served you faithfully."

Her words drifted off as her mind added in mutiny, And what good has it done? Poverty and fear, a bare living only. Her eyes, dark brown with amber flecks, watched the stone face half in hope and half in resignation. The hot air and the smoke that still lingered from the cooking pressed down on her as she put a hand to her forehead.

There was a touch on her shoulder as Argi pushed the remaining cake and her own portion of beer toward her. The slave girl was sturdy and heavy, several years older than CeLa, who was sixteen. There was a wealth of patience in the dull eyes as she pantomimed that her mistress should include this in the offering to Intar.

CeLa smiled and felt some of the heaviness lift. "I thank you, Argi, but we have given as best we can. Intar will understand. There is no need to deprive yourself. It is with the gods."

Argi looked long at the family god. She might have been adding her own prayers to those of CeLa. Then she went out, leaving the portions. There was no need to tell her further. Argi could be most stubborn, and perhaps it would make a difference. You never knew the whim of the gods.

CeLa lay down before Intar's shrine. She would watch away the night here. It might be that the god would be impressed with such daughterly devotion. The hours seemed endless as the noises of the street rose and faded. The sense of doom had returned more strongly than before, encompassing not only Nandar but herself as well. She let the past roll over her once more as she gave way to the familiar resentment and love.

CeLa could remember little of Nippur, the city where she had been born, the city which some said

was the greatest of all those in Sumer. They had
lived in a wide, bright house that was filled with
laughter. In those days Nandar had been a respected
scribe and scholar who talked often of the gods and
their mysterious ways, a wise man who believed in
learning and had already begun to school his young
daughter in knowledge beyond her years. Then her
mother, Lilda, had been delivered of the son for
whom she had never ceased to pray. Delight had
grown as still another appeared from her womb. Then
her life blood soaked the mats of the sleeping room
and the old woman who had come to attend her had
not thought to be quiet before a watching child's
queries.

All three died. Nandar attacked the woman and
nearly killed her. CeLa had nightmares for months
afterward. It was not long before they left Nippur
and went into the desert, where she was left at an
oasis with some of the nomads sheltering there. When
Nandar returned from his lone wanderings, he was
a dour, cold man who spoke only when necessary.
His earlier warmth had gone forever.

CeLa remembered the next few years as ones of
constant travel. Much of their time was spent in the
desert with those of the nomads who asked no questions. Some of it was spent working in the fields that
surrounded the cities near the rivers, when workers
were needed in times of flood and planting. They
had journeyed to Ur, where Nandar once again
worked briefly as a scribe, but his hands had begun
to shake so badly he could not continue. Their debts
had run up and finally they had departed because
they could not pay. More frequently in the past several years, Nandar had found sufficient work to be
brought to whatever hovel they were living in at
the time and CeLa had learned to inscribe the tablets for him. The pay had been drunk up promptly
until she learned to demand enough to live on.

For the past three months they had lived quietly in this rude house in Lagash, for it was no longer easy to wander as they had done. The times were becoming restless. Bands of plunderers were abroad, killing and stealing with impunity. War was always being threatened between the city-states and rumor bore news of it.

They had been more settled in Lagash than anywhere previously and CeLa had dared hope that this might last. Nandar had begun to study again, emerging from his drunken haze at times to reckon and write, setting CeLa harder tasks as her skill grew. The thirst never left him but it was muted. She walked about the city often with Argi beside her and became familiar with the shops, the temple courtyards, the streets of the artisans and the great docks. The river called her, the ships lured her and she dreamed of sailing down the mighty stream to the far lands of the gods.

Sometimes now, Nandar would tell her of the old legends when god strove with god for the love of goddesses or mortal women, of the darkness and light of Dilmun, of paradise and of man who was but the servant of them all. He had said, "And in the end it is all nothingness, a mere tale. We are but toys and wind." The jug had been raised many times in the days that had followed.

CeLa shifted on the floor and watched the gray light lift on Intar's face. One evening not long ago, Nandar had startled and frightened her as she placed the inevitable beer and cakes before him. He had looked directly at her, as if seeing her for the first time, rather than with the gaze that was so often opaque and staring, as if he saw only from within.

"This is no life for you, CeLa, it never was. The time has gone so swiftly . . ." He stopped and let the words trail off. "You are a woman now and unprovided for."

She was glad that she could mean the words as she said, "Father, the freedom of our life pleases me well. I am more content than many women, I think."

His hand shook as he poured out the beer and drank. "I have been foolish."

Nandar had always been slight of build but sturdy. In the past year he had begun to shrivel and his gaze would slide past those to whom he spoke. Only when he taught her or worked did his old authority return.

CeLa said, "My father, do you truly think that I would wish to be confined to the house only, preparing to tend it or another, my world bounded by the demands of hunger, thirst and cleanliness? You have taught me mathematics, the ways of the stars and the gods, of the lands beyond the river, of the writing and all that may be learned. Do not reproach yourself on my account."

She might not have spoken for all the interest he took. "I must see to your future, then it will not matter what else happens."

When Nandar set his mind to something, it was best not to interfere or attempt to dissuade him. Usually he would forget of his own accord or return to the comforting fog in which he lived.

CeLa was soothing. "You have much to consider, I know. Will you come and rest on the roof in the cool?"

She shifted now in the light of the new day and felt her eyes scratchy from lack of sleep. Faint nausea twisted in her stomach. Something had happened to him, she knew it now. She saw again the suddenly clear gaze he had given her on that night they had spoken, and the words that might have been sharp were simply those of the old Nandar: "She has been with me all along and I have not seen it. The gods have had their jest and we are the losers."

CeLa was not to know that he had seen Lilda in

her daughter; the bright amber-flecked eyes, curving dark brows, straight nose, smooth, lithe limbs, swirling dark hair—all were Lilda. But even more so was the independence of thought and the loyalty—all gone. He had laughed long and loudly before reaching for the jug and retiring to his safe world.

The next day Nandar had returned sober from a trip into the city and announced his plan to travel with the merchant. "The pay will be good and when I return we can make plans. I would see you safely wed, CeLa, your future assured."

She had protested but he was adamant. He had gone because of her and now whatever had happened to him was her fault.

The day drew on to be hot and heavy. CeLa set Argi duties about the house but she could not bring herself to go out seeking even the cheapest food. She went to the roof again and waited there even as the heat rose. It would not be long now.

It was early afternoon when the clatter below warned her and she descended to the ground just in time to see a tall, heavyset man whose hair and beard were carefully crimped approach her. His traveling clothes were stained but they were rich and in the latest style. The heavy red face was pocked, the small eyes hooded by folds of flesh. Two servants were with him; a slave carried his cloak.

"You are Nandar's daughter? I am Hanor, the merchant, returned only this morning from the voyage. I must speak with you."

Knowing that it was bad news, she could face the assessing look with composure as she led them into the courtyard. Her voice was level as she said, "I am grateful that you have come so quickly. I have only beer to offer you for refreshment."

He waved a ringed hand. "Is there another woman in the house?"

"Tell me." She faced him, small breasts moving under the thin robe, the compact body shivering. "He is dead, is he not?"

"Yes. He drowned when the boat lurched in a sudden storm only a few days out of this city. His body could not be found. We had to go on. You may take comfort in the fact that his end was swift and the gods merciful."

"How were his spirits? Was he well? Before, I mean?" Urgency rang in her voice. The blow had come and she still lived.

Hanor watched her covertly. He had noted the mean little house, her mended robe and gaunt cheeks. "He seemed well, lady, but I had no speech with him, you understand. I was told that he had been a good scribe. Naturally, he did no work, so there is no pay. But I felt that I must see you personally."

CeLa smiled slightly. She was probably being cheated. She would never know if Nandar had been drunk or not, but he would never have sought conversation with such a one as this. Her father had done what seemed best to himself and there it must rest. She felt sorrow rise in her as she inclined her head.

The merchant was discomfited. "If you are in need, perhaps help can be arranged."

"I am grateful to you, but there is nothing that can be done. You will understand if I ask that you go. I must be alone for a time."

"I can send someone to be with you. Another woman can be most helpful at such a time. Food, soothing wine, then I can call on you again. Alone as you are, there will be much that must be done."

His gaze licked at her and she saw his hands move convulsively. She stepped back, spread her legs and folded her arms in front of her as she said, "I have no wish for further dealings. You have given me the news and offered help, which I have refused now and for the future. No. Let it be at an end."

Red flamed in Hanor's face and his eyes narrowed but he did not pretend to misunderstand. "As you will have it." He called angrily to his followers, who moved after him as he stalked to the door.

CeLa went into the little shrine and stood tearless before Intar. She could not think of the future now, only the past. Perhaps the great gods had willed that Nandar die and their own deity could do nothing. Her pain and her vigil, Nandar's own years of loss were as nothing, nothing, as were all before the will of the great ones. She could not stay here and think such thoughts; offense would be taken.

The image looked placidly down at her, however, and she held both hands out in entreaty as she said softly, "Grant him peace in death, for he never found it in life. Give him safe journey. He died long ago."

She bent her head then and wept at last for her father.

2

Invocation of the Goddess

CeLa and Argi spent the next several days in mourning. The slave girl was devoted to her mistress and tried to do the washing, cleaning and meager cooking duties that CeLa, hating them as she did, usually delegated to her; the girl found release in hard work that dulled the mind. During this time CeLa did not go outside the house except to the roof in the cool hours after midnight. Time seemed to stand still; everything was changed, yet all seemed as before.

Then one morning CeLa was awakened by Argi's urgent gestures. The landlord, Ba-Nur, had come for the rent and she must face him with the small stores she had, which were not enough for one person, let alone the two of them. Wearily she rose and went out.

Ba-Nur was an old man and shrewd. He had heard of the scholar's death and sympathized, he said, but what could a man do? He too must live. He rubbed his bald head and his chins moved like wattles as he watched the girl.

"I will give you what we have. Then if you can wait several days until I can earn more . . ."

"I have already waited far over the appointed time. Now tell me, how is a young girl such as yourself to earn what is due?" His voice rose as his bulk shifted from side to side.

CeLa stood very straight. She would not divulge that information; the scheme that had come to her in the night might have been put there by Intar himself. "Give me five days and you shall have what you require."

"I am a man of business. I well understand your sorrow but you must know that I could rent this house and more like it for double the price that I charge you. People are flocking to the city now that the battles are beginning to come closer to Lagash."

CeLa did not care about the skirmishes that were always going on. Determination edged her voice and the fierceness in it made new fires light in Ba-Nur's loins that even his new and fourth wife had not been able to kindle.

"Five days is little enough. What can you lose?"

"You have need of a protector. Much can happen to a young girl alone." His eyes glittered as his tongue moistened thick lips.

CeLa wanted to laugh in spite of her concern. She had fended for Nandar and herself too often to fear now. He had always been there, however, as a buffer and consolation. She could not antagonize this man yet, so she said, "I will think about what you have said, Ba-Nur. Still, give me the time I have asked. For the mercy of the gods."

The landlord took his leave then, already thinking what a choice morsel the scholar's daughter would be.

CeLa sat long in the stillness after he departed. It was the future with which she must be concerned now, with the fact of surviving in this world equipped only with her wits and the learning Nandar had given her. The mist had left her brain and the guilt was beginning to fade; it was not in her nature to look back.

The morning air was fresh and cool, the sky cloudless as CeLa, with Argi respectfully behind her, made her way toward one of the small marketplaces close by a lesser temple of the gods. She wore a loose tunic of common weave, a shawl over one shoulder, battered sandals and a wrapped headdress to shield herself from the sun and to disguise her womanhood. Argi carried her writing materials. It was CeLa's intent to offer her services as scribe to those transacting business of such importance that it must be written down then rather than memorized and recorded later. Surely, enough could be made in this manner to enable them to live until she could decide what the pattern of her life was to be.

They settled near one of the walls away from the temple grounds and the compound controlled by the priests. The implements of her trade were set out, and Argi stood ready to call attention to her work if a customer should chance by.

It was good to be in the world again and CeLa felt her spirits lift as Lagash roused itself for another day. A man went by driving several sheep and goats on the way to the temple area. Behind him straggled a boy with quantities of wool. A donkey-drawn cart followed. It too was heaped with goods. Two men dressed in rough, wrinkled tunics pushed another cart filled with fish. A swarthy woman had begun to display some gaudy jewelry nearby and a storyteller was already making expansive gestures. A young girl set down a wine jug and filled a proffered cup before taking the extended coin. A family arranged pots and clothing, to lure the customers. The smell of grilling meat from a nearby cook shop caused CeLa's stomach to tighten hungrily.

The sun grew hotter and the flood of people increased. Soon the wall no longer shaded them and CeLa shifted the hot turban she wore, longing to remove it. Nearby two men began to argue heatedly about shipments, errors and the calculated harvest. A tall man paused briefly beside CeLa and Argi to say, "You are newly come to these precincts? I have

not seen a scribe here before. Might you not do better within the compound, rendering service to the
gods and the priests?"

CeLa drew back slightly, for his manner was one
of authority. Nandar had worked among several scholars who had recommended him to others. She knew
that her ability was not equal to his, yet scribes were
honored for their learning and it was rare to see one
in the marketplace. Now she bent her head and
tucked her hands in the folds of the shawl. Her voice
was husky. "A vow of humility, sir, that must be
served out."

He lifted ringed fingers to his neat beard but his
eyes were piercing as he said, "Then I will question
you no more. Such an example is to be commended
in these decadent days."

He passed on and CeLa felt the sweat trickle coldly
down her back as she watched. There was no reason
to be afraid. The exchange had been most casual,
but the warning had come and she breathed a quick
prayer to Intar for safety.

The argument between the two men had progressed considerably during the past few minutes. One
put his hand on his dagger, then started forward,
but the other called out, "Stop. You know the penal-
ties for fighting so close to the temple!"

"You are afraid! Come away then, and we will settle this!"

The first man, a rotund, richly dressed tradesman,
snapped, "Don't be foolish. Come, the scribe shall
record our differences and we can settle them in the
courts. Or do the men of Umma settle their disputes
in other ways?"

Even though she was new to Lagash, CeLa understood such a thrust. The cities had been enemies for
years in arms, trade and culture.

They came to stand angrily beside her, both speaking at once, demanding attention as a crowd began

to gather. The man of Umma glared at his rival,
then commanded her, "You shall record for me first,
scribe. Write swiftly now."

She took out a fresh clay tablet and a newly sharpened reed stylus, then said slowly, "Tell me the gist
of what you will say. I will shape it."

He stared incredulously at her. He was short and
thin, his clothes hung with jewels, his manner sharp.
Now he turned to the other and gave a sneer. "I can
tell you this, in my city we do not allow the lower
classes to speak to us in such a manner. I will teach
him to speak properly, then you and I will settle
our business."

With one swift gesture, he caught CeLa by the
arm and pulled her up. The turban went to one
side and the long black hair fell shimmering in the
sun. She grabbed for the shawl but it was gone and
the tunic gaped open to reveal a smooth breast. The
onlookers laughed but some gave cries of horror.

CeLa jerked the tunic up with one hand and
brought the tablet down on her attacker with the
other. Rage enveloped her and she gave no thought
to the danger of a public brawl. She had been thwart-
ed enough. After the pain and loss of the last few
days, it was bliss to release her feelings.

Tempers flared easily in the heat. It took little for
the crowd to find grievances. The man of Umma
dropped CeLa's arm even as she hit him, but someone caught him in the face with a heavy hand. He
fell to his knees. The fat merchant cried, "Spy! You
spy for your city and she is likely with you. You
sought to take advantage of our justice!"

The cry was taken up. "Scribes are not women.
Take her!"

"Call the soldiers! We are betrayed!"

And more deadly still, "Kill them!"

CeLa dropped the tablet pieces that she held and
took up the dagger that she always carried. Argi held

one of the triangular-tipped styluses, although it would avail her little against the angry crowd that seemed to be growing in numbers.

No one heard the chariot until it was upon them; the two donkeys drawing it had made little sound. Suddenly, however, the guards surrounding the occupant, who sat alone on a small fixed seat, parted and one roared, "Stop this at once!" At an unseen signal, the six of them moved forward and drew their swords.

CeLa stared even as the crowd did. The brawl was forgotten as they looked at the woman in the chariot. She had risen to her full height, at least as tall as the tallest man there. Her headdress was of beaten gold and covered her hair entirely. Jewels flickered and shone in the sun. Her tunic of blue and gold was elaborately flounced and flowed over her body. An intricate collar of jewels was wound around her long neck. Points from it touched her full breasts. Her mouth was wide, arrogant. Dark brows arched as she demanded, "What is this that you demean the very dwelling of the god? Do you think he will look kindly upon those who do so?"

There was such a silence that CeLa could hear the fowls clucking and scratching in the pen by the far wall. The black eyes met hers, held, moved on and returned. CeLa gave her look for look. The silence drew out, it seemed that they were struck dumb.

The woman said, "Disperse these people. Shut down the marketplace. Such happenings are offensive at a time when all our efforts must be obtained to dispose the gods, all of them, favorably toward Lagash." She spoke with such an intensity that those nearest the chariot moved back, watching her with awe.

A woman cried, "Intercede for us, Sirna. Call on the Mother for us."

The cry was taken up and repeated. The dark woman stood tall and proud, not deigning to heed.

She lifted a hand and they fell silent. The finger pointed straight toward CeLa.

"Come to me, girl."

The people moved away so that a straight path opened before the girl. CeLa stood unmoving as Argi pressed close.

"Shall I have you fetched?" The tone was almost conversational.

"Had you that in mind?" CeLa could not have said what made her answer so to such an important personage as the woman must surely be. She thought herself a fool, then knew it for pride, the pride that had stood well for her when there had been nothing else.

"I will ask you to come with me to the temple of she whom I serve." The intonation had not changed but one flick of her finger had altered the first movement of the guards.

"Why, lady? What do you wish of me?" She put out a hand to Argi, who caught and held it. "I am of the poorest of Lagash and do not know your goddess."

The crowd gasped and began to mutter. The woman laughed and this time the dark eyes were incandescent.

"The Mother of us all. Ninhursag. She has many manifestations." The glow left her eyes and they were cold again. "You are not of Lagash."

"No." CeLa was puzzled anew at the power that radiated from her questioner. "Once of Nippur. Now a wanderer."

"I would speak with you. Afterward you shall go as you wish and not be the poorer for it." This time she asked freely, with no hint of command in the rich voice.

CeLa could not resist her answer even though she knew the anger she risked. "I will come because you now ask. My slave must come also."

The woman looked at her without expression. "It is well. The guards shall bring you to me in two hours' time."

Two of the guards stepped to CeLa's side; another took Argi's arm. The others moved back to their places as the servants in back began to clear the marketplace. The chariot swept away as they followed after.

The temple stood on a mound that was terraced and topped by a ziggurat. Surrounding it were the usual grounds and compounds where business was transacted, artisans worked, classes were taught and archives kept. They entered by a passageway from the back and were almost immediately swallowed up in a maze of passages. The dark woman and her followers had vanished earlier. CeLa and Argi were taken to a small, bare room and were given a bowl of water for washing, a handful of dates and some strangely heady wine by a woman servant who did not speak. The girl vowed she would ask no questions, but she was beginning to wish she had not dared to challenge the priestess, for such the dark woman must be.

"You are summoned. The slave remains here." The servant had returned, her face expressionless as she waited for CeLa to follow.

CeLa smoothed her fingers over the unruly hair, adjusted the ill-fitting tunic of coarse cloth, lifted her head and said, "I am ready."

Once again she was enveloped in passages where there was little light. They passed through a little room filled with carved, round-eyed figures set in the walls and even in the ceiling. Musical instruments stood about and jewels shone in some of the eyes. Finally they went between two high, clammy walls, the space so narrow that they were forced to turn to the side in order to pass, and came out into a well-furnished chamber. Couches were set about; an elab-

orate frieze of gods and men took up one wall; woven
mats lay on the floor; a table was laden with fruit,
cakes and wine. A thronelike chair stood in the center of the floor and in it sat the dark woman, wearing a loose garment of white and gold, a tiara of
jewels glimmering in the unbound black hair that
fell curling to her waist and below.

The servant knelt but CeLa did not, nor did it
seem expected. Instead she bent her head slightly and
said, "I thank you, lady, for your hospitality, but I
am at a loss as to why you have so honored me."

The woman smiled and the power of it lit her
with that strange incandescence once more. "I am
Sirna, priestess of Ninhursag, representative to her
and her voice in this land. She is the source and the
light. Honor to me is honor to her."

CeLa stared, then felt her gaze waver, for Sirna
had begun to sway, taken up in the intoxication of
her words.

"How may I serve you, lady?"

Sirna's voice was matter-of-fact now and slightly
cool. "It is imperative that we who serve here know
what goes on in the city, be it small matters or large.
Such a brawl as you were in has a cause. This is
not the time to stand about in small factions. Tell me
of it, tell me of yourself."

CeLa found herself sitting on the couch facing the
chair, eating, drinking and talking. Her earlier anger
vanished in the warmth that came from the priestess.
Nandar, the travels, her youth in Nippur, the veiled
demands of Hanor and Ba-Nur, the very aimlessness
of her future, all came out.

"I wanted only to earn enough money to live until
I could decide what to do. I had thought to seek a
position as a scribe in the temple or royal archives
but I doubt they would take a woman. Still, I must
try."

Tiny points of flame burned in Sirna's eyes. "The

goddess demands many servants, CeLa. I think you could serve her well. Lagash is in peril but there can be safety and more, if we will to take it." Her voice trailed off but the huge eyes fixed on the girl's and CeLa knew suddenly that she looked at danger.

3

The Mother of Life

CeLa stretched languidly as she threw back the softly woven coverlet that had covered her naked body. Three days of good food and wine along with rest had done much to lift the haunted look from her eyes and restore her spirits. She touched her hip bones and felt them less prominent. A sense of well-being permeated her as she glanced around the room.

It was long and narrow with a separate alcove for sleeping. The floor was of red and black tile made from clay; the walls were whitewashed. On one of them was painted a maiden offering fruit and wine to a goddess whose features were hidden by a cloud but whose female body was sensual and proud. Tablets Sirna had sent her stood on a table nearby. They were from the archives of the temple and told of the remote past when gods and men spoke freely with each other. A small image of the goddess whose temple this was, Ninhursag herself, sat in a wall niche. Before her sat dishes of food and jars of wine.

A slave glided smoothly in just then and bent her head to CeLa as she put down her burdens. Cakes, a light wine, some spicy meat and cucumbers; more food than she usually ate or saw in two days, thought CeLa wryly.

The girl was saying, "When you have refreshed yourself, lady, and bathed, the priestess Sirna asks that you walk with her on the terrace."

CeLa responded in kind. "It will be my great pleasure to do as she asks."

The slave withdrew and CeLa paused to wonder at the strangeness of her time here in the temple. She had not seen Sirna since their meeting day but the hospitality offered was surely far in excess of that routinely dispensed to the unfortunate. She remembered Sirna's glowing eyes with the savagery in their depths, the repetitive language, the intensity of manner, and knew that she must walk carefully.

Water was brought, first warm, then cool. Two silent slaves washed her despite all her attempts to dismiss them, saying simply, "We were bidden, lady." A loose robe of white was skillfully draped from her shoulders, the waist caught with a jeweled pin. A wide band of gold held back her dark hair and pins secured it at the nape of her neck. CeLa looked at herself in the polished orb held up to her and said involuntarily, "I have never looked so in my life."

Oils and perfumes had been rubbed into her body and face. She had soaked in soothing baths during her stay and now much of the weather-beaten look had left her. Her softened skin glowed with youth and freshness, her eyes sparkled with vigor. She looked once more at herself and thought that Nandar had been right. She was a woman ready for the making of her own life.

Before leaving the room, CeLa looked at the image of the goddess who was crowned with leaves and held the palm of fertility. She was far from Intar now and could only hope that this great one would look with kindness on the supplicant who took from her.

"Show me what I can do here, Lady, to walk in my own way and in my own worth."

The prayer came unbidden and she murmured the words to herself but she saw the slaves exchange nervous glances as they hastened to guide her on her way.

They went again through a series of passages that led to a terrace open on one side to the pouring light of day. Steps went down and up from it. There was a broad section between the two staircases and on it stood the cloaked figure of Sirna. CeLa looked at her for a moment; she seemed oblivious to their approach. Great columns decorated with brilliant colors only slightly faded by the winds and sand upheld this level of the terrace. There was a statue of Ninhursag in an alcove to one side. Beyond the columns CeLa could see the sprawling city, the lively compound and the faint glitter of the river.

Sirna turned suddenly and once again CeLa was struck by the beauty and power of the priestess. She too wore white with a headdress of the same color. On her breast was stamped the same branch of fertility that the image of Ninhursag held.

"You have rested well during these days, I see. I am pleased." She held up a bare hand as the girl started to speak. "You need not be concerned for your slave. She works in the kitchens, as I understand she did in your home, and she seems well content."

CeLa said, "I have much to thank you for, lady, but we cannot continue to accept your hospitality. I must seek to earn our living, the landlord must be paid. Already you have helped us greatly."

The dark eyes bored into hers as the straight nose wrinkled. "It was understood, was it not? I said that the goddess needs worthy servants. You are young, reasonably fair, virgin and intelligent. You have known adversity and privation. There is reason for you to be grateful. The landlord is paid, the house is doubtless rented again. He was told that you had left the city. Hanor the merchant heard the same."

CeLa whirled and faced Sirna in a fury. "How

dared you seek to arrange my life in such a way? I
have no will to serve your goddess, and my life is
my own to handle as I see fit."

The priestess did not move but the little points
shone in her eyes as she said, "All live only to serve
the great gods, CeLa. Your life is theirs, not yours,
and to doubt that is to blaspheme. How do you know
that the hand of the goddess has not been over you
since you entered Lagash?"

She felt a chill run down her back as Sirna spoke.
Her tongue froze before the words of rebellion could
leave her mouth, and she heard again the taunting
words of Nandar as he spoke of the uselessness of
the life of man. Here in the temple of the greatest
of all goddesses, she, a mortal, had said and thought
such things as might be the death of her.

Sirna saw, and her voice was gentle as she spoke.
"I knew when I saw you standing in the marketplace
that you belonged here. The Mother spoke to me
and I but obeyed, as you must."

The hot wind blew against CeLa's flushed forehead. All at once she felt awkward and foolish. An
image rose in her mind as it often did. She thought
of herself in one of the high reed boats sailing down
the river near Lagash, on to the Tigris or the Euphrates and the waters beyond. Free. Free to ride
on a camel into the wide desert to the oases and to
wander as she might. Their wanderings had made
life with Nandar worthwhile. She saw that now and
knew that to herself she could not lie. She opened
her mouth to say something of this and saw Sirna's
eyes, deadly and fixed on hers.

"It seems that I have been given little choice in
this." She spoke mildly, carefully.

"None." Sirna waited for the rebellion to pour out.

CeLa looked out again toward the distant walls of
the city, anywhere to escape Sirna's implacable stare.
Logic told her that it was foolish to think she could

resist, even more foolish to want to do so. The only recourse for a woman was marriage. If her husband died and left her property, she then could have a life of her own and none could say her nay. If she entered the service of the goddesses, it was not likely that she could rise to a powerful position, but at least comfort and security were hers. CeLa did not doubt that with her learning she could do well here. She knew with all the power within her that danger was within these gates and that her freedom was not the only thing threatened.

"Forgive me, lady. And ask the forgiveness of the Mother. I have not yet overcome the sorrow from my father's death. You are right, of course. I have been fortunate."

The deep voice was hypnotic, honey-sweet. "Feel no sorrow. Your father serves now in his way as you do in yours. Do not mistake me, CeLa. The goddess will not have an unwilling servant."

"And the alternative?" She could not resist the question, which hung clear and revealing between them.

"It would not be feasible for you to remain in Lagash having spurned her goddess." Sirna spoke smoothly, watching her.

CeLa turned from her and went to stand before the goddess in her alcove. "I will serve her right willingly if she will have me." Her words were as smooth as Sirna's had been but in her thoughts she prayed, I do not lie. I but dissemble, for I am afraid.

Sirna came close to CeLa and the girl caught the odor of costly fragrances as she said, "Welcome to this house. Now go and rest, for there is much to be done." She clapped both hands together and the slaves came running.

As they went out the door, CeLa heard Sirna's voice lifted in chanting as she knelt before the image. There was a note of passion and urgency in the

chant that made her skin prickle, for there was no
mistaking the overriding triumph it held.

The days after that were full for CeLa and she
seldom saw Sirna. After the early morning rituals of
worship were completed, she was taught by a priest
who was so old that only determination and love
for his subject maintained him. The old stories of
the pantheon of gods and goddesses were reiterated
and emphasized, with those of Ninhursag paramount.
The duties of man were sternly delineated, both in
this life and after death. Throughout the repetition,
CeLa gave him her full attention, as she had been
bidden to do.

Then came the special rites: the observances of approach, the interpretation of dreams, the movements
of the stars and their meaning, the sacrifices suitable
at various times of the year, the flooding of the rivers
and the changing of the seasons as ordained by the
gods—all these were taught by priests of an age to
be remote from temptation. Although CeLa had
known much of this, the knowledge had been frag-
mentary, and she absorbed it all now eagerly.

The best time of all, however, was when she was
taken to the separate building that housed the archives where many of the temple scribes worked.
There she was allowed to study the tablets on any
subject at leisure. She read history, law, poetry and
legend, even the temple accounts. But those which
fascinated her the most were those which told of
travel into the far lands: Magan, Meluhha, the Silver
Mountains, the haunts of the gods themselves, trackless journeys into the desert, voyages of many moons
to another great flowing river called the Nile. The
exploits of Gilgamesh, King of Erech, were both
written down and told at every place men gathered.
Here she once more followed him as he, both divine
and human, crossed the seas and the mountains in
search of life without end.

When the cool of evening came, she walked in the temple gardens, which were kept well irrigated and green. Palms rustled overhead, flowering plants of all types reached toward the tiny ponds and the tinkle of musical instruments was heard. Another image of the goddess overlooked all.

At first CeLa had thought that she alone came at this time of day and that others might come at well-regulated times. But now and again she saw other women and girls, robed like herself in white, drifting about. One of them, a girl of her own age, was sitting on one of the benches placed invitingly around as CeLa approached one evening after she had been in the temple for some three weeks. As she caught sight of the girl, who started to rise hurriedly, CeLa said, "Don't hurry off. Stay and talk to me." She was surprised at herself, for the company of others had never been particularly sought by either Nandar or CeLa. Now, however, she realized how anxious she was to speak to another person of all that had happened in this strange place. She was not prepared for the expression of sheer fright that came over the other girl's mobile features as she stood erect and straightened her draperies.

"It is forbidden. I must go." She looked at CeLa with fear and fascination.

CeLa moved directly in front of her so that she could not continue on the path or turn back without going into the pool. "Why is it forbidden?" Her voice felt rusty from disuse in normal conversation after speaking only when the tutors allowed it or to the slaves who followed her constantly. "Are we not all in the same service?"

The girl stared but CeLa saw that she shook with what could only be terror. "Please let me pass. If I am found here in converse with one such as you, I dare not think of the consequences."

Anger licked at CeLa but she forced her voice to

remain soft. "One such as I? What does that mean?"

She was not prepared for the expression of sheer horror that came again in minutes and manifested itself in the jerking movements of the slender body or for the halting words that finally came, sending a shock of fear over her own body.

The girl said, "The Chosen are set apart for the great rite of the goddess. You know this and seek to toy with my ignorance."

CeLa caught her arm and felt it tremble under her fingers. All the sincerity she could muster went into her voice as she said, "But I do not know. I have been isolated since I was taken from the streets by the charity of Sirna and asked to serve the great one. I have been told nothing and was not aware that I was a member of a select group for some special service. Tell me what it is!" It was a demand.

Wide black eyes looked into hers even as the full lips shut tightly. CeLa saw that she would get no answers here. With a strength born of panic, the girl jerked free and ran as hard as she could toward a door on the other side of the garden.

It was very silent in the area as the faint sliver of moon rose. CeLa stood still as she thought of the way she had been kept from others and the watch maintained by the slaves who had not been so cautious this evening. It was strange too that of those in the garden none had ever come close enough for even casual conversation. Enough of this mystery! She would demand to see Sirna, force an explanation. Her palms were suddenly wet and she knew that she was afraid of the dark priestess.

A soft voice spoke suddenly beside her. "Forgive us, lady, for not being here with you. The slave who attends you here mistook the time and will be punished for it." It was one of the slaves who usually paced beside her silently, impervious to questions or comments. Now the voice hardened as the woman continued, "None have troubled you here, surely? All has been quiet?"

CeLa forced herself to become calm and turned slowly to say, "Very quiet and peaceful. I am suddenly very sleepy and would retire to my couch." She held herself very stiffly so that her body would not shake.

The slave thought her suddenly haughty and protested, "You will not be left unattended again, lady. I promise it."

CeLa knew that suspicion was diverted even as she gathered her skirts about her ankles and prepared to stalk away. "I certainly cannot find my room without assistance. Guide me there instantly."

"Certainly, lady. At once."

CeLa knew now that some danger was very close. All her senses were alert and poised, as they had been since she had first seen Sirna. This talk of rites and the Chosen frightened her inexplicably. There was no one to ask about it and she could not approach Sirna. Her fate must hang on her own wits and courage, virtues which were fast leaving her.

She tossed long on her couch before an uneasy sleep took her, a sleep filled with swirling shapes that called and cried to her as she fled before them into an inferno. Fire and water lifted as she fell and jerked awake to find herself dripping with sweat. Even her hair was soaked.

There was to be no more sleep for CeLa that night. The air had the feel of that last darkness before the dawn. A slave slept across her doorway; another was within call. A wall torch burned before the goddess in her alcove. The girl sat up in the half light and used the coverlet to dry her trembling body. As she did so, she remembered the words she had read in the archives days before and which had seemed only of casual interest at the time.

"The Mother is life incarnate, even so is she death.

In the shadow world she demands as in the fleshly one. In her are both met—thrice blessed is the mortal who walks both roads in the great choice."

Then had followed the carving of the goddess holding a skull and a knife, balanced on the other by her symbols of motherhood and fertility. Great breasts had been both sensual and eloquent of life.

CeLa knew then, with all the instinct of a threatened animal and with all the logic that Nandar had taught her, that death awaited her in the temple of Ninhursag, Mother Goddess of Sumer.

4

Upon Whom the Hand Has Been Laid

The knowledge that burdened CeLa must not be allowed to show, but she knew that the night had left its mark on her from the sidelong glances the slaves gave her and the increasing sharpness in the old priest's drone at the morning lessons. She felt her fate coming closer, yet was seemingly powerless to prevent it.

She heard the distant sounds before the priest did—trumpets, drums being beaten, shouts and cheers. Sandals slapped the floors in the corridors that were normally hushed at this hour. Then came the echo of singing and the blare of the temple trumpets. The door to their chamber opened and a young priest came in to bend respectfully before the older one and whisper in his ear.

He stood up, assisted by the younger, and waved at CeLa. "Go, woman. Your slave waits outside. I am summoned to council."

Boldly she said, "What has happened?"

Both priests stared at her in surprise. It was not proper that a woman should speak before her superiors, and certainly not so lowly a one as this newest handmaiden of the goddess. Then the younger one could not contain himself, so important did he feel.

"Abdar, the high priest himself, has returned from secret negotiations with his fellows in another city which is unnamed. The future of Lagash is said to

hang on these talks. I am sent to summon all priests
to come at once."

His fellow gave him a quelling glare and he subsided as they went out after directing CeLa's slave
to take her back to the women's section of the temple.

CeLa spent the next few hours in her room, to
which food was brought. The slave who waited on
her simply repeated, "You must remain here for
now. These are the orders of the priestess." Demands
for information brought nothing else, but there was
fear in the woman's eyes and her movements were
jerky.

Exhaustion took its toll and CeLa slept finally,
without dreams. She woke refreshed and found that
in some strange way the edge of her own fear had
abated. The unknown was, after all, the unknown.
She did not doubt her instincts and knew that she
must remain alert, but she no longer felt frantic. To
what god she owed this, she did not know, perhaps
the Mother herself, but she was grateful.

Her slave entered with wine just then and said,
"Lady, we must hasten. All are bidden to watch as
the high priest is welcomed by the Lady Sirna in
formal ceremony."

"Where has he been?" The question was idle. CeLa
had studied of the ancient days but knew little of
the current news. Possibly some threatened skirmish
between neighboring cities, with priestly intervention
sought. Lagash had undergone a savage battle some
years ago in a dispute with Umma over water rights
and much of the city had been damaged. The king
of Umma had held sway over Lagash and added her
name to his steles, his official tablets. It had been a
bitter time and only recently had the animosity begun to cool. This much she had learned from her observations when she first arrived in Lagash, but battles were not uncommon, though this had resulted in

much destruction, and neither she nor Nandar had been very interested.

"I do not know. It is said from a great mission."

Later CeLa walked down a winding passageway she did not remember with three slaves in attendance. She wore the inevitable white but this time a gauzy veil was suspended from a crownlike headdress and a heady fragrance drifted from the oils with which she had been lavished.

They joined others dressed as she on a long balcony that overlooked a small courtyard that abounded in images of the goddess. Two richly ornamented and inlaid chairs were placed on brilliant mats. Behind one stood several priests and behind the other were several of the older priestesses. CeLa looked about her and could not help but see that, crowded as the area was, many of the other women were isolated by the slaves around them.

Suddenly the great temple drums sounded, trumpets blew, then a silence fell. Into that silence walked a tall, bearded man with straight shoulders and a proud bearing. He stood in front of his chair, his face hard and set. CeLa stared down at him in sudden awe. Abdar, the high priest, was the man who had spoken to her in the marketplace that day, he who had remarked that no scribe had been seen there before. Those who spoke of his journey had seemed to think it had been far. Why had he wandered about without the panoply of his great office? Even now he was not richly dressed. Only a band with a rich jewel placed on his head set him apart. Yet power and strength exuded from him.

The drums rose again and this time timbrels and flutes joined to do honor to Sirna, who was resplendent in golden draperies edged with blue. Jewels hung in her ears, flamed in her bound hair and cascaded down her neck. Her tall body moved in perfect rhythm as she came up to Abdar, bending her head only slightly even as he touched her fingers and guided her to the waiting chair. They sat down and now the musicians waiting nearby advanced to begin the hymns of praise to the goddess.

It was the heat of the day and although the ceremony was not unduly protracted, to CeLa it seemed to go on forever. The ritual invocations, the citing of the blessings bestowed and sought, the sacrifice of the birds and the libations of wine, the joining of these two mighty servants of Ninhursag in harmony, all paced on. CeLa yawned cautiously behind a sheltering hand, almost forgetting the night terrors. Then she was jerked back into reality, a reality that was all the more deadly for the brilliant sun and the little breeze lifting the damp hair from her forehead.

Sirna was looking directly at Abdar, who was gazing off into the distance. In her stare was such malevolent hatred that her beautiful face was momentarily changed into a mask out of a nightmare. Could he not see it? CeLa wondered that Sirna could so show this in public. Almost as though she felt the girl's gaze, Sirna inclined her head so that she was once more the smooth, serene priestess of the Mother. But the black gaze snaked upward and CeLa betrayed herself by jerking back.

Apparently no one else had seen, but now CeLa was acutely aware of the careful way Sirna and Abdar kept from touching and the icy formality in their parting bows. All knew that at times the goddess honored her chief servants by her presence in their bodies in divine union. But here it seemed that a kind of contempt was offered and accepted. CeLa told herself that she was imagining things. What did it matter to her if temple intrigue were rife? She had best gather her wits and begin thinking of some way to escape this place.

In all her time in the temple of Ninhursag, CeLa

had been watched and supervised in ways both delicate and overt. Sirna ruled supreme in her own area,
as befitted the high priestess, but her influence extended into the areas of wider power as well. In the
next few days it became more and more clear that
the affairs were shifting. There was an all-pervading
air of tension. Tempers were short, people hurried
back and forth, there was much consultation and
discussion. It affected the girl in that she was often
left alone in the particular section of the archives
that she frequented. Scribes and clerks worked in
other parts of the building but they were concerned
with their own pursuits. Slaves were assigned to clean
and polish, to be there in the event that their masters wished refreshment or had duties for them, but
even in the state of constant alertness required they
would seldom notice a small girl dressed unobtrusively.

CeLa did not really know what was causing the
general unrest but she meant to use it to her own
advantage. The white garments laid out for her
daily were the mark of whatever role Sirna had set
for her; to wear them was a badge. Fortunately she
had retained the old robe she had worn when she
first came to the temple. For sentiment's sake, she
had said, when they sought to remove it. Now she
could only think that even in this place Intar still
watched over her.

The next evening she did not walk in the garden
but moved restlessly back and forth in her room until far past the usual hour for sleep. Suddenly she
called one of the slaves to her and demanded, "Sleep
is far from me. Send someone to the archives and
fetch me the tablets I was working with this afternoon. I will return them when I go there tomorrow."

CeLa had learned that if she commanded in that
hard voice she would generally not be refused, especially if the request were simple. Now the slave

girl, unknown to her by name for they were rotated every second night, took several steps back and looked at her mistress in fright.

"Lady, only the high priestess can remove tablets from the archives."

"You will not wish to disturb her to ask her." CeLa saw the chill come over the girl and hated that she must continue. "Do as I say, else I shall tell her myself that you have been recalcitrant. I do not think she wishes one of the Chosen to be disobeyed."

At the use of the term the slave turned paler yet and CeLa longed to shake whatever information she possessed out of her.

"I obey, lady."

"As well you should. They are on the table in the corner where the most ancient records are. Hasten with them."

The girl's reaction told CeLa that something of her position was known to even the lowest echelons of the temple. The fear she exhibited was similar to that which Sirna, for all the power of her will and the charm she often chose to use, seemed to engender in people.

Several hours later the girl returned with the tablets and carefully deposited them before CeLa without looking at her. CeLa then spent much of the remaining hours of the night ostensibly staring at them while going over her plan, such as it was. It was full light before she allowed herself the luxury of rest.

It was the time of afternoon rest when CeLa wrapped the tablets carefully in the old soft robe and started for the archives. Her slave was a new one, awed and nervous. CeLa snapped at the girl several times and saw that tears were held back with an effort. She was not likely to hover.

They passed few people as they moved through the corridors, and the big dim rooms of the archives were

almost deserted. CeLa reached her corner, put down
the tablets and settled herself as if to remain for
hours. The slave came as if to stand behind her but
jumped as CeLa rounded on her.

"How can I even try to understand these with you
constantly making noises and moving about? Get away
from me!" She sounded petulant to her own ears
and not at all fearsome, but it was otherwise to the
younger girl.

"Yes, yes, I am sorry." She scuttled away, almost
tripping in her rush.

CeLa was shaking in her own turn. Her hands left
clammy prints on the surface of the tablets she held.
There was no help for it; she must continue with
her plan. Slender and risky though it was, it was
still the only means she had been able to devise. It
would have to do. She had tried to go against the
logic that told her she imagined the danger, but the
instinct was too strong. Prayer was useless in the
very household of the goddess who must surely have
meant this fate, whatever it was, to overtake her.
Intar was but one god before the mighty and who
knew but what his favor might leave her as well?

CeLa sat straighter, outwardly composed as she
set her own tablets for copying, but underneath she
was remembering Nandar's sour conviction that man
was but a plaything to those he worshiped. If that
were so, and who could know, it was best to trust
oneself as far as one could and not wait for the whim
of a god. Blasphemy, said one part of her mind. Save
yourself, said another. It was Nandar's daughter who
obeyed.

Slowly she freed the tablets of their wrappings,
held the robe down by her feet, waited an agonizing
moment, then rose and moved behind one of the
shelves and then another. Nothing stirred near her.
From a far corner an old man snored peacefully, the
sounds almost muted in the ancient calm.

CeLa crouched down farther and jerked the white draperies from her body. It was the work of a second to pull the robe over her head and settle it loosely around her waist. A white circlet had held her hair up and back. She pulled it off and wrapped it with the material, then thrust it all into a crevice made by several heavy tablets that she had arranged the previous day. She could only hope that no one would seek out these low shelves for a time. Now she loosed her hair and plaited it roughly back, then smeared her face with the dust of the floor. Her feet were bare; she had often walked so in preparation for this day. With luck no one would recognize the handmaiden of the goddess in the lowly slave who had been sent into the archives with a message.

Behind these shelves was a door sometimes used by the priests. In all her time in the archives, however, CeLa had seen fewer than five or six enter by it. Everyone else used the main entrance. It did not really matter where it led so long as she was able to escape and put some distance between herself and the immediate area. Surely it could not be a dead end, since she had seen it in use.

There was no time to think further. CeLa crept close to the entrance, pulled at the handle, and the door slid noiselessly open. She moved silently through it into blackness.

She paused on the rudely cut steps, waiting for her eyes to become accustomed to the change from light to dark. Her breath came in uneven gasps and her heart hammered. Her whole body seemed stiff. Now that the first step was taken it was almost impossible to take further risks. She wanted to huddle down and wait but there was no time.

CeLa forced herself to scuttle down the several steps that led to a passageway only slightly less dark. She could touch the walls on either side by extending

her hands from the wrists. Something slid across the
floor in front of her and she suppressed a shriek by
clamping her teeth into her lower lip. At least she
was going down. There must be a separate way out
of the archives, for that building and the temple were
joined.

She came at last to a larger hallway where there
was talk and the slap of sandals as people went to
and fro. Now came the test of her disguise. She must
walk among others as though she knew where she
was going down. There must be a separate way out
was no way to know which passage led out; it was
blind chance.

A large woman carrying a load of the draperies
worn by male and female alike came waddling by.
She was followed by a small boy carrying more of
them. Far behind her came two men, somberly dressed
from what CeLa could see, deep in conversation. She
slipped out and began to walk some few paces behind the woman, as if part of the procession tending
to the washing.

The woman was less oblivious than CeLa had
hoped, for they had gone only a short distance when
she stopped to adjust the wide sandal she wore and
caught sight of the girl.

"What are you doing, girl? I've not seen you here
before." The voice was penetrating, the tones flat.

In agony CeLa heard the footsteps of the men behind her stop. The boy peered into her face and began to giggle. She made her face dull, her eyes worried as her toes began to twitch in the dust. "Looking for the kitchens. Lost, I guess. The man told me
to go work in the kitchens, said I would be fed."

The woman leaned closer, assessing her. "Who
told you that? You're a long way from the kitchens,
I can tell you that." She laughed raucously.

CeLa thought hurriedly. "The man from here who

buys fresh things in the market every day. I said I
was hungry and would work hard, that I wanted to
see the goddess. He said . . ."

The woman was losing interest at such a common-
place happening and her bundle was growing heavier. "Well, come along and I'll point you in the right
direction. I don't know what this place is coming to,
hiring girls off the street that way. You'll need a
bath before putting in an appearance anywhere, but
that's not for the likes of me to say, I'm sure."

She babbled on and CeLa followed meekly in her
wake, thankful to be close to someone who so obviously belonged here. The hurrying footsteps increased behind them, then the men elbowed past the
laundry woman, who gave vent to further expostula-
tions even as she shrank against the wall. CeLa heard
their words in that brief moment and her blood
chilled.

"Other physicians must be summoned. If he dies
and that slut rules, Lagash is doomed."

5

Judgment of the Gods

CeLa felt in that instant that they must mean Sirna. She could imagine no other in the temple who might excite such vehemence. But who was near death? She brushed it from her mind. What did it matter so long as attention was occupied elsewhere? But the incident was a grim reminder of the danger she knew she faced.

They walked up a slight incline into the blessed air of twilight. CeLa had not thought it would take so long for her plan to work out. It was doubtful if the alarm had been raised yet; the slave had been thoroughly cowed. The normally bustling courtyard was quiet as they went toward the temple and along the side toward the gates that led to the kitchens.

CeLa's escort was fuming, "Dirtier and dirtier every day. What do those great ones do that demands so many changes of clothes and headdresses? I don't get more help but they can still take such as you to be one more pair of useless hands in the kitchens. You're too small to be any good at washing. I ought to protest. I ought."

The child shifted his bundle and moved closer to her. CeLa looked about for the cause of the strange silence. The woman ceased talking suddenly and all three looked at each other.

"Something has happened." The fat woman's chins began to tremble. "It's never this way at this time of day."

CeLa looked toward the gates through which people, carts, processions and supplicants ordinarily flowed. They were locked, and barricaded. On the various levels of the ziggurat and terraces the last rays of the fading sun caught the gleam of weapons from the guards who stood where none had stood before. She heard her lout's voice say, "What is it? They'll know in the kitchens." It was no use to try to get out of the temple now. Safety lay in numbers and it was certain that all the slaves and other help in such a place as this could not know each other.

They jostled together as they hurried for the wide door to the kitchens. It was filled with people, but all were silent and still. The area was large, with several hearths, high, wide shelves filled with supplies, a great wall lined with pottery jars. Pots and pans of various types took up another section and there was a wide stone area set apart for the preparation of food to be cooked. In one corner was food evidently to be readied for the next meal—onions, barley for cakes, cucumbers, fish and birds.

Heads turned as they entered. The fat woman whispered to the first person she encountered, "What is this? What calamity has come upon us?"

The man turned and CeLa saw that he had been weeping. His headband was awry and his mouth twitched with the effort of speech. "My Lord Abdar, the high priest, is stricken. It is said to be mortal."

CeLa forgot her guise as she demanded, "He was well only recently. What manner of illness is it?"

They stared but the present matter was too grave for idle speculation. The man who had told them of the illness said now, "We have come to petition the goddess for his life. Yes, and to seek our own gods as well."

CeLa wondered at this, for it was not often that a high priest was a tangible entity, a living person, to the people of his household. Usually he was the voice of the god he served and none other.

Their informant was continuing, "The tax collector sought to take thrice over from my son who is a fisherman with a large family. Time and again this happened. To whom shall a poor man turn? He has not the ear of the king. The high priest himself gave ear to me when I called out as he passed in the street. The matter was soon righted and I was given work in this temple."

The fat woman said, "We were all given extra food and clothes in the fearful times after the battle with Umma."

They grew silent then and CeLa perceived the truth of much that had filtered to her while they lived in Lagash. In this city there was a freedom that had not been known in other cities. The hand of the tax collector was not as heavy. Temple and ruler were wary of each other but did not generally prey upon the other's rights. Even the poorest were considered to have some degree of dignity. She thought of the history she had read and of the battles that all men will fight. Whatever the reasons for the loosening of the reins, it was apparent that the high priest had been concerned for the citizens of Lagash.

The fat woman spoke twice before CeLa heard her. "I am Nardo, chief laundress here. What is your name?"

"Tia. My uncle recently died. He worked outside the walls in the fields but his place was quickly taken by another. I came inside to look for work but could not find any. In the market I met the man who sent me here."

It was a thin enough story but CeLa gambled on their agitation to let it pass and she was right. The man who had talked of the kindness of the high priest turned back to them.

"I am Ard, clerk in the treasury. I do not know what work can be found for you while all activity is suspended, girl, but I do know that we waste time in talk that should be spent on our bellies before the goddess."

CeLa wanted to question him further but dared not call attention to herself. She stood staring before her until Nardo snapped, "Come, Tia. We will go apart here and beseech the Mother for the life of her servant."

The girl followed Nardo to a less crowded corner of the kitchen and listened as she began the ritual prayers in a thin, wailing voice. Others came to join them and soon the air was full of the supplications of the faithful. CeLa cried out, too, but was well aware that she might anger the goddess by turning aside from the fate given her. Or was it perhaps that she was indeed chosen to rebel in order to meet what was ordained? Her swiftly ripening sense of self-preservation made her yet more fervent.

Time passed and her stomach began to growl angrily. There was food in plenty on the nearby hearth, but if she ventured to help herself she might be noticed unfavorably. She pressed her stomach and repeated the prayers once more. It was no use. Weeks ago she had been as accustomed to hunger as any other poor person, but good food eaten regularly had taken its toll. It had been long since the morning barley cake, which she had only nibbled on.

Cautiously she slid out and back from the press of people. A few quick steps brought her to the hearth, where she snatched up a hard cake and bit hungrily into it. Her teeth rattled on the edge; it must have been left there days ago. The noise in her stomach increased in volume as she set the cake down and turned to look for another. So intent was she that she did not see the hand extended until it

THE WINGED LION 53

touched her shoulder. She jumped back with a street
oath.

"Take this cake. It is fresher."

She looked up into the unsmiling eyes of a tall
dark man in dusty clothes that proclaimed him a
laborer. His beard was unkempt, his black hair was
half hidden under a turban and his swarthy skin was
burned even more so by the sun. His nose was aguiline
and proud, his brows arched over fierce black eyes
with a shimmer of gray in their depths. They were
arresting. She could barely wrench her gaze from them
and when she did it was to notice the firm leanness
of a body that was well disciplined. His lips were
as finely carved as though by a sculptor.

"Thank you." She bit the words off ungraciously
but took the proffered cake and downed it hungrily.
No one was paying any attention to them, so CeLa
turned openly to the long shelves in the general direction where she had seen food earlier. This time
she took part of a bird as well as a cake and then
a peach that stood in a basket close by.

The man had not turned away as she had expected
but came closer, still watching her. His voice had
the slight trace of an accent but she could not recognize it.

"Do you not share the grief over the high priest?"
His tone was conversational and light but there was
a snap in the question.

CeLa could not answer at once, for the juice from
the fruit was dripping down her chin and she was
forced to wipe it with her already dirty sleeve.

"Of course, but that does not mean that I cannot
be hungry also." It was the first full sentence she had
spoken to him and she saw his eyes narrow as if in
curiosity. She felt a faint chill run over her back and
knew that he did not miss the reaction.

"I can see that you were indeed hungry." Again,

the merest touch of accent. He was smiling now, his
teeth shimmering white against the dark beard.

CeLa looked up at him. "Do you find hunger amusing?" She felt the beginnings of anger even though
she knew that the man's master probably lingered
here, leaving the servant free to roam about, and he
but sought to pass the time. Her nerves were giving
way in the prolonged suspense and her increasing
fear of discovery.

He put a long-fingered hand on her arm and she
jumped. His eyes were contrite. "I did not mean to
offend you, mistress. My tongue went ahead of me
as it often does. We are all touchy here tonight, I
think."

He did not take his hand away and as CeLa continued to look at him, she felt it burning on her
flesh and the blood seemed to course more swiftly
through her body. Her tongue felt dry in her mouth.
He too was not unaffected, for she saw the shadow
that crossed his face and a pulse began to beat in his
temple. It seemed that all else was shadows, that they
stood alone in a vast and windy space as they swayed
toward each other.

She managed to say, "I am not offended. As you
say, this is a difficult time." Her heart hammered
savagely and she knew that he must sense her discomfort.

He pulled back from her then and a mask seemed
to come over the carved face. Only the dark eyes
bore the memory of pain. Just so had Nandar appeared once when he spoke of Lilda. "I think I see
my master yonder. The goddess guard you." He
touched her shoulder and again the fire ran down
her arm. Then he was moving lightly away.

CeLa walked back toward Nardo and Ard, who
seemed not to have missed her though she felt she
had been gone for hours. She glanced around for the
stranger but he had vanished and she tried vainly

to suppress a sense of loss. It was foolish to speculate
about what might have begun if she had truly been
only a maid from beyond the walls and he the servant he appeared to be. Instinct told her that he was
more.

Time crawled now. None of the others wanted to
leave the company so they huddled together as the
hours wore on. She watched but the dark man did
not return. She knew that what happened this night
would affect all their lives and doings. They could
not return to their homes because of the barred gates,
but those who had quarters inside the premises did
not make any effort to go to them. As frightened as
she had been in the long day or was when she considered the dubious future, CeLa felt comfort in the
shared wait. She put her head down on her arms
and let the world blur into haunted dark eyes touched
by dawning warmth.

She woke with a start to the clatter of sandaled
feet, the expectant murmur of voices and the sharp
sound of hands clapping. Three men, two of them
priests, the other a soldier, stood on the high steps
that led from another part of the temple. Their faces
were somber, their manner grave.

The whispers of the people stopped as the soldier
clapped again for attention. CeLa rose, the better
to see. Her legs were cramped and prickly but she
forgot her momentary pain as the older of the priests
came forward.

"The high priest, Abdar, is dead. It is the will
of the great ones and not to be questioned. He will
grace the netherworld."

He waited until the babble of mourning and excited comment slowed, then held up an admonitory
hand. Even across the room, CeLa could see how it
shook.

"Go now, all of you, and rest. The gates will not

be opened as yet, for the city must not be excited. You will have many duties to perform on the morrow, for it is likely that the king himself will come to pay his respects."

They turned then and left as they had come. Beside CeLa, Ard was shaking his head in sorrow. "He was struck down so quickly, I cannot understand it."

Curiously she asked, "Will the king indeed come?" With such a spectacle it seemed likely that one small slave might be able to dash out without notice.

Ard laughed without humor, the sound dry and unexpected. "The mighty King, Lord of Sumer, not the least of Umma and Lagash, is far too busy pursuing conquests in the south to return for the death of a good man."

Nardo was horrified. "Silence, lest you bring the wrath of gods and men alike down upon us."

CeLa said, "What am I to do now? I do not know where I should present myself in the morning and everything will be in an uproar. Nardo, you spoke of needing help in the laundry. I am capable and, after all, no specific duties were given to me."

The fat woman looked at her speculatively. "The next few days will be terrible indeed and there will be even more demands on me. No one could blame me if I used you."

People were beginning to thin out now that the worst was known. The three stood in a clump near the corner, their voices pitched low.

Ard was saying, "You don't sound as if you were a kitchen servant, Tia. Have you had learning?"

CeLa felt chills prickle the flesh on her arms. Was she to be so easily given away? "When we worked in the fields by the walls there was an old scholar who had sold himself into slavery for his debts. It amused him to teach me and several of the other children. He said it made him remember happier times."

"Ah, was it so? Can you read, then?"

"Of course not. He just talked about legends and the gods. I didn't really understand much of what he said."

Ard was mildly interested and would have talked longer in the effort to remove his mind from pain. Nardo, however, was exhausted and elated at the prospect of having help for an indefinite period of time. She caught CeLa's arm, called good night to Ard, and moved briskly out of the kitchen.

During the next two days CeLa worked harder than she had ever worked in her life. Great piles of the white draperies were brought to a bare little room just off the equally bare one where she and Nardo slept. Water was supplied by slaves who carried endless buckets of it. She kept the fire burning to heat it, then carefully washed the delicate fabric and carried it away to be hung in special areas set aside for the purpose. Nardo worked in another area, presumably doing the same thing.

The temple was a kingdom in itself, populated by craftsmen, scholars, laborers, slaves and servants. Many of them lived on the premises and very seldom went into the city proper. It was ruled by the goddess and those who served in her name. Even the conqueror from Umma, the king who ruled much of Sumer as well the old enemy, Lagash, might not make demands of the temple. Abdar had directed much of the policy with the king's wishes in mind, realizing that acceptance of the inevitable was necessary for the continued survival of the city, and he had been instrumental in many of the restorative measures enacted for Lagash. Abdar had been a remote sort of man, well liked and admired. Those who knew him at all had come to love him, but the city had seen him as the symbol of authority.

CeLa learned all this and more from Nardo as they sat in the evening cool. The woman was a gos-

sip; she kept up an endless run of chatter about this
person and that. The information about Abdar and
his policies was delivered just as she must have heard
it while passing officials in the hall.

"And he had best watch his delight in the boy
singers now that Sirna is supreme. Anything less than
complete devotion to duty will never do for that
one."

CeLa was not interested in the official's predilec-
tion for youth. She wiped a hand across her hot forehead and hunched her shoulders to ease the ache in
them. The mention of Sirna stirred the fear for the
future that had been pushed aside by the slavery of
the past days.

"Is it usual for the high priestess to rule? Will
another high priest be chosen?"

Nardo laughed. "The Lady Sirna is a worthy representative of the Mother. All the city knows this
and she is greatly admired. There is none to say
her nay."

Remembering the powerful woman and the pull
of her will, CeLa could well believe this even as she
thought of the nebulous fate that had awaited her.
She spoke carefully, "There is much that I do not
understand, Nardo. I heard someone speaking of the
lady only the other night. They mentioned those who
are called the Chosen and said that she was very
intimately concerned with them. Do you know anything about that?"

Nardo turned to CeLa and her eyes held the same
fear that the girl had seen in those of the slave in
the courtyard. Her voice shook slightly as she said,
"I have been here many years and known many secrets, but if you would live you will not ask such
questions. It is forbidden!"

"I did not mean to trespass in forbidden areas. I
was only curious. The words were dropped very ca-

sually. I did not know." CeLa saw that Nardo knew more than she would say.

"Those who speak so have often vanished. The ways of the great are not our concern. Remember that." Nardo glared at her one final time, then heaved herself up and was gone.

CeLa sat very still, no longer hot or tired. Deadly fear permeated her being once more and she knew that she must find some way to leave the temple before she died there.

6

Lady of Love and War

Early the next morning CeLa was arranging more of
the wash on the special lines where the sun could
strike it. She would return in an hour to move the
pieces about so that they dried evenly. Her mind
was as busy as her hands and as swift.

She had wandered near the gates of their side of
the compound after the conversation with Nardo
the night before. It had been natural enough, she
thought, for a servant to move about a little after
his day's work. Certainly she would attract little attention in the sweat-stained robe, her hair tangled
and greasy. The gates were open and the people of
the city passed through freely. A closer inspection
showed that all were observed by guards standing
nearby. Now and then a person would be stopped
and questioned but it was done so easily that the
human flow continued unabated. She had feared to
watch for very long but the pattern was established.
At the next pair of gates she saw that this still held
true. The guards were looking for someone. It might
or might not be herself. She doubted that it was, but
an assumption could not be made.

Now, in the clear light of morning, her face freshly
washed and her hair bound back, some of the dirt
soaked from her robe, CeLa knew that she would
take the chance for escape that evening. Surely she
would be successful if she merged with a group of
people who appeared to have been buying and sell-

ing in the compound all day. Her decision had been
made in the wake of the paralyzing fear of the night
before when she had realized that action must be
taken, that she could not stay in hiding. Far better
to battle than to live in fright. She had never thought
of herself as impulsive—life with Nandar had required planning and forethought—but feelings such
as she had experienced in the temple of Ninhursag
were like none she had known before.

Her spirits lifted and she hummed a bit of song.
The low tone carried to the ears of a temple guard
who was wandering over the premises he had been
ordered to check. So far everyone fitted the lists he
carried. Later, he knew, his report and others like it
would be evaluated by his superiors. In this restive
time it was best to be thorough.

CeLa looked up a moment later and saw the query
in his face as he demanded her name, duties and
manner of coming to the temple.

"Tia from outside the walls. I have been here about
a moon and my duties are as you see."

"Your name is not given here." Proud of his ability to read, he called out the names. "The laundress
Nardo has no helpers. Who chose you?"

CeLa looked at him and saw that his suspicions
were aroused. What was she to say? Would Nardo
help her? She temporized, "I was not thought suitable for the kitchens."

"You have not answered my questions. Come, girl,
you waste my time!"

"And you waste hers! Why have you stopped my
helper from her work? Do you have any idea of the
work that I must do, helped only in part by those
incompetents who can be spared from other jobs?
How dare you question her? I rule here!" Red-faced
and furious, Nardo advanced on the guard, who nim-
bly retreated, for her temper was well known.

CeLa would have laughed at the squabble of authority if the situation had not been so deadly for her. As it was, she stood her ground and thanked Intar, who must surely be watching over her to bring Nardo just at the moment her own ingenuity was failing.

The guard said now, "Everyone must be accounted for. In this section she alone is not. Rail about as you will, Nardo, I must be answered."

The fat woman was at a loss and her hands began to twist in her robe, which was wet across the front and at the hem from her work. CeLa saw her hesitation. The present danger must be removed, then she would deal as best she could with Nardo. She did not know if the woman would fall in with the story that had just come to her but she must try.

She said hesitantly, "I followed the temple steward in the gates and asked him for work in the kitchens. I was hungry and there was no work in the marketplace. I was told I might help there for a short time, but the very first night I had a falling down spell, which I have often, and was told that this made me unfit for service. I was weeping in the grounds when Nardo, out of kindness, stopped and said that I might work here, that the goddess needed all who could serve. Is it not so, Nardo?"

Nardo looked at CeLa and the girl saw the shrewdness in her eyes. "It is so. She has had fewer fits and may prove to be a good servant. I saw no use to speak to her further until I saw the quality of the work. The steward in charge of this section has lost nothing and I have gained a much needed helper."

The guard shifted uncomfortably, then backed farther away as he watched CeLa. "Well, if it is as you say, this must still be recorded now. The records must be accurate."

"Leave us to our work then, and do what you must. Be assured that if reprimands are in order it must be further recorded that I do the work of five others and this girl is necessary." Nardo was growing angry again. Her arms began to flail about, the muscles bunching.

"I can see that all you say is true." The guard glared at CeLa and turned hastily to leave before Nardo should further lose her temper.

"Thank you for helping me." CeLa felt the blood hammer in her veins and her whole body was tense with excitement.

Nardo was staring at her curiously. "Who are you, Tia? Why are you hiding?" There was no animosity in her voice and CeLa remembered her propensity for gossip.

"I serve the Mother, Nardo, and am specially commanded by her. Can you believe that all this is necessary and that the utmost secrecy must be maintained? I am not what I said, that is true, but your help will be recorded in the annals of the temple."

CeLa thought of Sirna's manner and tried to adopt the priestess's quelling gaze. Had she but known it, she had presence enough for Nardo as she stood there in the dirty robe, her profile lifted to the sun and her eyes more amber than black, fierce in their intensity.

Nardo moved back and spread both hands. Her manner was humble as she said, "Lady, are you from the high priestess herself?"

CeLa looked her full in the eyes and said flatly, "I serve the Mother. Her will governs all that I do. It is sacrilege to question further."

The girl was unprepared for what happened next. There in the lines of flapping draperies in the walled courtyard, Nardo knelt before her, putting both hands on her head as she moaned aloud.

"I am sorry, lady, I did not mean to question the will of the great ones. Intercede for me."

CeLa wanted to raise the great clumsy figure and

speak soothingly but she dared not. This unexpected gift must be utilized.

"You must go from me now and tell no one of this. Act as you always have done, and if the guard returns, say that you have sent me on errands of some urgency. Do this for at least the next day or so, then you may say that I have run away or some such. Secrecy is vital."

"I will obey. You have only to command." Nardo gazed up at her and CeLa saw the impassioned earnestness in her eyes.

"Good. You may go now." CeLa waited until the woman had walked shakily away, vowing obedience with every step. Then she sat down in her turn and allowed her stiff muscles to relax.

For a few minutes CeLa tried to assess her situation rationally but the sheer blessed relief of release from tension overcame all else. She knew that she must leave the temple without delay, that the small span of time given to her could not last. Nardo would be bound to babble of what she had experienced and other ears might not be so easily fooled. She remembered the fat woman's swift, cunning eyes then, and thought herself well warned. One must thank Intar and use one's wits as she had done.

There was no longer any point in lingering. CeLa knew that she must find a suitable hiding place until some of the people began to leave the crowded temple grounds. She thought swiftly. It would be strange to see an idler. She must seem purposeful. Fortunately for her, CeLa would go relatively unobserved in the great rush of activity as priests and people alike prepared for the ritual burial of one who had served the goddess faithfully. She had considered this earlier, after the guard had begun to question her. Did they have some reason for checking? What of the sinister comments she had heard

in the corridor and the disrespectful comments about
Sirna?

CeLa shook her head in confusion, then caught up
the dragging ends of her robe as she hurried from
the washing area, eyes down, a frown of concentration on her face—a slave given a task that must be
remembered and performed instantly.

Time moved weightedly for her that day; fear was
constantly at her back. She had time to notice that
although there was a great amount of rushing about
and frenzied calling, there was a general air of apprehension. People stood in little groups, gesticulat-
ing and whispering, then moving watchfully apart.
Soldiers were now more in evidence, and they too
moved in groups with alert eyes.

At last CeLa went back toward the general area
of the kitchens and took one of the narrow passageways that seemed to lead back into the bowels of the
temple itself. She would try to rest here until the
evening. Surely she could find some small niche in all
these twists and turns. She walked more slowly now
as her eyes gradually became accustomed to the deepening darkness. Her robe flapped around her ankles
and she pulled up the ends to secure them at her
waist. It was cooler and she felt the sweat begin to
dry on her back.

The passage continued to go down but the walls
were straight with no break. Anyone coming along
would see her and have the right to demand what
she did there. Still, it was only early afternoon and
it was far better to be out of sight in an obscure passage than to lurk in the compound. She would take
her time, go a bit farther, then gradually retrace her
steps.

There was a clattering sound behind her. CeLa
whirled, flattened herself against the wall and waited,
holding her breath. It was not repeated and the girl
forced herself to think that possibly a rock had fallen,

for the passage was far older than any of those she had previously encountered. She walked a little faster now, conscious of the smoothness of the stone on her bare feet. It was as if many feet had walked here at one time. A faint drift of incense came to her, too, as the slant of the floor became more pronounced.

CeLa stopped and stood very still. All her senses cried alarm but there was no sound. It was time to turn back, to flee for safety. She would go and simply stay near the mouth of the passage. Her mind made up, CeLa turned to go back. In that same instant, she heard a low snarling sound far in the distance. Coming as it did in the previously quiet area, it seemed magnified in intensity. Her head jerked in that direction, then back in the direction from which she had come.

CeLa cried out in horror, her mouth suddenly so dry that only a mewl emerged. She launched herself in panic at the slight bend in the narrow passage but it was too late. A wide slab of rock was gradually descending from the ceiling and settling into place. The final crunch and thud ceased as the doorway to release was cut off.

She stood staring for minutes after the dust had settled in the passage. Somehow she resisted the urge to tear at the stone and scream. There was no way to go now but forward, forward to whatever awaited her coming. She knew that she would not leave the temple and its grounds that evening. Perhaps she never would. Self-pity tore at her and tears filmed her eyes.

She whispered, "Intar cannot hear me. The Mother, Ninhursag, knows that I rebelled against her priestess. Great gods, what am I to do? Guide me!" Obedience to the will of the gods, known or unknown, governed everyone, but Nandar had been a cynic and his daughter had acquired some of the same quality. Even now in her extremity, CeLa could not yield

herself utterly as might be demanded. "I am not
meant to serve in your temple, Lady Goddess. Do
not penalize me for that."

Almost as if in answer to her, there came a series
of snarls and then a full-throated roar that rang
against the walls and sent the girl shaking to her
knees. The odor of incense was heavier now and it
mingled with the rank smell of wild beast. CeLa
sprang up and ran down the corridor. Anything was
better than groveling there in the dust.

The passage slanted again, grew dark, then gave
way to an open section on one side that had bars
over it. Beyond that, farther on into a dimly lit area,
came the sound of chanting. CeLa could only see
one thing, however—the great lion, tawny-maned and
fierce, pacing in his wide cage, coming nearer to her
as the human scent of fear reached him.

The bars looked strong to CeLa. It did not seem
that he could break free of them. Were there others,
she wondered? And why were they kept here in the
temple rather than in the royal preserves to be set
free so that the king might hunt? She stood irreso-
lute. The lion paused in his turn, standing with his
head faintly raised, his savage eyes on hers, the tip
of his tail twitching.

CeLa folded her arms together to stop their shaking and deliberately took her eyes from him as she
walked swiftly by the barred area. The low snarls
followed her but there was no rush to attack or any
sign of movement from the lion. The rush of courage that had taken her this far persisted now as she
moved on stiff legs into the short passage that led to
the next room.

The chanting stopped as CeLa approached and a
voice began to mutter unintelligible syllables that
were interspersed with a chilling laughter. She crept
noiselessly toward the door and peered around it; so

caught up was she that she would not have known
if the lion himself were loose.

The room was small but so filled with gold and
jewels that flamed in the light of torches that it
seemed twice its size. There was a raised platform in
the center on which a richly dressed figure lay. Its
hands were at its sides, the head crowned with an
ornate headdress. At the feet was the raised symbol
of the goddess. Nearby were tablets, ornaments, boxes
of jewels and draperies.

CeLa knew that this was Abdar, the dead high
priest, being prepared for his journey into the netherworld. He must go as well equipped in death as he
had been in life, for who knew what the great ones
would require of their servant?

There was a movement in the shadows as the laughter came again and Sirna came into the light. She
wore a gauzy pleated skirt and a halter of the same
material, both encrusted with gems. Her hair fell
down her back in shimmering waves. A crown of
palm fronds and gold held it back from her face. Two
live snakes were curved over her arms and waved
their heads hypnotically as their tongues flickered.

She looked down at the body and held her arms
wide, moving them back and forth as she laughed.
The torches blazed higher in the wind caused by her
movements. CeLa clutched the stone wall, unable to
move as the terrible gist of the words came to her.

"Abdar, my enemy, do you find it chill in the dark
world? Had you thought to visit it so soon? My
soothing potion was meant to ease your travel-weary
body. It did so, did it not?" The voice rose until it
screamed, then subsided to the barest whisper. "Did
you think I would let you stop me? More fool you!
Now we shall see who rules with the Mother! You
would have deprived her, now are yourself deprived.
Wisest of men! Protector of Lagash! Dealer with the

usurper! Truly my hand was guided!" Her laughter curled up again, triumphant and savage.

CeLa thought of the lion in his cage, less savage than this demonic woman who had murdered the high priest of Ninhursag and delighted in it. She tried to move her own cramped body so as to slide back into the shadows, but it would not obey her. In that instant one of the torches flared higher, Sirna turned and her fierce eyes met those of CeLa.

7

Despoliation

CeLa saw the recognition in Sirna's eyes and a darker emotion as well. There was no place to run and nothing she could do. If Sirna had not intended her death previously, she surely intended it now. With a bravado she had not known she possessed, CeLa pushed away from the wall and stood erect, giving Sirna gaze for gaze.

The priestess waved one hand, causing the snake on it to writhe. A swarthy slave darted out from one corner and advanced on CeLa. She had time to see that his nose and lips had been cut off before he was upon her, turning her about and binding her hands behind her back all in the same swift motion. Then she was jerked up, carried and thrown to her knees before Sirna. The slave melted back from the light as Sirna began to laugh again.

"Foolish one, did you truly think to escape? Such lies as you told! You had scarcely left the laundry before Nardo was clamoring to see me. One of the guards watched you from then on. When you strayed into this passage he retreated, knowing that it would be death to come farther. My slave was near you the rest of the way."

CeLa rose unsteadily, the tight cords already burning into her flesh, but she would not quail before this woman. "What do you want of me, Sirna? I only want to be free. I heard little of what you said here.

I assure you that temple affairs matter nothing to me."

The priestess leaned close to CeLa, who could smell the feral odor of her and see the wildly hammering pulses in her throat and head. "I am supreme here and your fate is ordained. You shall be punished before you go to meet it, however. The goddess is not pleased that you sought to avoid her."

"What do you intend to do?" CeLa was proud that her voice did not shake, that she could stare coldly into the huge black eyes.

"Do!" The laughter came again, all the more hideous in this place of death and decay. "The slaves who attended you, CeLa, who were responsible for you and yet let you escape. The girl you spoke with in the garden that evening. Do you wish to know their fate? Do you wish to know what happens to those who oppose my will? Why do you think my slave is tongueless and earless as well?"

"You had them killed? For so slight a thing?" This time CeLa's voice did falter.

Sirna caught her shoulder and pinched it in fingers as hard and cruel as the slave's had been. "Had them killed? No, pretty one, I did it myself and gloried in my obedience to the Mother."

One of the snakes slid down her arm, very close to CeLa's. The girl saw the movement. Everything swung before her and blurred. Sirna slapped her face so hard that her neck jerked and she fell again to the floor.

"Get up before I lose my patience. I have waited long for you."

CeLa struggled up again and faced her tormenter. "What do you mean? You will have me killed, I suppose, or do it yourself?"

"There is much pleasure to be had before you face Ninhursag." Sirna came close to CeLa and jerked the dirty robe apart so that the girl's breasts were ex-

posed. She bent forward and cupped them in her
hands, ignoring CeLa's attempts to flinch away. Then,
before CeLa could move, Sirna leaned closer and
took one of the nipples in her sharp teeth, biting
down, then releasing it almost in the same motion.
Her eyes blazed into those of CeLa and her breath
came in short gasps.

CeLa forgot that her life span was short, forgot
that this woman was mad with lust and power. She
spared a second to wonder if this was the meaning
of the Chosen and of Abdar's death. Her own anger
consumed her as she spat directly into the hungry
face.

The next blow sent her almost to the edge of darkness. She was jerked from it by the swift motions
of the slave as he wrapped a gag of harsh cloth
around her head and took her to an inner room
where he tossed her on a thick mat. He pulled the
rest of the robe from her body, leaving her bound
and naked before Sirna, who had followed them.

The priestess had divested herself of the snakes,
which coiled nearby. Her tall body was also naked
in the gloom and she was laughing to herself as she
laid practiced hands on the shrinking girl. CeLa
struggled at first until she saw that it only inflamed
her seducer, who again bit eagerly at her breasts and
explored the tender parts of her body with mouth
and hands. She lay quietly then, letting Sirna do as
she willed even though her whole being revolted.

Suddenly the movements of Sirna's body shifted.
Now she began to rub and thrust in a gentle yet soothing way. Her hands moved over CeLa's stomach and
up, then down, down to the center of her sex and
turned it into molten flame with her mouth. Again
and again this happened until CeLa felt her mouth
crying out against the gag and her bound hands moving in their own rhythm.

Harsh laughter pulled her up from the sludge of

pleasure. Sirna's face was twisted and distorted with passion. "You will cry for my body before I do this again to you, little one. Cry in longing and abandon for what you have missed!"

CeLa was expertly turned over then so that her bare buttocks were in the air, her face in the dusty mat. She could not cry out in pain when the smooth, hard object was thrust into her anal area, going harder and deeper each time even as a hand squeezed and kneaded her flesh. All the while, the bubbling chuckling laughter went on.

Struggling caused enough pain to blind her. CeLa forced herself to go limp, her mind to think of the reed ship on the river drifting toward unknown lands. She at the prow and the warm sun on her shoulders. She had often sustained herself in this way in times of need in the past—during Nandar's weeping quietly over his watered beer, during endless work in the fields and lately in the temple—and it seldom failed her. This time, however, her body had proved itself not her own as it responded to passion and cruelty. Humiliation touched the core of pride that was CeLa and gagging vomit rose in her mouth.

The contortions of her body and the choking gasps roused Sirna from her own passion. She gave a cry of disgust and pulled free. In a moment the slave was bending over CeLa, jerking the gag loose.

The girl gave way to her sickness then and later to shudders and moans. Some flicker of her mind told her that surely this could put an end to even the most impassioned episode. Her chest and ribs began to ache; her head was an anvil of pain.

"Call the women and have her cleaned up. Guard the door to her cell. Have this mess taken away, it offends me." Sirna gave the commands in a sharp voice and the slave scurried away to obey.

CeLa felt her head lifted and pulled back. Her eyes were streaming and her mouth was smeared as she fought to get her breath. Sirna stared at her as though she were a lizard or a water bug. Her words were almost indifferent.

"In other times it would have been my great pleasure to show you more of the delights of womanly contact, especially since you have known no man to pollute your body. Even if you had escaped, you would have been taught to take no pleasure in a man. The touch would have filled you with loathing. But now the time approaches and you belong to the goddess."

Beyond her pain and discomfort, her mental confusion and despair, CeLa could still fight for that part of her which remained inviolate. She moved farther from the gods who ordered the lives of men as she said in a whisper, "You are wrong, evil one. I belong to myself alone."

Sirna moved convulsively, every line of her beautiful body rigid as her face twisted into a travesty. In spite of herself, CeLa pushed herself back to shield her body from a blow. Seeing it, Sirna laughed, the sound deathly in the bare room.

"You fear pain, do you? Not for you the cup that soothes. You, CeLa, shall go willingly to what awaits, even as all shall do. But you shall know all that occurs and still be powerless. You sought knowledge and shall obtain it. That I promise you! For my goddess, I promise." She raised a ringed hand and, before CeLa could dodge, lashed her heavily across her bare, tender breasts. "And that is for myself! And this also!" The other hand caught CeLa again and she fell forward in blinding pain.

There were footsteps at the door and through her daze CeLa heard Sirna say, "She must be ready within two days. If she is not, you will join them in the pits."

There were gargling sounds and mutters, then CeLa was rolled onto a litter, and a cloth, soothing and cool, was placed on her face. The cords were cut from her wrists even as a cup was held to her lips. Past

caring, she drank and felt the warmth move into her
blood. Nausea and pain faded a little as she lay limply, willing herself to endure until she was able to
cope with all that had happened to her in these few
short hours.

Time blurred for her after she was settled in her
new prison, another bare little room filled principally
with a ledge where mats and draperies made her comfortable. It seemed that there were always hands guiding food and drink to her mouth, voices whispering,
"Rest." She turned over in the restful darkness, slept
and woke to sleep again. At times she breathed scented water; at others she knew that her hair was being
washed and polished with a soft cloth. Once she heard
a lyre being strummed and a soft voice singing, then
a cup was held to her lips and she drank without willing it.

CeLa came fully awake for the first time in a long
time. The dream had been so close and vivid. The
ship had drifted high on the waters of the brown river
and the odor of fish in the sun came up to her. A bird
catapulted down, then rose again. She started up in
the unfamiliar surroundings, then lay back suddenly
as memory came rushing back.

The voice was close by her door. Evidently the
guard was changing in the deep night, for she heard
him say, "It is tomorrow that the ritual begins. We
are promised great sport later. I must rest so as to
be ready."

The other laughed. "I think we shall enjoy the
rule of the high priestess."

Footsteps clattered down the corridor, then the
door opened to admit one of the dumb slaves who
carried a cup in her hand. CeLa feigned sleep even
though the slave tapped and pushed at her. It was
not hard to do since the last dose still ran sweet and
heavy in her veins. She moved drowsily in the bed,
yawned in the general direction of the slave and

pushed her head farther under the draperies. CeLa
knew that she had been kept drugged but her mind
would not function except to tell her to use any pre-
text so as not to drink the contents of that cup.
There was a final jerk on her shoulder; she moaned
again and the slave gave a sigh of exasperation.

CeLa heard the soft movement of bare feet on the
stone floor as the slave moved into the corner and
the gurgle as the liquid was poured out. The woman
was taking no chances for the reprisals that would
be dealt out if Sirna discovered her orders had not
been obeyed. CeLa lay unmoving, for she felt eyes
on her and guessed that the slave watched. Finally
she moved away, the door was shut and the guard
rattled his gear as he let the slave pass.

Now the task of making her body her own again
must begin She did not know what had made her
rouse in time to avoid the new dose; she must count
herself fortunate that the slave had not forced her.
The muscles in her arms and legs were flaccid and
unwilling as she turned and twisted in an effort to
gain control. Her mind kept drifting and swinging
in arcs of light as she willed it back to the task in
hand. With the lifting of the lethargy CeLa forced
herself to remember in detail all that had happened
to her with Sirna. She dug her nails into the soft
flesh of her upper arms in an effort to remain alert
and think. It would not be wise to try to get up. At
any moment someone might come to check on her.
Her battle must be fought here and as she was.

Time drifted as CeLa kept her body in constant,
writhing movement and her mind in concentration.
She knew that she must be ready to take whatever
opportunity presented itself, for it was not possible
to have any illusions as to her fate. There was the
tramp of feet in the corridor and a short, hissed conversation punctuated with a laugh. It would not be
long, CeLa knew. She twisted over until she lay on

her stomach, then put her face in her hands and prayed.

"Intar, if you have followed me in this house of the goddess, if you care for me still, help me from this peril. Do this and I shall build a temple for you that is all your own. Lagash shall see me no more if I live, but you shall be worshiped wherever I settle."

It was bold to speak thus to the gods, she knew. But they who gave humans their foibles and who had them in plenty themselves should surely understand. What was Intar against Ninhursag? Was it not better that she pray to the goddess for courage to go willingly to whatever fate had been set out for her? CeLa twisted again in fear, then in awe.

Her prayer was answered, for her body moved at her command and the dizziness, the lethargy, was gone from her mind. She was weak, it was true, but that would fade with time. If she were granted time.

There was a light step and her door began to open. CeLa had time to stretch out and simulate sleep before the slave had reached her. It took all her power of concentration to lie quietly, breathe regularly and evenly. She felt the slave's silent scrutiny as the minutes passed.

Just as it began to seem truly unbearable, that she could not lie there another second even if they killed her for it, there was a purposeful tread, a hard hand on her shoulder, and a swift voice demanded, "Wake, lady, it is time!"

CeLa moved languidly, wearily, basing her performance on the way she had felt the night before. Opening her eyes, she saw that the woman who bent over her was in early middle age and, from her dress and ornaments, was one fairly high in the service of the goddess. The woman peered into the girl's eyes and CeLa forced herself to gaze back in an unseeing manner. The woman released her and she fell back against the cushions.

The woman whirled on the slave who had stood by. "Fool, you have given her too much of the drink! Look at her, she is barely roused and it is but three hours until the ceremony. You shall be punished!"

The slave cowered away. CeLa saw the horror on her face as she frantically pantomimed a ritual of bathing and preparation. The woman's eyes were calculating as she turned back to the girl. Before she could turn away as if in exhaustion, the woman seized CeLa's arm and pinched the tender area just above the elbow. The metal-shielded fingernail bit deeply but CeLa did not flinch or move. The look in the dark eyes had been the same as that in Sirna's and she had anticipated the move. It was well for her that she had, for now the slave was being berated once more.

"Fetch stimulants, cold and hot water. She cannot go this way." The voice hardened with pleasure. "I shall personally see to your punishment when this is done."

The slave shuddered but ran to obey. The woman continued to watch CeLa with an unblinking gaze and the girl knew that the slightest false motion could give her away. She closed her eyes and feigned sleep once more.

No fewer than five slaves entered suddenly, carrying water for the bath, trays, draperies and dishes. One held a cup of gold to CeLa's lips. The liquid it contained was hot and frothy; she had no choice but to drink. As she did so, another was prepared. Almost instantly she felt new vigor and power. Cakes and newly cooked fish were placed in front of her and she ate slowly, trying to draw out the time when her fate must be faced.

The hawk-faced woman sat down in front of her and said, "You are better now? Yes, I can see that you are. Do you remember anything?"

CeLa did not know what it would be wisest to say;

she allowed her voice to tremble. "Very little. Such dreams as I have had! I am still weary from them. Will I be allowed to rest soon?"

"There are temple duties that are required of you first. You must be obedient and perform them." There was a rasp in her voice and the dark hunger looked out of her eyes.

"Duties?" CeLa heard her voice light and vague as she swayed. The slaves thrust another cup of the stimulant into her hand and she drank eagerly.

"Aye, this is the day that the high priest journeys into the netherworld, the day that Sirna has chosen as most auspicious for the great farewell. He shall not go unaccompanied." She laughed, the sound ugly in the stillness.

CeLa held her face still with a great effort but inside she was screaming. Now she knew the fate of the Chosen of Ninhursag.

8

Allotted of the Gods

The silent slaves moved around CeLa as the hawk-faced woman withdrew. She was bathed, her hair washed and polished until it hung long and gleaming over her shoulders. A flounced skirt of white was belted low over her slender hips. A longer tunic covered her arms and breasts, then fell away to her golden-sandaled feet. A pair of golden bracelets, intricately designed, curved up her arms.

While the activity was going on, CeLa sat still, knowing she could do nothing but hoard her strength and hope that it would build. She knew she would fight for her life, fruitless though it might be. One of the slaves inadvertently pulled a strand of hair as she administered yet another combing to the shining mass. It hurt and CeLa started to shift her head. She could not. She tried to lift her hand and it would not move. Her body was helpless as she sat unmoving, a slight smile on her lips. Her mind was clear and sharp but her physical being was a prisoner.

"It is time. Bring her." The hawk-faced woman returned, stood in front of CeLa, adjusted a golden chain attached to the belt and moved one of the bracelets on the immobile arm. Then she looked at the girl and smiled.

CeLa knew that panic showed in her eyes just as she knew that this woman gloried in what she did. Was this to be her end? Was her life that had just begun to be sacrificed in some bizarre plot or ritual?

She exerted all the force of her mind and strained against the power of the drug, but it was hopeless.

One of the slaves took her arm and pulled gently. She rose and walked obediently beside the woman, not of her own volition but as if strings were attached to her limbs. The hawk-faced one, whom CeLa had heard called Horta, bent her head for the placing of a rich coronet upon it, then took her place in front of CeLa and began to pace slowly forward. The slaves took CeLa to her place a few feet behind. Two walked beside her to guide that smooth walk that was not her own, and seven others went behind. She heard the sound of a lyre as they moved along.

They walked slowly and sedately through narrow corridors that widened as they went upward to a central hall that could easily hold six and more groups such as theirs as they moved abreast. Guards in rich livery lined the area and they were heavily armed. The sounds of music became louder, more discordant, but with a challenge to them. CeLa could not look about her, but it seemed that they must be approaching their destination.

Their procession stopped suddenly to let another group enter the corridor. Three girls were in its center, dressed as CeLa was, and propelled by slaves. As they went by, CeLa saw that their faces were smooth and set in half smiles, their eyes cloudy and glazed. They seemed to have taken leave of their bodies. Her blood chilled, for she knew that they were drugged beyond what she had been. Whatever their fate, it was obvious that the drug made it seem they went in joy and gladness. She tried once again to command her body but it would not obey except to move in the gliding gait of the others. She heard the call of the music and the shuffle of sandals, then the corridor ahead of them filled with groups such as her own. It would not be long now.

The walk seemed to go on for a very long time as the corridor leveled out, then plunged sharply down. They must be underground and beyond the walls of the temple, thought CeLa. A slow chant had begun behind them, its rhythm reminding her of the inexorable rivers as they flowed to the sea. The chant was punctuated by the thump of a drum in cadence, a sound that seemed to carry an ever-increasing sense of the doom that awaited. There were no words, only the hammering and the rising sounds accompanied by their feet as they moved.

CeLa was beyond prayer and hope, into a world of struggle as she tensed her unmoving muscles and willed her mind to take control of her body. "I will fight this even to my last breath. I will not go supinely to what waits." That it was death she had no doubt. Sirna's eyes had told her that when she entered the temple.

CeLa knew herself well enough to know that it was not pride or courage that sustained her will to fight. It was endurance, that tough quality she had learned from living with Nandar, who in the end had been unable to cope. Terror possessed her utterly; only by swinging her mind away could she retain her sanity for the little time that remained. It was unbelievable that she should cease to exist while warm blood yet moved in her veins and her caged mind could yet conceive of freedom.

The air was cool on her face as it blew from an open door at the end of the corridor. The processions were moving in single file now and the chant was louder, the dirge note more pronounced. She was taken forward in her turn into a wide, long room that seemed at first to be filled with people. As she advanced, however, she saw that they stood on another level at least five feet above the floor, which was lined with mats. They wore crimson, gold, purple and brilliant blue. Jewels flashed in the light of the

torches that reflected the grave faces of the onlookers. Light shone down a shaft at one end of the
room; it seemed to come from far above.

CeLa was taken by Horta now and escorted slowly,
gravely, in time with the beat of the drum, toward
one of the walls where other girls dressed as she
stood. She was placed in the front row and turned
to face the other end of the room. As she was being
positioned, however, CeLa had time to notice that
the eyes of the girls were as vague and unrealizing
as those she had seen earlier. They knew nothing,
whereas she was to experience all. Was this a final
trick of Sirna's, a master touch to torment one who
had tried to flee? Or was it simply her own avoidance of the drug in the early morning that now left
her numb but keenly aware? It did not really matter,
CeLa thought. She was to die in any event.

The gorgeously clothed and jeweled body of Abdar lay on a raised platform of stone and bricks.
Around it were piled weapons, tools, dishes, chests,
clothes, musical instruments and tablets. On the
other side she saw a light chariot with the bodies
of three donkeys resting nearby. A ceremonial chair,
stool and table stood close at hand. A lion, carved
in gold and inlaid with silver, stretched great wings
from a pedestal. Several men servants stood unmoving
by the body. It did not take more than a look to
know that they too were drugged. Ten soldiers, lances
gripped in their hands, lay on the floor directly in
front of them. They were dead, apparently from
their skulls being crushed. With her heightened
senses CeLa could see the dark blood congealing
around their heads.

The music began again; it was both doleful and
promising. The drum sounded louder and more ominous as it was joined by the beating of a metal gong.
A harp melody threaded in as six priests carried an
image forward to the center of the room and set it

on an ornate throne brought in by slaves who staggered under its weight. The waiting people bent down before the revealed face of Ninhursag, Mother Goddess.

CeLa stood with the others, but of them all only she could see with clarity. The statue was of beaten gold and crowned with a headdress of jewels and feathers. In one hand a lance had been placed, the other held a dagger. The carved lips were fixed in a savage smile and points of light winked in the huge eyes.

"Hail to the great one! Hail, Ninhursag!" The company cried with one voice again and yet again.

The great drum was beaten and roared forth three times. It was followed by the blasting of trumpets, and then a woman's strong voice rose above these to cry, "Welcome the Mother as is worthy of her, by homage and obedience to her will!"

"We so do!" "Guardian of Lagash!" "Great one." "Command us!" The cries rose in the room.

Sirna had entered from a side door and stood at the side of the goddess. Her breasts were bare, as were those of the image. She wore a flounced skirt of some thin metallic-appearing material that parted as she moved. Snake bracelets curved up her arms, and on her head was a tall white headdress with a plume of blue. Golden earrings swung to her shoulders. A cape of the thinnest white cloth billowed from her shoulders and was held by a thin band of jewels around her neck.

CeLa stared at her and could not but acknowledge her beauty even as her own fear increased. She watched as Sirna bent before the goddess, then straightened, held out her arms and cried loudly into the sudden silence as her trained voice filled the room with its power.

"We have come to send our high priest, Abdar, on his way into the netherworld. Behold! The household that shall travel with him—the servants, the animals, the goods, the jewels—all are worthy of his greatness, all are worthy of this man who sought to placate and exercise calm judgment in the wars of men. These young women, some of the fairest of this city and beyond, are pure and learned. They will serve him well in the world beyond and go willingly with him as it is most pleasing to the goddess. By honoring her servant, we honor her. It is right that we should do this."

"Aye, very right!" the company called after her as she stood like a flame in the sheath of light and jewels.

CeLa knew that she should not have been surprised. It was so obvious now. Sirna had planned to kill Abdar but had not dared do it openly because of his popularity. So she had used poison and had designed this elaborate burial rite complete with human sacrifice. It was barbaric, a thing not known in Sumer in any of the literature that Nandar had taught CeLa or that she had read in the archives. Surely the gods did not demand such a sacrifice even of their kings whom they set up to rule men? Were they not just gods?

"Ninhursag has spoken to me this very morning, in the stillness of the dawn. She is displeased, even angered. I dared to ask how we had offended and was commanded to give her words to you, her people!" Sirna's voice fell almost to a whisper and she crossed her arms on her breast.

A moan swept over the people and they knelt while one voice, braver than the rest called, "Tell us, Sirna, that it may be put right."

The great drum boomed. CeLa felt gooseflesh rise up on her as the light of the torches seemed to sway in the little wind that rose. A chill fell on the room.

Sirna lifted her head and her face wore the savage smile that illumined the face of the image. Her voice was a hollow roar that echoed the temple drum, but there was a snarl in it that seemed not of the world of men.

"So speaks Ninhursag to her servant Sirna. 'I have seen how Lagash lies supine under the heel of the destroyer, Umma, and its king, for these years. Abdar sought to placate and I have taken him to me, for this is not pleasing in my eyes. Sirna speaks with my voice and woe unto Lagash if I am not obeyed!'"

The company stared at the priestess, their faces contorted with fear. CeLa looked at them and her gaze slid past and up. She saw parts of the ceiling, which looked freshly made. Slanting beams supported what appeared to be bins of great size filled with some sort of material. These were arranged directly over the area where she and the other girls stood. The purpose eluded CeLa; her mind skipped back and forth, an effect of the drugs, she guessed.

The throbbing voice was continuing. "The goddess spoke further to this unworthy one. Her words are on the stele of my heart and are thus: 'The upstart of Umma calls himself Lord of Sumer. That power by which he sought to destroy shall in time destroy him, for there is come out of the north one who has subdued that land and has taken several cities in our own. Lagash must hold its council, send messages to the upstart of Umma and provoke him into open war with the northern ruler. They will destroy each other and Lagash shall rise to her former greatness. The way will not be easy, but I shall support those who are with me and those who are not shall die. I have spoken!'"

The temple drum boomed again and again as the torches shot up in flame that reflected the tall figure of Sirna, who stood, arms high above her head, eyes blazing, beside the goddess whose face shone red in the light.

"Do you obey? You who are the most powerful men

of Lagash? Do you heed the words of the goddess?"
Sirna's call rose even above the drum.

"We hear and obey. Command us!" The company
was as one.

"Then remember how it was those years ago when
Lagash fell before Umma! That time of bitter destruction when temples were ravaged and fire gutted
the avenues. When the gods were despoiled and the
bodies of the citizens lay putrefying in the streets. Remember the insults to the great ones! Remember,
men of Lagash, and know that the Mother has never
forgotten nor will she forgive. Abdar is dead because
of that and I am commanded to lead in his place."

After every sentence Sirna paused and the drum
boomed portentously. Her voice rose and soared as
a frenzy came upon her. Sweat poured down her body
until she seemed soaking wet. The long shadow of
the goddess fell upon her and men gasped in awe.
Soldiers moved into place behind her, their weapons
at the ready. Others positioned themselves at the
doors.

"Remember the great days of Lagash and Ninhursag!" Sirna began to extol the far past as the citizens
called out her name and that of the goddess with
each pause. They were bewitched, drunk on words
and acting.

CeLa forced her mind away from the bizarre setting. She would force it to her will. She concentrated
fiercely on moving her fingers, her toes, even her lips.
Memory had returned sufficiently so that she remembered Sirna's promise that she should experience all,
yet be unable to do anything about it. It was a fate
past all hideousness, to die while paralyzed yet with
her mind clear and rational. CeLa knew that she
could kill Sirna with the greatest pleasure. How could
such a woman live and prosper? "Playthings of the
gods." Nandar's voice was sardonic in her mind.

Sirna and the horror of the whole situation faded

as CeLa fought with her gathering strength for a
chance at life. She followed the muscles and bones
of her body with her mind. The coursing of her blood
seemed swifter as it pounded at her temples and
pulsed in her neck. There was no time to think of
the horrors in store; imagination palled before the
reality of what she saw. For CeLa, reality was the
stone her body had become. She strained until sweat
beaded her forehead, although the motionless bodies of those near her were dry.

I will move. I will walk. I will live. A chance only,
not death in this manner, a chance, blessed gods!
Over and over the litany hammered in her brain.

A chorus of cheers punctuated by the thunder of
the drum jerked her into awareness. Sirna's face was
a mask of savagery as she waved daggers in both
hands. Almost at a signal, a young man in the first
flush of youth was brought in. His face shone with
adoration as he looked up at Sirna, and CeLa
thought, almost inadvertently, that they were lovers.
He came close to her and knelt, smiling.

Sirna, her own face radiantly cruel, cried, "The
other face of the goddess is blood and revenge! All
whom you see here will go to slake her blood thirst
even as Abdar journeys forth to her. But we must
be prepared to sacrifice for Ninhursag's favor! Lives
are nothing! Sacrifice is all!"

Even as she spoke, she raised both daggers high
and brought them in a crisscross movement over the
bared throat of the young man, who fell at her feet
in a welter of blood. Then a sacred frenzy fell on
Sirna and whipped her to the floor, where she lay,
a shimmering statue at the feet of her goddess. The
company was very still in the presence of such divine
honor. The soldiers turned the points of their spears
down and the crackle of the torches was the only
sound in that chamber of death.

CeLa strained one last time, for it seemed that in

any instant the sacrifices would begin. Every person in that chamber would die for Sirna, she knew. She was beyond rational thought now; her one hope was to wage some kind of fight and not to die helplessly.

Sirna came to her feet in a slow movement. She had dipped her hands in the blood of the young man and now she lifted them up before the image as she called, "Will you accept this sacrifice as a token of faith? You shall be well served! I, Sirna, swear it!"

The drum boomed slowly, then dwindled to tiny taps. A flame glowed dull gold on the far wall and reflected on Sirna's bloodstained hands. Points of red fire shone in the great eyes of the goddess.

Sirna spread her arms wide and turned to face the company as the red flame spread over the entire face of Ninhursag and encompassed her priestess. "The sacrifices are accepted. Let them begin."

CeLa fought against the binding potion that held her prisoner as the mute slaves, accompanied by several grave priests in white, came toward the women of the Chosen. It was time to die.

9

Sojourn in the Death-Pit

A hand touched CeLa's shoulder, another her arm, and her body moved at the touch. At the same time, four other girls were taken with her back toward the wall. There was total silence in the chamber as this was being done. The girl caught a glance from Sirna. The priestess seemed hypnotized as she stood tall and powerful in the light from the torches.

CeLa saw that the girls were being directed to lie down on their sides, all facing in the same direction with their faces to the wall, their hands folded near their faces. When it came her turn, she felt a tingle run through her legs as they were arranged. She felt the scratchiness of the floor and it was sharp to her body as she lay there.

The first row had become the first one to face the wall. As the five girls were arranged and the slaves stepped back, two of the priests came forward to place palm branches of the goddess in the hands of those who were shortly to meet her. Then the harp and lyres began to play softly, while the soft tapping of the temple drum began to build in intensity.

CeLa could no longer see the others, for her head was very close to the wall. She still fought to move; she would do this until the last moment of breath. There was no doubt that the drug was already bringing peaceful death to the willing sacrifices. She had seen the slowing of response in the girls nearest her in the row and that they breathed more shallowly

even as their eyes glazed further. Already they were
near the goddess whose sacrifices they were.

There was no such anodyne for CeLa. She was conscious again of every prickle and rough place on the
floor, and her nose itched. She thought wildly that it
was ridiculous to think how delicious it would be
to scratch it when soon she would be beyond caring
about so foolish a thing. She knew that she had been
afraid for so long that it had become almost a way
of life for her; it was possible to be in deadly fear
and yet think of the humor in small things.

The shuffle of sandals came near and another girl
was positioned down in another row which began
almost at CeLa's feet. They were to be packed into
a small space then, and Abdar's body would lie in
the open space surrounded by his goods and jewels.
It would not be long before the ceremony was done
and they were left to finish dying while Sirna returned
to continue her plans for power.

There was a small stone directly under CeLa's side
and her flesh was being bruised. She jerked away
from it in a small, swift movement that went unseen.
The movement had been involuntary and for a few
seconds she did not realize what had happened. When
she did, she closed her eyes and let the world fade
as she concentrated fiercely. The minor discomfort
she had experienced, the prickling of her flesh, this
had been a sign of returning sensation.

CeLa did not see or hear the placement of the
other girls close to her. Once begun, the power of
movement was returning swiftly to her body that had
been held motionless for so long. She was almost
instantly able to tense and release, tense and release
muscles that were cramping. It seemed that her
blood flowed faster. Her teeth were unlocked and
she could feel the pangs of thirst. The dreaming sensation was gone from her mind as clarity of thought
returned.

CeLa was first conscious of a great thankfulness that her body was her own again, then of wonder that the drug was wearing off. Apparently the dose that she had managed to avoid taking was the crucial one. Sirna would surely have wanted her immobilized yet aware even as the sacrifice took place. She had no idea what she could do to struggle against the mass fate; for the moment it was enough that she could feel.

She carefully turned her head a small fraction. The standing group of girls had vanished and all lay compressed within a few feet for each, compactly arranged. A slave was approaching with the last girl. There was complete silence in the chamber and the light of the torches seemed to flare and fade, concentrating on the image of the goddess and Sirna. CeLa cautiously slid both hands around until they rested flat on the floor under her. She was so close to the wall that it lay in shadow; her movement went unseen.

The girl was arranged. The drum began to beat heavily, the deep booms thundered out over the temple area and Sirna's voice rose with it as the darkness deepened.

"Go, men of Lagash, go to the shrine of Ninhursag where I shall shortly join you to worship and then we shall meet in council. This is a holy place and none shall live in it."

Her words ended on a scream of pure frenzy. There was a crashing, roaring noise, a rattling and thumping of debris. CeLa looked up to see the roof caving in. The bins had fallen. They were filled with earth and bricks of mud in huge quantities. Chaos reigned, but there was no human outcry, only the chant of Sirna and the drum.

CeLa's action was almost instinctive. She jerked her legs up under her and rolled toward the wall, into the corner, where she buried her head under her arms,

frail shelter that they were. Even in the horror of
the moment, she noticed that there was very little
weakness in her limbs. She expected every second to
be her last as the weight of the ceiling and the earth
continued to rattle down. A great pile fell almost
on top of her and some of the sand spilled over, but
it proved a shield in that the next part of the roof
to fall slid down rather than landing flat. In that
shelter CeLa clutched her knees and wept with fear
of being buried alive.

Silence was absolute in the death chamber and
had been for some moments before CeLa realized
that she still lived and could even see light above the
rubble that hemmed her in and had saved her life.
Sand and debris lay on her back and her mouth was
caked with dust. Her eyes burned. She sneezed, then
gradually unclenched her hands. She dared not move
for fear of bringing down more of the earth and
walls; also, she could not know if there might be
people watching to see if anyone lived in the mass
burial. It would be easy enough to stand on one of
the several ledges and oversee the pit.

CeLa did not know how long she remained in the
very cramped position. She could not think beyond
endurance and every breath she drew was precious
to her. She strained her ears but could hear nothing
as, in an effort to pass the time of waiting, she counted off numbers in her mind and inscribed them on
tablets there.

Several thousands later, CeLa dared to move slowly
and carefully as she flexed her legs, then twisted until she could peer out from the protected bastion
where she lay. As far as she could see, piles of rubble
covered the sacrificial pit. Directly above her and
at an angle, however, she saw bricks mixed with the
sand. These had fallen in a stack that might be sufficient to give her a foothold where otherwise she
might simply sink back into the morass.

Thirst raged in her. She felt bruised in a dozen
different places, and her legs shook with weakness,
but CeLa was only vaguely cognizant of such things.
The battle for life occupied her now.

The pit was not as deep as it had seemed when
they were brought in, but in the hours that it took
CeLa to reach the first ledge, battling sliding sand,
slipping back three feet for every inch gained, it appeared bottomless. She moved with her hands, toes
and stomach, going in a dogged crawl that would
not give up. Once the brick she clutched gave way
and she grabbed for the nearest handhold, which
turned out to be a dead hand from which protruded
a jeweled dagger. Beyond terror at this point, she
snatched the dagger and thrust it into the scrap of
cloth that still girded her loins, pulled upward on the
hand and moved over the body and on.

The slant of rubble that had fallen so lightly in
her corner continued upward so that her progress
was steady if laborious. Her whole body was wet
with sweat and she had bit her teeth so deeply into
her lower lip that she tasted the salt of blood. Her
harsh breathing was loud in her ears and she held
her mouth open for more air in the oppressive chamber.

The raw ends of her fingers suddenly touched a
flat surface. CeLa lifted her head, shook the sweat
from her eyes and stared at the passage level with
her eyes that ran off to the left and away from the
chamber of death. She pulled herself up the last few
feet until her whole body rested prone on the ledge,
then she looked down at the way she had come.

The pit was a sea of sand and bricks that sloped
down on the sides. There was no sign of any other
human life and no sign of what lay underneath. The
silence was one of waiting and evil. It was as if
Sirna's plotting had taken tangible form. A faint
light came from somewhere farther above and torches

burned in the recesses of the passageways, but shadows lay deep. CeLa half expected the sand to begin to move as those who had been so wantonly slain rose to protest their fate.

The girl forced herself to rise and move back into the passage. It did not matter where she went so long as she left that place. She was not thinking so much as reacting instinctively, the trapped animal seeking a place that was dark and safe. Midway down the passage, it came to CeLa that she walked on two feet, however hesitantly, and that she had escaped a terrible fate planned for her by one who knew all the nuances of cruelty and had not hesitated to use them. Her laughter was half hysterical as she whispered, "I still live! By all the gods, I still live!" Such was the wonder of it that she stood, well nigh naked, in the middle of the floor and shook with laughter.

CeLa caught herself in an instant. She could not afford the indulgence of laughter or tears; she remained in deadly peril. Deep anger swelled in her, however, and she said savagely, "If I live and escape from this place, I shall return and one day kill Sirna! This I swear, an oath of vengeance and blood!" She looked down at her bloody hands and torn body.

It had helped to think of ways to dispatch Sirna as she climbed out of the pit, and CeLa found that it helped now when she wanted to sink down and give way to the emotions that were beginning to surface. In the manner of a fugitive, she stayed close to the wall and moved along it as the passage moved slightly upward. She had no idea if it was day or night. All her instincts warned her to move as quickly as she could away from this place.

Her feet were soundless in that place of silence. There was no indication of the barbaric ceremony that had taken place so recently. The sweat on her body had dried and she could smell her odor in the cooling air. CeLa looked at the scratches and bruises

on her bare body; it was strange that they did not
hurt, but she was so wrought up from her recent ordeal that escape took precedence over everything else.
Escape! The word was like a drumbeat in her brain.
What she would do when and if she reached the
outer courts of the temple was another matter. Her
exhausted mind could not go beyond the present.
She moved mechanically, a bloody wraith in the
gloom.

The passage curved suddenly. CeLa went stumbling almost into the arms of a man who was moving
as cautiously as she. They swayed for a second in
mutual surprise, he struggling to keep his balance,
she in gathering panic. He snapped out an oath in
a strangely familiar voice even as one arm caught
hers.

With that restraint, CeLa broke. After all she had
endured, it was unthinkable that she should be taken
back to captivity just because of a chance encounter.
Anger blinded her as she felt her cracked lips draw
back in a snarl. Her hand closed on the dagger still
in the band of her torn skirt. She drew it out in one
swift movement and rammed it straight at the stomach of the man who held her.

He moved just enough so that it penetrated the
fleshy part of his side. Blood poured forth but CeLa
raised the dagger again and this time aimed for his
neck. He dodged but was not quick enough and the
sharp point went into his upraised arm.

"Bitch! What is the matter with you? Are you
mad?" He jerked back and wiped the blood away.

CeLa was oblivious to all but the fact that she was
shedding the blood of her enemy as she had sworn
to do. Rage and pleasure made her smile. This time
she would not be taken to the slaughter as an animal
to the pit.

"Die! Damn you, die!" She threw herself upon him
then, the dagger rising and stabbing. The relief of

striking back was so sweet. She hungered for the sight
of his blood flowing in expiation.

The man pivoted, slammed his arm across hers and
the dagger went flying as her arm lost all feeling.
He tripped her and she went sprawling, but as she
did so, she caught him around the ankles and he
fell on top of her. She attacked him then with her
teeth, bloody fingers, kicking and seeking his vulnerable male organs. All the while the snarl came from
her as she tried with all her power to kill this enemy. Just as she brought her knee up in the gesture
learned in street fights of long ago, his fist hit her
head and darkness exploded around her.

She woke to a heavy weight on her legs and pain
in her arms that were bound under her. She did not
open her eyes or give any other sign of returning
consciousness, but hopelessness came over her in a
wave. Why had she not died in the blessed relief of
the fight?

The weight on her legs shifted and then a tiny
trickle of water seeped into her mouth as a cup was
held to her lips. As it was withdrawn, CeLa opened
her eyes, gathered the moisture and spat it directly
into the bearded face bending over her.

He jerked back, wiped his face with one hand and
pulled her hair back with the other. She writhed and
struggled but could not move since he sat so firmly
on her legs.

"Stop this, you cannot possibly win. Promise to
behave and I'll let you up." The voice was faintly
amused.

CeLa stared at him in surprise. It was the same
man who had spoken so briefly to her in the kitchen
the night they had learned of Abdar's death. He
wore nondescript dark clothes and a turban hid his
hair but the beard, high nose and hard eyes were
unmistakable.

"Summon the guard if you have not already done

so. I will fight until I die. Would to the gods that I had killed you, servitor of the foul one!"

"I suggest to you that you are unable to do anything at present. I have called no guards and serve no one here." He tilted the water cup to his lips and brought it down. "Have some?"

CeLa felt the first flickering of hope. "You do not serve Sirna? But all in this temple do. Who are you?"

"I might ask the same of you." The dark eyes were hooded but his voice was casual.

"Let me go. You have no reason to keep me this way."

"No." It was flat and unequivocal.

CeLa kicked upward in a sudden movement that dislodged him so that he went sprawling. Her bound hands made her unsteady, but she rose up in time to kick once more at his jaw. He caught her foot in midkick and toppled her to the floor. Her head cracked on the side and she felt darkness spin around her even as he pulled her to face him.

"You are a savage fighter, girl. What has happened to place you in such a situation? There is hardly a place on you that is not bruised. Still, you fight on. Many a man would not do such." There was admiration in the hard voice.

CeLa lifted her face to his. Her blinding anger was gone and the bitterness of defeat corroded her. "If you would honor such, let me go."

"I cannot."

"Why? What harm could it do?"

The intent gaze shifted to survey the passage, then returned to her. "I must learn of the one called Sirna; it is a mission for my master. It is safe to tell you that much since you must now come with me as my prisoner." His manner was that of one used to command, a natural arrogance.

"I have been the prisoner of Sirna and have vowed her death. If you seek to accomplish that, I will join with you willingly. I am as I am now because of that slut and whore."

He looked down at her and knew that she spoke the truth. "Will you tell me what you know of her so that I may weigh this matter for myself?"

"You spoke of a master. Sirna rules here now that she has slain the high priest. I will tell you what I can if you will let me go afterward."

He was surprised and there was real sorrow in his words. "Abdar dead? How?"

"A bargain for a bargain." CeLa was beginning to feel better. Life was worth the price to be paid and she might win yet.

"Whatever else I may be, I am no friend to Sirna. Abdar was a good man. Tell me what you know. Remain with me willingly until I leave Lagash and you may go your way in peace. In return, I will help you to get free of the temple, which you have fought so fiercely to do." He spoke strongly, a man sure of himself.

"Done." CeLa too could make up her mind swiftly. But then, she told herself, she had no choice. "Release me."

He sliced the cloth that bound her hands and handed her the cup that still held water poured from a leather bottle nearby. He unwrapped the turban from his head, tore off a length of it, wet it and gave that to CeLa.

She wiped much of the dirt from her face and arms, then used part of the cloth to fasten her hair back from her face. It was impossible to do anything about her near nudity but his eyes were impersonal as he glanced at her before going back along the passage to the place where they had first collided. He bent down to retrieve a short, dusty robe from where it had fallen.

"You can wrap yourself in this. It's just about as dirty as you are."

CeLa ignored him as she adjusted the stiffening folds over one shoulder and around her waist. Some of the stains appeared to be blood but she was not

queasy. "Where do we go from here? You were going one way and I the other. I will not return from
whence I came."

For the first time he smiled at her and the gesture
transformed his stern face. "We are comrades for a
short time, I think. What is your name? I am Kir."

"I am CeLa. We must go from this place without
delay."

Her urgency infected him and his smile faded. He
caught her arm, but she jerked free.

"I have been prisoner too long and cannot abide
the touch of captivity. It would send me mad, I believe."

"As you wish." He shrugged and started back along
the passage. She followed.

A few minutes later they came to a fork from which
three wider passages opened. He went unhesitatingly
into the narrowest one and turned into an alcove
that was both dark and dusty from disuse.

"We can talk here. I cannot leave the temple without the information for which I came."

They had not seen another human being but CeLa's
nerves were drawn past the screaming point. "I cannot stay so close. Fool, do you still not understand!"
To her horror her voice began to shake and her
whole body followed suit. Kir said something but his
voice came as if from a great distance. She started
blindly out of the alcove but he stepped in front
of her.

"CeLa, listen to me." He put both hands on the
sides of her head and forced her to look at him, at
the gray flicker in his black eyes. He spoke soothingly. "I will take you from the temple. You will be
safe to return to your family. I have promised and
I do not break my promises. Sit here now and tell
me what you have endured."

One part of CeLa rebelled at being spoken to as

if she were a child, but the commonsense part of her welcomed his kindness. There was no way she could escape alone, therefore the horror must be relived. She nodded numbly and allowed him to lead her back into the alcove. She sank to the dusty floor and he squatted beside her, one eye watchfully on the door and his dagger at the ready.

CeLa glossed over her reason for being in the marketplace the day Sirna found her. Of Nandar she did not speak at all. The rest of it rolled out of her like poison, and when it was done she put her head on her arms and cried in long, whimpering gusts. She felt his arm encircle her shoulders and draw her close. She had not been held so since she was a very young child and his gentleness made her cry all the harder. Kir murmured soothing words in a language she did not understand and his hand moved slowly on her neck. Finally her shaken nerves were calmer even though she felt near to exhaustion from all that had happened. She looked up into Kir's face and was not surprised to see it drawn and harsh, although his eyes were warm with compassion.

"Better now?" His voice was soft.

She nodded dumbly, half ashamed of her outburst.

Kir said, "I have seen strong men give way after having endured far less than you. You will be the better for this release. Can you answer some questions now?"

"Of course. I am fine."

"Did Sirna say the name of the northern king?"

"No, what does one ruler or another matter to the lives of the poor?"

Kir laughed but the strain was obvious. "You have more than fulfilled your part of the bargain, CeLa. You may rest assured that the information you have given me will in the end ruin Sirna. She will not triumph, however much she tries to mislead the men of Lagash. This tale will be given abroad in the cities. Many knew Abdar for a fair man; the gods are just and cannot will that this go unpunished."

CeLa laughed in her turn. "I besought the goddess even as Sirna screamed out her will. I suppose I am answered. I still live."

Kir touched her hand in comfort. "It would be well for you to hide for some few weeks at least. I do not think there will be a search, for how could anyone have escaped the sacrificial pit? It beggars the imagination. Truly the goddess was with you. Rumors will start about Sirna soon, such rumors as will topple her. Then you can pursue your life once more."

"Are you in the service of the king?" The thought struck CeLa that despite his disreputable appearance he carried a visible authority.

"The king?" The question caught Kir off guard and he swung round to face her.

"Of Umma and Lagash. He whom Sirna calls Lord of Sumer. The king." CeLa was tart in her answer now that the storm was past. It was a blessed relief to think in terms of freedom and hunger and thirst. She knew that Kir planned to leave her in Lagash, but she had already begun to scheme to get him to take her to another city. If he served Umma, she would be beyond the reach of Sirna. She would not remain in Lagash for any reason.

"No, my master is beyond these and you would not know his name. I have been bidden not to reveal it."

"As you will."

Kir came close to her and touched her face with a hard hand. "Come now. We are two slaves bidden to perform a task to which we are hurrying. If we are stopped, I will speak. You, I will say, are my wife and mute."

"Which is doubtless why you chose me!"

They laughed together in a lightening of tension

and relief from fear, joined for the first time in a camaraderie of sharing.

CeLa and Kir walked steadily upward for a short time, then moved along the passages that seemed most light. They passed few people—a sleepy guard nodding before a door, a slave carrying water jars, an old woman mumbling to herself as she shuffled along. After all the fear and scheming, it seemed almost anticlimactic to ascend a final flight of stairs, push open a door and emerge furtively into the night air, which nonetheless had the smell of dawn.

"Wait here." Kir guided her toward a small shelter built away from the wall, possibly to house stores of some sort and now fallen into disrepair. "I will get food and drink. At this hour I doubt anyone will be watching the kitchens."

CeLa hid behind one of the tumbledown walls and kept watch with her dagger in one hand. Weariness threatened to overcome her utterly but she dared not give in to it. How long had it been since she'd rested? For that matter, how long had it been since the sacrifice? Days, hours? A step sounded and she braced herself, but it was Kir returning.

"I think this must have been a day and night of celebration. Several people lay about drunk, there were no guards to be seen. The gates are securely locked and guarded—I did notice that—but they will have to open them when morning comes. Until then we will rest here."

He had brought cakes, cucumbers and beer. CeLa's stomach revolted at first but she forced herself to eat and drink. Kir satisfied himself quickly and went to stand guard. She found her strength returning with every bite, but with it came the lassitude of extreme weariness. Sinking down, she put her head on one hand, held the dagger in the other and gave in to sleep.

CeLa was roused by a hand on her shoulder. The

morning was burning hot and she could feel the
sweat running down her back. Every muscle was sore;
it hurt even to turn her head. Her mouth was dry
and sticky.

"Is it time?"

Kir looked the very picture of a peasant or slave
in his dusty robe and flapping turban. Only the chiseled lips and arched nose belied the impression. He
said slowly, "As good a time as any. Are you ready?"

In answer CeLa struggled to her feet, moved her
limbs carefully and took up her place behind him
as they went out of the place of concealment.

The normal bustling crowds of the courtyard and
marketplace were absent today. A few sellers sat near
their produce and other wares, slaves went about their
business of buying and soldiers went by in groups,
yawning. It was early enough so that the fishermen
who came to sell their catches were still straggling
through the partially opened gates in search of the
buyers who were usually waiting for them. As CeLa
and Kir approached, one of them was talking to the
man with him.

"Business will be bad today. The high priest was
entombed yesterday and the mercy of the goddess
sought for us all by the high priestess."

"Better we had stayed in the city, then."

There were three guards at the gate but they
glanced at those coming in only casually. One of them
stepped in front of Kir when he saw that they wished
to go out.

"No one leaves without being checked. Where are
you going?"

Kir stood very still, as did CeLa, who was several
paces behind him. His voice was low and shaky as
he said, "My old mother lies ill in the Street of the
Lizard. My woman and I are summoned."

The guard glanced at his fellow. Both were big
and burly, their eyes bleary from the excesses of the

night. "How was the message carried to you? No one was permitted to enter or leave while the ceremonies were going on."

"The day before. My nephew called it through just as the gates were shut at sundown. Please, may we not go now?"

"Where do you work?" The guard was bored and the sun was hot. This might provide sport.

Kir had brought CeLa another robe from the kitchen, which she had draped over her head as women sometimes did to keep off the sun. Now she pulled it closer and began to moan through her teeth. The sound was highly unpleasant. Kir turned to face her, but she seized his arm and moaned louder.

"What is the matter with her? Is she sick, too?" The guard's head was beginning to ache all the more and it was hours before his relief.

"Ah, she has been afflicted all her life. She cannot speak but she is much attached to my mother. When she gets upset, she has fits."

The guard retreated. "Fits are sent by the goddess."

Kir was respectful. "Even so, sir. May we go before she too grows worse?"

Fearfully, the guard swung the gate wide. "Go quickly."

They shuffled through and out into the street, which was oddly quiet. Conscious of the fact that eyes might be watching, they went slowly until they turned the corner and several buildings hid them from the temple. Even then they walked only slightly more swiftly.

"Why did you do that? Your interference placed us both in jeopardy." Kir was angry and the sharp edge of his voice angered CeLa.

"He was set to bait you. Surely you could tell that. I but sought to divert his interest, and it worked. It was you who endangered us with that talk of fits. Suppose they had thought to take me before an official of the temple in the event that the goddess did truly speak through my fits?"

"What else was I to call that performance of yours? You should have kept silent as a woman should." He increased his pace and stalked ahead of her.

"I gave you good battle, Kir the arrogant!" CeLa threw the thrust at him and was surprised when he whirled to face her.

"What do you know of me?" He glared at her, his face rock-hard under the drooping turban. "Where have you heard of that?"

"You are arrogant. Is that so strange to you?"

He looked at her for a few seconds, then forced his lips into a smile. "We must not quarrel now that we are about to part. I did not mean to battle with you, CeLa. You are a good comrade."

The words rang falsely to her but they could not stand in the narrow street and argue. Soon they would attract attention.

"It does not matter. I too am at fault."

They walked on for a time, then Kir said, "I will go out the gates at the height of noontime while many others will doubtless be about. Do you live near the Gate of the Dawn?"

"Not far from there. I will go with you to the gate and bid you farewell."

"That is kind of you but you need not. Are you sure that you will be all right?" He fumbled in his pouch and withdrew some silver. "Take these. Be careful. I will think of you."

CeLa said, "I thank you, Kir, but I have no need of your silver. We have been friends, have we not? Remember your vow to bring Sirna down. Accomplish it if you would please me."

Kir laughed. "Sirna will fall as the barley before the wind, that I promise."

They moved through crowds that were becoming more numerous as they neared the gates. CeLa was

thankful to be among people again, to smell sweat,
to hear the chaffering of merchants and the clatter
of everyday life. Never again, she thought, would she
hold life so lightly and carelessly. The girl, Nandar's
daughter, was a woman now, a woman who must
make her destiny as best she could. Her heart hardened as she prepared for what she must do.

A merchant with a string of donkeys was haggling
with the guards at the gate. A line of workers in the
fields outside of Lagash was moving slowly along,
while a pompous official and several of his entourage
fumed in the back. Some soldiers stood nearby, ar-
guing about a past battle. A group of children played
idly in the shadow of the walls.

A breeze lifted the hanging section of Kir's head-
gear and he raised his arm to mop away the sweat.
His profile was strong and dark in the pouring light.
CeLa felt a pang of guilt but quickly stifled it as
he bent to her. His lips were on hers then and molten
warmth seared through her body. Her arms lifted to
his shoulders and she felt the quickening of his own
response. Hurriedly, he set her back from him.

"Ninhursag give you life and happiness, CeLa. We
shall not meet again but I shall honor you in my
prayers. You have done much more than you know
to bring justice to this land of Sumer."

He touched her hand, smiled into her eyes, and
as he did so, she saw the quirk of what looked to be
an old arrow wound on the edge of his cheekbone.
They stood silent as the sounds of the official and
his party rose at the gate. Abruptly, Kir turned and
started away.

"Stop. I go with you." CeLa heard the authority
in her voice as she walked up to him with a firm
step.

"You are mad to speak of it. Go back." He spoke
in a low tone, for they had come very near to the

guards at the gate where the official still complained in a loud, petulant voice.

"I go with you." She was level with him now and her voice lifted.

"By the gods, why? I do not want you. You cannot do this thing." His eyes were savage as they bored into hers. His words were biting.

"I have no kin in Lagash. The city will soon be torn by war. You know that as well as I. I will travel with you to the first city we come to. Ur, Uruk, Umma—it does not matter. I can make my way but I cannot travel alone."

He pushed her aside with a rough hand. "Out of my way, woman."

CeLa lifted her voice in the last gamble. "Are you a spy for Umma then, that you speak so?" The clear words carried the name of the hated rival to the official at the gate and he looked toward them. The same king ruled both cities but Lagash would never forget that she had been sacked by his order.

Kir hissed at her, "You will trap us both, fool!"

"You have praised Umma to me, sir. That makes you suspect in this city." She put both hands on her hips and stared up at him.

Two of the soldiers came up as they stood there and in a moment the fat official in his white robes followed them. His face was mottled by the heat. Little pig eyes glared from under his elaborate headdress.

"What manner of talk is this before the city gates? Are you rabble not aware that orders have come from the high priestess herself that we are in danger? That Umma may attack us? It is no secret; she has forbidden congregation in the streets. The name is not to be mentioned. I could have you imprisoned." The smell of fear came from him as he confronted them. "Answer me, rabble! What is the meaning of it?"

11

The Oasis of Zol

The altercation had begun to attract the bystanders, who drifted closer. The soldiers had their hands on their weapons. The watching children grew quiet. CeLa saw this and her gaze darted to Kir, whose eyes blazed at her even as he bent respectfully before the official.

"A thousand pardons, great one. My woman here is jealous. I did but talk with the seller in the marketplace and she must make a great fuss. A pig of Umma, she said. That is gross insult and I shall beat her when we reach home." Kir's voice was whining and his hands twisted in his robe.

"You are a pig of Umma, the worst thing I could call you. Fondling that girl and she letting you! Is it for this that I have borne your children and worked in the fields?" She advanced on him, her hand raised.

One of the soldiers stepped between them. Another waved at the crowd as he called, "Just some peasants having an argument. Get on along now. Hurry."

The official glared at them. "Where do you live?"

Kir waved vaguely in the direction of the fields outside the city. "Not far, great one. We meant no harm. We know nothing of great matters."

"Get out, rabble. Such as you should never leave your mud huts. You are lucky not to be in prison."

CeLa cried, "Men are all alike. Is it all right then for him to do as he wishes and insult me?"

The official nodded to the soldiers, who took her

by one arm, pushed Kir ahead of them and marched together to the gates. CeLa fell to the dust with the force of the shove she was given and the people watching roared with laughter.

Kir stalked ahead, ignoring her. She jumped up and followed him, conscious of many watchers. They went on this way until the road bent away from the gate and they were lost in trundling carts, soldiers moving about, lines of workers in the fields maintained by the city and merchants going out on business. The two attracted no interest, for they meshed perfectly, except for being dirtier than many.

CeLa exerted herself and caught up to Kir. "I'm sorry, but there was nothing else I could do. I could not remain in Lagash."

He spoke savagely. "I offered you silver. You could have made arrangements. A shop perhaps. A merchant would have found a woman possessing property in her own right to be interesting. But no! You must jeopardize all that I struggled to win. And for what? A whim!"

"I gave you the information you sought. It is not a whim to know that I would have died had I remained in the city. You do not know Sirna."

He laughed. "She thinks you dead." He stopped and looked down at her. She felt her flesh crawl as he did so. "You have outsmarted yourself, however. I do not go to a city but to a private meeting place, a hard journey from here. I could have left you in Lagash. If you babbled, it would have done no harm, but now I cannot risk it. You travel with me. Afterward it will be decided what to do with you."

The impersonal tone of his voice shook CeLa but she forced her voice to remain calm. "I have asked little of you in all honesty."

"If you cannot keep up with me or if you give me trouble, I will kill you. I should do it now but you fought well. Remember that we are even when next you seek to use me." He walked faster than ever and CeLa was forced to run to keep up.

The blazing sun of midday beat down on them as they followed the winding trail out into the dusty countryside. The rains were done and the canals cleared. It was the scorching time, the time when men moved slowly, glad of the coming of night. The workers in the fields owned by the city and those tending the irrigation, driving the oxen, hoisting the water, planting the crops, at least had their own security, thought CeLa as she tasted the grit in her mouth and felt the burning of her feet in the battered sandals Kir had found for her before they left Lagash.

Nothing could dampen her relief at leaving the city, however, and her body soon began to adapt to the punishing pace Kir set. The soft weeks in the temple had been tempered by her recent battles. She had always been wiry and strong. It seemed she was to need that strength now. If she fell down in the sand and died there, CeLa knew that she would not call out to Kir. Foolish pride, said her mind. She turned her head, feeling her hair dripping wet on her neck and in the turban. The walls of Lagash rose dark in the distance. At this rate they would be out of sight of it before dark.

One foot in front of the other, the refrain continued to beat in her thoughts. Kir never looked back. She might not have existed for him. His shoulders were straight, his stride free and easy. He was a man born to this country. Angry as she had been at him, CeLa could feel pride that such a one had helped and complimented her. Tired as she was now, she felt an odd prickling of her loins, akin to the pleasure she had felt when Sirna had so used her. She understood the hungers she had experienced too, for

Kir had raised them again. The terror that had flattened her for these many weeks had lifted and CeLa welcomed the return of life.

It was midafternoon when Kir finally paused beside a lone palm tree that gave only scanty shade. They had left the area of the cultivated land with its crops, canals and planted shade trees and were heading for the hilly, dusty, barren lands through which travelers made as much haste as they might. Here moved nomads, traders, soldiers seeking fresh battles in the ever-warring cities. Few traveled alone and certainly none moved as did Kir and CeLa, on foot and ill-equipped.

He handed her the leather bottle and watched as she took only a few sips before passing it back. The tone of his voice was mocking as he said, "You are weary? You will come to regret your insistence, I think."

"My father and I went between the cities. You have no reason to taunt me." CeLa felt her anger rise and knew that she must not give way to it. It annoyed her that she had felt desire for this man whose eyes flicked over her with amusement. "By the gods, I will save my breath for walking. You know why I insisted on coming and it was not for love of your company."

The tart words made Kir's head turn sharply. His eyes were dark, ringed with weariness and dirt. Sweat showed through his robes. CeLa knew that she too showed the ravages of the past days. They might have been strangers as they faced each other, with no thought of what the other had endured.

"We must go faster." Kir put the bottle back on his belt and began to move swiftly toward the east.

Questions rose to CeLa's lips but she shut them determinedly, tasting the dust caked there. Sooner or later even Kir must stop for the rest they both so desperately needed. She could only hope it would be before she collapsed and before the scavengers of the area found them. She concentrated on the broad wet back in front of her and moved in the same steady rhythm. Thought faded as she walked; more than anything else CeLa wanted to live, and she knew that if she fell, the arrogant man ahead of her would leave her where she lay. The mission on which he had been sent consumed him utterly. While she had been the source of information, she had been useful; now she was worthless to him. Their shadows stretched long on the flat land, but CeLa thought only of endurance.

This was a country she had never seen before. Most of the cities she and Nandar had visited or heard of had had vast areas of cultivated land with networks of canals and herds or crops maintained upon them. Even the barren areas into which they had occasionally gone had not been far from the civilizing influences. Nandar had told her that eventually all the land would be under control and producing, a veritable paradise of growth, if men ever learned to live together in peace. "But such is not the will of the gods," he had added with the bitterness that had come to be CeLa's own at such times.

When the fierce heat of the sun gave way to the shading of evening, Kir halted near a small hollow in the earth, barely large enough to see. "We rest here for the night. I will watch, then you. We must appear to be only weary wanderers, unworthy of a glance by those who seek for prey."

CeLa started to protest and felt weariness rise up so strongly that she was incapable of speech. She drank once more of the water that now seemed to be so little, then sank down on the spread robe Kir had indicated. The world spiraled around her and she knew no more as exhaustion finally took its toll.

It seemed no more than seconds later when Kir woke her, falling immediately upon the pallet she had vacated. CeLa was numb, her senses seemed paralyzed, but she was yet sensitive to the quiet of the flat land around them as the little wind brought sensations of coolness to her nostrils. The canals were far away but they carried their rich, damp odors to her. There was no sound, only the bright wheeling heavens and the still earth. Sleep dragged at her but the thought of Kir's anger and the sure knowledge that he would leave her made her sharply pinch the delicate skin on her wrists so as to stay awake.

With the first pink light, she shook his shoulder impatiently, only to have him roll in the opposite direction, one hand on his dagger and his body poised for a leap. She jumped back in her turn and looked at him angrily.

"It is dawn. I thought you might want to get started before the heat becomes so severe."

Kir straightened up and looked through her, his eyes dark with urgency, lost in his own concerns. "Time is short. You were right to wake me, but heat or not, I must make rendezvous at the appointed time."

After that it was a battle against time and the heat. As strong and determined as Kir was, even he could not sustain such a pace in the blistering midday. He begrudged every second that they paused, but CeLa had vowed to maintain his own speed and she did so, though at great cost to mind and body alike.

By the evening of their first full day of walking, the water gave out. They had eaten the last barley cake as they moved, soon after first light. CeLa was swiftly conscious of the raging thirst that possessed her, but she sought to put it from her mind. Kir stalked ahead, as firm and determined as ever. She could only follow as time wheeled on. Sleep became no more than a stupor for the very short time that they were able to rest. Hours were not measured in time but in breaths.

CeLa's tongue was swollen large in her mouth; her head hammered and her eyes burned in their sockets. It was ironic, she thought, that she had escaped the pits of Lagash to die in the wilderness. She stumbled and almost fell. A small cry came from her cracked lips as the world spun around her. Kir swung round and she thought of his angry words with the threat to kill her. Surely he could not have meant it?

He bent over her in the heat haze and she saw that his own eyes were inflamed, his lips puffed large. "Get up and walk. I will not be delayed."

"Leave me as you wanted to do." Her whisper was loud in her ears.

"We are too close to our goal. I cannot risk the possibility that you might be found by those dangerous to my master. Get up, I said!"

Exhaustion burned in her and she did not think she could walk another step. Her head dangled loosely and the world swam.

"Did you spend all your courage in the pits of Lagash? I think ill that I counted you a brave woman. You delay me at your peril." The taunting note was in his voice again and his prod at her was almost disdainful.

CeLa felt rage sweep through her. "The gods curse your stupid cause as I do." She struggled to her feet and swayed drunkenly.

"You waste my time with this wailing. Come or I will drag you until we both die!" He jerked at her arm. She pulled free and staggered after him into the miles and the never-ending heat.

Now anger drove CeLa to put one foot in front of the other, regardless of her pain and exhaustion. Had she the strength, she would have thrown herself upon him with teeth and nails. As it was, she invented punishments, each more spectacular and savage than the last, while she watched the strong figure ahead of her. He turned frequently to watch her and each time she met his gaze with her chin up, her eyes defiant.

It seemed a mirage at first. The scrawny palm trees and the glitter of water from several separate small pools, a dusty mound off to one side and several camels standing patiently. CeLa rubbed her eyes with gritty hands, causing them to burn all the more. She opened them again and the vision remained even through the lines of heat that shimmered in front of her. She did not dare to hope and so walked straight into Kir as he stood at the top of the little rise. Words parched her mouth as she forgot her anger.

"Real?" She could say no more.

He turned to her and his black eyes were brilliant, a faint gray light piercing in their depths. The desperation had faded from his cracked and gritty face as he answered, "The oasis of Zol. I am in time."

Nothing thereafter would be as glorious to CeLa as the taste of water, taken sparingly at first, sipped cautiously, and then more swiftly. She could not leave it but lay at the side of the pool with her fingers touching the water. She unwound and soaked the long end of her turban, then applied it to her face as she tried to cool its burning surface.

Kir had drunk little and gone almost immediately to the goat-hair tent set up a safe distance from the pools. CeLa barely noticed; nothing mattered but the water. He had left the leather bottle with her. Now she picked it up and retreated to the far side of the pool, where in the shadow of one of the palms, she unwound some of the wrappings from her body and poured the cool water over herself.

The sun was setting and shadows stretched long. A tiny breeze rattled the leaves of the palms as CeLa,

feeling more alive with each flood of water, pushed
her hair over her shoulders and let it stream down.
Her small breasts jutted through the thin material
of the robe and lifted with the movements of her
arms. A ray of the fading sun touched them as she
lifted the bottle and drank deeply, her eyes closed in
delight.

A shadow detached itself from one of the trees
and flung itself upon her, ripping the remainder of
the robe from her body as she tumbled to the ground.
CeLa shrieked once before a hard hand closed over
her mouth. She looked up into a fearful face as they
struggled, his male organ erect and hard as it pressed
against her naked body. Horror made her lie still
for a moment.

The man was not bearded but one side of his face
bore a huge red mass that grew out of his mouth
down into his neck and up into one eye. It was veined
and pulsating. It was so large that the other side of
his face was drawn down and twisted. She thought
it looked as if he had eaten the entrails of animals
and had not yet finished his meal. The body that
grappled with hers was large and misshapen, the
hands overgrown and hard. These impressions passed
over her and faded as she fought and kicked without
success. The huge organ pushed her wide. His hand
slipped from her mouth as she twisted and gave one
last scream. Her broken nails clawed ineffectually
and her heels drummed at the sand.

Suddenly the splaying weight was jerked from her
forcefully and thrown back. She jumped to her feet
with the instinct of a cornered animal. Kir, short
sword in hand, faced the apparition that now lum-
bered toward him as it muttered unintelligible sounds
of rage. Kir was a tall man and muscular, well restored with water and wine from the nomad's tent
from which he had emerged, but he was no match

for the thing that loomed at least three heads taller than he. CeLa caught up her own small dagger from the pieces of the robe where they had been flung.

Even as the apparition lunged at Kir, slamming him back against the bole of a palm tree, she drove the dagger into the huge bare back. The beast gave a bellow of rage, shook the dagger loose and turned back to her. She circled backward as if to draw attention away from Kir, who took that opportunity to rise and lift his sword again. The thing gave a shattering bellow of rage and stretched out its long arms.

Kir rasped a command. "Run while you can." Sweat stood out on his arms and forehead but a little smile curved up one corner of his mouth.

CeLa wondered at his apparent pleasure in battle even as she was thankful that he fought at least partly for her sake. The concern in his eyes was not for himself alone. That knowledge gave her the courage to say, "No, I stand with you." Her voice was rock steady even over the terror that held her.

The man-thing bellowed again and started toward them. There was no more time for words. Kir danced to one side and CeLa the other. It would only be a matter of time, however, until both were worn down. The nomad and his wife were old; they could not help even if they would. Kir and CeLa were alone in this losing battle for their lives.

The apparition was very close now, the growth on his face shaking redly in the last light before darkness. Suddenly there was a whirring sound, a long gurgle, then it clutched its chest and fell prone in the sand, a long arrow piercing the huge body.

CeLa leaned shivering against a tree but Kir ignored her as he stared out into the darkness where a tall figure with a drawn bow was cautiously approaching.

12

Campaign

The figure came into full view while Kir stood with his sword at the ready. He would take no chances even with one who had undoubtedly saved their lives. CeLa pulled one of the largest tatters from the robe over her lower body, conscious that it hid little but past caring.

"What was that?" The incredulous voice of their rescuer came toward them as he neared the huge body that lay where it had fallen. "I heard those screams and thought it some strange animal until it turned that awful face."

He was a tall man, dark and burned by the sun, in early middle age. In addition to the bow and arrows, he carried a dagger and short sword. His clothes were loose and dark but a rich jewel glimmered in one ear.

CeLa spoke from the shadows. "We thank you for our lives. It came so suddenly . . . a demon of the desert perhaps."

The man looked at her disarray and a smile began in the depths of his beard. "We must pray that there are no more like him."

She saw flickers in the dark eyes and knew that he thought she had been interrupted with a lover who had fled in fear. He moved closer. As he did so, Kir stepped close to his side.

"She is right, Sokar. Our thanks."

The man turned to face Kir, his face changing into

stern lines as he saw the haggard appearance. One hand lifted in a quick gesture that was repeated instantly by Kir. CeLa felt sudden tension rise in the charged atmosphere as the release from the terror of the past moments faded and a new threat appeared.

The man, Sokar, looked at Kir and there was a faint thread of scorn in his voice as he said, "It is the fourth evening that I have come. One does not expect such of Kir the Arrogant."

CeLa felt her flesh tingle. So had she called him, though half in play, and he had rounded on her in surprise and anger.

Sokar was continuing, "The little flotsam of the desert has distracted you, I see. Are there messages then, or do you come empty handed?"

Kir was standing stiffly but in the light of the rising moon CeLa could see the pulse hammering in his throat and the angry line of his mouth. His words, however, were calm. "This is not the time for personal differences or anger. You have saved our lives but I suggest that you not stir that antagonism that has ever stood between us. Let be until such time as we can settle it." The sharp edge of fury showed slightly. "Then I will hold you fully responsible."

CeLa stood still, her own anger rising as she heard the casual way this man had dismissed her. Her pride still smarted after the treatment Kir had offered her. What could she have done? A pox on all men who considered a woman of no more import than a thing to be used and tossed aside!

"We came as swiftly as we could and have often been in peril of our lives," she said aloud. "I suggest that you hear what Kir has to say before venturing such opinions."

Two pairs of incredulous eyes swung toward the nearly naked girl who stood proudly in the light and shadow of the night, her hair a dusky torrent down her back, her eyes dark pools of anger.

Sokar was the first to recover as he said smoothly, "Your pardon, both of you. I can see that I have been overhasty, but our orders were explicit."

"So they were and I have all the information that is required. It is urgent that it be given without delay to the king, for it may mean that he will wish to alter his battle plans. Summon your messenger that he may be sent ahead of us to warn him." Kir spoke authoritatively, the snap of command in his words.

It was light enough for CeLa to see the flush that rose in Sokar's cheeks above the beard. "By the gods, Kir, I summon no one until you have told me what you have learned. You have stood by his side and spoken freely with him, drunk of his wine cup, well and good. But this is war and I have been chosen to lead this particular enterprise. Lead it I shall. Do you concede my authority?"

Kir put one hand on his dagger and his dark brows drew together in a scowl. Then he gave a half smile. "For now, yes."

CeLa felt the fierce antagonism between the two men and somehow knew that it went far back in their relationship. Who was the king of whom they spoke? What was the mysterious mission and the cause for which Kir had been willing to give both their lives?

Sokar was saying now, "It is well. Come now, and tell me what you must. Drink wine with me." He was generous in victory.

They moved away into the shadows of the palms, leaving CeLa beside the pool. She sat cross-legged on the bank and dipped her hands into the cool water. After the weariness and strife of the past, it was sheer blessed relief to do nothing for a little while. The tree fronds swayed against the dark sky as a breeze drifted across her face and the moon rose higher over the flat land. How peaceful it was here.

CeLa remembered how Nandar had spoken cynically of the growing cultivation of the lands with irrigation and of how, but for the continual warring between the cities, all Sumer might be so for the betterment of all people, even such as they. "But war is pleasure and comfort, a thing not to be forgone." She had deplored his words then, but now she knew that he was right.

Sokar and Kir were walking back and forth not far away. She heard the low hum of their voices and caught something of the urgency in them. The light poured over the rise from which Sokar had come and glittered on the body of the monster that had so nearly destroyed them. How strange were the ways of the gods! She had endured much that only a few moons ago would have seemed incredible to the girl who lived quietly with her father in the little house in Lagash. Now she was prepared to struggle once more for the right to live her own life. Whoever these people were that Sokar and Kir served, surely the addition of one girl to travel with them as far as a city would not matter. She pillowed her head on her hands and slept.

It could have been only a few minutes before a hand on her shoulder brought her upright. Kir was standing back, an angry scowl on his face. Sokar squatted beside her, his manner wholly changed from the cheerful disrespect of earlier.

"Kir has told me that you wish to be taken to a city and left there to pursue your own life. He has promised that this shall be done."

CeLa lifted amazed eyes to Kir, who glared back. Obviously he had not told Sokar of the trick she had played on him.

Sokar continued, "Your wishes shall be honored, of course, but I would ask this of you. Will you hear me out?"

Kir snorted but Sokar ignored him. CeLa looked
into the handsome face before her and saw that it,
like Kir's, was drawn with weariness and anxiety.

"Gladly."

"Soon war will engulf much of this land. Indeed,
the impact has already been felt and cities have fall-
en, but the great campaign is even now preparing.
There may be danger for you."

CeLa was suddenly weary of subterfuge and guile.
Her words were sharp as she said, "Speak straightly.
What are you asking? Whom do you serve?"

It was Kir who answered, "Sargon the Mighty,
Sargon, King of Agade and ruler of Akkad. Soon to
be ruler of all Sumer." There was the rattle of lances
in his voice.

CeLa sniffed. "One king is like another. What does
it matter?"

Sokar drew his breath in with a hiss, but Kir
laughed outright. "Sokar commands here, as he has
said. CeLa, he has decided that this tale of yours is
incredible, that this sort of slaughter you describe
vanished hundreds of years ago. We know of Sirna
but we did not know the extent of her power. I was
sent to treat secretly with Abdar, who was noted to
be a reasonable man who sought peace. We wanted
to ally Lagash with us while her ruler seeks to further
his lands by battling in the south and while he
thinks that Sargon yet fights in the north, as we
have led him to believe. Now that plan is lost."

He paused for breath and Sokar spoke hurriedly.
"I would have you tell this tale to Sargon himself.
He will know the truth."

"He will know it anyway, from you, his emissaries."
CeLa knew that she would have to go, for they had
no intention of setting down in a strange city one
who knew all these things, but she would play the
game out a little longer.

Kir's eyes flickered at her and she knew that he

understood even as he said, "Of course, if you are adamant . . ."

She did not want to anger Sokar and she knew that the desperation of both men was very real. What manner of man was this Sargon that such devotion to him was forthcoming? In Lagash the ruler was not held in high esteem and was openly hated because of the cruelty that he, being of the hated Umma, had brought to Lagash.

Sokar said, "Will you come willingly?"

"Does so much depend on my personal recitation of these things I have endured? Will your ruler not believe the word of his trusted friend Kir?"

Kir looked at her but she knew he was not displeased that Sokar was being forced to show his hand.

"He will be able to tell much from your manner and words that is not possible from such as Kir and myself. Even I find it incredible. We fight among ourselves in this land but we are civilized. The gods do not demand so much of us."

CeLa was silent as Kir snapped, "We have wasted hours in this foolish meeting. Believe me well, Sokar, time is precious. The king will not be pleased that we waste it. The girl comes with us, of her own will or without it. Is that not so?"

Sokar turned to CeLa. "Forgive me, but that is the way of it. I would not have spoken so crudely to one who has suffered as you and who is so fair, but it is war."

CeLa knew his remarks for practiced flattery but the trite excuses for any inhumanity man might choose to render to his fellows sickened her. She said slowly, "I do not think one king can matter more than another but I am both penniless and homeless. If I do this of my own will, I will ask payment. A wage upon which to live, that I may set up my own business as a scribe in one of the cities that your ruler will so thoughtfully liberate. I will ask enough to buy materials, a house, furnishings and clothes. That is my price, you who serve Sargon, and unless you pay it, my body will stand before him but my lips will be mute."

Sokar was at a loss for words but Kir answered her. "As all women do, you have set your price. Well, commander of the mission, what is your answer?"

"Only one answer is possible." Sokar had recovered his dignity. "I do not blame the girl. She is alone and apparently friendless. CeLa, in the name of Sargon of Akkad, I promise that you shall have what you demand."

She too could be generous. "And your ruler shall have knowledge of the perfidy of Sirna."

"By all the gods, we have wasted enough time. Let us go!" Kir did not look at CeLa but she had heard the flaying contempt in his voice and wondered at it. Now he strode toward the rise as Sokar gave a high whistle that was quickly answered by another.

CeLa waited as the little group that came toward them was quickly sorted out. There were four men and four onagers—the asses often used for travel— and a separate man who, after a swift consultation, set off at a run that seemed to gobble up the miles. That would be the messenger, trained for such duties, whom Kir had wanted to send earlier. Two men were left to bury the monster. CeLa was set in back of Sokar on an ass and they set off across the rough ground at a surprising rate of speed. Sokar had given her his cloak to hide her nudity but his help was impersonal. His touch as he lifted her up was the same. Did he think she should have helped them for sheer pleasure? How strange. She yawned, leaned against the hard back in front of her, oblivious to the stare Kir gave her, and fell asleep.

It was full dawn when CeLa woke to find herself in front of Sokar, held by him in one arm. Apparently they had moved about in the night and she had not even roused. Her mouth tasted of brown fur, the corners of her eyes were matted and she felt grimy, but her bone-exhausting weariness was gone. Memory came back to her with a rush and she recalled the bargain she had struck. Here was provision for her future; here was safety. She did not know if the mysterious king could be trusted, but Sokar had sworn in his name and she had seen the little flames in his eyes that told her she was fair to his sight. CeLa had seen that look before and knew that it could be worked to her advantage. Only Kir had looked at her with the honesty of a comrade; only he had been friend. Now he found her of no interest, for he still felt that she had betrayed him there at the gates of Lagash.

CeLa's eyes burned with sudden tears. What else could I have done? she thought. I survive by my wits or not at all. She thought of the foulness of Sirna's touch and her own response, then knew that she had hungered for Kir as for a cool wind in the heat.

She shuddered and Sokar looked down at her. "We have come far in the night and the animals are exhausted from their burden. Can you walk with us, Kir and me, or would you prefer to stay behind with the men who will bring them at a slower pace?"

CeLa laughed and for once her delight was real. "You offer choices that are no choices, Sokar. Am I really to think that you would leave me behind when, according to you, your master waits breathlessly for my tale?"

He was affronted. "The bargain is made. We trust each other, do we not?"

"Of course, but what surety have I that when I have done all that you ask, I am not simply sent away, another beggar in the wake of an army?"

"You have the word of the king whose representative I am." Sokar set her down from the ass and she saw that he was angry. His orders to the men were curt and they obeyed hurriedly.

Kir came up to join them, his eyes hooded and unreadable, his carved face blank. "How much farther?"

The land lay flat before them but now in the distance she could see the outline of hills or mountains. They shimmered in the already heavy heat. A large bird hung motionless in the still air. CeLa felt sweat trickle between her breasts in the muffling robe and thought that if she ever came into her own, she would bathe and change clothes several times a day for the pure joy of it.

Once again they walked in an unchanging pattern, one behind the other, at a speed that seemed to eat up the miles. They did not speak, for to do so would take up breath needed for movement. CeLa had hacked a piece of the robe off and wound it around her head to ward off the fierce heat of the sun. She reflected wryly that in the past few moons she had spent more of her life naked, or very near it, than many a child. If she won through to safety, it would be a great tale to tell in her old age. She smiled inadvertently. As a woman of property, she could take a husband if she wished, but the freedom to choose was hers. A lover, perhaps, but not a husband to make demands and seek to manage what was not his.

"You find contemplation of the future exciting?" Kir had come up beside her, his dark eyes taunting.

Stung, CeLa faced him so that he stopped suddenly. "Why do you persist in deriding me, Kir? Am I to grovel before you because of a trick that has, in the end, done you no harm and saved my own life?"

Sokar was moving ahead of them and could not hear their words. His back was straight and proud.

Kir was so close to her that she could see the little pulse hammering in the hollow of his throat. She

wondered what it would be like to set her lips to
that place. The familiar anger was in his eyes—it
never seemed to leave them—but she read puzzlement
there as well.

He said, "Believe me, CeLa, you will wish to all
the gods that you had stayed in Lagash before all
this is done. You are a foolish girl. You lied to me,
moreover, and now you think that you will find adventure." His hand went out to push her away from
him.

She caught it. "Kir, can we not at least be friends
as we were in the temple of Ninhursag? What is
done cannot be changed after all."

He pried her fingers loose and pushed her from
him all in one gesture, but she could not miss his
response to her touch before his control took over.
His voice was hard as he said, "Sokar is the leader
here. He thinks you will be of use. There is no more
to be said on that score. Friends? You delude yourself surely." He laughed and it seemed to have real
mirth. Then he strode after Sokar in long steps, his
head high and shoulders back.

CeLa felt her pulses hammer even as, for the second time that day, tears burned in her eyes and
throat. There had been no anger in his parting words,
only a great weariness. She could not doubt that he
meant them. But with a wisdom as old as time, she
knew that he fought his own interest in her. Had
he not fought to save her life? No matter that he
would likely have done as much for anyone else,
even a stranger. They had shared life and death; indifference could not be between them. She walked
on behind the others, remembering Kir's actions on
the journey to the oasis. His words had been harsh, his
actions savage, but she had been so angered that she
forgot her bodily discomfort and so had endured.
He had known how to help her even then and she
could not doubt that he had done so deliberately.

Hot wind swirled the sand around her feet and sweat beaded her forehead, but she was oblivious as she recalled his lips on hers, his arms around her at the walls of Lagash. What was this strange power, this fire, that bound her to Kir the Arrogant? She yearned for him, longed to be within the sound of his voice and the sight of his eyes. She had seen other men, certainly, and talked with them in the wanderings with Nandar. None of them had touched her interest, though some had smiled boldly at the shy girl.

CeLa paused suddenly as she remembered the tales of the heroes, the legends of the men who walked with gods and were made as they, the stories of the mighty kings of far-off times. Nandar had told her such stories since her childhood; was it so strange that the man who had saved her life, who had given her tenderness and courage in the bitterness of her fear, should walk now in her dreams? He was the first man who had touched her woman's flesh and aroused it. Cruel he had been, but were the gods not cruel also and for less reason?

She shivered in the heat, for she knew, without knowing how she knew, that their futures were intertwined and that this was the will of the high gods themselves. Kir was the man she had dreamed of in the long nights, the hero of her dreams made real. "Let him turn to me, great ones!" She spoke the words and knew that they were heard.

13

Sargon of Akkad

Time was endless after that. It seemed to CeLa that she had walked this land all her life, endlessly plodding in the blistering heat, her emotions in turmoil.

"I am a fool to care for him, a fool to see his face before me. Far better to cultivate the interest that Sokar has shown in me, however slight." CeLa knew herself better than to believe such thoughts, however. Perhaps the sun had touched her; perhaps the goddess planned a punishment. Her thoughts seemed to weigh her head down. Her mouth sucked eagerly at the dry bottle from which water had long vanished and her cracked lips began to flake as she ran her dry tongue over them.

It grew dark. The moon rose and grew pale in the sky. The land was silent and still behind them, rocky and high before them. They had reached the mountains and were in the foothills where the walking grew harder with every step.

Suddenly an arrow whizzed directly in front of Sokar and caused him to stop. Kir and CeLa did the same as they almost fell over each other in their exhaustion. Sokar gave a low, half-warbling whistle as he held his hands out in front of him. The others did the same.

"Advance." The command came from a gaunt, bearded man muffled to the eyes in a mantle. A bright sword reflected in the moonlight. There were three silent guards around him.

"By the orders of the king, I, Sokar, have returned and seek to give my report."

"And these?" The sword waved in the direction of Kir and CeLa.

Kir stepped close, his size seeming to dwarf the questioner. "Samu, commander of the armies of the king, can it be that you do not know me? Am I so changed from the days when we sported in the Silver Mountains and you told me tales of the great seas?"

The older man peered hard at Kir and his sword dropped to the rough ground even as his body remained alert. "Kir, it has been many years, has it not? I have heard much of you and prayed to the goddess to protect you."

CeLa moved closer in her turn and the sharp old eyes assessed her as they turned to Kir, who anticipated a question not to his liking as he said, "We have come with urgent messages for the king and must deliver them without delay. This woman has valuable information and must be with us."

Samu smiled, a grotesque splitting of leather lips. "Your messenger lies even now insensible, so exhausted was he from the run across the hot lands. The king sleeps, for you were not expected before the high sun tomorrow at the very earliest."

"Wake him." Kir made to stride past Samu but Sokar stepped in his way.

"I was given command and authority here. Do you seek to command in my stead?"

"We waste time." Kir shook free.

"Rest and refresh yourselves for the space of a few hours. Then you will be conducted to the king. He was up for the past day and night before going hunting in the wildness of these mountains only this afternoon. Dawn will be soon enough." Samu's words were conciliatory, but his eyes blazed at those who sought to usurp his authority.

"As you wish." Kir spread both hands helplessly. "I cannot rest until my mission is discharged. Let the others do as they wish. Will you lift a cup with me, Samu, in honor of the old days?"

"Gladly, Kir." He clapped the younger man on the back while Sokar watched sourly.

CeLa was conducted to a shelter made of hides and rocks that was close by. It was small but there was a crude bench, an ornate chest and a pile of robes to serve as a bed. A small girl who seemed to be all eyes and hair stood beside a leather bucket filled with water. Food and wine stood on a nearby rock.

"I am Pina, lady. I will help you wash."

CeLa tried to decline but so great was her weariness that words would not come as she sank to the rock and reached for the wine. Pina quickly handed her a container of water with which to wash it down. The heady stuff made her giddy and the world swung in flickering circles by the light of the small torch glowing just outside. The meat, whatever it was, stuck in her throat, but she chewed grimly while Pina washed her and rubbed her dry.

"Rest now. I will call you when it is time."

The soft voice rang in her ears as CeLa collapsed on the robes and drew the cloth over her naked body. Laughter came from just outside. A voice called in a strange language and was answered in her own. There was the sound of tramping feet, and a melancholy song beseeched the favor of the goddess of love, Inanna.

CeLa felt oddly at home, in spite of her aching body, and she drifted into sleep thinking, not of Kir, but of the great boat moving down the Euphrates.

"Lady, lady, it is time!" Pina hovered over CeLa in the first dim light. "You must hurry."

CeLa gave herself time for one annoyed thought at the whims of rulers, though she had known none.

The hard common sense she had acquired in the years of wandering told her that here lay her chance. She must not lose it. Willingly, she let her helper dress her in a loose green robe belted with gold. Her dark hair was combed back from her forehead and held in a caul of gold that flickered with gems. Leather sandals were placed on her feet and a gauzy cloak fell from her shoulders.

Pina held up a polished copper mirror for her to look. CeLa stared at a face she had seen only in water until she went to the temple of Ninhursag. Her mouth was firmer, her eyes appeared more deeply set, her skin shone more darkly from the sun.

"You are fair." The young girl gave her own assessment.

"You are kind to me. I am grateful." CeLa smiled and saw it reflected in Pina's own.

She drew her breath in deeply as she followed the soldier into whose keeping Pina had given her. The dawn air was sweet and fresh with a hint of chill that was very welcome to one who had been baked in the sun for days on end. They were in the edges of the mountains where rocks and small trees abounded. Several small shelters such as the one where she had spent the night stood in a cluster not far away. The silent guard took her past these up to a larger one that was also crudely made. He spoke to the sentry there and CeLa was bidden to enter.

"Come, walk behind me." Her new escort was fully armed with sword, dagger and club at his belt. They went through a narrow fissure in the rock of the side of the mountain that had seemed gigantic to eyes bred to the flat Sumerian plains.

CeLa was engrossed in staring about her and did not see the stray rock before stumbling over it. But for the strong hand of her escort she would have fallen headlong. She could not bite back the small

oath that escaped her. The young man laughed and
in a second she joined him.

"Only a little way now. Watch where you step."

The passage was beginning to remind CeLa of the
temple and sick fear touched her for an instant. "The
air is stuffy in here." The smoke of the torches was
making her eyes smart, but she did not want to rub
them and dislodge the kohl Pina had put there.

They rounded a turn. The air grew clearer and
suddenly a wide space opened up in front of them.
It was bounded by outcroppings of rock yet free
to the air and light. A tall man might easily walk
under the ledges. A fire burned to one side and its
light showed another passage leading back into darkness. Looking up, CeLa saw guards patrolling the rim.
Food and drink as well as a tossed-aside cloak lay
on a rock near the fire.

She turned to ask the young soldier a question,
but he had vanished. She was alone in the bowels
of the Zagros Mountains. Cautiously she advanced
to the center of the room. Truly, this might be a
place where the gods met when walking the earth,
so secret did it appear. The first ray of sunlight
speared down just then and CeLa followed it with
her eyes.

The man had walked so quietly that she had not
heard a sound. Surprise kept her staring. He was in
his early middle years or slightly younger, simply
clad in a tunic of coarse cloth, his dark hair bound
back with a fillet of silver. A wide sword was at his
waist, and his feet were bare, as were his arms. But
it was his face that held CeLa. The lips were full
and sensual, faintly red. He wore a short beard, elaborately done in ringlets, that emphasized the strong
chin and jaw. His eyes were direct and powerful,
glittering with force.

He halted a short distance from CeLa and waited.

She jerked herself from her trance and went to her knees as one did before the gods. Her hands were shaking; what perfidy to stand gaping at the king—for it could be none other—who held her future in his hands.

"Rise, CeLa of Lagash and Nippur. I bid you welcome to one of the many houses of Sargon of Agade."

CeLa remembered that Kir had spoken briefly with Sokar of one of his journeys to Sargon's capital of Agade near the Euphrates in the northern kingdom of Akkad. She had wondered at the time what had brought Kir into the service of what seemed so powerful a ruler. Then the familiar anger had risen and she had blotted him out.

Now she lifted her head, straightened and looked into the compelling eyes. "I am the servant of Sargon." Where was Kir? For that matter, where was Sokar? Was she to be left alone to give what information she must? Her blood chilled. She opened her mouth and shut it abruptly.

Sargon gestured toward the ground where a cloak had been spread. "Sit. Wine will be brought presently."

It was a command. Numbly, CeLa lowered herself onto the cloak as he sat on the bare ground in crosslegged fashion.

"Tell me about Lagash."

CeLa tried again to speak and could not. He saw her discomfort and slapped both hands together.

"By the gods, woman, Kir told me you were of surpassing courage, a comrade with whom he would be proud to fight. There is nothing to fear."

He sat boldly, as if an image of the god of the mountain, and CeLa felt the power in him. He inspired both awe and fear. A thought flickered randomly: A true match, he and Sirna. Behind that came the warm realization that Kir still honored what he called her courage, her own strong will to

survive. She felt proud that he had spoken well of
her to his ruler.

Suddenly it was easy to say, "Forgive me. I was
overawed by one so powerful." There was enough
truth to it to be palatable but she saw the dark eyes
cloud.

"Leave your flattery and fine words for the throne
rooms and the sycophants. Speak truly." He crossed
his arms in front of him, watched her piercingly and
waited.

"As you will have it." CeLa began her tale with
the death of Nandar and the plight in which it had
left her. The recitation spun out, wine was brought
and she drank the richness of it without knowing as
she lived again the fearful days so recently past.

The man before her did not move from his position even though the tale ran into hours. His attention was complete as he assessed her voice and bearing, probed for the strength and truth of her character.

CeLa was oblivious, for she was again in the death-
pits of Lagash, fighting for her life. Her hatred of
Sirna spilled out in venom. She did not detail the
sexual abuse she had undergone, nor did she speak
of her own shameful pleasure in it, but the intima-
tion of it was in her tone. Her listener marked it
well.

At last the tale was done. She stopped and drank
deeply of the wine, tasting it this time, savoring it
in her parched throat.

"You have done well." Sargon rose effortlessly to
his feet and waved one arm. "Summon the others."

CeLa rose as he did. She felt a curious lightness,
as if a weight had been lifted. It had been thus when
she told Kir of her perils. She still felt the same
toward Sirna, that would not lessen, but each time
she spoke of it, it became easier to bear.

Sokar and Kir approached now and stood before

Sargon, who acknowledged them with a gesture. They had washed, changed clothes and eaten. Kir looked as if he had not slept and she doubted that he had. His face was dark and grim, in contrast to that of Sokar.

Sargon said, "You were wise to bring the woman to me. The delay it has caused me was justified, Sokar. Had it not been, you would have felt the weight of my punishment."

His tone was conversational but Sokar paled as he bowed. CeLa had no doubt that the king could be utterly ruthless and she felt a little chill dance up her spine.

"Go now and begin to ready the men for departure. Report to Samu. He will have duties for you."

Sokar's mouth thinned at the abrupt dismissal but he bowed again and went swiftly out.

Sargon clapped Kir on the shoulder, the warmth in his voice in marked contrast to the tone he had used with Sokar. "My friend, I have missed you. It has been many moons since we drank and wenched together." He poured out wine into one of the cups, drank deeply and offered it to Kir, who took it, saluted him and drank in his turn.

"I have missed the company of my king." Kir's words were utterly sincere, with a depth of feeling CeLa had not heard before.

"I will withdraw shortly to take counsel of the gods and to plan my strategy. There will be a meeting of my captains in the afternoon, a feast this night; we march soon." Sargon slammed one fist into the palm of the other hand and the black eyes were savage with the lust for power.

"This time I shall march at your shoulder as of old." Kir spoke offhandedly but CeLa saw how the muscles bunched together in his shoulders as he leaned forward.

"I have not told you this, Kir, but my armies stand

even now at the gates of Uruk. Some of them sailed down the river, some came overland. My spies circulate rumor of my might in Ur. Others have given me reports of Lugalzaggesi, Lord of Lagash and Umma, he who calls himself Lord of Sumer. He is in the far south, near the sea, little knowing that soon my armies will march against him. I travel swiftly and lightly between my forces that I may miss nothing."

"Let me fight with you." This time the longing in Kir's voice came home to Sargon, and CeLa felt her heart wrench.

"I will decide soon. Your skills as a warrior are great, my friend, but the gods have given you the healer's knowledge and touch, the scholar's wisdom. You may render better service elsewhere. Do not press me."

Kir inclined his head and as he did so, Sargon's gaze passed over it and came to rest on CeLa. She saw from the surprise in his eyes that he had forgotten her.

"Take your woman with you, Kir. I am grateful to her."

Bitterness ripped out of him then. "She is none of mine, my lord. As you know, women are for bed and inn only. I believe that Sokar struck a bargain with her."

"Bargain?" The heavy brows drew together in a scowl.

"If I may speak for myself?" CeLa voiced her protest. "As the great king knows, I am alone and must find my own way as best I might. I but asked a sum of money large enough to buy a dwelling wherein I could pursue my business as my father the scribe taught me. I would live in a neutral city and be at peace with the world, studying and reading. Surely the information I have brought is worth that."

"The information you have given me will bring

down Lagash and Umma far sooner than I had hoped.
The gods do not demand human sacrifice. In time,
CeLa, you shall have what you ask. That and more.
But now, as of this time on, you serve in the armies
of Sargon. When I have no more need of you, then
you will be free."

CeLa heard the arrogant words and saw the smile
on Kir's face. Had he manipulated this? Fury took
her as she cried, "But I do not care who rules Sumer. Let me go!"

"That choice was made when you left Lagash. Go
and calm yourself. I cannot abide a wailing woman.
This affront will be forgotten but look to yourself in
the future!"

Sargon turned and stalked away, leaving CeLa to
stare after him as Kir's laughter rang in her ears.

14

The Mission

CeLa spent what remained of the morning and the early afternoon lying on a rock in the shade of a small stunted tree within sight of her shelter. The girl, Pina, watched from a distance. She had tried to accompany CeLa but had been ruthlessly commanded to leave. One of the guards kept her discreetly in view.

The breeze blew softly over CeLa's flushed, angry face as she recalled how Kir had laughed as she ran past him, heedless of the startled sentries. She had heard the bitter note in it and was glad to know that he too was unhappy. She was fiercely glad that it appeared he was not to have his wish to fight. The king was a demanding master, yet Kir counted him friend. Now she was part of this. What could a girl do in the conquering armies? She had no doubt that they would conquer; power was strong in Sargon. Now she had offended him and lost whatever favor she might have gained.

There was a clatter as a pebble dislodged beneath her. She sat up and looked into Sokar's eyes. Politeness was beyond her as she snapped, "Now what is it? Have I not endured enough for one day?"

"Believe me, CeLa, I am sorry. It was such a simple request, I was sure that he would grant it."

"Well, he did not, and I am trapped. It is my own fault that I trusted the words of others."

"Can you forgive me?" The brilliant eyes looked

warmly at her and she saw the admiration in them. "If you can, will you sit beside me at the feast this night?"

She laughed and her self-pity was gone. "Am I bidden to it?"

"Of course. A woman of spirit is admired in Akkad. You need not fear the reprisal of the king. He will use you but you must fight for what you will have."

"As you do?" The barbed words were out before she could stop them and the warmth froze on his face. "I do not mean to be cruel, Sokar. It is just that I think Sargon would have yielded had Kir asked it; instead he baited me and gloried in it."

"Do you love him, CeLa?" The question came so softly and naturally that she might not have heard it the first time.

"He helped me in a desperate time. You saved both our lives. I care for you both." CeLa was being cautious, for she did not trust Sokar; there was something devious about him even in his most open moments.

"Kir is a dangerous man, CeLa. Many women have sought him. The king would have chosen a fair bride for him but he would have none of it. He seeks out the ugly ones, the scrawny and the pocked, those who walk the streets. The fair and the high born are as nothing before him. He studied medicine in the temple and with the wise men long ago; it is said that he even cut up the dead, but that I do not know. He will not practice the healing art and has not for a long time. He seeks only war and battle."

"Why do you hate him, Sokar?"

His words spewed out as though it eased him to talk. CeLa remembered how her own pain had lessened in the telling of it. She put out her hand and his closed on it.

"Doubtless it is an old story, a thing that happens

every day. My sister and I came to the court of Sargon several years ago when he was fully established. I had been soldier in many armies, a mercenary if you will, while she lived with our relatives. She was beautiful but very timid, wise in the ways of women but not of the world. I took service with Sargon and became close friends with Kir, who had been with him even in the days before the palace revolution in which Sargon triumphed to become king. She fell in love with him, a passion so strong that even he could not repulse her. She knew what he was, but loved him in spite of it."

Sokar paused for breath and CeLa saw that he shook with the memories.

"He had dallied with those of the lowest that gave him his perverted pleasure. He took her and gave her their disease. She died in agony, stricken by the gods for her shame, a disease of the female organs, said the priest at the temple who came to her. She died of Kir, my beautiful sister, younger than you, who had harmed no one."

CeLa did not immediately voice the thought that came to mind, that it could by no means be proven that the girl had taken the disease from Kir. Perhaps there had been others. Instead she said, "Surely he could have turned from the charms of his friend's sister.

"I taxed him with it. We fought and both of us were sent from the court for a time. Soon, however, Kir was back with a fine tale to soothe the ears of those willing to believe. I should have left then, but the call of gold and conquest held me. In time he will pay. For now we tolerate each other."

CeLa said into the aching silence, "I pray the gods will give you surcease, Sokar."

"I should not have brought up all this; it is long done. Forgive me." He smiled at her and the past receded from his eyes. "Look, yonder is the little

wench. She seeks to prepare you for the festivities,
I think. I will come for you at dusk."

They sat for a moment longer, then he left as he
had come and CeLa went to give herself to the min-
istrations of Pina.

For all that this was a crude mountain camp set
up and taken down on the march, CeLa could only
marvel at the garments laid out for her after she
had been bathed in buckets of warmed water hauled
in by one of the guards. There was a long, well-fit-
ting robe of delicate lavender that left one shoulder
bare. Her waist was belted in gold; sandals inlaid
with it were on her feet. Long dangling earrings hung
to her shoulders, and her neck was bare. A curving
bracelet of gold covered one arm from elbow to
wrist; carnelians winked in it. Pina arranged her hair
high off her neck and wove more golden strands
through it. CeLa looked into the mirror of metal
that was held for her and once again knew the woman
there for a stranger.

"You would not think that short hours ago I appeared to be a waif of the desert. Pina, you are a
marvel at all this."

The young girl said in her quiet way, "My mother
taught me. When she died, I took her place in the
service of the king." Her eyes glowed at the mention
of Sargon and CeLa guessed that she worshiped him.

Sokar's eyes told CeLa that he admired her but he
said merely, "We are vastly changed, are we not?"
He wore an elaborately flounced short skirt, as was
the fashion. A wide golden collar circled his neck
and fell onto his chest, his beard was carefully bar-
bered and scented, and a new jewel hung in his ear.

The feast was to be held in the same natural chamber where CeLa had talked with Sargon that morning. Torches flamed along the sides and in the center. Food was laid out on robes of sparkling white
and there were great bottles of wine being poured

into jeweled cups. There was game, fish, a great
roasted animal in the center of the display, fresh
fruits and even a dish of sweets. Men sat cross-legged
or leaned on one elbow as they sampled their wine.
CeLa saw two other women, both older but more
richly clad than she, and speculated as to who they
might be. Quickly she counted some thirty or so
people. Kir was not among them.

There was a sudden silence, a pause in the talk,
and Sargon entered with Kir behind him. The company rose as one, then sank back as he waved a
hand. "Sit, we are comrades all. Eat, drink your fill,
then I will tell you my will."

In the richly dressed company only Sargon still
wore the rough tunic of the morning. A medallion
glinted on his chest and caught the light; it was a
likeness of Inanna, the goddess to whom he had
vowed fealty long ago. So powerful was his presence,
however, that one knew instantly that one stood in
sight of the king.

But it was Kir who held all CeLa's attention. He
wore a simple white tunic unadorned by any jewelry. A leather belt supported a long, thin dagger.
His beard was gone completely. The hard modeling
of his face showed more clearly; the arch of his nose
and the chiseled lips were more prominent. His hair
was shorter and closer to his neck. He seemed both
older and more dangerous to CeLa.

Kir glanced up and caught her stare before she
could turn her eyes away. His face was expressionless
but she felt a flush rise to her cheeks as she fumbled
hurriedly for the wine cup Sokar was holding out to
her. She felt Kir's gaze and made herself smile be-
guilingly at Sokar as she thanked him.

They chattered and laughed together as the meal
progressed. Someone was playing a lyre in the darkness under the ledges. A singer sang of old battles
and of those yet to be won. Sargon ate heartily, Kir

very little but his cup was filled often. CeLa felt the draining tension leave her as Sokar told one amusing story after another about his experiences as a mercenary. Soon it became easier not to look in Kir's direction and she could tell herself that she could ignore him.

There was a crashing chord, then silence as Sargon rose, tall and powerful in the torchlight. Once more CeLa was reminded of Sirna in the death-pits, but this voice was even and controlled, sure of its audience and the expected reaction.

"Soldiers of Sargon, I would have you know of the information I have received this day, brought by those who have risked their lives in my service."

CeLa saw how the soldiers reacted, the warmth of their response, their oneness with the commander, as Sargon spoke briefly of all that she had told him that morning. She saw the horror on all faces and heard their muttered cries of protest.

"When Uruk and Ur have fallen into our hands, we will move to the south, there to engage the lord of Lagash and Umma, the self-styled Lord of Sumer. My spies shall go abroad in Lagash, whispering against this priestess and undermining her power so that she shall be no threat to us. At the same time they shall speak of us in slighting terms, as if we are no danger. The hatred between the cities must be fanned so that if the king flees back to them, he will find only division where he had expected unity. We intend to make sure that word of this deed is put abroad in all Sumer, as well as the motive for it."

He paused to take a gulp of wine. It was utterly still in the rock chamber now as all eyes rested on him. CeLa forgot all else as the assured voice continued.

"The gods are with us as they have ever been with me since the days I served in the palace at Kish and later ruled there. They have made me lord of Akkad, ruler of the mighty city where legions sup before me. So it will be with Sumer. He who doubts it may leave my table. To the victory!"

Now the cries came as from one throat. "Sargon! Sargon! Favored of the gods!" Kir stood up, raised his cup and called, "Victory!" It was repeated a dozen times.

Sargon vanished as quickly as he had done that morning, leaving his followers to drink and talk. CeLa sat uncomfortably for a short time as Sokar fought an old battle with the man on his left. The other women had departed and she wondered again what positions they held in the camp. There was a touch on her elbow and she looked up to see a young soldier standing beside her.

His voice pitched so that only she could hear, he said, "You are summoned to the king, lady. Now."

CeLa stared at him in surprise, then her eyes swung to Sokar. The soldier shook his head; she rose and followed him out of the chamber and down a narrow passage that gave onto another small room lit by the glare of a torch.

Sargon sat on a chair that seemed too small for his frame. Idly CeLa wondered where it had come from. Did he travel to war with all the comforts? Kir was with him, his face black with anger, the pulses in his throat and temple jumping. The look he gave CeLa was one of pure fury. All the tenderness she had had for him departed and she returned the glare in equal measure.

The king was all business now. The conviviality of the feasting chamber had departed. He had been studying a map on two separate tablets before him. Now he looked up and said, "Within the space of four days, the two of you and several others whom I shall select will leave on a mission of great delicacy and seriousness that can be imparted only to those in a position of great trust."

CeLa stared at him. Then, as Kir said nothing and the king seemed to expect an answer, she asked, "What is this mission, sir?"

"I take it you are willing?"

"As you said, the choice ceased to be mine when I left Lagash. You know my wishes and have denied them." CeLa knew the audacity of her words but could not restrain them.

Sargon was not offended. "I have promised that Sirna shall fall and in the end you may have your choice of reward. I will have no unwilling recruits to my cause. Serve me or remain as scrivener to the army."

"I am the willing servant of Sargon." This time CeLa meant it, for here was opportunity and honesty, a chance to make her life instead of always being used by others. Kings always used people, she thought cynically; she would use the favor gained. One could want a worse master than this ruler of Akkad.

"And you, Kir, my friend, my almost brother? What do you say?"

Kir faced him. "By the gods, you do not yet rule in Sumer! There is much danger to be faced. What good can a mission to Egypt do at this juncture? They will laugh us out of Memphis."

"You go too far!" It was a bull roar.

"There has ever been honesty between us, lord king. Would you have it otherwise? And what need is there for this woman? Her depth of knowledge is not even known. She is tricky and full of deceit."

Sargon turned to CeLa. "I am sending you and the others to Egypt to test out the possibility of a trade agreement to be implemented as soon as I am fully established here. I approach them as king of Akkad but who knows how far my power will stretch in time? Information will be recorded and sent back to me by courier, ship, any method that can be devised. You, CeLa, will be taught as much in the next several days as can be taken in. You will be the official recorder of the journey. Kir will be the commander, the negotiator, the wily one. All of you whom I choose will be spies."

Kir said, "I would fight with you when you take the ruler of Lagash and Umma to the holy city of Nippur in chains and are there proclaimed Lord of Sumer and Akkad."

Sargon said wearily, "I will not command, my friend, but the mission cannot wait."

Silence hung in the chamber. CeLa averted her gaze from Kir's dark face but Sargon stared forcefully at him. The tension stretched long before Kir spoke as if the words had been wrenched from him.

"I do not like it, I do not agree, the woman will be useless. But I cannot refuse my commander and I will not refuse my friend. I will go and render you good service. Now I go to get drunk!" He bowed to Sargon, ignored CeLa and went rapidly from the little room.

Sargon said, "If I am great and still to be greater in this land, it is because the gods have given me such servants. He is a brave and loyal friend."

CeLa's voice trembled as she said, "I know."

Something of her feelings showed in her voice and the hard eyes softened momentarily. Sargon turned the full weight of his attention on her as he said, "Kir has endured much, lost much; he is my true friend but he has not yet learned to find freedom in the present. Walk gently before him, CeLa of Lagash, for there is that in his eyes when he looks at you that has never been there before."

"Aye, he hates me." CeLa felt her voice tremble.

"Not so. He battles within himself."

She looked up at the king and wondered once again that she should be standing here talking so intimately with one who would one day hold all

Sumer in his hand. Sargon smiled and his dark, formidable face was suddenly lit with warmth. She felt his power then and knew why he was so confident.

"With a few men such as Kir at my side, I will be invincible." He snapped his fingers and a soldier appeared almost instantly to hover just beyond the pool of light that surrounded them. "Remember my words." He turned back to the map that was close to hand and seemed already lost in concentration.

CeLa said to his silence, "I will remember all that my lord Sargon has said." The ritual words came easily to her now and she said them with all her heart. "I am the willing servant of Sargon."

His hand lifted in dismissal but she knew that he had heard. She felt a surge of happiness as she followed her guide. Whatever the demons that haunted Kir, whatever the bonds of the past that enthralled him, she knew now that she could wait, for hope had come to her with Sargon's words. Now she had a mission, a cause and an opportunity to be with the man who attracted her so strongly. The world lay before her. She who had walked with death had the chance to love and live. She would make the most of it.

15

The Vow

Early the next morning Pina took CeLa into the recesses of the caves once more. Apparently these were
the main headquarters of the armies for the region,
although CeLa had seen no more than the men at
the feast. The room she entered was little more than
a fissure in the wall. She could see several tablets
placed to one side and something that might be a
map was in the process of being drawn on a fresh
tablet close at hand. The torch placed on the wall
might have been left from the night before, for it
gave only feeble flickers. The air was stuffy and
choking.

"You are the woman I am to instruct?"

The surly voice came from behind CeLa and made
her jump. She turned to see a young man, clean-
shaven, eyes hooded, watching her from the entrance.
Her temper flared.

"I was bidden here, yes. But who can learn in
such quarters?"

"Go and wait outside. I will bring the maps. I
cannot think this will take long." He looked beyond
her and his hands twitched.

She tried to ignore his manner, for they must work
together; she could not go into the mission ill
equipped. Whatever the adventure, she must give
herself to it with a whole heart. "I am CeLa, late
of Lagash."

His expression did not change as he said, "And

I am Utar, first of the scholars of Agade, adviser to the great king, now apparent instructor of women."

He turned his back on her and began to gather the tablets together. CeLa made her way toward the front of the caves, telling herself that she must learn what she could and adapt to this new world in which she must now move. She settled on a convenient rock nearby in the sparse shelter of a bush, one of the many that grew in these mountainous areas, and surveyed the scene around her. The morning air was fresh and cool, the sun not yet high. Her mind idled. For a few minutes she was content.

The few shelters, such as the one she had spent the night in, were constructed so that they backed onto rocks and appeared so flimsy that they might be demolished in minutes. Several men stood talking before one and she recognized them from the night before. The camp was quiet otherwise. Behind her lay the mountains as they rose faintly purplish; in front were the foothills and the beginnings of the flatlands that would in turn give way to the fertile farmlands of Sumer.

Utar came up beside her and thumped down one of the tablets. It was a crudely drawn map and, from the quick glance she took, appeared to be quite old. He followed her look as he said, "We must begin. I have other and more pressing duties."

"Leave the materials with me. I am quite capable of understanding them." CeLa thought that he was impossible. It was ridiculous to think of his claim that he was the first among scholars! This was a child's resentment and she regretted that she answered in kind.

He did not answer her now for a long moment. She felt a flush rise in her cheeks as the dark eyes raked her face. Then he said, "Ah, you did not tell us that you speak Akkadian?"

"The foremost scholar of the king should know

that maps are a universal language, should he not?"
CeLa rose to her feet, suddenly conscious that Pina's
tunic was too small for her.

"The foremost scholar of the king knows that the
worth of a woman is not measured in her brains.
Your tongue is sharp, lady. I would curb it. The lord
Kir is not known for his patience."

The maliciousness of the attack caught her by surprise, but her reaction was as swift. Her upraised
hand slammed against his face with such force that
he staggered back and would have fallen except for
the boulder at his back.

Quick tears came to her eyes. She wanted to run
but knew that there was no place to go. She could
not face the powerful ruler and protest that her
teacher was not to her liking. A chill went through
her at the thought of Sargon. They were all as clay
in his hands; even as in the gods'. Curse her fierce
temper! Sweat ran down her back and blood pounded
in her temples as she moved to do what must be done.

"Utar, forgive me. My hand was overquick. Both
of us have been commanded and must obey. If you
will instruct me, I promise that I will learn rapidly."

So might the boys in school speak, she thought.
But Utar stood erect now, his eyes sharp with anger.
CeLa knew that she had made an enemy. He had
only resented her before; now he hated her. He
picked up a tablet and ran his finger along it until
he touched a mark close by a long line.

"Here is that city of all cities, Agade, capital of
Sargon the Mighty. From here, in time, will all the
known world radiate. Here, woman, is the beginning
and the end of all power, the source and the light."

CeLa saw the light of the fanatic in his eyes as
he recited what seemed a holy incantation and her
thoughts flickered uneasily to Sirna. Was she to see
the woman and her spell in everyone she met? Un-

easily she sat down and looked where Utar pointed
as he launched into a description of the wonders of
Agade, the thousands of men who daily ate their
meals before the great king, of his power and the
wonders accomplished and yet to be accomplished.
It was a rush of words that left no time for questions, but CeLa knew better than to venture them.
Utar's thin face was now lit with pleasure. He had
forgotten her as a person; she was a vessel for his
knowledge.

He built a picture of Egypt in CeLa's eyes. Several of the older men at the court of Sargon had
journeyed there in their youth and much of his information was taken from their observations. The
caravans and traders of the desert as well as the
venturesome ships had taken the far trip and Utar
was well versed in their lore.

"The great river flows down the land, the united
two lands as they are called. There is prosperity and
flourishing trade. The tombs of the kings rise out
of the sand and their gods welcome them in council.
The river brings the renewal of life even as it does
here."

He added now, the light of vision in his eyes, "Not
for many years has any man of this land visited there.
Who knows what wonders there are to see? What
knowledge to be gained? Warriors see one thing,
scholars another. It takes the balanced eye to see
all and to record it for the great one."

CeLa wondered that Utar was not to be sent on
this expedition. Surely he was the logical choice. His
anger at her was explained but not the clearly exhibited venom. She lifted a hand to push back the
heavy hair from her face. The warm wind touched
her arms and in the distance she saw the shimmering heat haze. The camp was quiet but she could
guess at the councils taking place.

Utar seemed impervious to hunger and thirst as

he talked of the trade routes, crops, methods of tilling the land, ships, rulers, slaves and buildings. Time
drew into afternoon as CeLa's head swam with facts
and considerations. He stopped once for breath and
she rushed into the gap.

"Your knowledge is vast, Utar, and I am grateful
for such instruction, but may we not rest in the heat
of the afternoon?"

Malice flickered in his eyes as he said, without inflection, "You had best become used to work, for it
is the order of Sargon that you learn both Akkadian
and Egyptian. If you are to be of use to him, it is
well to obey."

CeLa would not let her temper rise again. "Do we
meet then in the cool?"

"I have taught you quite as much as the weak mind
of a woman can absorb in one day. Likely you will
not remember it past the next new gown that is
bought for you." He did not give her time to reply
but snatched up the tablets and walked swiftly away.

In the release from concentration and tension, CeLa
felt her stomach knot with hunger. Her throat was
parched and her hands shook faintly. She decided to
make her way back to the shelter and rest. Surely
Pina would come soon with food. It was the pressure
of events, the knowledge that the unknown must be
faced without a friend, the uncertainty of her life
that made CeLa suddenly and uncharacteristically
fearful. She walked slowly around the boulders toward where the shelter seemed to be and did not,
in the depths of her thoughts, see that she was going
astray. Was it for this that she had escaped the
machinations of Sirna? Was she never to be free to
lead her own life? These questons plagued her day
and night; they had done so ever since her escape
from the pit. Her head hammered with them but
she could not feel that she was other than a toy in
the hands of the gods—gods so far from her own

understanding that she might as well walk in lone-
liness. Who knew what gods lived in these mountains? Ninhursag had many faces, but at least she
was familiar. What of Intar? Would he have come
this far to watch over her? Her eyes burned as she
fought to keep her face from twisting with the desire to weep.

Suddenly she tripped and fell so hard that the
breath was almost knocked out of her. One hand was
under her stomach. The other clutched a rock. Her
lip was bruised and she felt a trickle of blood. She
lay in a type of cleft; the upthrust rock edge had
caught her foot. Small as the pain was, it was too
much when taken with her other feelings. CeLa wiped
her fingers across her mouth as dirt and blood mingled with salt tears. She turned her face into her
arms and began to sob in earnest, knowing only that
she must have release. Everything came up then in
her memory as she wept for Nandar and all that had
happened.

A hand touched her shoulder gently at first, then
pulled harder. Without raising her head CeLa
snapped, "Leave me alone." So engrossed was she in
her own misery that she forgot the strangeness of
the mountains and the fact that men of the army
were unused to the company of women. The hand
touched her neck and slid away. There was a stagger-
ing movement, then a voice she knew mumbled something indistinct. It came again.

"Wine, that will help. Got to get it. No path."

She sat up and mopped the tears away. Kir was
standing close to her. An empty leather bottle lay
at his feet and his eyes were blurry from drink as
well as exhaustion. His face was puffy and distorted,
the clean line of the lips marred. As she watched, he
put a careful hand on a nearby boulder and bent
to pick up the bottle. He shook it in disgust, then

hurled it away. She was forgotten, she saw, for he stared at her in surprise.

"CeLa. Everywhere I go. Do you trail me? King's orders?"

She rose shakily to her feet, thankful that he did not remember the state in which he had found her. "Will you walk back to the camp with me, Kir?"

He seemed to be in a daze as she put out her hand to him. "Can't see?" He staggered and almost fell. "It comes again. She is not happy in the nether-world, she blames me. She should blame me. The skill of the gods did me no good." The swift voice trailed off, then rose as he began to curse in Sumerian and moved to a language she assumed to be Ak-kadian.

CeLa took his arm firmly. "Come. You will do yourself an injury if you fall about this way."

He gave a harsh laugh. "That is forbidden to me. Have I not tried?" The cursing began again, the words seeming to be torn from his lips.

CeLa tugged at him and this time he came will-ingly. His eyes were rolling, his legs growing flaccid. She knew from long experience with Nandar that he was not far from collapse. Whatever the demons that taunted him, she could not doubt that they were powerful. Forgetfulness was not a draught given to those who sought it.

They stumbled a little way farther, but the area was very stony and the rise to the camp steep. Kir muttered something, leaned against CeLa, then slid to her feet in a heap. She was sorely tempted to leave him to sleep it off but could not do so. What if he were wanted? On him, whether she willed it or not, depended much of her future. A drunken man sleeping in the heat was prey to man and beast alike. So she told herself as she looked down at the carved face, the hawk nose and long-fingered hands. That

part of CeLa that could always see clearly told her
that her fate was joined with that of this man and
her will, no less than his, could not alter that.

She knelt and pulled him into a more comfortable
position, then went hurriedly to find Pina. The camp
lay across two small valleys and she realized that
she had been lost when she looked down to see activity beginning in anticipation of the lessening heat.
There was no sign of the young girl, however. She
was not within the shelter or about the cook fire.
CeLa pulled the cloak and mats into some semblance
of a bed and took a long, refreshing drink of water
from the jug close at hand.

Two soldiers were standing idly by as she emerged.
She went up to them, conscious of her streaked face
and disarranged robe. Their stares were curious but
veiled.

"Help me, if you will. The king's friend Kir lies
in the little valley yonder. The drink and the sun
have felled him and he needs a bed, shade, water."

They looked at each other, then back at her. Some
understanding passed between them as one said,
"Shall he be brought here to your shelter, lady?"

She did not hesitate. "Of course."

Again that strange look. "As you ask."

It was a long trudge over the rocks to Kir and
back again. The soldiers seemed almost dwarfed by
his dead weight, for he was a powerful man, but
finally he lay stretched out on her bed in the shelter.
They brought more water and food for her, then
took their leave. CeLa sponged his face, briskly at
first, then more slowly until it was almost a caress.
He moaned, shifted to his side and she knew that
he slept more normally.

Night came on but no one came to them and the
business of the camp seemed far away. CeLa lay down
on a hastily improvised pallet but sleep would not
come. She tossed and turned, invoking all the fa-

miliar images of the rivers, but it was no use. It seemed very late when she turned for what seemed the thousandth time and looked into the open eyes of Kir.

He touched her face with one hand, pulling her unresisting body close with the other. She saw that the wine still held him in its grip, but his face was clear and open, unlike the man of caution and watchfulness that she knew. He half smiled as she watched and murmured under his breath in the language she did not know. The smell of sour wine mingled with the odor of leather and wide spaces. CeLa's breasts tingled and the warmth between her legs increased as his questing fingers trailed down her neck and into the hollow of her collarbone.

She knew that Kir was far back in his own past, in a happier time, and that the one word he spoke over and over was possibly the name of the woman he had once loved. The light in his face and the tenderness in his hands told her that. A pang of anguish came over her even as her body longed for his. She wanted so much to yield to this burning sweetness that seemed stoppered within her. His hands had loosened her robe and gone to her thrusting nipples. He bent his dark head to the pulse in her throat and she floated in desire.

"Inanna. Inanna." Kir spoke the name of the love goddess against her flesh and the yearning in it tore her heart.

CeLa pulled gently back, putting his hands from her, though it took all her power to do so. It was all she might ever have of him, this man she knew she could love as well as want, but she would not have him falsely. It was pride in herself that upheld her from this passion of the flesh, but it was also caring for him that could not use a love long done.

"It is not the time, Kir. The gods wait. You must rest now." Her voice was very low as she retreated.

He sat very still but a pulse moved in his cheek and he did not follow her. Even as she watched, he drew himself into a ball, knees to chest, and darkness came over his face. He lay unmoving in the flickering shadows.

CeLa whispered the only comfort she had for herself. "Until you want me for myself, Kir, and no other. If you never do, then I shall still live. I will it so."

16

Preparation and Farewell

"Why am I here? What does this mean?"

The angry voice shattered the heavy sleep that CeLa had finally fallen into. She felt her legs cramp and her entire body felt stiff. She stared up at Kir, who was swaying over her, one hand to a head she knew must be bursting. He was scowling. The warmth of his expression in the night might have been a dream.

"Answer me, woman!" He flinched as he said it. The sound of his anger must have made his head worse, CeLa thought, for he picked up the empty jug and hurled it against the flimsy walls that were only now brightening in the dawn.

CeLa laughed; she could not help it. He might have been facing a fierce enemy instead of one small girl and a monumental hangover. He was so tall that the shelter roof forced him to bend his head and he seemed to encompass the whole of it.

"You were drunk and wandering. I found you and the soldiers brought you here to sleep. Your legs gave way and you could not get up."

She laughed again at the expression on his face, incredulity mixed with pain. Had matters been otherwise between them, she would have tried to reassure him that no dignity had been lost, no foolishness committed, as she had often done with Nandar in a manner calculated to soothe. But she owed Kir no kindness; thus, she sat and watched as he tried to regain his equilibrium.

"Why did they not take me to their quarters? Why was I brought here?"

"I thought you might need looking after in the night." She said the simple truth and could not regret the impulse of kindness that had prompted it, although she knew that she had wanted to be with him no matter what the cost.

"I was drunk, nothing more." He spoke boldly but there was a slight inflection of anxiety on the last words.

It was in her power to wound, but CeLa, remembering the tenderness of his voice in the night, could not do it. "Nothing more," she agreed.

Kir stood still for a moment, then moved very carefully toward the door. It seemed that each step hammered in his head and when he spoke, his voice was low, although each word struck CeLa separately.

"I had meant to speak to you when I felt better, but it would have been necessary to seek you out in front of others and I did not want that. Now, because of this incident and your foolishness, there will be talk as well as laughter in the ranks."

"Sokar has told me of your predilections." She had to hit back.

"We are enemies and one day will settle our score with blood, but that day is not yet. Now the will of the king must be obeyed. Our personal differences must be set aside until the mission is done. Sargon knows that I regard it as unwise to send a woman on it and in such a position, but we are commanded."

"Do you so worship him?" CeLa found it hard to believe that anyone could entertain such caring for the powerful man who bent them all to his will.

Kir's face darkened and one hand twisted convulsively over the other. "For the last time, stay away from me! I will suffer you because I must in order to carry out the mission, but if you disobey me, you shall feel the consequences."

CeLa blurted out the next questions before she could stop herself and was instantly ashamed. "Why do you dislike me so, Kir? Is it because of the business in Lagash? Surely I have explained that?" She had left herself wide open to him, the prey before the predator.

The cold eyes rested on her for a brief instant, then his lips quirked as he said, "I do not care for you enough to dislike you, CeLa. You did not act as a comrade should, that is true, but you are culpable as all women are culpable. I have known many of them and hope to know many more in their proper place on my couch, pretty toys all. Do you think I do not know that you wish to try out your wiles and charms on me? Do you think I do not know that you seek what you have come to think is the unattainable? Sokar has told you much, as you have said. You have fastened your fascination on me and are foolish to have done so. I have known much of this in the past."

Humiliation burned in CeLa. Had she been so transparent then? A silly girl goggling after the first man with whom she had had contact and some closeness? Was that all it was? Questions framed themselves and faded as she sought to save face before this man who had seen so clearly, who yet was so filled with pride and pain. He stood there, proud now even in his drunken aftermath, aloof. Her body shook at the sight of him and she knew that he knew, once again, how it was with her.

Her voice did not shake as she spoke, giving her an obscure pride that was in itself sustaining. "You think greatly of yourself, Kir the Arrogant! By the gods, they called you well. You shame all women by this attitude you hold. Be well assured that you have nothing to fear from me; I but serve in the mission

as you do, because I am commanded by your king,
who would have done better to have kept the promise made in his name. That to leave me in a free
city with a portion upon which to live. *There* is dis-
honor; had I been a man, I might not have been
used so. You have mistaken me, Kir. Do so no longer!"

His face darkened, then twisted with a spasm of
pain. "Remember what I have said, CeLa. You will
save yourself much grief." He thrust back the skins
from the door and went out into the morning.

CeLa had learned to be a realist in the years with
Nandar. She did not know if she loved Kir, but she
longed for his touch and his caring, for his approval.
He had seen her passion clearly but that she would
never admit. It remained now for her to turn from
this and bear herself with as much composure as she
could. She was not the woman to yearn after a man
who would have none of her.

There was a swift movement at the door and Pina
entered. Her small face was flushed and her discom-
fiture evident. "Lady, forgive me for not seeing to
your needs but I dared not come while the favored
of the king remained with you. I will go now and
fetch food and water."

CeLa was blunt. "The whole camp must think that
he slept with me. Is it not so?"

"Yes, lady. It is rare for him. Usually his pleasures
are taken in the cities and all that they may offer.
It is known that you shared danger together." Pina
stared at CeLa in some awe. Kir had a reputation at
the court of Sargon that men envied and that drew
women.

CeLa came close to Pina and rapped the words out.
"He was drunk and unable to walk. He slept here
only and took his leave with a great head. I am for
no man's pleasure, certainly not Kir's. Spread that
over the camp. Say further that we work together by

order of his king and that only. Now, go. I both hunger and thirst!"

The young girl flushed again and hesitated. "I meant no harm."

"See that you speak as I have said. Do you understand?"

Pina nodded and slipped away. To her mind the awesome Kir of the dark face and this sharp-tongued, fair woman were well matched, but she would not voice this opinion among the several girls she knew, not after CeLa's commands.

It was midmorning before CeLa went to Utar at their meeting place of the day before. This time she wore a loose, simple white robe that Pina had brought when one was demanded. Her hair no longer fell loosely down her back but was bound on her neck with bright cords. Her face was more remote, its planes more pronounced.

Utar had brought more tablets this time as well as quills for inscribing fresh ones. He glowered at her. "You are late. Did I not inform you yesterday that my time was valuable, that there is a great deal to learn? Did your adventures of the night exhaust you?" His little eyes were malicious.

CeLa seated herself, took up one of the tablets that appeared to be in Akkadian and set it aside. There was a dignity about her that was easily felt as she said, "You were commanded to instruct me in the things useful to us on the mission, Utar. Do so. I will hear no more of such spiteful words, nor will I indulge in the ridiculousness of yesterday. If it continues, I will complain to the king himself."

Utar stared at her in silence. It was her morning for being forceful, thought CeLa wryly. As she had been put in her place, so did she put others. It was not a pleasant thought, but if she intended to survive in this new world into which she had been thrust, then such moves were necessary.

Utar put a tablet in front of her, held another so that she could see it and said, "You wish to be instructed? Then listen and learn." He launched into one of his lengthy explanations that CeLa could now recognize as his own way of saving face. After this morning's events she could sympathize with such moves and understand them. She listened with an intensity that would not have been possible yesterday.

The next few days fell into a pattern for CeLa as she drove herself with a determination much like that used in the temple of Ninhursag. There had been no further angry words between herself and Utar; now they were pupil and teacher together as he tried to give her the smallest beginnings of knowledge of Egyptian writing and speech. The curving, decorative signs and pictures, like and unlike Sumerian, spoke to her analytical mind, and she was able to take the idea of sounds by signs the more easily as Utar translated the ritual texts and prayers that, but for the strange names, might have been Sumer's own.

The work was exhausting and it was frustrating for CeLa to realize that all this was but the barest beginning, for all the knowledge had been obtained over long years. Language, history and the great river remained constant as Utar continued to emphasize that she must know what she did not know in order to record the journey more precisely.

They worked from earliest light now until dark, pausing only to rest for two short periods. CeLa would walk with Pina for a time before tossing herself on the pallet to sleep a sleep that was sometimes broken by dreams of Kir as he spoke the words of her humiliation. Pina had said no more, nor had Utar, and these were the only people with whom CeLa had any contact. She was aloof in her turn, knowing that the project into which she entered was her protection, at least for a time. How it would be if she were to meet Kir was another thought; she

could only hope that pride would maintain her until
she had enough sense of her own worth in this strange
world to make her way in it.

She ventured one evening to ask Utar a question
that had long troubled her. She would never like
him or find him bearable for a protracted period
of time, but she deeply respected his knowledge and
the hunger for more that drove him. It was highly
likely that he felt the same about her, but she knew
that he no longer regarded her as one of the wenches
who simpered after Kir.

"Why is so slight a scholar as I being sent on
a mission of such importance, Utar? I can see that
you cannot be spared from the councils of the king,
but it has ever seemed strange to me." It was flattery
but she longed to know and he had a great enough
opinion of himself and his importance to believe her.
Of his scholarship there was no doubt, however.

He paused in his arrangement of the tablets and
looked assessingly at her. "Who can fathom the ways
of those whom the gods have touched?"

It was the ritual response, perfectly appropriate,
but here it indicated either ignorance or secretive-
ness. Utar was never ignorant. CeLa kept quiet, having learned that he would speak at his own pace.

Now he was continuing in a reflective manner,
"The king allows no talent to waste. He uses men
and women alike. It may be that in some small way
he regards you as useful. It is not for us to question." He put the tablets in the special bag provided
for them and stalked away, leaving her to stare after
him, no wiser than she had been.

When she reached the shelter soon afterward, Pina
was looking at the contents of an unwrapped pack-
age that appeared to have been carried a long way,
from the disreputable look of it. The girl turned
with relief to CeLa.

"I am ordered to have you in readiness to leave at

dawn, lady. These are to be your attire." She waved
at the pile, which now seemed to be several robes
and turbans in a coarse weave and not new. "Can
you tell me where you go?"

CeLa looked at her in surprise. The question
seemed artless but Utar had told her earlier that only
those of the special council around Sargon knew of
this journey and its portent. If their absence were
noticed, it would be assumed that they had gone to
another city or with another segment of the forces.
Once again CeLa had marveled at the confidence
that could lead an invader deep in the territory he
wished to conquer so to divide his armies and yet
send out expeditions to a land so far distant as to
be almost legendary. Caution made her wary.

"I am not told as yet. It does not matter; I grow
weary of instruction." She picked up one of the
robes, held it up and put it down again. They were
dull brown, fading into sand colors, and the sandals
were the sturdy sort worn by those who toiled for
a living, not the stuff of ambassadors from one king
to another.

"Those are clothes of the common ones." Pina
looked again at CeLa, who saw that this time her
servant's eyes were calculating, watchful.

"I would rest now." CeLa was curt. She did not
know with whom or how she was to travel, or any
of her actual duties. It might take moons to reach
Egypt by whatever method they took, although Utar
had half indicated that it might be by caravan.

Pina waited, hovering. "I will be sorry to see you
go, lady. If you return, will you ask for me as your
servant?"

"Why do you say 'if'? Surely you mean 'when'."

"Forgive me, my tongue twists." She moved toward
the door then, turning back only to say, "I will rouse
you at the given hour."

CeLa wondered if in her tiredness she had read

something into voice and actions that was not there. Clearly this sudden departure was as much a surprise to Pina as to herself, yet it was almost overdue, for the king had spoken of a matter of days. Her words to the young girl had been true. It did not matter as to the destination or circumstances of the journey. The driving work of the past days had given her a thirst to know more. In that she was Nandar's daughter; she had the tools, now she would use them.

She sponged her face and smooth body in the water that stood close at hand. Her stomach curved back softly. The muscles under her rib cage were hard, the legs rounded and strong in their turn. CeLa's life had been one of adaptation and adjustment. It showed in her body and in her acceptance of the fluidity of her circumstances now. She bound her hair back and up in a knot secured with cords. It would be one less thing to do in the morning.

She had slept for a time but her coming awake was almost instant as she sensed that someone was in the shelter and watching her. She forced herself to lie very still as the person bent over her, watched, then as silently moved away. Fear held her paralyzed and she dared not even open her eyes to take a quick glance.

There was a footstep and a soft flurry of movement. Then a man's voice whispered, "This is not the time. Wait."

Another whisper answered him but was quickly shushed. CeLa shifted as though in her sleep and moaned. As she did so, she risked a look at the flap of the door. A bundled figure stood there, whether male or female she could not tell. The smaller one was Pina. She had not been mistaken.

"All the wine was not drunk. Go." Pina held the flap aside and the figure melted into the blackness. She followed it and CeLa was left alone.

Something of the quality of the darkness told her that dawn was not far away. She put her hand on the dagger under her head and waited for the new day that was suddenly full of menace.

17

Into the Wilds

Not long afterward, CeLa went out into the half
light and followed the guide who had come for her
as he went around the boulders and beyond an outcropping of rock to where several figures waited. A
group of asses were tethered nearby. Pina had looked
in to wake her, then had vanished. CeLa had pretended to rouse and yawn but every sense had been
alert. Whatever the happenings of the night, she
knew that she must be on her guard. Perhaps someone plotted against the mission, or perhaps a woman
of the camp thought she had engaged Kir's affections
and meant to remove her. Who could know? At any
rate, she welcomed action.

The guide turned to her now and she saw the
movement of a beard in the folds of cloth that provided ample protection from prying eyes. She draped
her own cloth in her turn and looked toward him.

"We move as swiftly as we can without arousing
curiosity. Our goal at the moment is to put as many
miles as we can between the camp and ourselves this
day. Tonight some of these things will be explained
to you." He spoke in a low, hard voice that did not
allow for questions.

"I understand."

"Good."

None of the group was recognizable. Certainly
there was no sign of Kir, who had been designated
as leader. She mounted the ass and dug her toes into

its side as the little group, some ten in all, moved into single file. There was no conversation or even such scattered words as were customary on the start of a journey. CeLa felt as if she moved in a dream from which she might soon wake; only the feel of the animal's skin against her legs and the jouncing movements told her of reality.

They threaded their way toward an open area where the rocks were fewer and the path more even. The mountains curved away on both sides in dark splotches of shadow that grew more massive in the distance. Beyond was the beginning of the uncultivated land that seemed so near now but would take them hours to reach. CeLa was next to last in line. Behind her followed her guide and after him came the pack animals laden with parcels in cloth and leather bags. They might be a party of traders or travelers between the cities, a common enough sight in these unsettled times.

She looked back in the gray light toward the direction of the camp. As she did so, a flicker of movement took her eye and brought it up to a high rock where a cleft was almost unnoticeable. Two figures stood there, wrapped in cloaks. They were very tall and stood without moving at first. Then one lifted a hand and held it out almost in benediction. The light grew clearer at the same time. CeLa's eyes hurt with straining and she shut them for a minute. When next she looked, the figures were gone. The man behind her followed the direction of her gaze and now shook his head as if in warning. Obediently she looked ahead at the brown-clad back in front of her and tried to adjust her weight to the movements of her mount.

They hugged the shadow of the mountains all that day as they moved steadily toward the north at a pace that ate up the miles. After the inactivity of the past days, CeLa was glad to concentrate on the un-

changing scene before her instead of the growing
cramps in her legs and buttocks that soon caused discomfort. The sun wheeled above them in the cloudless
sky and beat through the covering robes, but there
was to be no pause for rest and refreshment. CeLa
took a few sips of water from the jug in her pack and
ate a flat barley cake that tasted like dust in her
mouth. Her lack of sleep the night before was beginning to affect her and her mind began to raise up
fantastic speculations as to what the incident might
have meant. She thought back to the figures she had
seen in the cleft and believed it entirely possible that
Sargon himself had come to bid a silent farewell to his
latest expedition. Had the other man been Kir?
Where was he? Had the plans been changed?

By the time dusk came, CeLa was exhausted in
mind and body, longing only for the comfort of a
pallet, however hard, that did not move and sway
between her legs. The first rider held up a hand; the
others circled him and then began to dismount. They
were in the flatlands now, with the mountains loom-
ing in the distance. The camp would be spread in
the open but in all this land there seemed none to
see.

She swung down cautiously, feeling her legs buckle
and then grow firm under her. The man who had
guided her that morning came up beside her and
pulled the turban from his head to reveal hair threaded with white and a face that was scarred from temple to ear as if from an old sword wound.

"I am Laz, one of those who journeyed to Egypt
in my youth, now fortunate indeed to return." His
smile was open and friendly, his voice welcoming.

After the enforced silence of the day, CeLa was
thankful for human contact. "And I am CeLa, sent
by the king to be the recorder of this expedition and
honored by it." As she spoke, CeLa felt a sudden
gratefulness toward Sargon, who had not hesitated

to use a woman or denigrated her talents as so many had done with women, deeming them unteachable. Nandar had laughed at such ideas in the days before laughter left him, proclaiming that they were on the wane in the enlightened cities of Sumer.

"Come, you must meet the others." Laz went before her to the others, who were spreading out robes, taking long pulls of water or wine, stretching their legs and talking in low tones.

Some seemed to know each other but most did not. In the quick exchanges and assessments, the open sighs of relief that the first day was ended, CeLa noticed the women first. One was tall with very dark skin and hair that seemed a fuzz over her head, her voice rich and deep with a trill of laughter in it. She stood proudly with the air of a great one. Her name was Raba; she was not young but there was no way to tell her age, for her face was unlined. She came from a far country, CeLa knew, for Utar had spoken briefly of people who looked this way and with whom Egypt warred.

A girl in her early twenties, taller than CeLa with a long, rangy body and loose hair, came up. Her mouth had a wry twist to it and her eyes were bright. "I am Zama and this is my husband, Idi. We are navigators, star readers, tellers of tales."

Idi was a serious-faced young man with an elaborate little beard who mumbled a greeting almost under his breath, then smiled so that he seemed to be lit from within. He was very shy, CeLa surmised, and left the talking to Zama, who was rushing on now.

"We're all very good at something, you know. That is why the king is sending this expedition. Everyone was taken separately and privately for explanations. He could have ordered us. It is so exciting. We may be gone for years, did he tell you that?"

CeLa, who had been ordered and still did not

know her place in such company, could only say, "It was very sudden. I suppose I do not yet understand."

Zama laughed. "There will be time, CeLa. I can look at you and tell that we are to be great friends. Here, my hand on it!"

CeLa took the warm, calloused fingers in hers and smiled into the friendly eyes. It was impossible not to like this lively girl. Long ago in Nippur, CeLa had had a close friend, but there had been none since and she had often felt the lack. She was not usually outgoing but tended to hold herself in reserve, a product of years of caution. Now she responded freely in her turn.

"It has been long since I called another friend, Zama. I am honored." The words seemed stiff as she spoke them but her heart was there and Zama knew it.

Idi spoke in his soft, hesitant voice. "She will do enough talking for us all, CeLa, but I too bid you welcome."

They sat down on the pallets and began to share each other's food, handing CeLa dried meat, a date and some sharp, heady wine. She in turn offered the inevitable barley cakes that were wolfed down. The journey and the excitement had made her very hungry. Conversation lagged as they ate and drank.

A footstep close by made the three look up. A hard-muscled man with hollow cheeks, bald head and shaved face stood back a few paces. His face was hard and serious but his voice had the rich timbre of one who has trained it long in the ritualistic prayers. CeLa would have known him for a priest by that alone.

"I am Cusar, servant of Inanna and Sargon. Welcome to this company. May her blessings be with you all."

Idi spoke their names and added, "And her bless-

ings with you, Cusar. May she travel with us into the
strange lands where we venture."

The dark eyes snapped with fervor. "I have daily
importuned her for the greater glory of him whom
I serve as do we all. The omens are favorable but
she demands all our prayers. See that you do not
neglect them." He stalked away and they saw him
bending over three soldiers who were passing a bottle
of wine back and forth, laughing as they did so.

A little man with wizened features and a shrunken
body paused beside Cusar and spoke rapidly to him.
They saw the stern face soften and heard the burst
of laughter in which the soldiers joined.

Zama leaned toward CeLa. "That is Otu. He
knows the desert and this land as thoroughly as I
know my own face. We worked with him in preparation for this journey. There is none wiser or more
clever."

"He looks so frail, almost ill." CeLa stared through
the deepening gloom at the bent figure.

Idi laughed. "It is said that he can outlast the
king himself on a long march."

"So many people! How will I ever remember them
all?" CeLa spoke ruefully, glad to voice her doubts
to these two who seemed to understand. "Who is
that yonder who sits apart?" She inclined her head
toward a still figure whose clear profile was raised
to the sky as if in contemplation.

Zama seemed to be aware of everything, so sure
was she of herself, a quality CeLa envied. "He? That
is Jagon the poet, the adviser on etiquette, the singer
of honeyed words, the maker of songs, boon companion of the king. He does not often deign to notice
lesser mortals."

CeLa laughed and the sound was good in her ears.
"Such a goodly company. I wonder what I do in
its ranks."

Idi caught the uncertainty in her voice and said

gently, "We were told that you have great knowledge of the history and legends of Sumer as well as an aptitude for languages. Moreover, that you had survived fearful experiences that might have caused a lesser person to fall. You were well chosen, CeLa. Do not doubt it."

Zama said, "We heard that Kir, who is our leader as you know, had taken much interest in you." Curiosity flared in her eyes, which assessed CeLa frankly.

So it had come. Had she been a fool to let down her guard with these two? Was the shadow of Kir to follow her even here, when she thought that she had beaten her heart into submission? She chose her words carefully.

"You have doubtless heard much of what happened in Lagash and how it was reported to the king by Kir and myself. I could no longer remain there and he acceded to my request for a place of safety. There is no more than that."

Idi sought to turn the conversation even as CeLa was thankful for the perception that led him to do so. "When do you think Kir will join us?" he asked. "I knew that he was to remain behind for consultations with the king. He has always wanted to go into battle rather than serve on these missions."

CeLa thought that she had been right that morning as to the identity of the watchers. Kir had taken the opportunity to try once more to release himself from an onerous duty. Curiosity made her say, "It seems strange that Sargon would not yield to the express wishes of one who is close to him."

Zama said, "Sargon has one will and that is his own. It is what will make him ruler of this land and all others that he chooses. Doubt it not."

Remembering the fierce face and commanding presence, CeLa could not question her. She stretched and sighed. "I am very weary. Surely I will soon grow used to this method of travel."

Idi and Zama laughed with her as she winced and tried to move to another position. It was good to share, CeLa thought, and comforting to be no longer alone. Strange thoughts for the daughter of Nandar, but she was conscious now of her own needs and could not be ashamed of them. Perhaps her feeling for Kir had begun to teach her that. It was a sobering thought and one worthy of perusal.

In the shadows just beyond, Laz rose and spread his arms in a beckoning gesture as he stepped into the open space, calling for their attention. The moonlight glittered on his scarred face. His voice was low and compelling.

"We all know that we go on a dangerous expedition that may take many moons. Some of us may not return alive. The balance of power may have shifted in Egypt since our last reports arrived, for that was long ago. The secrecy of this mission was placed in jeopardy in the days before we left the camp. You can imagine what might happen if it became general knowledge that negotiators had been sent out before our king is fully established as Lord of Sumer and Akkad. We are specially chosen and specially commanded in this great adventure."

He paused and CeLa saw that his words were effective, for the company sat straighter, attentive to his every word. The one exception was the silent poet, Jagon, who had not moved since she first saw him.

"We go as a caravan across the great desert and will be guided by special contract with some of those with whom Otu has dealt. We will be traders and merchants then. As we go across the land of Sumer, we will be members of a small village who have been driven out by bandits in the wake of the armies of Sargon, who, we shall say, is everywhere invincible. We must maintain constant watch, especially as we leave this land. No one can tell us what to expect beyond the desert, but we are all resourceful and capable—otherwise we would not have been chosen for this task. It remains only for us to accomplish it as best we may for the honor of our king."

The resonant voice of Cusar lifted. "And for the greater glory of Inanna who has lifted him high."

"Inanna, great goddess." They spoke as one. CeLa lifted her voice with the others, remembering how Kir had called the name of the goddess of love and passion in the night. She knew that Sargon had taken her for his patron goddess and that her monuments stood in Agade by the hundreds. So had Utar stated the wonders of the city of his ruler. CeLa herself could not hope for the favor of so great a goddess, but might not the servant of Sargon attain some small favor? It would be comforting to be able to worship again, but doubtless her offense in fleeing the fate set down for her by Ninhursag had been duly noted by the recorder of the gods.

Laz was continuing, "We must be one with each other, our survival depends on it." Jagon had not shifted from his position, CeLa saw, and thought that the words must be wasted on such a one as he. For her part, she was eager. "Go now, my friends, and rest. We travel even more swiftly on the morrow."

As she lay down on the pallet and pulled her robe close against the chill, she saw the soldiers pacing in watchful circles around the camp and guessed that they would take turns in the night. Idi and Zama were close in each other's arms. The dark woman, Raba, was standing in the moonlight looking toward the south, her face serene. For the first time since Nandar's death, CeLa felt a sense of belonging and unity. Her fierce independence drew back a little in caution as tiredness overcame her and she slept.

18

The Hand of Inanna

It was late afternoon of the next day when the rider first appeared on the horizon, an ever-growing speck against the bulk of the mountains. Laz and Otu conferred briefly, slowed the pace of the travelers and spoke to the soldiers, all of whom were in their early twenties, strong and capable. Weapons were set at the ready, though unobtrusively. CeLa had been riding beside Zama, listening to the high, restless voice telling of the wonders that might be expected on this journey. In her turn, she had told what she remembered of Nippur and her life there.

"It is in Nippur that Sargon will officially become the Lord of Sumer, for the city is sacred to Enlil, and until he is proclaimed there, he will not be truly accepted." Zama spoke this by rote but the same longing had been in Kir's voice when he spoke of the final battle.

"By all the counts, when we return he will have been ruling there for a long time. Utar told me of the wonders of Agade. I find it strange that he could leave it for so long." Once again the visionary eyes of the king rose before her and she shivered at the dreams of conquest, a small person caught up in empire. She had started to voice something of this thought to Zama, but the rider had been sighted just then.

CeLa felt the tension rising as he came ever closer. Her hands were clammy on the halter she held and the dagger was ready under the folds of her robe. She knew that the others felt the same way. One man might presage a company of others. All did not share Sargon's confidence in his own invincibility.

A high whistle came down the line and Otu's slightly cracked voice called, "It is Kir. Our leader finally joins us." Delight and welcome rang in his tones.

CeLa whispered to Zama, "How can he possibly see that far?" Strain as she might, she could only distinguish an ever-larger moving blot on the horizon. The mention of Kir's name had set her heart thumping and she half expected Zama to hear it.

The other girl laughed at her incredulity. "Otu's sight is the keenest of any in the armies and has always been so. He is called the keen sight of the great king and bears that official title."

They halted now and sat in a semicircle to wait. The sun blazed down without the relief of a breeze. CeLa wiped her wet face with the sleeve of her dusty robe and caught Idi's eye as he did the same. Time seemed to crawl by but no one ventured any conversation or questions. CeLa did not know by what means Kir had planned to join them but it was evident that this arrival was contrary to the expected procedure.

She felt eyes on her face suddenly and turned to see who it might be, though she was too shy as yet with others than Zama and Idi to venture a comment. She encountered the dark gaze of the poet, Jagon, who seemed to be looking through her, for he did not alter either stare or posture. The folds of his turban were loose but concealing about his face and neck so that his features could not be seen. His body was tall and powerful, however, and he had the quality of perfect stillness. CeLa had a sudden premonition of danger, a chill down her back even in the heat, as she turned back to watch with the others.

CeLa held her body erect, her face stiff, in the last few moments before Kir arrived. Let me not give myself away, great ones. Let me hide what I feel so that in time I may come to accept what he has so truly said, that he has no feeling for me. Her mind whispered the words to any god who might happen to hear.

Then he was among them, tall, grave faced, bold of bearing, as he spoke in low tones to Laz, Otu and Cusar, acknowledging the introductions to those he did not know and greeting those he knew. Idi and Zama were among these last and his smile of recognition was warm.

"We shall sail the great Nile together if the goddess wills it. Both of you are thrice welcome."

Zama replied, "It is the greatest of all adventures, Kir, and we are proud to be part of it." Her eyes watched eagerly as Kir turned to CeLa and the girl knew that she had indeed heard stories of what might have passed between them.

"CeLa, record this journey well." His face was impersonal, his voice cool. He but welcomed another soldier to the ranks.

"Be assured that I shall." She heard the words as if from far away and despised the pang that came over her as she looked into his eyes.

He turned away and called to Otu, speaking urgently to him as they began to walk up and down. CeLa stretched her stiffened body and reached for the thin wine that was used for travel. The liquid coursed down her parched throat. With it, her head cleared and she was able to think more clearly. Zama apparently had seen nothing amiss. CeLa realized then that the intensity of her own feelings had blinded her to reality. The simple truth was that others had their own concerns that were paramount. She need only watch her own behavior, stay away from Kir's presence as much as possible, do the work she was sent to do and all would yet be well.

Her musings were interrupted by Kir's call for the others to join around him. He did not smile now as he issued his orders. "We must make as much haste as possible. I was to have joined you later but was warned by the king to say that our mission is suspected. There are dissident elements in his camp who may well have counterparts in the armies of Lugalzaggesi. They may have been warned; we simply do not know. At any rate, we do not want the expansion plans of our king to become general knowledge. We must be alert and watchful. Thus, we travel all this night by a different route and all the next day as well. Otu knows of several paths that fortunately are not in general use; he informs me that one of these will take us near our first destination. Prepare yourselves for a grueling journey."

CeLa again felt the warning of danger. She had no wish to call attention to herself but this went beyond the personal. "Kir." He swung toward her and caution leaped into his eyes.

"What is it?"

Hurriedly, before she could lose her courage, she began to relate the events of the night before their departure—the words of Pina, the strange person in the shelter and the warning to wait. As she finished, the others broke out into a babble.

Kir held up one hand and silence was absolute. "You did well to speak, CeLa, and well to bide your time that night. This shows that our suspicions are not unfounded. Let us make what haste we can now."

Days and nights blurred into each other after that as they moved in the paths found by Otu. They might have been going in circles for all that CeLa knew. The mountains faded in the distance as they traversed the uncultivated lands and came down into the central section of Sumer, where the fields of the great cities sometimes extended for miles and the harvests were tended with expert care. Now, however, the recurring wars caused much of the land to lie fallow as people withdrew to the safety of city walls and guards.

At times they saw others riding or walking, but always at a distance. The three soldiers, Beto, Wizi, and Zurlil, took turns remaining behind so as to check for followers. Always the report was of none but the vigilance never slackened. Kir, Laz and Otu went in front, always watchful, talking a little among themselves as their eyes searched the horizons. The dark woman, Raba, stayed to herself, sometimes humming in her strange language. Jagon spoke to no one, nor they to him.

CeLa had finally seen his face one morning as he prepared for the day. It was a strangely disturbing one, lines and planes that jutted yet came together boldly, thin straight lips and tufted brows over eyes that seemed to see things others could not. He looked to be about Kir's age but his skin was so smooth and supple that it was hard to tell. There was an excitement about him that CeLa found hard to fathom. Zama had told her of the high esteem in which he was held and that his strangeness brooked no questions, only acceptance.

CeLa rode by Cusar early one morning and paused to ask, "Where do you think we are now? I feel as if we have been moving for many ages."

"I believe it will not be long before we approach the Euphrates River and cross to the oasis where we will meet the caravan with which we are to travel. Two or three days, no more."

Cusar was taciturn in his manner for all his readiness to break into sonorous language, settle an argument or recite a precedent. CeLa had at times longed to ask him questions such as plagued her about the various aspects of Ninhursag and Inanna, but as the memory of her ordeal in Lagash faded from her dreams, she was reluctant to raise it again as would surely be required. Zama had asked several times about it, but CeLa had given short answers and finally Idi had intervened with one of his soft remarks that put an end to all discussion.

Cusar's eyes were sharp, however, and he said now, "Are you troubled, CeLa? Is there any help that I can give you?"

How to explain the feeling of unrest, of danger, that daily pulled at her, that made her jump sometimes when Zama put a casual hand on her shoulder or when the dark gaze of Jagon looked back toward the vanished mountains? She fumbled for words.

"There is a strangeness at times, I cannot express it. I think I am afraid for us all."

He smiled at her. "We all know something of your fearful experience in Lagash. I would think that as time passes you will be healed of these fears. The goddess is not insensible to the foibles of humans. Did the gods not create us for themselves?"

He launched into a long homily that CeLa could not in decency depart from. She sat while the ass ambled on and Cusar recounted the trials of Inanna with the other gods, the difficulties of mortals who fell into ways of error and of the ultimate goal to serve the gods in life as a preparation for death and beyond.

Zama rode by in an attempt to extricate CeLa from this sort of thing, for which Cusar was renowned, but it was useless. He was warming to his theme now as he clasped her bridle with firm fingers, delighting in the audience that had delivered itself willingly into his power.

Suddenly there was another figure at Cusar's side.

This one did not wait politely. It was Jagon, all indifference gone from his eyes, a sharp incisiveness
in his manner.

"Cusar, you know these things, my new epic needs
an ear. Listen." He spoke to CeLa, his voice hoarse
with an inflection that was not of Sumer. "Go away,
woman."

Fury licked at CeLa as she glared at him. "For
one whose tongue is of honey, I would say that your
manners have the bee's own sting. Were you taught
such rudeness, poet?"

She saw Cusar hide a smile behind his hand as
Jagon's brows drew together in an anger as sharp
as her own.

"I wait for your departure."

"Gladly." She pulled on the rein and drew back,
then turned the ass toward Zama, who was riding
with Idi a short distance back. A final glare at Jagon's back was pointless, for he had begun to recite
in Akkadian to Cusar with as much power as the
priest had had when speaking to her.

Idi said now, "There are legends about Jagon's
rudeness even to the great king himself. He is a
genius, touched by the gods, and beyond mortals. He
will tell you so if ever he deigns to speak to lesser
ones such as ourselves."

It was a piercing comment for the gentle Idi to
make and CeLa found it unsettling. Unsettling too
was the effect the savage black eyes and manner had
had on her. She was weak in the knees, angry and
fascinated. She wanted speech with this man and,
in sudden truth, she wanted to feel his hands on her
body. Gods, I am depraved, she thought. What of
her feelings for Kir?

She began inane chatter with Zama; it was better
than her own thoughts. But the fear did not leave
her and this time there was none to whom she could

voice her thoughts openly. She could only be grateful for the friendship that these two offered. Otherwise she would have been totally alone.

By early afternoon the next day they arrived at
the bank of the Euphrates and took shelter at a tiny
village some miles up from the city of Uruk, which
dominated this section and was thus to be avoided.
Otu, a master at avoidance, had come ahead with
one of the soldiers to make arrangements for the
company to rest and refresh themselves for the night
while readying themselves for the next leg of the
journey. Their mounts were to be given in payment,
later to be sold in Uruk. Their price would include
ferrying across the river in the round-bottomed boats
now pulled up on the bank. It was not likely, Otu
reported later, that questions would be asked, for
many were fleeing these days.

"I have said that we seek relatives in one of the
oases bordering the desert, among them my son who
fled when our village was overrun." He paused, justly
proud of his abilities at subterfuge.

That night saw the first roof over their heads in
weeks. CeLa and Zama bathed again and again in
the river, washing their hair and letting it flow over
their shoulders. It was bliss to put on a clean robe
and feel its lightness, bliss to move freely without
cloak and turban.

After Idi and Zama retreated to find some privacy
of their own, CeLa found herself restless and unable
to sleep. Raba slept heavily and instantly in the separate room they had been given. Carefully CeLa
made her way outside the mud hut and down the
little path to the river, which stretched wide and
free before the sliver of moon poised high and reflected in the water. Some palm and fig trees tended
by the villagers tossed their branches in the little
wind. A rich, marshy smell rose from the mud at her
feet and across the river little campfires gleamed.

CeLa stretched luxuriously as the thin robe molded itself against her slender body and her black hair rippled in the faint light. Her breasts lifted, small and high, as she raised her arms. The robe was slit at one side and her bare flesh shone provocatively through it. She had meant to bring a thicker covering with her but it was late and she had seen no other movement.

Suddenly a hard hand closed over her shoulder and spun her around to push her against the bole of a tree. Savage lips found hers and ground into them as the length of a male body pressed down on her and a leg sought to push her own apart. CeLa fought with all the fury a cornered animal would exhibit, but her attacker was too strong. He grappled at her breasts and tore the thin robe. She managed to free her mouth long enough to give one high shriek that was instantly muffled—but not before she saw the face of her attacker. It was Jagon, he who had fascinated her by his aloofness, and of whom she had thought hungrily only that afternoon.

Sickened by her very self and by the gloating light in his eyes, CeLa relaxed long enough to fool him into loosening his hold temporarily. *Lady goddess, be with me, free me from this fiend!* The thought gave her courage and she brought her knee up with all her power as she aimed the hard edge of her hand at his throat.

Jagon was quick enough to divert her knee with a movement of his own but the blow brought enough pain so that he released her and fell back before her hand could reach his vulnerable throat. CeLa tried to run but tripped in the edges of the robe and fell flat. All passion gone in his pain, Jagon snarled out a curse.

"Bitch! How dare you place your hand upon me! I am Jagon. You shall pay for this!"

He lunged at her. She rolled aside and tried to

scramble to her feet, but he threw himself on top
of her in combined murder and lust.

A voice she remembered came out of the shadows
then. "Leave the woman alone or my blade shall
sheathe itself in your back."

CeLa had been answered.

19

Confrontation

Jagon was so intent on his prey that the words uttered did not reach him at first. It was CeLa's breathed cry that gave him pause as she looked beyond him into the grim face of Kir.

"I will not say it again, Jagon."

Jagon pushed CeLa to one side and straightened up slowly, his fury evident as he said, "Why do you interfere, Kir? A woman should be honored that I wish to take her."

"Obviously, I am not. Your opinion of yourself is so great that I doubt your skill can exceed it." CeLa tried to be calm but her voice rose in an anger as keen as Jagon's own. "I am not a gutter wench to be toppled, you scum! How dare you force yourself upon me!"

Jagon laughed without amusement. "Women are receptacles, relievers of men, bearers of children."

Kir cut in. "You will leave the woman alone, Jagon. Now and from this time on. Seek your pleasures elsewhere."

"She walked well nigh naked beside the river. Her eyes have sought mine as I sat composing my epic. A whore's invitation."

CeLa opened her mouth to refute this, but it had gone suddenly dry. Kir's hand lashed out and Jagon fell back holding his jaw, his eyes incredulous.

"Listen, both of you. Nothing will interfere with this expedition. I am the leader, commanded by our

king and given sole authority. There is no disputing
that. I can send the great poet and the lowly scribe
alike back to Agade if I will. Jagon, touch her again,
or trouble any of the others, and you will find this
no idle threat. CeLa, there will be no invitations,
subtle or otherwise. Is that understood?"

Jagon stood up and wiped the blood from his
mouth. "Well understood. I owe you both a reckoning. Remember my words." The dark eyes moved
from Kir to CeLa and back again, the glitter in them
reminding CeLa of the demons that sometimes pursued her in dreams. He turned and vanished into
the darkness, seeming a part of it so easily did he
move.

CeLa braced herself for Kir's anger, telling herself
that she must defend her actions boldly, that she
was not a servant girl to flinch before the master's
anger. He could not think that Jagon had been right.
She remembered her flickering eyes and was ashamed
once more, but her head was high as she turned to
face Kir.

"I thank you . . ." The words trailed off as she
stared at Kir in amazement. He had picked up the
dagger from the ground where it had dropped when
he hit Jagon and was wiping it on the edge of the
mantle he wore. His face turned toward her and she
saw that he was laughing silently, a laughter that
reached his somber eyes and transformed him into
a youth, into the man who had called for his love
in dreams.

CeLa was prepared for anything but this. Her lofty
avowals faded as she stood in the night wind, the
remnants of the thin robe hanging about her. Out-
rage overcame her that he could find near rape so
amusing.

"Perhaps you will tell me the joke, Kir, that I
may share it. The last minutes have not been as enjoyable for me as for you."

He laughed again, this time aloud. "The face of Jagon! No woman could do such a thing to him! He has ever taken what he fancied, so great is his skill, so much is he a master of his art. You have made an enemy, CeLa."

"He does not care for you either, I notice." She pulled the robe tighter about her and hoped the moon would stay behind the cloud. Ridicule was as hard to bear from Kir as indifference; she was thankful that the brunt of it rested on Jagon. "I wonder that such lawlessness is condoned. The man is a brute."

Kir sobered. "He is that. There are stories of virgins new to the court, older women past their prime . . . he can be charming. But he will not harm you now."

This time she could say with all her heart, "I am grateful, Kir."

He looked at the curves of her body and her flowing hair. One hand went out to her shoulder and his voice was stern. "Do not go about this way. It is foolish when we must travel as we do. Nothing will disrupt the mission."

CeLa quivered at his touch and he jerked away. They stood looking at each other in the soft, blowing darkness. Then his hands were on her body, touching her breasts, exploring her softness, feeling the warmth of her yielding places. His mouth found hers. Their tongues wound together as they drank of each other. CeLa could not breathe. She was drowning in him. Her arms were around his shoulders and fire flamed in her loins. She could not get close enough to him. The blood hammered in her veins and her moans were lost in its sound.

Kir spoke her name in a quick rush of breath as his arms held her even more closely. She heard his heart hammering and knew that her own answered it. His manhood thrust against her loins and she yearned for him even as his mouth drank hungrily of hers.

There was a sudden splash from the river and they jerked apart in almost guilty haste. The fading moonlight showed Kir's hawk profile and gleamed on his jet hair. CeLa felt a flush mount to her face as she averted her eyes. They scanned the dark waters but there was nothing. Kir was the first to speak.

"The goddess has warned us. Jagon might well have doubled back to watch." His voice was soft and his eyes still held the warmth of passion. "We must finish this another day."

She stared at him, fully expecting him to lash out at her again or to disavow their passion with a scornful laugh. "Will we, Kir?"

He bent toward her and even in the pale light she saw the flames in his eyes and the flare of his nostrils. All her senses hammered and she wanted nothing more than to return to his arms.

"Will you come when I call?"

"You know that I am bound to obey the leader of the expedition in all things." She kept the words light out of necessity.

He put his hand against her neck and the gesture threatened to break her hardwon composure. "I am not Jagon, CeLa. I do not command or coerce." His fingers moved lightly and she felt her skin quiver under them. "Guard yourself, lady."

"And you, Kir." She took the hand that he held out and this time they smiled at each other in anticipation.

Later CeLa lay in the little room she shared with Raba, knowing that the dark woman was awake for all that she was very still. Not for the first time, she wondered what her secret was. Sleep was not for CeLa; her mind raced with the implications of what Kir had said. She knew that she would go eagerly to him when he called but he must seek her out. She would not lay herself bare before him again. Jagon's assault on her had been brutal but exciting. Now she knew the measure of that man. Restlessly she turned her face into her arms. It had to be faced, she knew. Was Kir's sudden interest in her sparked by Jagon? Was Kir the sort of man who wanted only that which was sought by someone else? She could not believe that, but previously he had spoken cruelly to her and ignored her. Still, his kisses and his hands spoke of long-held passion.

She sighed and turned on the pallet as her feet and legs cramped. There was to be no rest for her at all and she would look a veritable hag on the morrow. Thoughts of Kir must be banished from her mind before she began to weep. Anger swept through her in a spurt of relief as she remembered Jagon. Presumably he was one of the great ones of Sargon's court; she had heard them all speak of enlightened Agade, the capital of Akkad, but the women of Sumer were not treated as cattle as this man had treated her. Perhaps she should have stayed in Lagash, after all.

Kir's face rose up before her once more and she forgot Jagon, for wisdom told her that the flickers of interest she had felt for him were but retaliation for Kir's seeming indifference. CeLa knew that the core of the person she herself was remained yet inviolate; for now that knowledge must suffice.

It was very early when the party gathered its few belongings and went out to the round-bottomed boats placed at the river's edge. There a ferryman from the village waited to take them across, as had been agreed. The morning was brilliant with sunlight and the heat had not yet risen fully. The river gleamed blue, then dark as it moved toward the distant sea. Palm fronds blew in the breeze while the tillers in the fields close by lifted their faces to it. The rich smell of mud and fish mingled with cakes cooking on the fires before the huts.

CeLa lifted her own face to the freshness, feeling the night fears and speculations fade a little in the reality that yet another leg of the journey was about to begin. The others were quiet, immersed in their own thoughts. Jagon kept apart as always, but she could not repress a shudder at the sight of his cowled figure. All her senses sought Kir, but there was no sign of him.

She sat down in the little craft with Raba, Idi, Zama and Cusar, along with the ferryman and two villagers. The other two boats followed and CeLa felt the old delight of water travel that had always come when she and Nandar, along with her mother, had traveled the rivers in long-gone days of happiness.

One of the villagers began to sing a lively tune of farming and fine expectations. His fellows bawled out the chorus lustily as the oars flipped through the water. CeLa envied them for a moment as she thought of her own restless life and the vast uncertainties yet to come. Not for them the plotters in temples or the shaky favor of a king who would pass. Their lives were bounded by the rise and fall of the river, the tilling of the crops and the favor of the gods. Some drops spattered on her bare arm, touching it with coolness. In the shallows at the receding shore she saw several young women bathing and dandling their children, gossiping about these strangers in their peaceful life.

CeLa's spirits began to lift as they moved slowly across the wide expanse of the river. She could hear Nandar's soft, dry voice again as he told her of the place where the two rivers met and emptied into a greater gulf from which adventurers sailed to other

lands fabled and strange. She recalled that she had
cried to be a man and do likewise. Now she was part
of a great plan that might well become legend if
it was successful. In all honesty she could not wish
to be one of the loitering women by the shallows.
By whatever favor or whim of the gods, she, CeLa,
was involved in the press of events.

A bird cried above them, the ferryman and his
comrades ended yet another of their half-bawdy songs
and the boat scraped on the bank as one of them
jumped out to help pull it up. The Euphrates was
crossed. Beyond the strip of palms and tilled land
lay the desert and the men of the caravan who were
to meet them.

They sat in the shadow of one of the palms and
waited for the others to join them while their boat
moved back out toward the opposite shore. Cusar
bent to Idi as he said, "Now we go out into the
desert for two full days of travel before our meeting. Let us hope and pray that all has gone as
planned. I shall direct special prayers to the goddess
when we pause to rest this night."

"Do you think we have been followed?" Zama put
the question despite Idi's frown. Cusar frowned slightly. He had been addressing his remarks to Idi and
did not like being interrupted by a woman.

Idi answered her. "There would be little need. In-
formers might be posted in the villages we would be
likely to visit. They would know that we must cross
the great river some place."

CeLa lifted a hand to shade her eyes as she half
listened to their speculation. The other boat bobbed
closer. Her eyes ran swiftly over it, then went on to
a darker shape in the sparkling light. Kir and Otu
were in the next boat with the ferryman and another
man. Both were talking earnestly, the sound of their
voices carrying to those who waited.

Cusar was speaking again, his voice a rich roll.
"We must be on our guard, of course, but the journey through the desert will be fierce indeed. As Idi
has said, watchers have only to be posted in the obvious places. Otu is wise in these matters." He turned
abruptly and walked away. His lips still moved, however, and they knew that he spoke with one or more
of the gods who must be besought to watch over them
in what might be great peril.

There was a whistle from Otu just then and they
went to join the others at the water's edge. Kir had
dismissed the ferryman and now he turned to them
all.

"I dared not ask for many provisions, lest we give
ourselves away. We must make do with what we
have until we meet as arranged. We will go down-
river from the village and head out into the desert.
The journey will be hard. Try to conserve your
strength by a slow pace, no useless talking or excitement."

He looked up and CeLa saw the battle gleam in
his eyes that she had seen in the corridors of the
temple in Lagash. Instinctively she knew that this
was as meat and drink to him.

"We must work together for the common good, all
of us, forgetting that we are separate individuals. If
we do not, then not only will we not accomplish our
mission, but also we will die separately."

Despite the hot sun, CeLa felt a shiver run over
her body and down her spine. Raba's dark skin was
suddenly paler. Idi and Zama moved closer to each
other. Laz and Cusar exchanged glances while the
soldiers drew closer together. It seemed an ill omen
that the air lay heavily on them and that no sound
broke the hush.

A spirit of apprehension hung over them all that
day and became even stronger when they turned
from the green strip of land beside the Euphrates,

passed over the sparsely settled, tilled areas on this side and headed out onto the flat plain that would eventually give way to the desert proper. Cusar's ritual invocations of Inanna and the gods who served her did not help matters that night when they camped in the open, leaving the soldiers to watch. The rolling phrases sounded as if they came from a gong, repeating themselves without meaning or variation. CeLa caught the looks from some of the others and knew that she was not alone in this feeling.

Kir sat alone, his dark face hidden in the shadows. His head jerked up as Raba approached him and spoke softly, urgently, in a voice that sounded as if it were water flowing in a torrent to the sea. Her usually impassive face worked as she gestured. He listened and then answered in the same language. Angered, Raba turned away and rolled herself in her robe for sleep. Kir stalked out into the night.

CeLa walked across to Laz, who, with herself, had been the only spectator of the little scene. The others had been caught by Cusar and urged to continue the fervent prayers to the goddess. She wondered now if they felt as she did that the heavens were empty this night.

"What did she say to him? It must have been dire indeed to judge from the look on his face." She kept her tone light and conversational but fear rang behind it.

"She spoke in her native tongue." He moved as if to go, but the faint light of the waning moon glimmered gray on his scarred face and she saw that he felt as she did.

"You understood it."

"Yes." The word came hollowly.

"Tell me, Laz. I will simply be the worse for not knowing. Did not Kir say that we must share each other's burdens? All one company?"

"It was wild talk only." His eyes shifted from her and strayed to Raba, who lay some distance away.

"Then share it with me, for I can tell that you too are troubled."

He sighed. "I am not the man I once was. Glad I am that this leadership belongs to Kir and not to myself. Very well, CeLa, perhaps you are right. Raba, as you likely know, is from Nubia, which lies above the cataracts of upper Egypt, a fierce and harsh land. She has been a slave in Egypt and a servant of some dark god of whom I know little. In her own land she was a seer of great renown. It was not as in Egypt, however. Apparently only in freedom do her powers come, and then rarely. Sargon spoke with her several times, then set this mission and promised her an escort to her people. He did not say, but I believe that she foretold the future for him and he believed her."

CeLa was doubtful of this. That hard, confident man seemed to believe only in himself and the favor of Inanna, but even the bravest must bow before the gods.

"Raba said—" She paused and waited.

A drift of cloud covered the moon's edge and the brilliant stars seemed to recede as he spoke the words of the Nubian seer.

"Death lies in wait for us in the desert. The form of it is not perceived but it comes with the hand of a friend. We are doomed and our mission is useless. If one or more live, they will be scarred and destroyed in time to come. Once we crossed the Euphrates, the doom was sealed. So it has come to her and so it is true."

"She has seen her own death?"

"That is hidden. We are warned, she said. What is to be done about it is not within her scope. She awaits the will of the gods."

The words drifted on the air as if marking themselves on stone. CeLa felt deadly, creeping fear and longed to flee from it even as she knew there was no place to go.

20

Trumpets of Doom

All the next day they trudged into the face of the changing land that was now red-brown soil mixed with drifts of sand and some few rocks. The sun beat down and there was no wind or clouds. All their breath was saved for walking; their bodies were wet under the loose robes that seemed to weigh heavily. CeLa tasted the grit on her lips that would not be dispelled even with the carefully rationed sips of water that each person was allowed three times during that endless tract of time.

Kir marched ahead, speaking to no one, his face hidden by a fold of his turban. Only his eyes, dark and hooded, were visible. CeLa saw that he, no less than they, watched the horizon and started if someone came too close. Raba walked in back, her arms folded over her bosom, resigned to the fate she had predicted. Kir's hand was on his dagger and the other men followed suit.

The sun was sinking into the vast expanse of flat land before them when Kir stopped and held up his hand for attention. He loosened the face covering and tossed it back. The fading sun glittered on the flat planes of his cheeks and threw into relief the high arched nose.

"We will rest here for the night. Tomorrow will see us at the meeting place. We will have wine and comradeship this time tomorrow night." He paused and the words fell flat.

There was a high keening cry from Raba and the repetition of one word in Nubian. CeLa knew instinctively that the word was death. So did the others and they moved away from her in a widening circle.

Kir lifted both palms up and out, seeming more a bird of prey than ever as he roared, "One more word or sign such as that, woman, and I will leave you bound on this spot!" He repeated the words in Nubian and Raba shrank back before the look on his face.

Zama was trembling. "She has foretold doom, I know it."

Idi shook her arm roughly. "Foolish one, hush."

"You cannot say that you have not felt it. All of us have." She put her hand over her mouth and stared at Kir.

He called for the soldiers to open one of the packs he carried and to spread out cakes and wine. His tone was brisk as he said, "Let us remember who we are. People of Sumer and of Akkad, servants of the great king and thus the favored of Inanna. Do the gods of Nubia haunt this land that we quail in fear before them? The seer is far from her land and her ways. Take courage, eat and drink."

He sat down and lifted the wine jug. They watched for a moment, then Otu and Laz joined him. CeLa sat cross-legged and reached out a steady hand for the jug as she said, "I am parched. Leave some for the rest of us."

Cusar frowned at her but Kir laughed, the sound almost normal in the reddening stillness. "Aye, lady, you are bold. Drink to it." His eyes met hers and she saw warmth in them.

A new voice spoke then, a husky voice with music in it. "Our leader has said it well. Let us remember who we are. I, Jagon, will tell you."

He stepped to Kir's side, a small lyre in one hand, his body bare except for the short wrapped skirt customarily worn by those at leisure. He stood with a natural arrogance and waved them to be seated with his free hand while Kir watched with a faint smile. No longer the recluse, no longer the seducer or fighter, Jagon was that for which his name was famed throughout Akkad, the sweet singer with the gods' own power.

"I sing in the name of Inanna, lady of love, supreme in the worlds of gods and men. I sing in the name of the mighty king, Sargon. Hear now, my words."

Time and substance faded for CeLa as she walked in a world peopled by gods and kings, with journeys over far and trackless seas to paradise and the shadowy underworld, with battles and questions and passionate love. One man and many, all strove with gods, all were high in pride and honored for it. They gave respect where due but walked with heads high.

The light faded and stars wheeled overhead as the desert chill rose. The lyre spoke softly, then boldly, but the main instrument was the compelling voice that rose and fell in a saga that might have come from the gods themselves. CeLa was herself an instrument played as skillfully as any at a great feast. So were they all. The fear that had been at her back was thrust away as the king marched down the land to claim all that had been promised to him as he rose from a lowly position to rule over the cities. Before the holy city of Nippur he was welcomed by the god Enlil, whose city it was.

"And the might of the king stretched from Egypt, beyond Dilmun and the mountains, over the seas, even to the feet of the gods themselves. Great was their pleasure and many the blessings bestowed upon him and his followers."

Jagon's voice died away. The company sat very still and CeLa was conscious for the first time of her cramped legs folded under her. She shifted to ease

them and others did the same. Someone sighed. A
robe rustled as it was drawn over shoulders hunched
with strain.

Kir's voice was low and steady as he rose to clasp
Jagon's hand. The poet's eyes seemed sunk into hollows. He swayed on his feet. "You have taught us
much this night, Jagon. We are grateful."

Jagon nodded, then his eyes swung round to Raba,
who met them unswervingly. She spoke several words
and stopped, her head bent. Kir responded and turned
to them all.

"She says our gods walk with us, that Jagon has
called them together. The vision of Sargon is a true
one."

Zama laughed aloud with pleasure but CeLa saw
the frown on Laz's face and guessed that whatever
Raba had said, it had not been that. She did not
really care, for in one aspect Kir was right. The fear
that had pressed on them, suffocating rational thinking, had gone, banished by the genius of one man.

The haunted eyes looked into hers and suddenly
CeLa could forget the rough grapplings of the night,
the savagery of a man who saw only himself, for he
had saved them this night.

"I salute Jagon." The words came unbidden to
her lips. She trembled, for she thought that he might
take them amiss.

The light of the gods was still on Jagon, however,
and he looked beyond them all, weariness apparent,
as he sought his pallet, spread some distance away.
CeLa thought he had not even heard their praise
and gratitude.

The release that had come upon them all now
took the form of quietness rather than joviality. Kir
walked alone but within easy reach of the camp.
CeLa felt unbearably weary and sought her own
pallet, but sleep would not come. The vision painted
by Jagon had been too forceful. She could dislike

the man yet honor the power he had. Once more she
could appreciate the wisdom of Sargon, for each
member of the expedition had a particular place to
fill. "He brought us together tonight, gave us a personal pride." The thought ran through her mind as
she drifted toward sleep.

By nightfall of the next day they had penetrated
ever more deeply into the desert without a sign of
those they were to meet. The foot travel had taken
toll of even the most hardy, and their pace grew
slower with each passing hour. Food was barley cakes,
of which there were many; but the meager store of
wine was diminished and water was doled out sparingly. It too was vanishing rapidly. Otu had ranged
far ahead of them all day, keeping two of the soldiers at his side. Kir and the other soldier kept to the
rear to maintain watch. It was useless; the sands remained empty.

As they made camp, Otu said, "We have not come
astray, I know it as I know this country. Tomorrow
we must go on."

There was no dissenting voice. Their choices had
been made long ago and reaffirmed the night before.
This time they gathered close, talked, laughed, exchanged wild stories of improbable happenings. The
future might not have existed. Jagon and Raba sat
apart, their voices stilled.

The sun seemed to stand still in the sky as the
incredibly long day drew toward afternoon. Laz and
Cusar carried no water at all, having finished it the
day before. Otu had drained the last drop that morning and appeared scrawnier than ever as his cheeks
pulled into his sunken face. Zama had begun to
breathe heavily and leaned on Idi several times. It
was Laz who finally called out to Kir and brought
the straggling column to a halt.

"I think we must plan. Something has gone amiss and we go to our doom in this waste."

Kir was deadly. "Your plan? You have one ready?"

The tough old man jerked back as if slapped. "I do not challenge your authority. By the gods, Kir, you know that! I only say, give what water and wine as can be spared to two of the soldiers. They are hardy and used to privation. Let them return to the Euphrates and bring help."

"And the mission?" The tone was conversational. The others listened wearily, too tired to pursue the lines of argument.

"Messages can be sent to Sargon, supplies returned to us, other arrangements made. I only suggest. Yours is the decision to make."

"I have made it. We continue as we have done."

Water shone in little droplets on the part of Raba's face that was exposed to the sun. Her body was oddly tense as she stood next to CeLa. They began to move again and the girl went up to Laz, who was staring fixedly at the flat expanse of sand in front of them. Off to the sides, dunes rose on the horizon.

"You thought only of our safety, Laz. I thank you for that."

He looked at her and the faded old eyes held something of the flatness in which they traveled. "You are kind. He will mark me coward but it cannot be helped. The seer spoke of the death that waits. She said it again after Jagon finished. It will come despite his words, I know it."

CeLa knew it too, with that crawling of the flesh that sometimes speaks more truly than reason or logical thought. Laz turned back to the endless plodding toward the dropping sun.

At first the figures seemed to be part of the swirls of sand or the strained imagination as they moved steadily closer on long-legged beasts that might have

come out of a nightmare. CeLa rubbed her burning
eyes, ran her dry tongue over cracked lips and looked
at the others who had stopped at Kir's low order.
Otu stood straighter as he strained to see.

"I cannot tell. Their faces are not familiar but we
are on the direct line for the meeting place as agreed.
If it is they, then they are a day late."

"Be ready." Kir's order stiffened them and CeLa's
hand went to the dagger.

There were three of the muffled figures on the
ugly humped animals with the strange faces and toes.
CeLa stared in relief and dismay at the way the riders clung to their backs, seeming almost a part of
them. They were very different from the wild asses
Sumer had tamed and from the patient donkeys that
were common facets of everyday life.

One of the riders called out in a guttural language
to Otu and was answered in the same tongue. He
swung down, threw back his cloak to reveal a belt
filled with two short swords and a curved knife. His
followers waited, hands at their belts. Kir moved up
beside Otu and stood waiting. Several more phrases
followed, then the leader looked at Kir, who nodded.
The stranger faced them all and his words awoke
fear once more.

"I am Darzad, one of the leaders of the caravans
that move through this desert and one of those who
was to meet you last night as arranged by Otu. Yesterday morning we were attacked by a contingent of
armed men at an oasis where we rested. There were
some fifteen of us, for we planned to join yet a
larger group so as to better shield you. It was not
robbery. They sought to kill us all. We three alone
remain."

"It is as we feared. We are betrayed." Cusar came
to stand beside Kir, his face dark with anger. "How
did you escape to find us?"

Darzad flushed at the suspicion in his voice. "We slew some of them, took their camels and fled. Their day will come."

Kir touched the man's shoulder, his voice warm with sympathy. "You will contribute to the swifter coming of that day if you continue with the plan. Our enemies will not be expecting that to happen and our mission must continue."

Darzad swept the company with a practiced look. "Our bargain was made with you and it will be kept. Several hours from here there is an outcropping of rock that we have sometimes used as a meeting place. Supplies are kept there. We can rest and try to plan how best to join a caravan." His voice was brisk and assured but there was a hardness in it that did not bode well for those who had murdered his men.

Kir said, "It is well done."

The men dismounted then and, by gestures, demonstrated how the strange beasts could hold two persons at one time. The women and the weariest of the travelers would ride first. Zama backed away as an inquisitive snout reached for a corner of her robe where it crossed her shoulder.

"If I were not so tired I would almost rather walk!"

Water was passed about and they drank freely. Nothing had ever tasted so good to CeLa. She thought wryly that for a lover of the water she spent a great deal of time in dust and sand. The thought made her smile and as she did so she looked up to see Jagon watching her, little points of lust flickering in his eyes.

She whirled around to avoid them and encountered a hand on her arm. One of the riders was motioning her toward the camel, that strange beast she had never heard of before. Another camel sat in place and Zama, laughing in spite of her fear, stood ready to mount. Darzad was still talking with Kir and Otu, his back turned. The man took her hand as he readied himself to lift her up. As he did so, his cloak swung open slightly and she saw the seal around his neck.

CeLa jerked away in one swift movement and screamed with all her might. The dagger seemed to leap into her hand as she faced the man, who gaped at her.

"He wears the seal of the followers of Sirna! The crowned Ninhursag with the skull face bearing the emblems of war. They are the betrayers!" To her dying day CeLa would remember that image in the death-pit with the priestess in her mad frenzy before it, thumping drums signaling the approach of doom and high trumpet notes lifting above it all.

Kir's own sword was instantly at Darzad's throat. CeLa would think of that trust later with warmth; now it was enough to see the apprehension that came into the man's eyes as he said sharply, "The woman's wits are glazed by the sun. What foolishness is this over some trinket?"

Kir moved close to him. The sword flicked aside the folded turban where it lay around his neck preparatory to being pulled up against the sun. A seal of lapis lazuli with the same image worked in gold hung on a thong there.

"Explain this or you die this breath." Kir pushed the sword into the soft flesh.

Darzad stood still. "It is but a trinket, a bauble. You try my patience and we waste time."

The sword did not waver as silence mounted. The rider on the camel shifted position and Idi caught up the reins before he could reach them.

"The truth, Darzad!"

"I have told it to you. I now withdraw my offer of help and my bargain. The woman is mad. My men and I will go. We have suffered much and are of no mind to suffer more at your hands." His voice was controlled and full of dignity.

Kir looked at the others and then at CeLa. She saw the beginnings of doubt. "Don't you see? They killed the men of the caravan and doubtless others are with them. It is they who followed us and that is why we felt as if we were in danger. They worship the death aspect of the goddess and that is why they wear that symbol. I told you of her power! By the deathless gods, must we all die because you cannot believe the truth?"

Cusar came close to Darzad then and jerked the image loose. "It is true there is such a cult, old beyond belief, which says there is but one side to the Mother Goddess." He mused down at the image.

There was a faint trumpet blast in the distance. Figures came rushing toward them on camels, and Darzad began to laugh in triumph.

21

Caravan to the Two Lands

The sound of that laughter hammered in CeLa's ears and for an instant the death-pit was very close. They stood heedless of the menace that was approaching as Darzad surveyed them, his manner scornful.

"We are in the ranks of your king and know his plans while we ourselves are unknown. We will send him to the netherworld for his foolishness to think that he could rule in the land of the great goddess. My men have slain the unbelievers and now come to deal with you." His laughter was cut off by a gurgle as blood splashed red in his face and poured down the front of his robe. It came from the dagger in his throat that had been flung with such force that it protruded through his neck.

Jagon stood with hand still uplifted, the sun shimmering on the naked blade of his short sword as he turned to the other riders, who cowered away from his look.

"Die now as you have killed others!" He thrust toward the nearest one, who fell to his knees in entreaty. There was a rattle of swords as Kir's came across that of Jagon and sent it flying.

"Fool! You could have ruined our chances for bargaining. What good is he to us dead?"

Jagon's face flamed with fury. "Cowards buy their lives."

CeLa drew in her breath at the insult but Kir

laughed. "So the tales have it." He turned to Otu. "Call to them that we wish to parley."

The riders were very close now. CeLa counted ten, dressed in black robes and hoods, their swords shimmering in the sun, their eyes fierce above the masking cloth that hid their faces. Darzad's men stood still, menaced as they were by the sword of Jagon. Otu called out again and again but there was no reply as the hooded figures neared the party.

Kir's voice came low to them. "We must fight, there is no choice." The riders circled them and paced the camels around in silence. Otu's words received no answer and finally he ceased as the minutes drew on and the eerie pacing continued. "Kill as many as you can."

In the moment that death seemed closest, CeLa gripped the little dagger, well aware that it would do little damage to a fighting man. Her eyes sought Kir's. Life seemed immeasurably sweet now that she was about to lose it. The sweat that trickled down her back and burned in her hair, the very sand in her sandals spoke of that life. The circle was drawing closer. Soon their enemy would howl in triumph and fall upon the party.

Kir looked back at CeLa then and his eyes were warm. It was as though he touched her intimately. She knew that her very soul was open to him and that this moment of sharing was a true union. She lifted the dagger in salute, her head high.

He laughed and it was a battle cry. His words were those of the leader of the expedition he commanded, but they were also for CeLa and she knew it. "Together, my friends, together we shall fight and die."

Jagon called back to them, "A fine tale this would have made, had I but lived to speak it." There was merry disdain in his voice and CeLa took time to wonder at this strange man whose very selves seemed at war with each other.

It was strange to CeLa that they all should be closer in the preparation for death than in the living of life. A cold hand touched hers; it was Zama's. She stood by Idi, his body seeking to protect hers. There was no sound except the camels' feet as they slid through the sand. The eyes of the riders looked through and beyond their prey.

Suddenly a wild cry split the air. Arrows seemed to come from nowhere as they pierced the breasts of Darzad's companions. Two of the riders held their bows at the ready in the event that the targets had not been reached. The bodies spun to the ground and their life blood gushed out. The circlers stopped where they were and one of them turned to face Otu, calling out in gutturals that were curiously flat.

Otu answered, his own voice lifting with incredulity. Instantly they swung down, sheathed their weapons, lowered the cloth from their faces, and the one who had spoken to Otu came to stand before Kir.

Otu translated. "They are an offshoot of the tribe of those we were to meet. They arrived on the murder scene too late to save any lives but they did see the murderers scatter. Their forces were divided and have gone in search of revenge. The leader, Manto, wanted to destroy Darzad, who seems to have been a particularly bloodthirsty sort. When he saw us, he thought that we were of their party. Only the body of Darzad held him off. We came very close to death, my friends."

Jagon gave Kir a triumphant look. CeLa caught Zama's hand and Idi put an arm around them both. The air of life shimmered around them and CeLa breathed a prayer of thanks to Inanna, whose hand had surely been over them all.

"This is a dialect I do not understand," Kir said. "Ask him if he would be willing to guide us to a

caravan going toward one of the oases on the way
to Egypt. Do not say where we go."

Otu gave the essence of Kir's words to the leader,
who gave a savage grin and spoke at length.

"He says that if we can travel night and day, two
to a camel, we will be guided to such a place and
his own word will commend us to those of the caravans. We have slain the evildoer, he says, and are
therefore right in his eyes."

For the next three days and nights they moved
across the endless desert. CeLa lost all track of time,
for she felt the sway of the camel even on the very
few times they paused to relieve themselves or walk
about. She learned to sleep leaning against the person in front of her and to take her own turn at
wakefulness, though these beasts needed no guiding.
It seemed ages ago that she had shared a time with
Kir. Now he was remote and distant, the leader concerned totally with the safety of his expedition as
he walked apart or conferred with the men, his face
dark and sober. He spoke to her now and then, but
his preoccupation left no room for intimate conversation. She understood; for her the days passed in
exhaustion and blurred dreams. For the moment it
was enough that they walked in the same path and
that he was not indifferent to her.

The oasis was a crack in the desert—one tiny pool,
a scraggy palm and a collection of rocks. A large
dune stood to one side and more loomed to the west.
It seemed a trackless, forgotten place but the party
was only too delighted to reach it safely.

CeLa remembered only hazily her pleasure in gulp-
ing cup after cup of water while the world rocked
with motion even as she stood on the sand. Then
there was sleep that came as with a bludgeon, sleep
so deep that dreams could not penetrate. She woke
once to great thirst quickly satisfied by the cup at

her elbow. Two guards paced slowly back and forth
while the others lay in separate mounds of exhaustion. She looked at them fondly, easy tears of tiredness coming to her eyes. Her people, closer than any
she had ever known, with whom she had endured
much. The thought of Kir touched her gently and
she lay back, this time to dream of the boat on the
Euphrates and him beside her.

It was a full seven days before the caravan directed
to them by Manto arrived. Time passed slowly for
the party as they waited, for they were forced to remain at a constant alert, knowing themselves unable
to resist any full-scale attack. CeLa, who had thought
that she might never get enough sleep, soon found
that it came hard enough. She was conscious too of
Jagon's eyes and knew that the time would come
when he would seek her out again. In spite of herself, her blood ran more swiftly at the thought. Kir
had ignored her since their communication. He spent
most of his time talking with Otu as they paced
back and forth.

The caravan appeared in the early morning light
of the eighth day. It was composed of a string of
vicious-looking camels, some twelve men muffled in
robes but well armed and watchful, four women who
kept their heads bowed and rode in the rear and
five soldiers whose skins were only slightly paler in
color than that of Raba. They wore leather helmets,
carried strangely curved short swords and remained
apart from the others.

Kir and Otu went out to parley, returning shortly
with the news that the others had waited to hear.
Otu said, "They are to meet another caravan many
moons' ride from here at the oasis of Sadmar, a principal place for trade of goods and gossip. We may
join them if we can travel at their pace and do not
encumber them. I have explained that we are from
the same village, have been oppressed and seek a

new life elsewhere across the desert. Manto bore this out as well as the fact that we can pay well. They have honor, these desert dwellers. I think we are as safe as might be expected."

The pattern of all their days was set by the next. Up at first light, ride all day with only a brief pause once, camp in the lengthening twilight, the members of the caravan to their own way and Kir's to theirs. They slept, cooked and ate separately in small tents made of cloth and animal hides that could be swiftly dismantled and assembled. It was a strange life, bounded as it was by the largely silent riders, their own closeness, which grew in their isolation, and the vast stretching sands overhung by the brilliant sky. CeLa's body soon accommodated itself to the swaying rhythm of the camel and she felt one with it as they moved across the endless miles in a journey so long as to have no imaginable end.

One afternoon they paused earlier than usual to make camp. One of the caravan leaders had spoken to Kir that morning and their conversation resumed now. When Kir came to his own people, he was smiling, the light for once reaching his dark eyes.

"It seems this is a day to rejoice and thank their gods for some favor granted long ago. There will be a small feast and we are bidden to join the festivities. I need not tell you that we must remain cautious; nothing must jeopardize our relationship with them."

His eyes rested on Jagon, who seemed restive but said nothing. Once again CeLa could feel the antagonism between the two men. Sooner or later it would rise up the more strongly for the necessary suppression. Fear stirred but she pushed it back. After the endless riding any release was welcome and the proposed feast a delight.

The golden moon hung high in the sky as a shrouded dancer moved carefully in a ring of watchers. A lone voice wailed while heads nodded slowly. Off to the side one of the women buried the bones of the desert animals that had been roasted earlier. The people of the caravan sat by themselves; Kir's party was scattered out among them in an effort to be friendly. All had eaten and drunk together, clapped their hands in an effort to catch the strange beat of the discordant music and tried to overcome the language barrier. A sense of alienation remained, however, for these nomads knew but one way of life and sought knowledge of no other. Otu was the exception. He sat now with the leader as they drank the sour wine and their voices rose and fell with the music.

CeLa recalled the pleasure of the morning and her own eagerness at some change in the routine of daily travel. The least grimy of her robes had been shaken out and donned. It was a thin brown cloth girdled by a bright cord, and her dark hair swung freely over her shoulders as the warm breeze lifted it. She sighed with boredom. Was this repetitive ceremonial to go on forever? Her ears ached and her body was cramped, yet she sat as far back as might be deemed polite. These people held her life in their hands and must not be offended. So much for anticipation, she thought as she gave a bone-cracking yawn.

"If this is a celebration, I would greatly fear to attend one of their ceremonials for the bereaved."

The sardonic voice spoke almost in her ear and she jumped. Turning, she looked into the amused eyes of Kir, who crouched slightly behind her, his dark cloak almost blending with the sand. His profile was pure in the light that glinted off the planes of his face. His dark eyes were fixed on her with such intensity that her mouth went dry. Beyond them, the singer paused, lifted her voice into a higher wail and dropped it swiftly into what might have been a dirge.

CeLa whispered, "My head is ringing with that. I thought they were a silent people." Her heart hammered against her ribs and she felt little prickles of sweat start on her forehead.

She saw the flash of his white teeth as his lips quirked up. "They make up for it on such occasions as these. I do not think that I am alone in wondering what marvel of beauty lies under the shrouding cloth of the dancer, even though I am sure she must closely resemble one of the mud flats of the Euphrates. Anticipation is all. I shall, I think, propose the use of such a custom in our city of Agade when we return."

His hand lay near hers on the sand. He was so close that she could feel the warmth of him. She said, "How long will the ceremony continue, do you think? It seems to have been hours now."

"Into eternity. Their gods must be deafened by now."

She giggled and with that release of tension felt Kir's hand on her wrist. She leaned toward him and their eyes met.

"Will you come, CeLa?"

"Yes." The word was wrung from her. The time had come.

The drumbeat rose heavily in the night as the singer and others began to wail more rapidly. A fire was leaping now and the attention of all was focused on it. Bottles were lifted while here and there forms lay back in the sand or drew closer together.

Kir drew CeLa slowly back with him as a cloud drifted over the moon and the darkness of his cloak blended in with the sand. She neither knew nor cared where they were going; it was enough that he had sought her out of his own volition, that his hand held hers and they shared this moment.

The little cluster of dunes flanked by two waist-

high rocks was quite close to the camp but offered
them privacy at this time when everyone's attention
was elsewhere. Kir spread his cloak behind them and
turned to CeLa. She looked up at him and saw that
his control was still strong, for his face was impassive. Only his eyes were brilliant with warmth. A
muscle jerked in his cheek. Hunger rushed up in
her and her blood drummed in her ears. They stood
gazing at each other for a timeless moment, then
they were in a close embrace without seeming to
move.

CeLa felt her blood turn to fire as his lips sought
hers, moved away to her throat, up to her neck and
back to her mouth. Their bodies melted together
even as their tongues intertwined. Her arms were
around his shoulders and her fingers moved in the
darkness of his hair. One of his hands went to her
breast, touching the nipple lightly at first, then more
strongly until both stood full and high. She felt the
growing wetness in her loins as her legs grew weak.

They sank to the ground in their mutual eagerness. Kir pushed her back against the cloak while
he continued to touch her warm, secret places and
kiss her mouth in long, deep kisses. CeLa was in
a fever of wanting by now, but she was also conscious of a growing fear. She remembered how her
mother Lilda, had died in childbirth. She thought
of Sokar's tale of Kir and how he sought out only
those who could not compromise him. Her body went
rigid under Kir's stroking hands and her eyes went
to his flat stomach, the lifting shaft of power, the
dark eyes.

"What is it, little one? I will not cause you pain.
I know that it is the first time for you." His voice
shook slightly with his own passion and the effort
that pausing at such a time cost him.

"I am not afraid, Kir." Not afraid of you, cried
her mind. Not truly afraid of your body. I fear my

own feelings for you and that you may count them as nothing.

They looked into each other's eyes, then his mouth came down on hers and for CeLa there was no more thought, only feeling. His body settled against hers and she felt the first long thrusting, the faint withdrawal, a flash of pain and a fierce yearning. Her hands were on his shoulders, her head back as he thrust and lifted, waiting for the first response of her flesh. When it came, CeLa was at first frightened as she moaned and twisted in Kir's arms. He touched her face with warm lips, then moved in her gently and more steadily. She closed her eyes and rose with the staff of his body, rose to the heights and poised, then fell with the moment of release as into a warm crystal pool. They lay quietly together, shuddering in the aftermath of passion, as the cool breeze dried their sweat-dampened bodies.

In the shadow of the rock just beyond, the watcher stirred and risked a look as they lay oblivious to all but themselves. Then he drew the turban flaps more closely about his face as he moved cautiously away. It was well that he did so, for the savagery there would have cowed any man, much more those who had any experience of Jagon.

"We must go. It will be dawn soon."

CeLa opened her eyes to gaze into those of Kir as he bent over her. She felt the blood rise to her face as she remembered her hastily stifled moans of ecstasy in the night. His face was remote now, but she knew Kir well enough to know that this was a mask, a very effective one, by which he held others at bay.

"Yes, of course." She kept her own voice cool, though she longed for some word of tenderness from him.

They moved swiftly over the sand. Nothing seemed changed in the camp and soon CeLa was once more in the spot from which Kir had claimed her. As she sank down there, she looked up at Kir and smiled in recollection of the passion that had been between them.

He whispered, "Say nothing of this for the safety of us all." Now he was not her lover of the white, burning moonlight; he was the leader of the expedition and it was to him that she spoke.

"I would not be so foolish." Bitterness tinged her soft words as he nodded and moved quickly from her toward one of the kneeling camels where he would rest for what remained of the night.

CeLa lay back, staring up at the sky from which the moon had long since sunk. She relived every moment with Kir, remembering the gentleness so at odds with the hardness that he daily exhibited, the restraint used because of her maiden fear that had turned to passion with his tutelage, and the withdrawal from her now. Desire for him lifted in her veins and she clenched her fists at her sides. He had come to her this once. Inanna willing, he would do so again and then she would not be afraid.

Inanna, lady goddess of love, I know now why you are so well worshiped. A vast weariness came over CeLa then and she closed her eyes to dream once more of the boat on the Euphrates as it drifted to the sea. This time Kir, laughing and happy, his eyes brilliant with love, was beside her who had been alone all the days of her life and now was alone no more.

22

Evil in the Land

CeLa was preparing to mount her camel the next morning when she suddenly felt eyes on her back. She turned and met the malevolent stare of Jagon. There was a faint smile on his lips. Once more she knew that strange quickening of the blood that was somehow mingled with fear. Never had he looked at her so. How could he know of the passion of the night? Yet she felt that he did. She jerked her gaze away, annoyed at her own fanciful thinking.

There was a movement beside her and a low voice spoke in the guttural language that none save Otu and Kir could speak. It was Raba, her usually remote manner broken as her wide nostrils flared and her hands moved rapidly in a language of their own. Jagon had turned rapidly away and no one else was near them. CeLa shook her head and tried to speak slowly.

"I cannot understand you, Raba. All is well, truly."

The Nubian now spat words at her, rage in every syllable. The girl backed away but Raba followed, one arm lifted as if to strike her.

"Raba!" The cry came from CeLa's left and she saw that Otu had suddenly appeared there, Kir a few paces behind him. Otu spoke swiftly in the same language Raba used and the woman stopped as if rooted to the sand. She spoke two words in Akkadian, then ran toward the waiting caravan that was preparing to move off.

CeLa's eyes met those of Kir and she saw the familiar coldness there. The sweat was cold on her
body as the drumbeats sounded in her memory. "Demon" and "death." Did Raba see this for all of
them or for CeLa alone? She knew then that some
obscure doom hung over them all.

"We must depart. Let it go." Kir spoke swiftly to
Otu, who nodded in agreement. Both averted their
eyes from CeLa and she knew that this in itself was
a warning. Obediently she mounted and they moved
off across the desert in another of the endless days
of their journey.

Worry went with CeLa all the time now, but there
was none with whom she could discuss it. She was
very conscious of her essential aloneness as they
moved still deeper into the wilderness. She could still
banter with Idi and Zama or argue abstrusely with
Cusar in the manner of good friends, but she must
retain her own counsel. Kir remained aloof from
her and even avoided her pointedly on the several
occasions when she tried to have speech with him.
Raba made no other move toward her, but the few
times CeLa saw her, she noticed that the usually
warm, dusky skin was now gray and slack. Jagon
had returned to his self-contemplation and the girl
wondered if she had made much of little.

In the end it was Otu of the spare words and the
far-seeing eyes who told her what the seer had meant,
and he did not do it willingly. Their own company
had tended to break off into little groups as the
journey progressed but Otu kept to himself or, of
late, with Kir. Often he sat alone late into the night
and watched the unmoving sands or the wheeling of
the stars. CeLa had waked at times to see him thus
and had wondered when he slept.

It was at such times, there alone in the darkness,
that CeLa thought of what her life had been and
what course it might take in the future. It seemed

to her that she had had basically little to do with
it; she had been tossed by the whim of the gods.
She did not know that Nandar's cynicism had touched
her quite so deeply but she was, she thought, much
wiser for the experiences of the past few moons. That
same will that had made her fight for her life in
the temple of Ninhursag now drove her on to solve
some of the mystery that seemed to enshroud Raba
and in some strange way to touch CeLa herself.

She lay awake in the deepest part of the night,
watching the dim figure of Otu as he sat alone, upright as always. The others lay still. Only the silent
pacing of the guards some distance away gave life
to the moon-bathed scene. The impulse came to her
and she acted on it without thought as she rose cautiously and tiptoed toward Otu. Her mouth was dry,
her stomach fluttering, but the will to know was
greater than all else.

His head did not turn as she halted at his side,
but the whisper was dry as the sand at their feet.
"I felt you as you watched, CeLa. What do you want
that you must break your rest for it?"

She sank down in front of him, noting how wrinkled and seamed his face was. "I would know what
the seer said and why."

He said, "The gods will protect those who serve
them. You need not fear the Nubian."

"I fear only the lack of knowledge." CeLa spoke
smoothly, hoping that he would not challenge her
in the lie.

Otu swung his head from side to side and there
was a rough anger in his voice. "Raba was thought
to be necessary to our mission by the king; it seems
that she simply speaks of doom. She must be dealt
with."

CeLa did not doubt the manner of the dealing.
She had learned that much from Kir. A little sound
escaped her and the hard old eyes looked into hers.

"You have asked and you shall be answered. The Nubian's words concerned you alone. She warned that the woman of Sumer will cause destruction to the mission, that the shadow rests over you in the brightest of sunlight and that by you are the demons made bold."

CeLa stared at Otu in disbelief. "Can this be true? I cannot think that she has such power."

"You wanted to know and would have pressed until you had what you demanded. There is great strength of will in you." He stood up and she rose with him, the force in his small body making him tall. "You will tell this to no one. Raba will be spoken to. There have been enough disturbances."

"Do you believe her?" The question ripped out as CeLa tried to fight back the memory of the seeress's wild black eyes and contorted mouth.

"A wild woman of Nubia? I believe nothing she says but she will have her uses even as we all have. Go from me, I must rest. It must be a late hour or I would have kept my own counsel."

"Thank you for telling me." She stood very still as he grunted and strode away. Otu saw no demons, that she knew, but CeLa had come too close to demons who walked in human form. She shivered as she made her way back to her pallet. There would be no more sleep for her that night.

Once more time stretched in endless bands over the desert. CeLa lost track of time, which was marked only by the waxing and waning of the moon. Sometimes she and Zama would walk for miles in the effort to relieve the monotony of the days. The members of the caravan stared at first but continued to remain apart from these strange travelers who had paid so well. Questions were best not asked in the desert. Raba spoke and sang no more but kept to herself, shrouded in robes, her fire quenched.

They were walking in their usual fashion one morning when Zama sighed heavily and pushed the turban from her head so that the sun beat down on her face. Her hands were shaking.

"I must ride now, CeLa. I was foolish to push my strength. Idi must not know yet or he will leave me in one of the border towns to be protected."

"Are you ill? Why would he leave you?" CeLa stared at her friend in amazement. "Is it the fever, that you talk so?"

Zama laughed in spite of her efforts to fight down nausea. "I am to have our son, silly one. I suspected it before we left and I have been sure for some time now. The goddess has blessed my womb twice before but each time the child came forth dead. This time it will be different, I know it." Her small face shone with light as one hand went protectively to her stomach.

"Perhaps it would be wise to take care this time."

"I must be with Idi! When you love, CeLa, you will understand." The dark eyes went soft with dreaming.

That was the sort of remark that CeLa hated. It brought Kir too sharply to mind as she thought of the closeness shared by Zama and Idi.

Zama was continuing, "A man wants a son; he wants to see his shadow long on the earth. We will name him for the great king who will surely reward Idi according to his merits."

CeLa beckoned to one of the guards, who slowed their camels, then helped them to mount. CeLa listened to Zama's musings with one ear even as she tried to remove her thoughts from Kir's face in many moods. The sound of laughter floated back to them and CeLa lifted her head to see Jagon deep in conversation with Cusar, who was one of the few people the poet seemed not to antagonize. Kir rode a little ahead of them.

She hummed a lilting song of the water that she had often heard Nandar do full justice to while flown with wine. The sound carried over the still sands as Zama joined in, full of her own happiness. Kir turned abruptly to look back. His eyes met CeLa's and she saw the hunger in them, a hunger that suddenly matched her own in a power that flowed between them. He took up the song in a mocking tone that quite belied the sense of it and rode ahead, leaving CeLa oddly shaken and mute.

Usually the desert cooled at night in contrast to the burning heat of the day, but the next few nights it did not do so. The hot sands seemed to radiate back and the customary winds did not rise. The strain of lost sleep showed in the travelers' faces and they tossed and turned, waking early to dread the blaze of day. They talked little among themselves. It was enough of an effort to rise and mount the camels that also turned balky and had to be treated firmly.

In these long times of travel, CeLa had found that the desert itself brought peace in spite of the forebodings she felt. Her life with Nandar now seemed far away and the episode in the temple of Lagash but a fearful dream. Reality was the heat, the camel, the wet pull of her clothes against her body, Zama's look of pride, shared laughter with her and Idi over Cusar's sonorous pronouncements. If her heart hammered when Kir passed, it was easy enough to turn away. For this time apart, it was enough that he inhabited her small world.

The heat flattened them by day and night. Kir had passed the word that an oasis might be expected soon and this gave them hope of relief. It might also have made them careless when they stopped for camp that night. Even Otu took to his pallet with an audible groan of relief. Laz paused to speak to him and CeLa heard the words clearly.

"They say the wind will come soon. They feel it."
He dealt with the men of the caravan more than
any other in the daily processes.

Otu gave a short laugh. "I wish we might feel it
too. We will pause for at least a day's rest at the
oasis. Even such tireless ones as they must rest."

CeLa turned her head into the bunched-up robe
that served as a pillow. Her hair dragged wetly at
her neck and she strained it away from her head.
She felt as if she were smothering and resolved to
open the thin robe she wore even more after the
others slept. Even the familiar dream of drifting
down the Euphrates in the high-prowed boat would
not come. The desert was too real.

CeLa sat upright, her heart hammering, her throat
dry. She did not know what had roused her or even
that she had slept, but she must have, for the moon
was a fading sliver on the horizon and the stars had
a remote look. The others lay sprawled in sleep and
the camp of the nomads, arranged a short distance
away as usual, was still. All seemed as normal as
ever. Why then this unrest? This sense of alarm? Had
she dreamed without knowing it?

CeLa relaxed slightly and prepared to seek sleep
again. Possibly she had tossed until the heat woke
her. Her robe was wet in back and front. She loosened it and felt the welcome air touch her skin.
Hopefully she would be able to rest a bit more before the new day began. Her scalp prickled, however,
and the sense of wrongness returned. Without moving anything except her eyes, she scanned the camp.

It came to her with a shock. The two guards who
normally patrolled the camp and the nomad watch-
man were nowhere in sight, although they were always in view at night. The flat sands gleamed under
the pale light; their camels were dark bumps close
by. All was still, nothing seemed out of place, yet
where were the guards? A flicker of movement caught

her eye and she turned her head. Nothing. But it was
not her imagination, no idle fancy or dream planted
by a god. Danger was all around them. She heard
the angry squall of a camel, a sound that would have
gone unheeded any other time, camels being notori-
ously temperamental. Now it was a warning. She
saw a flowing movement as though a person were
trying to hide behind the beasts. It was enough. CeLa
jumped to her feet and screamed, the sound shattering in the quiet. There was no time for words even
if she could have formed them. She screamed again
and all her fear went into the sound.

Pandemonium resulted as the sleepers tried to get
up and to their weapons. Hooded figures rose up
from behind the camels, from behind the piled bag-
gage, from the desert floor itself, and poured over
them in a stream. Swords were bared, long knives
flashed, a woman's agonized scream seemed torn from
her throat, men shouted and cursed, a death groan
sounded close by.

CeLa bent down for the dagger she kept by her
even as she slept but a bearded figure howled in an
unknown language and tripped her so that she fell
heavily. He threw himself upon her and she could
smell his rank odor. Her hand found the dagger and
she drove it straight up into his stomach. His cry
was unearthly as he rolled from her. She did not
stop to see if he was dead but jerked the dagger free
and, holding it dripping blood in one hand, she
pulled the thin robe about her and ran toward the
place where Kir had been sleeping.

All about her the fighting continued. She could
not tell the numbers but it rapidly appeared evident
that her company was outnumbered. It was almost
impossible to tell friend from enemy in the dim
light, but somehow she knew that wherever he was,
Kir would be in the forefront of the fight. A knot

of men struggled silently near a sprawled body. They
did not see CeLa approach or hear her gasp as she
heard a familiar voice lifted in Akkadian curses. Kir
still lived. No other man could curse so richly and
still have breath for battle. A surge of delight ran
through her body and she launched herself at the
nearest back, clawing and digging, the dagger raised
to strike.

The man flung her to the ground but fell in his
turn and grappled with her. One of the others turned
from Kir and raised his weapon to defend his comrade, but he could not tell where to strike. CeLa
slid from the fingers that sought to take her life and
jumped up.

Kir's sword held the attackers temporarily at bay
because of the diversion she had created. He looked
past them and saw CeLa, smeared with the blood of
the man she had killed, her robe in tatters about
her legs, her eyes wild.

"Get away from here, you fool! Try to escape if
you can." He spoke in Akkadian, which the attackers
would not be likely to understand and which CeLa
could barely grasp.

She cried, "It cannot be done! Anyway, do you
think I would leave you?" She was beyond reason
and terror, governed now only by her passion for
him. One small girl would be of little use against
the robbers, for such they must be, but she would
die beside Kir rather than flee to what would not
be life without him. It was hopeless, for they would
catch her if she did not die in the desert.

They pressed in upon Kir and the two who turned
their attention toward CeLa grinned savagely as they
approached her from both sides. She held the dagger
outward and prepared to give her life as best she
could. The world narrowed down to this battle and
this man. There was nothing else.

Kir was losing his wind now and his voice came jerkily. "CeLa, use the knife on yourself! They do unspeakable things to women!"

"No!" She screamed the word between her teeth. While she lived she would fight.

"CeLa, you fool!" There was great pride in his eyes at that moment.

"CeLa. CeLa." One of the men close to her said her name in a strange language, then spoke rapidly to the other one, who turned and called out to those around Kir. Instantly, two others detached themselves and came toward her. She lashed out with the dagger but one caught her arm and twisted it behind her. Kir saw and lunged forward. A blow connected with his head and he fell backward just as one man thrust a sword into his chest.

CeLa screamed and pulled free. Oblivious to all else, she ran to him and bent down. The dark eyes opened and gazed into her tearful ones. A faint, almost mocking smile curved his lips as he whispered, "Death to all I touch." Blood rose in his mouth and spilled into the sand. He fought for breath. "I destroy—"

"Kir, I love you!" She put both hands on his and felt their coldness even in the burning heat of her own flesh. She was faintly conscious of the robbers standing around them.

"CeLa . . ." He twisted, his eyes glazed and he was still.

She went mad then. She snatched the sword from his limp fingers and lashed out at the nearest robber with all her considerable power. "Beasts! Carrion! Ox dung!" Tears choked her and she had no more voice.

The man's arm lay at his feet as he clutched his shoulder in disbelief. She lifted the sword again and brought it down on the neck of the robber who ventured close to his comrade. The blade, Kir's pride, struck bone and halted. They recovered from their shock and rushed her, using their hands, not their weapons. She spared a moment to wonder if they meant to kill her that way. With Kir dead, nothing mattered.

One of them hit her in the face and knocked the breath from her so that she fell back and away over a body. The world spun and rocked as she tried to regain her balance. They stood in a ring around her and watched as she tried to rise. Her fingers touched warm flesh and blood. She looked through tears, tangled hair and blood. Zama lay disemboweled before her, her face contorted by the pain in which she had died. She was naked, her lower body in shreds. CeLa knew that they had taken the dead body in lust.

CeLa vomited explosively then. The world rose up and faded away as she collapsed insensible at the feet of the murderers.

23

Lair of Death

CeLa drifted in and out of consciousness as her mind sought to evade the fearful knowledge of all that had happened. Once there was the strangely smooth ride on a camel, a bearded face bent over hers and chatter in a discordant language, her head hammering with pain, her voice calling out Kir's name, wine held to her lips and her own efforts to spit it away, nightmares of blood and death, a whirling as if in a storm of sand, then the vision of the great river in the light.

She opened her eyes this last time to find herself lying on a soft pallet in a tent. It was cool there and a clean, dry scent hung in the air. The tent seemed fairly large as she turned her head experimentally. Chests stood against one wall and brilliant materials drifted from one onto the floor where mats had been laid. One of the flaps was partly open and she saw the figure of a guard there.

Because knowledge must be postponed as long as possible, she looked down at the outline of her body, which was clothed in a thin white robe of such woven softness as to be almost nothing. She moved her limbs and twisted her fingers. Everything worked. She raised a hand to her face and felt its new angularity. She was surprised that she had not been killed outright. They must have an elaborate revenge planned.

"Kir is dead." She spoke the words out loud and

felt them drive into her heart like a dagger. There were no tears, only a deep, dull ache. Had she shed them all without knowing it? "Would I had died beside him!"

The words sounded loud to her but they emerged as the merest whisper. There was a rustling sound beside her and a woman's impassive face looked down into hers. The woman spoke but CeLa could not understand. She was in early middle age and heavy, but light on her feet. A cup was brought and proffered to CeLa with signs that she drink. The girl thought of declining, throwing it on the floor, bursting into tears, but her body still lived and it demanded sustenance. She stretched out both hands and took the cup of gold set with jewels. It was heavy and her hands shook as she set it to her lips. Instantly the woman's arm was behind her shoulders to support her as she drank the liquid that appeared to be a mixture of milk, honey and wine. CeLa felt the effects instantly as strength returned in some measure.

"Where is this place? Who are you?" She spoke slowly in Sumerian, then in Akkadian and finally in the barest Egyptian that Utar had taught her. The woman listened, shook her head and signed that CeLa should rest. The girl lay back obediently as the woman went out, closing the tent flap behind her.

Thoughts of the massacre she had witnessed came back to her and she knew that few of her party could have survived that onrush of robbers. At the time she had thought only of Kir, but her memory worked better than she had thought possible. Idi's body had lain beside that of Zama, the throat cut. Laz's scarred face had risen above that of an attacker and his triumphant laughter still rang in her ears. Truly, Raba had seen all this and they had given no heed. CeLa clenched her teeth and pushed such thoughts back. There lay madness and she was a survivor.

She must have dozed for a few minutes because her head felt musty and heavy. She shook it impatiently and reached for the remains of the liquid in the cup that did not satisfy her. How was it possible to be hungry when the man you loved lay dead, your friends destroyed horribly and your own death lay in wait? Still, there it was. Just so had death waited for CeLa at Sirna's hands and she had lived.

She heard voices raised, then the tramp of feet and a command outside the tent. She shivered with fear. If she had no trouble thinking of all the dreadful things they could do to someone who had killed several of their men, or at least seriously wounded them, how much more could these robbers know, since it was their trade?

Two men thrust another man into the tent so hard that he stumbled and almost went to his knees. They laughed loudly and turned back to stand at the flap, hands on their hips, eyes intent on the prisoners. The man whirled to speak but a brusque command made him turn again in CeLa's direction. It was Jagon.

A purple bruise ran down the length of his face on the left side and a rude bandage, already stained with blood, was wrapped around his neck. He limped as he walked. His proud face looked much the same but his brilliant eyes were no longer remote, for anger burned in them.

"CeLa, are you all right?" The concern in his warm voice made her shiver. If only Kir had stood in this man's place!

"Reasonably so. Jagon, what happened? Who are these people? Is anyone else alive?" Her voice faltered to a stop before the pain in Jagon's face.

He sat down on a cushion at the foot of her pallet. His eyes held hers as he talked and somehow

gave her courage not to scream the pain in her heart.
CeLa clenched her fingers into fists in the folds of
her robe while a whisper in her mind spoke Kir's
name over and over.

"They are robbers who wait near the oasis for
the rich caravans that sometimes pass by here. They
knew who we were and our mission. They had orders to kill, from whom I do not know, and those
orders were carried out. Our friends are dead, CeLa,
the victims of a plot."

"Why are we still alive?" It was an accusation she
had no will to hold back.

Jagon's dusky face burned under her eyes as he
said, "We will not be for long, be assured of that.
You live because those who watched you fight called
you a warrior woman, worthy of a more interesting
death. I live because I attacked the chief himself
with my bare hands and almost choked the life out of
him until I was knocked aside. Their sense of hier-
archy is strong, if you take my meaning."

"Kir? The bodies?" She could go no further.

"They lie where they were slain, CeLa. Food for
the beasts of the desert."

She looked at him and for the first time remembered that he and Kir had hated each other. Had
there been a flicker of satisfaction in his voice? Her
old distrust rose up as she kept her face impassive.

"May the gods guide them safely in the underworld, for they served well. Inanna give Kir peace."
It was all the epitaph they were likely to get, CeLa
thought bitterly. "May all the gods curse these murderers. May the flesh be eaten slowly from their bones
while they still live and may they be slaves in the
dark world forever."

"We are far from Sumer, CeLa." Jagon watched
her, his face expressionless.

She pulled her mind back and looked at him, survivor of a hideous attack, a man to whom she had

been drawn in spite of herself, one who would be with her in whatever ordeal was to come.

"Jagon, I am sorry. I did not mean to reproach you with life."

"You loved Kir."

The pain would not be with her long. Did the shades of the underworld know love and passion still? Soon she would join him, and the gods did not forsake those who suffered in their names. "Always."

"CeLa." Jagon put out a hand to her, then drew it back. "May I speak openly to you?"

"Of course." She stiffened. What would come now?

"I would not speak so in our mutual sorrow, but time is short. These robbers will not offer broken bodies to their gods. They will wait until we recover and are in seeming good health, then they will hold a great feast and destroy us. Dissimulate as I will do. Who knows what opportunities will come our way?"

It was the first hope CeLa had felt. "I will be very slow to recover, Jagon. You may be sure of that."

This time his hand touched her face and drew down its new thinness. CeLa shivered involuntarily and he drew back, his manner chilling.

"You must rest now, but hope is a strong medicine."

She lay back wearily as he moved away toward the guards. Weakness was pouring over her and she wanted only to sleep. She half shut her eyes, then suddenly they flew open. Jagon was almost at the tent flap and one of the guards was stepping aside, but it was not that that caught her attention. Jagon's limp was noticeably less severe and his head was held at less of an angle as he shook it. Perhaps he was better for having rested at her side while they talked. CeLa turned on her side and gave herself up to sleep.

The next day CeLa was taken outside in the com-

pany of the nurse or maid who had continued to
tend her and one guard who remained a discreet distance away. They were camped at a small oasis ringed
with palms and with dunes in the distance. There were
three separate pools with short distances between
them. Tents of hide and cloth were grouped around
the largest and camels were being tended beside
them. Guards were posted in every direction, walking watchfully back and forth. CeLa was allowed to
bathe, given fresh clothes and meat and wine of a
surprising quality. Then, with her back against the
bole of a palm, she sat for hours in the cooling winds
beside the pool.

The scene did not vary except that she was closely
watched. No one other than the maid came near
her. She did not see Jagon again for four days, all
of which followed the pattern of the first. Her
strength was returning in full measure but she took
care to move slowly and appear faint, sometimes re-
quiring the assistance of the maid to walk. She had
no way of knowing whether or not the woman was
fooled but it took all her effort to try.

The nights were long and painful at first. CeLa
wept silently for Kir—she would not do it in front
of his murderers—until she realized that her hold
on reality was fading and that she was dreaming as
if he had loved her in truth. Her own life hung in
jeopardy; if she lived, there would be time to mourn;
if not, then she would be his epitaph. After that,
she slept long and deeply.

On the morning of the fifth day, Jagon was brought
to her at the poolside by the same two guards. He
seemed thinner, the marks on his face less livid, and
his limp even more pronounced.

"How is it with you, Jagon?"

"Well enough. Our captors have told me that you
weep in the night, refuse food and find it difficult
to walk at times. They grow concerned for your

health. My wounds are tended by day and break open at night. I find it hard to retain my food. So far our plan is working."

"That is reason for thankfulness."

"I hope that you may find it so." He hesitated and looked at her for a long moment. The wind ruffled her dark hair and soothed the grief lines under her eyes. "I am bidden to tell you, CeLa, that this night they will house us together and that we must take each other as man and woman. They are elemental, these people, and believe that the cure for one loss is a replacement. Your feelings for Kir were evident. I told them that I was the father of Zama's child. Potency is highly thought of, you know."

"You will do anything to save your life, Jagon! What makes you think I will do likewise?"

Fury lit his face and she saw again the man who had tried to take her in lust and who had regarded her as little more than a vessel for his easement. "You are a fighter, CeLa. Do you think I would do this if there were any other way out? Do you not wish revenge on those who killed Kir? Do you want to die at the hands of such as these? We must obey, seem absorbed in each other, heedless of them. When their guard drops, as it must, we will be ready."

Tears came to CeLa's eyes and she bent her head. "Forgive me, Jagon. I know that you speak the truth. After all, we need only pretend."

He came to her and put his arms around her. She stood stiffly in the embrace. "You must know the truth. The maid will watch and you will be examined afterward So I have been told. If you breed a child, I will be ordered to lie with others of the tribe."

CeLa jerked back in disbelief. "What manner of man are you?"

"The same as you, my dear CeLa, a human being who will use the wits the gods gave him to survive.

You must show yourself willing or they will kill us
here and now. I had not thought you found me re-
pulsive for all that Kir had your heart." He put his
hand on her arm in a gentle manner for all the harshness of his words.

CeLa remembered with no little shame those flickering glances of awareness and pleasure that had
passed between them, the knife edge of hunger and
expectation that had sharpened as time went on.
Jagon was a mystery, a man of many puzzles and
greatly accomplished, a legend.

"I must be alone." She turned and went slowly
toward the tent, the maid and the guard behind her.
Jagon stood where she had left him, a bitter smile
quirking his lips.

Later that night CeLa paced up and down in the
confines of the tent, her thin white robe, loose and
knee-length, swinging out behind her. She had resisted all attempts by the maid to dress her in brilliant
colors and ornaments or to have her hair arranged.
It hung down her back below her waist, night dark
and rippling. She would do what she must, but there
would be no pleasure in it. CeLa knew that she
feared Jagon's depths and what she knew of his reputation did not comfort her now.

A brazier set near the door gave a little light. The
maid had taken up her seat in the shadows where
she could barely be seen. CeLa shuddered at the
thought of a watcher, but it could not be helped. If
only she spoke the language of these people! Any
communication would comfort her; she did not relish Jagon as an interpreter.

"CeLa." He spoke her name and entered at the
same time. His own loose robe was the color of the
sand. The bruise had faded from his face, leaving
the high cheekbones and planes of it prominent. He
still wore the bandage but his limp had diminished.

"CeLa." He came closer to her and put both hands
on her body in a curiously intimate gesture.

"Wait, Jagon." She drew back but he did not miss
the shudder of her flesh. "Let us have some wine
first." She poured it out from the jug into the cups
and gave him one.

He drank it in a single gulp and reached for her,
pulling her into a hard embrace. His mouth closed
over hers, his tongue sought her own and she felt
the ready thrust of his maleness against her near
nakedness. CeLa fought her repulsion, telling herself
that not too long ago she had thought eagerly of
just such a moment, had tantalized herself with just
such a communion with the elusive Jagon.

His mouth burned deeper into hers as he felt her
lack of response. She forced herself to put both arms
around him, to sigh with simulated eagerness. She
thought of the time he had tried to rape her. This
was worse in some inexplicable way. His hand went
to her breasts and rubbed the nipples in a painful
manner. He pulled her harder against him and CeLa
felt the sourness of vomit in her throat. She pushed
against him with all her strength and put her free
arm up in front of her face. He let her go so suddenly that she stumbled backward.

Instantly the nausea passed and she wiped her
sweating face with the hanging sleeve of her robe.
Now it was all to do over again. Doubtless the wine
so hurriedly drunk had caused such a reaction. She
looked up into Jagon's face and saw a stranger. His
eyes were narrow slits, his mouth savage and hard,
a pulse hammering at his temple. Fear licked at her
and she moved back.

"Jagon, I am sorry. The wine. The heat. I just—"
She stopped, knowing that words were useless in the
face of such fury.

He lifted both hands and jumped at her so sud-

denly that she had no chance to avoid him. Hard
fingers pressed the breath from her even as she
flailed and kicked at him. The world spun and faded
before her, then she was tossed aside as an old robe
might be. Jagon was standing over her, laughing.

"Too easy a death for you, CeLa. A pity, really."

She pulled herself up on one elbow and stared at
him as he called to the maid, speaking with easy
authority. "Tend her. Bring her to my tent at midmorning. Summon the council now."

"Yes, great lord." The woman spoke in the same
Sumerian that he had.

Numbly, CeLa looked into the face of her betrayer and knew that she faced Kir's murderer as
well as Sargon's traitor.

24

A Goddess Besought

The woman refused to answer any of the agonized questions CeLa threw at her but moved about bringing more wine, some cheese and little cakes, putting out water for washing and arranging a night robe at the end of her pallet. Then she left and CeLa heard her talking to the several guards who had newly come to the tent. The girl put a hand to her aching throat and sank back to rest. She would have need of it on the morrow.

Plainly Jagon was in league with these desert robbers or he could not have spoken so. In some manner he had caused all that had happened to them; he had toyed with and fooled her for some strange reason but her own body had told the truth. CeLa knew there would be no sleep for all the long night. She would likely die in a few hours, but the shock of the night's happenings had rendered her numb. She picked up the cup of wine, poured it out at her feet, then knelt to watch it sink into the sand where the mats had been moved.

"Inanna, lady goddess, I have not served you but it was your name Kir spoke in his sleep and you who brought the mighty king to power. If you hear me, if your strength extends this far, grant some measure of revenge against these enemies. Destroy them! Avenge my love!"

Her voice lifted in passion and was as quickly stilled as a little gust of wind blew out the remains of the light in the brazier. It might have been only that, said Nandar's voice in his daughter's brain, but CeLa felt oddly comforted. With that comfort came resolve; she would play out this game as best she might and watch for whatever opportunity might present itself. She would not go cowering to her own extinction, a thought not to be endured.

Time crawled endlessly by. Her eyes burned with weariness and her stomach churned and could not hold even a few sips of wine. She clamped her jaws together against the rattle of her teeth.

Do not let me show this fear before Jagon, I entreat you. CeLa instinctively knew that that would delight him, that his was a nature that took pleasure in the pain of others. Yet did she wrong him? Might he not have been forced even as she?

Her speculations were stopped by the appearance of the maid at the door. Guards stood behind her as she said in faultless Sumerian, "Come, he awaits you."

CeLa rose, her chin level, her body stiff. "Then let us have done with this acting. I would face my enemy and deal with him." She walked outside and the guards fell in behind her.

They walked into a part of the camp that CeLa had seen only from a distance since it was well spread out. Apparently these robbers lived well and saw no need to hide themselves. Several tents of brilliantly colored cloth were set apart from the duller ones of hides. One was crimson and blue with a white plume set on its highest pole. Guards paced back and forth before the entrance, hands on their weapons. CeLa took time to wonder how such an encampment could fail to attract the human scavengers of the desert, then remembered the savagery that had left her bereft and felt salt tears burn in her eyes.

One of the guards went before her and entered,

holding the flap aside for her. CeLa kept her face
immobile but her brain recorded the lavishness of
her surroundings even as her every instinct cried out
to flee.

Color was everywhere: in the rich hangings, on
the slightly raised pallets where soft robes lay, in
the hide boxes of jewels and weapons that took up
one entire side of the tent, in the inlaid serving vessels and wine container resting on the matting nearby.
The odor of incense hung in the air. Light came
down through one of the openings in the roof, which
also gave some freshness to the interior.

"Have you no words, CeLa? I had thought you
full of them." The light tone might have been the
greeting of a friend.

She turned and met Jagon's taunting gaze. Her
doubts about him were resolved instantly. He was
all the evil she had ever thought him to be. He sat
in a chair fashioned of the cedar wood so valued by
the rich. Pearls and gold gleamed on its arms and
headrest, which were carved in the shapes of beasts.
Sandals of gold and leather shone on his feet. His
robe of pure white linen was girdled with ivory and
silver. A golden circlet surmounted with a gleaming
black jewel curved around his head. He was like a
king in his own land.

"You give yourself great honor for a common robber and murderer, Jagon. I would have thought you
had more imagination." CeLa too could taunt.

It was a mistake. The savage eyes flamed as a
pulse beat in his temple and color moved to the
smooth planes of his face. CeLa realized her danger
but her tongue must buy her revenge for what had
been done to those for whom she cared. There was
no taunt that could touch Jagon now, she thought,
for he was totally alien to her. She must not let him
sense her fear or he would attack; the gut knowledge
of the cornered animal alerted her.

He said now, "My poor CeLa! Was I not con-
vincing enough for you? Were you so entranced by
the dead Kir that my touch made you flinch? I,
Jagon, for whom women and men have wept that I
turned from them? You shall pay for that insult before you die." His long fingers fondled a sliver of
a dagger that flashed with jewels in the light and
his gaze was hard on her. "If I knew Kir, and I did
know him well for some time, he would not willingly
have sought a woman like you. His taste, shall we
say, went otherwise."

CeLa heard her voice shake as she answered, "One
cannot command the heart, Jagon. As well seek to
order the gods themselves."

He laughed. "I do not care about your heart, CeLa.
My score against Kir and Sargon of Akkad was a
long one. You are but an incidental, a small toy with
which I shall amuse myself in the days to come, during which we must remain quietly here, away from
any caravans of the desert."

Surely the man was a demon! He meant to kill
her, that shone hungrily in his eyes. "What will you
do?" Her words sounded cool in her own ears but
sweat trickled down her back and under her arms.

"Much." His laughter rose up as CeLa shrank
back in spite of herself. "Come to me."

"No." She stood straighter, glad of this defiance.

Jagon flipped the dagger negligently through his
fingers and smiled his half smile that she had once
thought so mysterious. A sudden blow hit CeLa in
the back and she fell to her knees, the breath knocked
from her body. Dizzily she struggled to regain her
balance, only to be hit again. This time her face
struck the matting as the world whirled before her.
Jagon's voice seemed to come from a great distance
and it seemed very important that she listen carefully.

"Then I will come to you now that you are in

your proper place. I would advise you to lie quietly.
The guard does not really know how frail a woman
is. The next blow might seriously hurt you."

CeLa knew that she should try to rise but the
thought of another blow held her rigid. She heard
the slight creak of Jagon's sandals as he came close
and the sharp command as he dismissed the guard.
Then his fingers pushed on the back of her neck
and twisted her face to his. She opened her eyes and
looked into his own, where her doom lay.

An instinct as old as man told CeLa not to struggle, for the hurting rage was on Jagon. He ripped
the robe from her, clasped both hands over her breasts
and dug his nails deeply into the flesh. His teeth
worried her nipples, then went over her stomach and
into the mound of her womanhood, where they bit
down savagely. The shock stunned her for a moment
before the pain began and by that time the long,
hard length of him was in her dryness and pumping
steadily. He rose up slightly and held her arms wide
apart with his as he watched her from eyes that
burned with cruelty even as her blood stained his
white teeth.

It seemed that he would tear her apart as his loins
smashed down on her again and again. He pulled
up and out to the very tip of the organ and rammed
it home each time. CeLa felt warm wetness and knew
it was her blood. She could not cry out; it would be
her death if she did. Somehow she knew that and,
with it, that she wanted to live more than anything
else.

The pumping stopped and the great organ swung,
turgid and full, before her face. Jagon loomed over
her, a horror mask from the forgotten lands of the
cursed. Then his seed loosened and hurtled forth,
a sticky, hot mass that burned in her eyes and mouth,
revolting her and causing nausea to rise. She fought
it back with horror while Jagon sat back on her

bitten, mutilated body and rocked with mad laughter.

CeLa drifted in a retreating haze as she lay motionless on the pallet while two impassive women tended her, rubbing salve into the bites and applying cool compresses to her bruises. They had come to her as soon as Jagon rose from her. She had heard him outside calling thirstily for wine and had known that some small respite was to be given her. The relief of fainting or unconsciousness was not to be given; instead her thoughts pounded wildly in her head. Would he simply take her in this way and others more bizarre until she died?

Words formed on her lips and she half spoke them aloud, not caring if the women understood her and reported them to Jagon. "Lady goddess, let me live to kill Jagon. If I may be permitted to spill his blood, I vow all my life to serve you, be it long or short. Inanna, can you hear me?" The last syllables broke out of her exhaustion and she began to cry in long gulps that could not be ceased.

One of the women held a cup to her lips but CeLa savagely dashed it to the floor. "Get out! Leave me in peace! You but prepare me for that monster again." To her shame, tears started again as they left.

CeLa's body was young and strong. Her injuries were superficial and healed in the space of the next several days. No one came near her except one very old crone who brought food and water as well as ointments. The girl lay motionless on her pallet much of the time, plotting ways to kill Jagon. They were useless schemes, for there was no way to carry them out, but the time passed and her natural optimism came flowing back with each moment that she was left alone.

The next night she was waked from a restless, tossing dream to see the familiar face bending over

her. Her reaction was instinctive and swift; she spat
right into it, then curved her nails against the blow
she knew would follow.

Jagon wiped his face with his sleeve and said
mildly, "You would be savage if you lay dying,
CeLa."

She watched him narrowly. He was immaculate in
a loose white tunic, his feet bare, a golden circlet
curving about his arm. His eyes burned with excitement, seeming twice their natural size.

"What do you want?"

He shrugged. "It is the late hour and I could not
sleep. I remember too much when such times come.
I wish to talk and you have no choice but to listen
and do as I wish."

Truly some demon lay on him. Might this not be
her chance? She drew the thin robe up about her
shoulders and rose to face him. This man was capable of anything. She did not wish to fall into his
trap as she had once done, to her humiliation. "What
do you see in the night, Jagon? Those whom you
have wronged? The punishment that the gods who
love justice will finally inflict upon you?"

He crossed to the jug of wine that had been left
earlier with her food and poured generous measures
into two cups. He held one out to her. "Drink with
me."

CeLa knew that such gestures could not help her
but they were all the defense she had, the only way
her pride could bear all that had been wreaked upon
her. She slapped out at the proffered cup, dashing
it from her tormentor's hand.

"I do not drink with scum or with the entrails
of scum."

Jagon sipped from his own cup and watched her
without speaking. CeLa tried to summon up more
epithets but her mind refused to work. She could
not turn her gaze from his compelling eyes. Her flesh

began to quiver and one hand started to knead the other. Her legs trembled but she found it impossible to still them. A burning sensation rose up from between her legs and her nipples rose under the loose cloth. She put out one hand and a low moan came from her.

Jagon set the cup down slowly and retreated to the far side of the tent as if preparing to leave. CeLa turned partly toward the pallet and back again as she looked hungrily toward him. This ache must stop! He could not leave. She called his name in a low, throaty voice.

"What is it, CeLa? You are weary. I will leave you to your rest."

"No, no. You must not leave."

He turned to face her and said, "Beg me. Tell me what you want."

The burning increased. She jammed the fingers of one hand deeply between her legs and looked craftily up at Jagon. "This."

"Tell me." He moved a little closer. "But I really have no time for you now."

The words ripped out of CeLa, words heard in the streets, in the fields, phrases read and scarcely comprehended, some of the lore she had read in the temple of Ninhursag. Specific, detailed, greedy.

Jagon laughed at her fever and said softly, "If we did all that, my dear, we should need all the temple physicians of all the cities of this land. I do not think you ever spoke so to your beloved Kir, did you? Ah, but shall we try to fulfill your requirements as best we can?"

Kir. The fever slowed in CeLa and she recoiled. Long ago that name had meant something. Did it still? Jagon came closer and she inhaled the hot scent of him. He took her arms and pulled her to him as she quivered with eagerness. He turned her around slowly, then bound her arms behind her tightly with a leather thong. Holding up a wider one, he said softly, "It is the night and I promise you such pleasure that would make you cry aloud with delight. The camp must not be roused."

The burning was worse. CeLa did not feel the leather scoring her skin or make any sound of protest when he fastened the second thong tightly over her mouth. That completed, he turned her back to face him and ran his hard hands over her shivering body.

"Are you ready, CeLa?"

She nodded frantically and a moan escaped the gag as she rubbed against him. She arched her pelvic area out and up, twisting so that her breasts shook under the robe.

"Lie down, then."

She sank to the matting and spread her legs as wide as they would go, her entire body throbbing with the fire that burned her. Jagon bent down and bound her ankles together with another thong that he then brought up to fasten about her knees. Then he rose with one fluid movement and stood looking down at her with a smile of real amusement on his face.

"I bid you good night. I have business to attend to. Willing women bore me. Perhaps you will remember that in the future. Which reminds me, I owe you a token." He bent once more and spat full in her face. "Rest well."

The fire rose consumingly in CeLa then and she flailed against the bonds with all her strength, but they were so tight that she could not move or cry out. Images swirled massively in her brain as her body writhed. She managed to turn over on her face and began to rub herself on the coarse mat but the fire grew worse, flaming up unbearably. She gave one last convulsion, twisted, jerked and lay still.

25

The Ruse of Life

CeLa opened her eyes to filtered light, a warm breeze on her skin and the sound of a humming voice. She stretched experimentally, feeling the ache in her muscles and the exhaustion that permeated every bone in her body. Her mouth tasted vile and her lips were cracked. She tried to lift her head and was instantly conscious of the hammering in it.

The humming stopped. There was a flurry of movement, then a soft voice said in passable Sumerian, "Drink this, it will ease you."

CeLa looked up into the face of a dark woman several years older than herself. A purple scar covered one cheek and the eyebrow above was patchy, but her smile was warm. The girl looked down at the cup from which faint warmth rose and all the horror of that past time with Jagon flooded over her. Drugs in the very food she ate! She had crawled after that murderer as if she were a thing possessed; she had beseeched him to take her. Shame burned in her and fierce anger. Words etched themselves in her mind. Goddess, is this the way you heard me? Fool that I am to have asked your help. Rather would I live in the house of the dead. You are powerless here or have chosen not to help me. So be it.

She pushed the cup away with a feeble hand. The small gesture seemed to take all her strength. She noticed the healing marks of the thong on her wrist;

the cord had bitten deep. If she lived she would carry the marks.

"Seven days you lay as if dead. Your life was feared for. The drug is very powerful but what I give you now is safe. You need have no fear."

CeLa heard her voice rasp as she said, "And when I am well, it will begin again. Such is Jagon's way. It will continue until I am dead of his excesses."

The woman touched her face. "You will not die, lady, not until the gods call you."

"I have done with gods." The exchange had exhausted her and her body began to shake as her vision blurred.

The woman sat down beside her. "You cannot withstand another seizure. Drink and rest. When you wake, we will talk. You are not alone, CeLa. Many have walked this path before you. I am one such."

CeLa saw the truth in her eyes and the faintest flicker of hope rose. She lifted a shaking hand. The woman put the cup to her lips and she drank the heady brew. Almost instantly a feeling of well-being came over her and she floated free on the great river of her dreams.

CeLa slept and woke several times, each time drinking freely of the life-giving liquid that brought peace. She grew stronger with every waking and a sense of urgency quickened in her. It was time to face whatever new horror the future held. When the woman came again with the brew, CeLa turned her head away, pulling herself up to a sitting position.

"I will take no more of that, no more of that which makes me other than I am." As she spoke, she knew that one horror was done. She could not blame herself for what had been done to her, either by Sirna or Jagon. It had happened and was done. What mattered now was life, even more than revenge, for CeLa wanted desperately to live.

"You are better." The woman smiled and the ugly scar seemed to fade.

"Are you the servant of Jagon?" The words were more abrupt than CeLa had intended and the woman flushed but her intent eyes did not leave those of the girl.

"All here serve him." The answer was smooth, obedient, with no sign of the covert sympathy CeLa had felt earlier. "I will bring hot food now that you seem able to eat."

"Wait, what is your name?"

"I am Kalla." She stirred nervously and swung round as a familiar voice burned in CeLa's ears.

"That is enough, Kalla. I will speak with her alone." Jagon advanced into CeLa's sight and stood looking down at her. He waited until the woman had vanished, then said softly, "I think you have now begun to discern the pattern of things."

"Yes." She could say no more, for the fury she longed to lash upon him stopped in her throat. She trembled with the intensity of it.

"We will continue our exploration of each other in two nights' time. It should be interesting." The dark eyes watched for her response and his nostrils flared with anticipation.

CeLa could say nothing. She shut her eyes wearily, thinking that perhaps the aftermath of the potion she had been given caused it.

"How unlike you, CeLa. I am beginning to think that you are not worthy of all the attention I have lavished upon you."

She looked at him and through him, only vaguely beginning to think of something that might help. Her head lolled slightly, then jerked as he caught her chin with the tapering fingers that had once stirred her at the sight of them.

"Do not think to deceive me. You will be ready."

CeLa let her eyes glaze further and did not reply. He released her abruptly and strode from the tent. She heard his commanding voice outside speaking in a language she did not understand. The soothing tones of Kalla came to her vaguely as Jagon's anger rose. She lay limply back as Kalla called for food, this time in Akkadian. Then the other woman came in and sat down on the pallet at CeLa's feet.

"I have told him that you are yet very ill and that more time is necessary before you can approach him as he deserves. You heard his anger but even the mighty Jagon can do nothing against such illness. He will have his toy."

CeLa said, "I do indeed feel quite weak."

Kalla put a hand to her face and her mouth twisted as she said, "How, I wonder, will you be disfigured?"

CeLa felt a thrill of terror go through her. "What do you mean?"

"I said that you would not die. I did not mention that you might not wish to live after Jagon has had his many pleasures. He does not like willing women, as he has told you. All that is savage and cruel and perverse is delightful to him. Subterfuge is his game, as you have reason to know. When he is weary of you, you will be crippled in some manner; the loss of a breast, scarred as I am, a muscle in your leg cut so that you cannot walk, an eye gouged out—the ways are many. The women of this camp are few, but they bear his mark."

Her voice had been emotionless and flat. A sudden wind lifted up part of the edges of the tent and sand blew in as the light grew less, rising again with the passing of a cloud. CeLa felt no surprise. She had endured so much that horror dimmed. Caution made her wary now. Was Kalla simply the bait in another of Jagon's ploys?

"Why do you tell me this?"

"You remind me of myself long ago. A girl from a distant land, her young husband, the lure of travel, betrayal. An old tale." She put her hand to her face and CeLa noticed the strange way in which the scarred part remained immovable even as the rest reflected her emotions. "I have seen much and somewhere there must be an end."

"I do not believe you," CeLa said flatly. "I must rest now."

Kalla's eyes flamed. "I have bought you time. Yet I do not blame you. I will trust you with this much and you may betray us if you wish it. My life and the lives of others will rest in your hands."

In spite of herself, CeLa felt the first glimmerings of hope, although she knew the devious twistings of Jagon's mind. "Can there be betrayals in the very camp of the betrayer?"

Kalla ignored that and continued, "The great storm of the desert builds up. It is a time when all men burrow down and wait for it to pass, for who can foresee the will of the gods? It can be death to venture forth. This is the time that Jagon plans to devote to you. I and two other of the women know two of the guards who are disgruntled with the life here and complain that there is not enough booty, that Jagon takes only a select few with him on his forays. One of the women was stolen from Ur; her family is wealthy and will pay handsomely for her return. They feel it is worth a try. You may join us if you wish it."

Did she wish for life itself? To be her own person and free again, now knowing what freedom meant? There could be no greater blessing than this. She said, "Right willingly would I join you if I could believe that this were true. How can a few travel in a storm such as you describe? What of Jagon and his men? Will they sit idly by as we leave? It is a dream."

"Think on it and on the alternative. Jagon will be given some of the potion that you were given. Pray to all the gods it will kill him. My hand shall administer it as he readies himself to come to you. So great is his belief in himself that he fears none of us. As to the storm, the men are of the desert and know its ways. Better to fight than submit supinely." Kalla turned and left the tent, her stride bold and free.

For all the rest of that day and throughout the night, CeLa practiced tightening and loosening her muscles, flexing her arms and legs, sitting and standing for longer periods. When it came to be what she judged the depths of night, she dared to walk about, finding that her body responded better with each step. Kalla had brought roasted meats, fruit, barley cakes soaked in oil, and strong wine. There was so much that CeLa could eat her fill without fear that she might seem to be eating heartily. She bathed once in her small allotment of water, looking down at her smooth body, which still bore the marks of teeth and thongs, and wondering what Jagon would do to her if the plan failed. She touched a brown breast, watching the nipple lift rosily and harden. Would it be done with a heated sword blade? Once she had seen a slave whose nose had been cut off as a penalty for running away. She had turned aside, sickened. Or would it be an arm? Perhaps a woman's sex torn away. She had read of such things. CeLa forced her mind to a blank; in the late night one often thought of horrors that never happened. To think that way now would be to destroy herself. She knew that likely she was a fool to trust Kalla, but even the slightest hope was better than none. It would help to pray, but CeLa had gone beyond the gods. They eschewed this place of evil. There was only herself and chance, no more.

About midday an older, nondescript woman well

swaddled in turban and long, flowing robes brought
her a meal that CeLa, well filled from Kalla's offerings, declined. She lay on the couch and tried to
look even more sick than she might otherwise have
been. The woman made motions that CeLa follow
her outside, but the girl shook her head vehemently
and held out her shaking hands. The woman went
to the door flap, which was already moving briskly
under the rising wind and the sand blown against
it. She called out in guttural tones and three others
like her came hurrying to her.

They stood around CeLa like giant birds of prey
and before the girl could even attempt to struggle,
the robe was stripped from her and she was subjected
to a minute examination that took in her eyelids,
teeth and female parts. One of them touched her
stomach and then her throat, making the noises of
nausea. Nothing daunted, CeLa nodded her head
and pantomimed vigorously. Fear made her skin
damp and chill; sweat soaked the edges of her hair.
She knew the flesh had receded from her cheekbones
in these last days, for she could feel them high and
jutting in what Nandar had called her "hungry look."

One of them handed her the robe and she pulled
it around her naked body as they watched. She began a sudden spasm of coughing that seemed to con-
vulse her entire body. It was a trick she had learned
in childhood and many a bully had been routed by
it. Now the women drew the veils over their faces
and conferred together a safe distance from her, their
voices low and portentous. CeLa ended the spasm
as it had begun and lay still once more.

A sudden movement in the gloom near the flap
caught her attention. Jagon stood there, black-robed
and silent. Only the flickering eyes were alive in
his carved face. She shrank back, knowing now the
reason for the examination and hoping that her
performance had been adequate. One of the women

went toward him deferentially, speaking in a soft tone. Jagon spat at her in anger, gesturing toward CeLa with one hand on the curved dagger at his waist. The other women joined him. Over their heads he looked at CeLa and she twisted in spasm once more.

His deadly voice reached through her coughs. "By all the gods, bitch, you had best hope this plague kills you!"

She gave no sign but rolled over on her stomach and put her face in her hands as if exhausted. It was that way that Kalla found her a few minutes later. She put a cautious hand on CeLa's sweat-soaked back and then hastily withdrew it.

"Have the gods truly stricken you, CeLa? One of those who examined you is shrewd in the manner of illness and has aided many a child to birth. Another has mystic powers and draws wisdom from the moon demons. I have been commanded to remain with you until this is past. One of the other useless ones, as we are called, will bring us food and drink. Our lives are of no value to Jagon."

CeLa lay quietly for a moment. Dared she trust this seemingly earnest woman who offered the only faint chance to escape? What was there to lose? Caution held her back but she whispered as though unable to find full voice. "What do they think that I have? Some deadly disease? A visitation of the plague demon? I should pray that Jagon will be consumed utterly by it!"

She heard a little movement and thought that Kalla pulled her turban fold across her face. "There are tales of curses, blood guilt and destruction; Jagon has been cursed by many. He fears disfigurement, I know. Disease is always rife. This may be yet another."

CeLa spoke through the hair that muffled her face. "Go from me, Kalla. It may be your death as well."

"You are Jagon's. You will not be allowed to die

except by his will and I know that he is intrigued
by those he has not yet subdued." The ring of hatred was uncontrolled in Kalla's voice. "But you
shall not die from this, whatever it is, and our plot
shall yet be victorious. He has given us our opening and the storm grows."

"You cannot be burdened with a sick one." CeLa
hoped that she did not carry the ruse too far but
she must be as sure as she could.

"Rest now." Kalla moved away and CeLa could
only imagine that they were still watched to some
degree and she remained motionless until many minutes had passed. When she finally turned over on
her back, the tent was empty and only one brazier
burned low in the fitful light of a day half obscured
by the drifting sands already beginning to pile up
against the sides of the tent.

CeLa stretched and rose to walk about, sure that
all would keep a safe distance from whatever fearful ailment she was supposed to have. Kalla's words
about blood guilt and curses swam in her head. Had
she unwittingly revealed a vulnerable point about
Jagon? Disfigurement, indeed! How gladly would she
render him a monster of ugliness did she but have
the power!

A noise close by sent her scuttling for the pallet
but it was only a mass of sand scattered by the winds.
She moistened her lips and felt the tiny grains on
them. The coming storm could not be far away. All
at once she remembered a scene she had happened
upon with her parents long ago in Nippur, the holy
city of the god Enlil, and how she had been jerked
away in horror only to have nightmares for many
times to come. CeLa grinned savagely and her hands
came up to cross her breasts as the words she whispered
came from her heart.

"Jagon, you may yet know some small part of the
torment that you have caused others."

26

With a Great Curse I Curse You

The wind rose in the night and there was an eerie wail to it that made CeLa wonder if demons rode there. She huddled deeper in the tangled robes, trying to bury the decisions she must make, but the sleep she sought eluded her as the sneering face of Jagon rose up. Her thoughts turned into the wildest fantasies and fears as her head began to hammer with a dull beat. Her eyes felt scratchy and swollen.

She sat up with a jerk; it was no use trying to rest. If she was going to fight, she must be ready. Any idea, however foolish, was better than submission. She remembered the look in Kir's eyes when she had joined him in the battle that had been his death. She would carry that look with her into her own battle. A hair ornament lay on the pallet where it had been thrown what seemed days ago. It had tiny silver teeth that made marks in the flesh of her arms, breasts and stomach when she drew them hard over the areas. The blood came slowly at first but when she squeezed the little wounds it appeared more freely. She scratched at her face to open wounds there and rubbed on sand to irritate the skin. The wine dregs had gleamed purple in the cup. She rubbed it into the exposed areas and over her face. Then CeLa set her teeth, lifted the ornament and brought it down on the soft flesh of her inner arm, dragging it back and forth until the skin was torn and loose. She blinked the tears away; there was no time for

them. Sand, the wine dregs and some of the yellow
dye from a corner of one of the robes created the
image of suppurating wounds. They were only surface wounds but already the flesh had begun to ache.
Determinedly, CeLa shook her hair loose so that it
flowed over her face and into some of the blood.

It was still only faint light when the flap was
pushed aside and Kalla entered. She did not at first
notice that anything was wrong and her low voice
was jubilant as she approached. "The storm will be
very bad by tomorrow evening, at least so says the
guard who will go with us. They take a long time
to build but are quickly over so that if we can
leave during the worst— By the gods, what has happened to you?" She gave a little shriek and backed
away in horror.

CeLa longed to tell her the truth but caution forbade it. Time enough later when the camp settled
in for the storm. She could not bring herself to trust
any servant, however unwilling, of Jagon's. "I am
fevered. I cannot see clearly. The blood, it comes
when I turn. Kalla, I am so frightened!" That was less
than true, thought CeLa wryly. She was terrified.

It was so dim that she could not see the part of
Kalla's face that showed emotions, but the great scar
shone livid before the woman clasped both hands to
her head and began to moan in a fear almost as
great as CeLa's own. "The plague! Gods." Panic
mounted as she moved closer to CeLa and then ran
back. "For our sins, it is the river plague, the bleeding one. I have seen it."

CeLa had counted on Kalla to recognize the signs
of the dreaded illness that was familiar to those who
traveled the great rivers as she had done. It did not
come often, seemingly at the whim of the gods, but
when it did, old and young alike died in blood and
excrement, screaming with pain and fear. Few recovered and those who did had wasted limbs, twisted

faces and shaking bodies. CeLa had seen a man die
of it in Nippur before her parents had taken her
away. That year fully one third of the population
of the holy city had died before Enlil's wrath was
abated.

"Everyone will die of it. There is no cure. Better
that than Jagon. Better anything than Jagon." CeLa
half whispered the words, then looked through
smeared lashes to see if Kalla had taken the import
of them.

She had. Her face was malevolent through the fear.
"He was with you and you gave it to him! To me!
Curse the day you were brought here. He left me—"
Kalla stopped and watched CeLa closely.

The girl gave no sign of what she had heard but
continued to toss and moan. She let the fretful words
come. "The escape. Is it tonight? I want to go. I
must go. I must."

"So you shall, CeLa. So you shall." Kalla came
closer to CeLa and the girl could see that the soft
pretense was gone. Whatever Kalla was, she was
no friend nor ever had been.

CeLa twisted back as if with the fever and opened
her eyes wide. It was well that she did so, for the
slender dagger whirred past the place where her
throat had been and buried itself to the hilt in the
pallet.

Kalla gave a cry of rage. "You shall die. We can
bury you and he will never know about the plague.
Your body will be cleaned . . . you enticed him from
me!" She pulled at her girdle and drew out another
dagger, advancing on CeLa all the while.

CeLa jumped up, dodged the deadly aim, screamed
and ran for the door, knowing that her only suggestion of safety lay in rousing the camp, which certainly would not intentionally remain around so obvious a plague victim. The dagger caught her robe,
pulling it from her, leaving only the cloth about her

loins as she fell forward, still screaming, into the swirling sand outside.

Jagon's followers were used to the eccentricities of their leader and would not have heeded screams coming from the tents of the women, but to have one emerge, well nigh naked, covered with blood and sores, screaming of the plague and pursued by the scarred one, was more than curiosity and fear could bear. Storms were one thing, a matter to be borne stoically, plague another. The hooded men began to gather at a safe distance.

"The plague! The river plague! I have it and soon you all shall have it." CeLa tossed and twisted, the sand coating the wounds and making them all the more real. The wind buffeted her and jerked at the tents as the moving sand seemed to make the sun all the more pale.

Kalla reached CeLa and lifted the dagger she had retrieved from the pallet. She seemed mad from her own fear as she cried, "She must die, for our protection she must die." She faced the others and waited.

"Aye, that is so." The mutter came from some of the men.

"Kill the woman and all who have served her, then break camp." Another was more sure.

"The leader has been with her." The flat voice carried on the wind.

"Jagon will have the plague!" CeLa shouted the words and appeared to tear her face. All knew of the itching caused by the disease. The muttering rose ominously.

There was the twang of a bowstring and then another. Kalla fell at CeLa's feet and farther on, the man who had spoken of Jagon also dropped with an arrow in his chest. The others stopped to stare in consternation toward a nearby dune.

"Death to those who challenge me!" Jagon stood, tall and commanding, bow at the ready, several men behind him. "I will have no disobedience in my camp. Have I not said that the gods themselves protect me? Have you not known it? The woman is mine and she shall die at my will only."

CeLa heard this challenge to the very gods and a chill ran through her. The wind moaned and the sand spun finely between Jagon and his men. She wondered again at the very beauty of this man who had been so blessed and yet destroyed all he touched, for Jagon might have been a warrior out of legend as he stood there in his close-fitting brown tunic, a strap binding back his hair, his lips curved in a proud smile.

The mumbling of his men ceased and they looked up at him, tamed before his very insolence. Jagon came slowly down among them, looking neither right nor left, until he reached CeLa, who stood swaying near Kalla's body. He stood far enough away to be considered safe while he scrutinized her unclad body. She could see the smile fade and his jaw shift. For a moment the same panic came over him that had touched his followers. Then he recovered and said softly, "I had thought to have more sport of you. Now you shall lie here until your bones bleach dry and brittle, your flesh bleeding from your bones. Carrion!"

CeLa tensed. There were no illusions left. He would have her killed, either by abandoning her in the storm or maiming her and allowing the plague to do the rest. It no longer mattered, for she had lived to see his fear. She let froth come to her mouth and pitched her voice so that it came out deeply. "Woe unto him who touches me, for the affliction is of Inanna, who has come to me in a dream. I am bidden to say that you are cursed with the great curse of the gods, Jagon of Agade, for you have bitterly offended them with your pride and cruelty. Your beauty of face and form, the rare talents show-

ered upon you shall be taken away and you shall
bleed in the slow destruction of the gods. So has
Inanna spoken!"

Jagon stared at her and she saw his mouth quirk
downward in the beginnings of a laugh. The men
stood silent in awe. CeLa gathered her muscles and
launched herself at Jagon, her hands bloody from her
nails. He was caught off guard and fell heavily to
the sand, she on top of him, her blood on his face
and body. In an instant she was up and back before
the wounds could be inspected.

"I am the vessel of the goddess and carry out her
decrees. Cursed be he who touches me!" Foam flickered on her lips and she crossed both arms over her
bare breasts while blood trickled between her fingers and her hair blew back from her head. Jagon
struggled to rise but his fear was too great. He lay
prone in the sand, his hands scrubbing frantically at
the places where she had touched him.

Suddenly the wind died and a great stillness pre-
vailed. Even the camels were silent in the dimness
that had been caused by the whirling sand. CeLa
knelt in one swift movement, crying, "She is come
among us!"

"No!" The agonized cry came from Jagon. "No! It
is not written thus for me."

"You are cursed and so are all who remain with
you." CeLa rapped out the words as a little spiral
of sand spun at her feet, for the wind was rising
again.

CeLa knew that she dared not maintain this much
longer. Soon the spell would break. She turned to
the men and saw them cringe away. "Give me a camel
and provisions. I must go into the desert to die alone.
Such is the command of the great Inanna, whose
will I have this day carried out."

Jagon staggered to his feet, then fell down again,
his face already paler under the dark skin, his fin-

gers pulling at his tunic. Two of the men ran frantically to the camels and prodded one to its feet. Another brought a bag of barley cakes and a jug of
wine with water. CeLa reached down and stripped
Kalla of her robe and turban.

"Lady, your goddess is not our goddess but we
acknowledge her greatness. Intercede for us." The
man brought the camel and provisions as close as
he dared, then cringed back.

"I will live but it is not the will of the goddess
that that carrion should live." Her voice was hard
but it was difficult to keep the elation back. "I must
go now, for the sickness is deep within me."

They moved still farther back as CeLa moved to
mount the kneeling camel.

"Stop her. I command it." Jagon regained his feet
this time and there was only the suggestion of a
quaver in his voice as he put a hand to the dagger
at his waist.

"No, Lord Jagon. She is the messenger of the goddess herself, one whom you worship."

Jagon turned to face them and it seemed that all
his great pride had returned. "Is this the manner in
which you obey your leader?"

This time several voices cried out, "No longer.
You are accursed." The men did not approach him
but some began to murmur.

CeLa touched the camel to make it rise but before
she could do so more purposefully, Jagon came close
and ran a hand over her face. Then the men gasped
in horror as he held it up for them to see.

"Is the blood of the plague purple from wine and
a small facial wound? I think not. All sensible men
fear the plague but this is foolishness." He grinned
at CeLa now, all his confidence restored. "Do not
think to escape me; I take pleasure in so devious
a mind."

It was time for the last ploy. CeLa knew that all

her chances would lie here—death in the storm, but death in freedom, or death at the hands of a Jagon, who had been momentarily made to look a fool in front of those over whom he had exercised full authority.

"I sought to cool my face in the wine. The plague is all too real." Her voice was shaking.

Jagon said, "Those who are so afflicted have addled wits. Yours are not so and I see that the foam is gone from your mouth. You should have been a street mimer." He came closer and leaned forward to pull her from the camel.

CeLa rose halfway in the seat and bared the wound on her arm. The sand had irritated it even more and the flesh stood up angrily. The dye shone yellow and vivid in the light. At the same time, she moved the cloth from her breasts where she had earlier shielded them with her arms except in the fight with Kalla. Streaks of blood and yellow mingled together.

"By all the gods! You are truly stricken!" Jagon stared at her in amazement, all his bravado gone.

CeLa kicked the camel as hard as she could before he had time to look more closely. The beast rose as to the firm hand of a master. She pulled the cloth back in place and looked at Jagon.

"I am sick unto death, Jagon, and your own days are numbered. I suggest that you beg forgiveness of the goddess who has demanded your death in expiation."

Jagon was inspecting his flesh again but he lifted his eyes to hers and she saw death in them. "I should have killed you when I first knew myself drawn to you. Now you are my destroyer."

She longed to scream out delight at this revenge but she hoped that his own men would kill him that they might be safe. "Not I, Jagon, but the all-seeing gods who do not wish to punish the innocent along with the guilty."

"Intercede for us, lady!"

"We did not doubt. Only he!"

"His is the guilt. His alone."

Jagon turned to face his men while their cries mounted. He picked up sand and washed his hands with it after the manner of the desert dwellers. He did not again succumb to the first panic and CeLa saw that he was truly a brave man. Her hatred did not lessen; rather it seemed to grow as the voices of the dead called out to her.

"Here now is the command of the goddess Inanna. This man is an abomination in my eyes. As he had done to others, so must it be done to him. This is my justice. Let none seek to avoid it!" Her own voice rose to a scream as the wind mounted once more and she struggled to be heard above it.

"I will kill you first!" Jagon jumped at the camel, which moved back. "Bitch, you will pay. I, Jagon, swear it."

His men moved closer and she saw the glitter on a drawn knife that was far larger than his own dagger. He turned to defend himself and as he did so, CeLa dug her bare, hard heels into the sides of the camel, which turned to swing out toward the open desert. In a few strides it was free of the menace he posed and away from the approaching men.

CeLa turned around and called, "For Kir, Jagon!"

Jagon's curses were muffled by the wind and the snorts of the camel but CeLa knew that he had heard and would remember. Whatever came in the few short hours that remained to her, she would know that Kir was partially avenged. That knowledge was sweet within her as she set her face toward the west and freedom.

27

Lift Up My Face

The storm was swiftly worsening. In the hours that had elapsed since her flight from the camp of Jagon, CeLa had pushed the camel ruthlessly, overcoming its attempts to slow down or halt. Now they were down to a slow plod as the wind spun the sand up around them. A heavy curtain seemed to cover the land and she could see only a few feet ahead. Even with her face and body completely covered, CeLa still felt the slash of the sand as it cut through the thin places of the cloth. She had no idea where she was in relation to the camp. After the torment of the past days she was content to battle the storm. Her skin itched all over, sand was matted in her hair and her wounds were inflamed, but nothing mattered except freedom.

The wind rose again, this time with a howl that seemed human. It was hotter than ever but the sun was obscured by the fine, stinging sand. She felt smothered under the whirling menace. Suddenly there was a hissing noise as the camel swung its head around to nip savagely at her knee. She jerked away and tried to make the beast go on but it would not. CeLa felt tears burn in her eyes. Was she to be this close to freedom, only to fail because of a storm and a beast?

The camel knelt, turning away from the wind. CeLa had no choice but to dismount. Perhaps this was, after all, the wisest course. She would burrow

down beside it and shield them both as best she
might. There was no use attempting to go any deeper
into the storm now. It was with the gods, to whom,
in the final event, she must commend herself.

CeLa pressed herself close to the animal's body
and drew the rough material of the robe even more
tightly over her face. She compressed her arms and
legs so that she was wound in a tiny ball. Her breath
came slow and shallow but still she felt the graininess
of the sand in her nose and throat. Her head hammered in long, dull strokes as if struck by a gong.
The wind rose and she felt the beat of the sand on
her back. Just so had people been buried alive in
the secret wastes, the bones discovered years later
by wandering caravans.

The heat was intense and stifling. Sweat rolled
down her chest, a sour smell rose from her unwashed
body and nausea threatened. She fought it down,
her will stronger than that of the flesh. "I will live.
I will." She could not bear to dwell on her present
plight and the fact that, but for the storm, she would
have been well on her way toward one or more of
the oases that spattered this desolate land. She remembered some of Otu's talk and wondered how far
they had come before disaster overtook them. Why
had she not paid attention to the words he had
spoken and not mooned after the elusive Jagon in
the hope of rendering Kir, if not jealous, at least
capable of noticing her.

Her sand-clogged nose registered the vile scent of
the camel, along with the fact of an increasing in-
ability to draw in the little air remaining. Was this
the way it was to be after all her battle for life?
CeLa knew again the pressing desire to live. Once
she had thought that without Kir she would not
choose to live, but with all her growing awareness,
she knew how childish that had been. He had been
the first to stir her blood and heat her loins with

desire, the first to show her what the hungry thrust of a man could be, the way her body knew to lift and respond. For a time too he had given her friendship in a way that the lone child and the young woman had never known. With him, love had begun.

CeLa bit down hard on her lower lip, feeling the particles of sand crunch in her teeth. An agony of longing overcame her. Her life had been blighted and torn from her. If only she had not yielded to Sirna or demanded payment from Sargon. Inscrutable were the ways of the gods. Was she being punished for some sin of Nandar's? Had Kir thought her smirched by the temple rites that he could not have escaped seeing—at least in part? If she and Kir had met in any other way, would he have cared for her?

CeLa tormented herself this way for what seemed like hours. The weight of sand increased on her but she could not move, for her legs were cramped and her body almost bound. The camel still breathed in a shallow manner and it shielded her. Her physical discomfort was almost as great as the pain in her mind. She had no illusions as to what Jagon would do to her when and if he caught her. He was mad and brilliant; the agonies he had previously devised would be as nothing to those he would inflict on her now that there were true grudges to repay.

Preserve me, Inanna. If I live, that which I hold most dear in the world shall be yours. For now I have only my life and that is fast ebbing. But I will give you service, service above all the gods and goddesses of Sumer. Preserve me, lady of life and love.

CeLa could not voice the words but they rose with all her being. She somehow felt kinship with the goddess who had lifted mighty Sargon to power and whose name Kir had cried out with all the abandon of a lover for his beloved. Intar, her personal god, doubtless could not traverse the desert, and the other great ones were busy about the affairs of their world and this. But she had come on Sargon's mission and she loved Kir. Both served Inanna. Was it not highly likely that the goddess could be invoked with some hope that she might hear? CeLa told herself that she must believe this; it was better than giving up and smothering. She repeated the prayer again and again as the sand whirled, building a dune over her.

CeLa could not have said when her ears ceased to pound from the roar of the wind or when the light began to creep between her shut lids. The camel began to squeal and shift as it tried to rise from the position in which it had knelt. It seemed a dream that was ending, so near had she thought her end to be. CeLa wiped her fingers across her mouth, forced her eyes open and looked upward even as she pulled the robe back.

The sky was already clearing, though clouds of what must be sand still hung low in one direction. The camel had risen and piles of sand tumbled back from the place where it had been. As far as CeLa could see, the new ripples of sand rose in a pattern as definite and clear as the waves of the Euphrates. She pushed herself up to her hands and knees, wincing at the rush of blood to them. The sand trickled in the holes where she had been and she forced herself up to her feet. Once standing, she drew deep and hearty breaths of air, heady as wine after a long thirst. She could for the moment discount everything else except that she could breathe and was still alive. Nothing else mattered but this supreme joy in life.

The camel squealed indignantly and made swaying motions. CeLa looked down at the hollows in the sand where they had been and knew that the beast was in part responsible for saving her life. She scrambled up on its back and into the seat, then dug her heels into its sides. How long ago was it that she had been afraid of the great, ungainly beasts? A lifetime, surely. It moved away at a pace that increased rapidly despite the shifting sands. In her thoughts CeLa clutched the one thing that had kept her from raving in that sandy tomb—her belief in the life force. She said aloud, "The debt shall be paid."

The camel moved steadily on for the rest of that day and into the night. CeLa was bone weary and her wounds throbbed unmercifully but every step took her away from Jagon. In her darker moments it was easy to recall the tales of those who survived storms only to move in a circle until they died. Thought vanished finally before the supreme effort to maintain her seat on the camel's back; it was surprising, she decided, how simple survival was if you concentrated on one thing at a time.

The faint light that comes before dawn was lifting into the sky when CeLa saw the smudge on the horizon that indicated hills. She apparently had not doubled back because there were no mountains in the desert beyond the great river, certainly not for more miles than she could contemplate. Rapidly the smudge resolved into foothills and red brown rock formations that seemed to go on forever. The storm had reached here as well, for sand lay drifted on top of boulders and over little bushes that were almost bare of green.

CeLa knew that she must rest somewhere, and soon, or she would drop. The camel picked its way between two rock formations that were almost joined together at first glance but resolved on closer approach to a natural doorway leading to a shadowed area overhung by another rock. A larger passageway opened onto more hills and rock-strewn land.

CeLa pulled the camel to a halt and tethered it to one of the rocks that was small enough. She jerked the robe from its back, threw it against one of the formations and fell instantly into bottomless pools of sleep.

Squeals and snorts disturbed her. She called out, twisted and tried to avoid waking, but it was no use. Sleep pulled at her and the delicious relaxation of her limbs was like swimming in the river. She could feel herself rolling and tumbling in the water, opening her mouth to drink all that she wanted, cooling her parched tongue that did not seem to fit her mouth. The squeals came again and this time she came fully, swiftly, awake.

She looked into what seemed a demonic mask. Beady black eyes stared into hers and a wide mouth parted over toothless gums in a seamed and wrinkled face; the scrawny neck was festooned with necklaces of teeth and rocks, long fingers with bent nails supplied support for the cupped chin—it was an apparition out of every nightmare she had ever had. CeLa jerked back as the laughter began to trickle out. It rose to a higher note as the camel squealed, apparently not fancying the bubbling, lifting cackle.

"Who are you?" CeLa heard her voice, high and filled with panic, as she rolled back from the creature and gathered her legs under her in an attempt to rise. It was useless, for they were cramped from the long ride. She was forced to sit staring into the face that was still stretched in that mindless laughter. "Who are you?" She forced the words out again in both Sumerian and Akkadian.

The laughter faded and the creature stood looking at her, a scowl on its face. Fear faded as CeLa saw that it was a woman or, rather, what was left of a woman. Great diagonal scars crossed the chest where her breasts had once been. One arm bore faded sword marks. She wore only a short skirt and no sandals, even though the sand was hot. Her arms and legs were sticks; her head bore only a few tufts of hair.

Her skin was a shade or two paler than Raba's had
been.

The woman chattered at her in an unknown language that had no menace in it, then paused expec-
tantly. CeLa lifted away the robe from the wounds
she had caused upon her body and pointed to them.
She touched the dagger at her waist and made storm
sounds, all the while sounding the very fool to herself. Then she made a low, elaborate bow and waited.

The woman returned it and motioned that CeLa
was to go ahead of her as she held out both hands
to show that there was no danger. The girl shivered,
well aware that terror walked in strange places and
that anyone who looked as this woman did must
have run desperately afoul of god or man. She pointed to herself and said her name.

The old woman let that terrible laughter out again
and said a combination of syllables that sounded as
if it were "Gugal."

CeLa said it experimentally and was rewarded by
a split-lipped grin and the peace gesture again. She
held her own hands out in peace as she tried to keep
shivers of distaste from racking her body. Thirst
seemed to have been with her forever and now hunger was added to it. The world spun and she swayed
to keep her balance. She remained on her feet but
it seemed that a vast distance remained between herself and the old woman.

"CeLa." Her name came out roughly in the cracked
mutter but it was at least understandable. She was
taken through another crack in the rock that could
be barely seen and into a small area where several
bushes grew. A tiny pool was there and over it
swayed a stunted palm. There was the carcass of a
desert animal near the remains of a fire. A pallet of
cloth lay close at hand.

The girl sank down on the pallet and allowed the
old woman to tend her wounds. She drank the water

she was given and forced down a few morsels of half-cooked animal. Her stomach rebelled but she fought to retain the nourishment and finally won. All that she had endured rose up in her; body and mind could bear no more, and she slept heavily while Gugal whispered over her fire.

The next several days took their own pattern. CeLa even traced on the sands some of the picture writing of Egypt that Utar had so grudgingly taught her and tried some of the strange sounds of that language, but it was useless. Gugal only shook her head and muttered, indicating by sign language that CeLa was to rest and sleep. She herself spent most of her time huddled on a rock in the shade singing to the winds in a cracked voice. Food was obtained from traps set in the rocks that produced limp, ratlike animals that were savory when cooked over the fire. CeLa saw, however, that there were cakes and sweetmeats, even a cask of passable wine, hoarded in a corner of the overhang that sheltered Gugal. Where did these things come from? How far away was any type of town or tribe? Why did the old woman live in this manner and look so? CeLa's blood froze at some of the explanations her imagination offered and she slept with her dagger close to hand.

The moon god, Sîn, each night lifted fuller in the sky, illuminating the rocks and crags with his own silver light. CeLa often wondered what he was called in this wild land and if he shone down in the streets of Lagash that she had once called home. She spent much of the night outside during this time, awake and enjoying the convolutions of the land in the coolness. She had never seen any true mountains except those in whose foothills Sargon's army had encamped, but this terrain seemed to indicate the presence of others. Nandar had told her of such and now the adventurer in her woke.

Gugal tried with mumbles and signs to make her

sleep under a sheltering section of the overhang but she resisted with a firmness that she herself did not understand. CeLa's strength was returning, the bruises and cuts on her flesh were fading and daily she was facing acceptance of the fact that Kir no longer walked the land. Her mind was trying to evade the thought of Jagon; it was only in her nightmares that he moved, smiling and deadly.

On the night when Sîn hung round and brilliant in the east, CeLa was surprised when Gugal brought out a battered cup filled with wine of a deep red color. She offered it to CeLa, who took a few token sips, then passed it back. The old woman raged at the girl in her gutturals, pressing the cup on her and returning with one for herself. She drank eagerly and waited for CeLa to empty it. Her air was that of a great bird of prey waiting as she sat there in her ragged skirt and hideous bare chest.

CeLa put a hand to her mouth and yawned in weariness. The other hand trailed in the sand where she had poured the major portion of the wine when Gugal went to get her own. The woman helped her to rise with a wiry strength that surprised CeLa. She lay uncomplainingly on the mat under the overhang and did not appear to notice that rocks had been piled in such a way as to obscure the view of the little open area. In a few moments she allowed her breathing to become regular and deep, conscious of the fact that Gugal stood close by watching.

Soon the old woman's shuffle announced her departure. CeLa thought that the wine must indeed have been very strong, for sleepiness rose up in her although she had taken only a few sips. Probably she had a secret purveyor of food and wine from a desert village, possibly in return for a fortune mumbled out at this time of the moon or a whispered incantation against an enemy. She would not want CeLa to know about such a source, for she would be afraid that the girl would speak of it in the time when she went forth from this place. The old were strange.

CeLa dug her nails into her palms. She must not sleep; the small mystery would be pleasant to brood upon in the coming days. She knew she did not want to leave this barren place yet. Where could she go? She sighed, thinking it would help if she knew where she was in relation to Sumer. If only there were some way to get back!

It did not do to dwell on her present circumstances or on the past. Surely she could find some way to communicate with Gugal. She would try harder in the next few days. She sighed and turned over slightly so that she could see into the area without straining. Then she opened her eyes, shut them abruptly and opened them wide as she stared at the sight that met her amazed vision.

Gugal stood, not in her usual bent posture, but straight and proud, seeming inches taller. She wore a tall headdress that glittered in the light of the radiant moon. The scars shone terribly but with a majesty all their own. The short skirt swung full to her ankles; bracelets dripped from the outheld arms.

A procession came single file through the fissure in the rocks. There were several men as dark skinned as she, dressed in white robes that moved on the soft air. Three slaves carried in bundles and placed them at her feet, then knelt a safe distance away. Another led an ox, pure white and garlanded with branches, up to a flat stone. One raised a long-bladed knife as a young boy began to dance in what seemed a prescribed ritual. Gugal did not move. It seemed incredible that a woman of her years could stand thus, but so it was.

CeLa pressed both hands to her face as the truth began to dawn on her. Below, the savage rites began.

28

Head of a Queen

The low songs, the mad bellow of an animal in pain, swift-cadenced prayers and finally a cry of victory—all these came to CeLa as though muted. She peered through her fingers now and again but the tableau shifted and melted as the sacrifice was offered and accepted. Her leg began to itch mercilessly but she dared not scratch or even move. It did not take all her past experience to warn her that such observance must mean death. She had stumbled on the stronghold of some outlawed religion and Gugal must be the priestess or keeper of the shrine.

CeLa tried to calm the shudders than ran through her. Surely after all this adulation even the most devoted servant of whatever god or goddess this was would sleep. She herself would then take some food and water, the camel, which had been taking its ease since she had come here, and go into the desert that bordered these hills. Hopefully some of those she met would be neither mad nor possessed of religion. That wry gaiety that was sometimes hers thrust the panic down as she thought that somewhere in this land there must be folk who worked with the soil, gave the gods their due and expected proper treatment in return. She was overdue to meet them, it seemed.

The body of the ox was being carried away now. The members of the procession were kneeling before Gugal, who was speaking clearly in a language that

sounded vaguely Egyptian yet more familiar than
the sounds Utar had made. Her hands were uplifted
again in blessing. The moon glittered down on the
scene where blood had been spilt.

CeLa did not know how many hours she lay in
that cramped position even after Gugal made her
way, curiously light-footed now, to her own sleeping
mat. There was an air of brooding menace about the
place where CeLa had found safe haven and now
she longed only to be free in the desert again. Unbidden tears stung her eyes as she thought of how
it might be to walk safely in the world. She fought
them back; if she had wept before Jagon or Sirna,
she would have died. Gugal's snores rose finally and
CeLa relaxed enough to sleep.

The next morning CeLa felt the old eyes on her
but strove to appear natural as they made the morning cakes and drank the thin wine. Gugal looked the
same but CeLa could not forget the overpowering
figure in the night. She spoke again in the languages
she knew but Gugal did not even mutter a response.
Later the old woman dozed in the sun, looking more
than ever like a bundle of rags. CeLa moved about,
deliberately dropping a rock and coughing several
times, but there was no movement. Doubtless Gugal
was exhausted from her night's activities and would
not wake. It was a chance that must be taken. CeLa
knew, with all the power of the instinct that she
dared not question, that she must leave this place,
for danger was close.

She gathered up her cloak, found some of the cakes
and a sealed bottle of wine near the entrance, then
made her way slowly to the place where the camel
was kept. It was not there. CeLa retraced her steps
cautiously, thinking that in her days in this place
she had come to know it. How could she be mistaken?
There was only one answer and that obvious. The
night visitors had either taken the beast away or

used it in their rites. Her heart hammered in her chest and her legs grew suddenly weak as she turned to go back.

There was a rush of wind past her ear as an arrow thudded into the sand almost at her feet. She whirled around to see a tall black man wearing only a short tunic and a leather band around his head standing a short distance away. He held another arrow at the ready and his face was savage in the burning sun.

It was then that CeLa lost her temper. It might have been the very materialization of her fears or the fact that anything was better than not knowing what was happening. She cried, "Who are you? What possible harm can I be doing that you shoot at me, a lone wanderer over the face of the desert? What do I menace that is yours?" She heard the fury in her voice, knew that he would know it for what it was and braced herself for the next arrow through her chest.

The man spoke and his words were vaguely familiar, the tone one of command as he gestured with the weapon. She stood still and he advanced, pointing in the direction from which she had come. The command was clear enough. She had no choice but to obey; her brief show of courage had faded. Now she went slowly before him until the rock where Gugal rested was reached.

Her captor put the bow down and drew his dagger, which he held warningly on CeLa. He spoke to Gugal in a low, singing tone and bent before her in great respect. Then he stood to the side and waited while the piercing eyes looked at and through CeLa.

The voice that had spoken in the night said in a dialect that approximated both Sumerian and Akkadian without being either, "You saw all that happened last night and meant to flee."

CeLa stared. Inwardly she must have known all along that Gugal was not entirely a mad old woman living on the edge of the mountainous land and the desert. There was no point in denying it. She tried to speak but could not.

Gugal straightened up and her pose was one of authority, her voice that of one used to command. "Since you have seen, you cannot leave this place."

The black man touched the edge of his knife and said in the same dialect, "It would be an honor, my queen. Let me."

CeLa stepped back a pace as her tongue found instant speech. "I am a wanderer only. I know nothing of this land or your doings. I would return to Sumer if I could. Let me take the camel and go. I will speak of this to no one." She was babbling and knew it.

The man took in the fear on her face and laughed. "She is afraid. Such a one is no gift to the gods."

"Gugal, you have been kind to me. Let me go in peace."

The old woman turned to face her, the toothless mouth black, the white scars glaring in the light of the burning day. "Peace! Do not say such a word to me. I, who was a warrior, now am this! There is no peace but eternal war!"

CeLa felt the craftiness of the trapped rise in her. Death put off a few moments was better than death in the next breath. She said boldly, "Then tell me why. Tell me what this is all about. Let me carry the tale into the netherworld, there to address it to the gods who have not dealt justly with you on this earth." She thought to herself that if she could ever find people who were not mad in one form or another she would gladly slave in their fields. Then the wry question arose; since her life was measured in Gugal's next sentence, what did it all matter anyway? Would she see Kir in that world of shades?

Gugal's terrible face shook as she spread her arms wide in that gesture of totality. The dark man watched silently, his breath drawing in, his fingers moving convulsively on the handle of the knife. CeLa knew that when those arms came down, her life would end. A faint shadow circled above them and the cry of a predator rose as the hawk sought its prey. Time was stilled; it seemed to CeLa that she had stood here forever, poised on the brink of nothingness.

Then by whatever grace of the gods and her own wit, CeLa found her voice and, with it, respite. She cried, "I bear the scars of the world even as you do, Gugal. I can bear witness for us both in the world beyond worlds."

Gugal did not move but her eyes shifted to CeLa's face, down her young body clad in the loose old robe, to the battered sandals she herself had furnished. She laughed and the sound was harsh. "Your scars were well tended. Now you must pay for that. You are young and could be fair. You must pay for that too."

The dark man said, "I should be watching, lady, lest others come. It will be like killing one of the small creatures of the desert." His eyes gleamed and CeLa knew that he would relish destroying her.

"I have the protection of Inanna, goddess of love and life, great one of Sumer." CeLa spoke the titles as if they were an incantation.

"She has shown it poorly." Gugal spoke sourly but the anger of a moment ago was no longer visible.

"We but serve and put our feet in the chosen paths." CeLa spoke as she had heard others speak, not as she believed; Nandar had long ago seen to that. "Only tell me of all this, Gugal. My story for yours." She gambled all on the fact that the old woman must have been long without someone to share speech with. Those of the procession had clearly been her servitors. "I will trust the goddess to deal with me as may seem best."

A little wind rose suddenly and blew her hair

about her face. It died before it reached Gugal, who
stared fiercely at CeLa. The girl took advantage of
the small incident.

"She is here. Will you go against her?" In her own
turn, CeLa lifted her arms, crossed them over her
chest and waited. If this did not work, she would
simply seize the dagger concealed in the folds of her
robe and try to overpower the old woman until she
ordered the guard away. She had no illusions about
the outcome of such a maneuver; she was of such
a nature that she must fight for life as long as any
hope of it remained.

Gugal looked long at her, then lowered one arm
and pointed it at the guard. He sheathed his knife,
bowed his head, his whole body following until he
was prostrate in the sand. Gugal sat down on the
nearest rock and motioned CeLa to follow her example.

"You shall speak and I will listen. Then I will
do likewise. At the end you shall not avoid your
fate." She spoke with the hard authority that came
with years of command and CeLa did not doubt her.
"Whatever that fate is to be."

CeLa had hoped that Gugal's mind would drift as
those of the old ones usually did or that she would
tell her story first so that CeLa could then alter her
own tale according to what parts of Gugal were revealed. But it was not to be. Her quick tongue and
a chance wind had given her a chance at life. She
did not mean to lose it now.

"Hear me, Gugal, for the words I speak are true
words. If they are not worthy of the servant of Inanna, may her arrows pierce my flesh this moment."
The ceremonial words were lulling, as CeLa had
prayed they might be. Gugal was a priestess, that
much she knew, and had once fought in a great
battle, lost and now lived in bitter regret, practicing

strange rites in secret. That knowledge would have to suffice.

They sat in the still, hot afternoon with the shadows of the distant mountains seeming very close in the clear air. The only movement was of beads of sweat that trickled from CeLa's face and body as she talked against death. Gugal seemed not to feel the hard weight of the sun and the guard only rose to a kneeling position so that he could see his mistress and await the inevitable orders.

CeLa spoke of a temple battle in Sumer where the high priest had the priestess killed and the maidens banished. He had sought to kill CeLa also since she had been close to the priestess but had himself been slain by an agent of the king who wanted all the power for himself. Fearing the wrath of the goddess, the agent sold CeLa to the desert caravan whose members, after raping and having their sport with her, had abandoned her in the wilderness. At the height of the storm, the goddess had appeared to her in a dream to tell her that more trials would be required but she would eventually win through to safety and be restored to her temple. The machinations of the evil men would be punished.

CeLa let her voice trail away. It was a tale that almost certainly could not be as fearful as whatever had happened to Gugal, yet she hoped to enlist sympathy for a maiden serving a mighty goddess who had been abused by men. Once again CeLa remembered Jagon's words in the desert and how he had heartened them all. Would that she had even a tenth of such power now! She raised her eyes to Gugal and found the assessing look on her.

"I am an old, old woman and have seen much." She fumbled in the rags she wore, produced a tiny image and threw it at CeLa's feet. "Look at it."

CeLa picked up the exquisitely carved image. It

was the figure of a woman done in black stone with a high, fluting coronet of ivory on her proud head. The features were regular and disdainful, the breasts jutting and full, the naked body inviting. Womanhood joined with divinity in one figure no larger than her longest finger.

"She is beyond beauty. She is perfection." CeLa started to ask what goddess this was but instinct warned her to stop there.

It was good that she did so, for Gugal again wore a mask of rage as she said, "I am she."

CeLa tried to conceal her repugnance and only partially succeeded. She dared not move but whispered homage. "You are worshiped indeed, lady. I think that he who made this loved you greatly."

Across the years that separated them, CeLa heard the voice of her own pain for Kir's loss as Gugal cried, "And I him, yet he is dead and I live on."

"I know." The tears that CeLa would not shed for herself were close to the surface for the man she had only begun to love with a woman's passion and a young girl's worship.

Gugal said, "Beyond Yam, into the Land of Ghosts, and in my country there is a goddess enshrined forever in the temple of my fathers. He sculpted her and her head is as my own in this image, as I was then. Pilgrims came to see and worship the goddess and her embodiment."

The old voice paused and CeLa watched her relive the agony of long ago. Life was sweet. Might she not even yet live to see the shadows of evening? Gugal continued as the girl stared at the image and tried to imagine such beauty carved in living rock in the temple of a far land that seemed to exist only in legend.

"I, whom you now call Gugal, had a name so sacred that it might not be spoken save only by those closest to the mysteries. I was the queen-goddess-priest-

ess, chosen at birth and carefully reared within the
temple. At a suitable time a young man was brought
to me; I was initiated into the rites of love and later
bore his child. He was killed as was our custom so
that our armies might be victorious, our seed lusty
and our trading good. Every three years this was done
and had been so since our time began. All profited
from this and men vied for the great honor. I did
not question our way of life."

CeLa saw the pattern of what was to come and was
thankful indeed that she had muted her own tale.
From such pain as Gugal had experienced only madness could come.

The voice rose higher now and the guard shifted
restlessly, but his dagger was sheathed. CeLa's profile was etched in the sunlight, as pure as that of the
little image, and his eyes rested hungrily on her before returning to Gugal's face. The girl felt the look
but dared not turn away.

"When the third young man was brought to me
and we coupled, I knew that I loved him. He returned
that love and his talent flourished in the time allotted to him. When the time came for him to die,
I could not give him up. I decreed that my will was
law in heaven and earth; he had been blessed by all
the gods with so great a talent that he should not
die. We must have children of our union. The people cried out but when the land flourished, they were
stilled. Our love blessed all."

The glory of that long-dead passion flamed in the
grotesque old face and CeLa wondered if her feelings for Kir were that enduring. It was the sharing
that made for indestructible love, she thought, and
theirs had been so brief.

"A girl was born to us in the fourth year, a boy
in the fifth. Both died. Two of our best crops failed
and one of Egypt's armies penetrated even to our
distance to raid and pillage. We retreated and the

people once more muttered and called for the old
ways. I invoked the gods and all was silenced for a
time. We were happy, he and I, in those last days.
Then Egypt returned, hungry for spoils that were
so easily taken. When the call for sacrifice came, I
put on the garment of a warrior and we went to
battle. I led my people against the invader and we
fought until the stones ran red with our blood."

She put a hand to her face and CeLa saw that she
wept without tears in a hideous motion of jaws and
wrinkles.

"It was the greatest battle we were to know. I truly
lived then, for I believed the power of my great office was over me. The invader was repelled at great
cost but the power of my people was broken. Some
of them rose up to say that the gods were angry and
demanded sacrifice for my sins. My lover was killed
slowly, his parts scattered to the vultures. The priestess-queen, the embodiment of the goddess, they could
not kill. My breasts were cut off, the mound of my
womanhood destroyed, my teeth hacked out. I was
nursed back to life most carefully and sent away far
beyond the borders of our land, to live in exile. They
did not reckon with some of my faithful followers,
who came to me, destroyed though I was. The plot
was discovered; only I and a faithful few lived to
retreat over the desert. They and their descendants
have served since that time and I have lived on in
mockery, it has seemed. The land prospered and for
that reason some have sought to find and kill the
defiler, as I am known. The faith is kept alive here
but none must know that I yet live. One day my
body will lie beneath the great statue my beloved
carved for me and I will be at peace."

CeLa raised her tear-filled eyes and looked into
the anguish of a time forever gone.

29

Into the Dark Lands

There was silence for a long time in the windswept place between the rocks. Gugal wrapped both skinny arms around herself and rocked in ancient sorrows. It was hard to think that she was once a queen, yet CeLa could not doubt it, remembering the power and authority that was still hers.

CeLa said, "Lady, we both have suffered at the hands of others. Can you not believe that I will do you no harm?"

Gugal looked steadily at her. "I sought to keep you from knowing. It is your own fault. But I will say this. You may remain here with me as my handmaiden if you do not try to leave; if you do and are caught, he will make sure that only your bones are left." She flicked a finger at the guard, who moved to instant alertness.

Life was indeed sweet and CeLa knew that she could thank the vagaries of an old woman for that. She said fervently, "Lady, you shall have no more faithful servant than I in all these lands."

The days soon settled into a peaceful, unvarying rhythm. The handmaiden to the living embodiment of the goddess, as Gugal called CeLa now, had little to do except help prepare the sketchy meals, shake out the bedding, walk with her mistress in the evening's cool and listen to the long, rambling tales of the past. Sometimes she saw the guard; he or another always kept watch. The camel had vanished and

CeLa supposed that he had been taken away to remove temptation from her pathway. The one strong consolation she had at this captivity was that Jagon must surely have gone from this part of the land now. Likely he thought her dead in the wilderness or the storm.

Four moons waxed and waned. On the nights of the ceremonies, CeLa was sent far back into the rocks and guarded well. She did not want to see what transpired. The memory of the death-pits of Lagash was too close. Her flesh filled out, the scars faded and her hair lost the dull look it had had. Laughter came again to her lips and brilliance to her eyes. She slept long and deeply in the sure certainty of the next day's being just as the one before it.

Gugal grew more feeble with the passage of time. Often she did not rise from her pallet near the rocks but lay there drinking in the hot sun as if she knew her bones would soon lie white in them. She talked less of the goddess-priestess-queen she believed herself to be and more of the young man whom she had loved so deeply. When she spoke of his long legs, his thrusting manhood, his carved lips and the honey his mouth had brought, CeLa felt her own flesh yearn for Kir.

One morning they sat so and Gugal's sharp old eyes saw CeLa's longing. "You have loved as well. Tell me of him. It will ease you."

CeLa was cautious, for though she had grown fond of Gugal she did not wholly trust her yet. The future was something she could not contemplate. She knew only that nothing must disturb the necessary calm of spirit that she found here. So it often was with a wound, she had noticed.

"It was long ago, lady, and best forgotten."

"He has left his imprint on your flesh and his light looks out of your eyes. Speak. I command it."

CeLa did not have to alter much of the tale to

fit the one she had told Gugal earlier. In speaking
of that half-completed passion, it was necessary only
to say that they had been parted by his death in battle caused by a friend's betrayal. The rest of her account
was of the man she had known him to be—contradictory, confusing, loyal and brave. She did not weep
for him—that was done long ago and her pain was
a private thing—but the stopper of the hurt was
loosed.

"There could never have been another for me. It
may be so with you." The light, musing voice drifted
into dreams.

CeLa shivered to herself. She could not imagine
herself as a mausoleum for Kir. Her fierce spirit
would have rebelled instantly at such a thought. The
days when she had thought to earn a living for herself as a scribe and by studying the ancient lore
seemed now all the pleasure she might ever want.

That night she was awakened by a deep gasping
followed by moans. Gugal was sitting up, unable to
get her breath, the thin chest drawing frantically in
and out with her efforts. The thin lips were drawn
back in a hideous grin.

CeLa ran to her and knelt to support her, the
light body no more than the weight of a pallet in
her hands. "Lady, lady, how can I help you?"

Gugal could not speak but she made motions in
the direction of the guard, who generally came closer
to them at night. CeLa ran to search for him, heedless of the rocks that tore at her bare feet, conscious
of the fact that in all this time she had never known
a name to put to him. Now she cried out with terror
and he came running, his weapon ready.

Together they knelt at the old woman's side. The
death rattle was in her throat, the film of departure
over her eyes. Try as she might, the breath could not
reach through her straining nostrils and open mouth.
She mumbled something and the guard bent to hear.

She clutched his fingers, arched upward and fell back with a cry that might have been desperation.

"She is dead." The guard stood up and looked down at the crumpled form on the pallet. It was the deepest hour of the night and all about them the rocks were silent shadows in the darkness. The stars glimmered overhead and the faintest curve of the old moon lay to the east.

"I will weep for her." CeLa spoke truly. It would not be for her death—she had been immeasurably old —but for a life spent here in the wilderness, wasted and alone, a self-immolation. She thought then of her own plight now that the old woman whose word had ruled here was gone. This man had wanted to kill her. She could not doubt that others of the cult or tribe, whatever they were, would wish the same. A great weariness came over her. Was it time to end the struggle to live?

"There is no need, for she has gone to rule yonder." He waved one arm toward the spangled heavens. "The commands she gave are to be carried out."

CeLa saw the great jutting nose, the ripple of his muscles, and thought of the lascivious glances he had given her. Now it would begin.

"Her flesh will be burned, the bones placed to bleach on the highest rock. Her heart will go with us into the far land of our fathers, there to be buried before the image her lover, the god-lifted one, made all those years ago."

CeLa gasped, then said, "Those who drove you out will still thirst for your blood, will they not? And is that land not far away?" She wanted to cry out for her own fate but fear sealed her lips.

He said simply, "It is a thing we must do. There are few enough of us and she commanded. It is enough."

CeLa said no more as his voice rose in high lament for the goddess he had loved and served. When his

mourning was done, she would try to obtain passage
to one of the caravans, using her service to his mistress as her talisman. This decided, she bent beside
the still body in her own gesture of respect.

At first light, the dark man came to her as she
sat huddled in the shadow of the rock where Gugal
had so often sat. The pale sands shone in front of
her, the brooding rocks behind.

"You are to go forth with me as soon as you can
prepare."

"Where do we go?" She was composed but ready
for battle if it came to that.

He waved a hand in the direction of the mountains and looked at her without speaking.

CeLa was so relieved that he apparently did not
mean to kill her that she at first was dazed. Then
the import of the gesture took her. "I seek passage
to Sumer, to my city of Lagash."

He said, "The great one commanded that you be
escorted to the mountains by a secret way known to
us of old. I have traded in a village near the water
that bounds them. You can remain there for a time."

CeLa said, "I will not go. I am of Sumer." She
forgot caution, wisdom and sorrow in a burst of fury.
"I am sick unto death of having my life constantly
in danger, of having to sue for it; I will direct my
own pathway. I served your mistress many moons
and did it well. This much is owed me."

Akl—such was his name, given by Gugal—caught
her by the shoulders and shook her. "She saw more
than most. There is danger for you on the road to
Sumer. One searches for you to deliver you over to
the power of great evil, a man mightier than most
and touched with the golden fingers of the gods. Only
toward the sea is there even the suggestion of safety."

CeLa felt chills run up and down her spine. Jagon!
It could be no other. "When did she see this? How
do I know it is a true revelation of the gods?"

Akl said, "She was grateful for your companionship these last days and spoke of your fate almost with her last word. It was then that the vision came. It did not lie." His face hardened and CeLa saw that his patience was at an end. "If you go into the desert, you go alone. I have begun to prepare her body. Some several days must elapse before I go to my people in the settlement. If we travel rapidly, there will be time to take you through the mountains, but her commands came first always. The choice is yours."

CeLa asked one final question. "The man whose face she saw, does he remain in Sumer in the end?"

Akl shook his head. "No more is known. But he was of surpassing beauty and ambition, a fierce enemy."

She hesitated no longer. "I am grateful and I will go with you to the mountains." Why would Jagon pursue her still? One small girl when there was a kingdom to be won since Sargon trusted him? It made no sense. Still, she was being offered a chance and she would be a fool not to take it. The hand of Inanna was still over her, even in this remote wilderness.

They moved at a killing pace through the rocky landscape. CeLa had taken some of the stores Gugal had kept hidden as well as an extra robe and less battered pair of sandals. A turban was looped over her head to ward off the fiercest of the sun's rays. She was thankful for the time of peace she had had. Her body was restored and the prospect of a difficult journey did not alarm her. It was well that she had no qualms, for Akl was a man possessed. He had commands to obey and would waste no time.

Time blended into heat, aching muscles, a weariness that must not be yielded to, shortness of breath, bruised hands from the clutching of rocks and a complete absence of thought. Akl had spoken more to her in those brief moments than in all the moons she had served Gugal; now his natural silence resumed. CeLa could only hope that the journey would not be long. Surely he must return to break the news of Gugal's death to the others. Each day they walked and climbed until CeLa was exhausted, paused to rest for a few short hours, then rose to begin again. Akl showed none of the weariness she knew he must sometimes feel. He was impassive and she knew he would have killed her if Gugal had commanded that instead.

CeLa's ears were ringing one morning and she was finding it hard to catch her breath as they steadily moved up a trail between two walls of rock. The trail itself was barely wide enough for Akl's body and it began to seem impossible that this could lead anywhere. The air was cooler here since the sun did not shine down into these crevices, but CeLa, used to the wide expanses of the desert, felt hemmed in, pressed down, trapped.

Akl stopped before a sheet of rock that seemed to tower up to the heavens themselves. He spoke his first words in days. "You must follow behind me, for the way is both long and treacherous. You will not be permitted to see the end of this passageway into the lower lands; I will bind your eyes then and your oath must be given upon your goddess that you will not reveal what you know."

CeLa could only stare at him. The rock before them stretched out wider than the span of many men's arms. The trail twisted on around a curve, seeming fainter as it gained in height. This man could kill her here and now, leaving her body for the scavengers. Only his oath protected her. She would have sworn to far more than the simple thing he demanded now. She crossed both arms over her chest, lifted her eyes to the faint glimmer of sky and said, "It is sworn, by Inanna and all the gods, reigning eternally. If this be broken, then may the great one

smite me in that moment and may I wander palely
in the world beyond worlds. I so swear."

Her oath, made up on the instant, seemed to im-
press the dark man, who nodded his head gravely.
Then he lifted his hand and beckoned her to come
closer. She did not see his hand move casually at
his side but part of the rock moved away with a
shuddering noise and a black hole was revealed there,
a narrow crevice that, to CeLa, did not seem wide
enough to admit even her slender body.

She was to remember that journey in her nightmares. Akl moved into the hole, holding onto the
rim of the rock, reaching for a grasp with his feet,
then momentarily disappearing. His hand reached
out as if from the very bowels of the earth and he
called, "Come quickly." His voice sounded hollow
and distant.

CeLa drew back from the darkness instinctively.
The air of day, the fresh wind blowing in her hair,
the mountains that seemed so high to one of the
plain—all these were her world. How could she go
down into the dark, into a place of living death?

"Come!" The voice boomed at her feet.

CeLa hesitated no longer. She could not go back.
She pulled up the robe so that her legs were exposed
to the knees, fastened the skirt tightly around her
waist, folded her sleeves back over her arms and put
one hand in Akl's. "I am ready."

She stepped in and down to a ledge that appeared
in total blackness. Akl pushed one of the rocks above
their heads and all light vanished. CeLa shut her
eyes in terror, then opened them indignantly when
she heard his laughter.

"Follow me and put your feet in my steps, your
hands where mine have been. This path is very old
and it grows slippery."

"I am new to this mode of travel and await your
instructions." The brief spurt of anger gave her cour-

age. Akl ignored her as he adjusted his own robe for greater freedom of movement. "Are we near the journey's end?" she asked.

"It is far and we waste time. Come." He lifted a torch from some place at his feet and lit it with a deft motion.

CeLa stared about her in wonder. They stood on the first great step of a passage that went slowly down into what seemed a rockfall. The way was partly hewn out of the living rock and partly natural. Walls of rock seemed to rise and lower in the flame. In the distance she heard the gurgle of a stream. It was cool and a faint wind caressed her cheeks.

Akl went forward and she followed, careful to obey his commands. Their steps were slow and tedious, a frightening journey that seemed to go on forever. They went down, up again, across a ledge so narrow that CeLa scarcely dared put one foot in front of the other, guided only by the repeated word, "Come," of the man in front of her. When they were across, he lifted the torch and she saw the depths of the gorge fading into invisibility below. They walked through wide spaces where the mountains seemed joined by a giant and the night sky shone through. They entered caves so small that they were forced to get down on all fours and crawl for many minutes. Once they stopped in a rock chamber where formations shone in the roof in a tracery of such delicacy as to be fit for a queen. Another time they passed so near the surface of the earth that only a large growth of some pungent desert bush hid the secret path from discovery. Time faded again for CeLa and she walked through this strange world thinking only of the next movement and the caution that must accompany it.

They came to the rushing stream so unexpectedly that CeLa almost upset Akl, who stood beside it. He held the torch at shoulder height but even so she could see a sheer rise of rock at what seemed to be the trail's end. Darkness seemed to weigh them down. The floor of the passageway was clammy here and CeLa felt exhausted down to her aching feet. She was so tired, in fact, that Akl's words did not at first penetrate. Then they did and her voice glanced off the rocks in the horror of what she had heard.

"Into that? You are mad. I cannot!"

The dark face was imperturbable behind the flickering torchlight. "It is the only way. Enough of this talk. We must rest." He sat down and extinguished the flame. "An hour only."

CeLa sat in horror-stricken silence. He would not talk further with her, that she knew. She had no choice. She would have to go down into the cold stream and grope for the small gateway that formed the door to the plain beyond. There was no other way out. So it had been planned by those ancients long ago.

CeLa had swum in the rivers and dreamed of water travel, but she had a terror of immersing her head or possibly breathing water. Add that fear to her terror of the confined space and the darkness, she thought wildly, and she would die such a death as might make Jagon's revenge seem small indeed. She put her hand to her mouth lest she moan aloud and disgrace herself.

Below, the water waited.

30

Life's Crowning

"Plunge downward, let the water carry you. Swim strongly when its pull lessens. You will come up against a ledge. Thrust away from that and to the right. The crevice is there and your arms can pull you through. Rise with the water and I will be waiting."

The instructions sounded simple enough when Akl spoke them and made her repeat them, but when CeLa looked at the black water, her body froze with fear. She said now, "In the dark? How can I do all these things and breathe too?" She wanted to cry, to scream, but knew that she dared not.

"Get up. Follow my motions." Akl rose and demonstrated the movements she must make. He was graceful in the light of the dying torch and his muscles rippled under the smooth skin.

CeLa obeyed, wondering yet again what manner of man he was and what strange faith had bound him to the dead Gugal. Anything to take her mind off the dark coldness at her feet.

"You must move swiftly once you are in the water. Your body will know what to do." He spoke brusquely as he removed his robe to stand only in his loincloth and belted dagger. "Best leave all that here."

CeLa looked at the small pack she had carried—the cloak, food and wine. She set it down with regret, then unbound the robe and took it off. Underneath she wore only a coarse undergarment that barely reached her knees. This would have to suffice. She secured her dagger as Akl had done, then bound the little goddess in one corner of the turban she had unwound from her head and girded around her waist. She looked up at Akl and it took all her courage to say, "I follow."

The dark man's eyes softened in the first display of emotion she had ever seen in him. "My lady was right not to slay you that first day. Come!" He plunged into the water.

As he vanished, CeLa took a quick look around the cavern, seeing the heaped rocks, the passage winding safely back the way they had come, the guttering torch. Then, before she could think further, she jumped blindly into the stream, pushing downward as Akl had told her and moving with the power of it as she had often done in the great Euphrates.

The icy shock of the water numbed her at first. She had taken deep breaths of air but a feeling of strangulation threatened to overcome her. Akl's words hammered in her brain even as she opened her eyes to see only blackness. Terror would have overtaken her except for the strong pull of the water that carried her body even as he had said. In the instant that it lessened, she swam strongly and instinctively. Where was the ledge? A bubble escaped from her mouth and red swung before her eyes. She fought back the panic and groped frantically. A rocky protuberance hit her side. She twisted to the right and felt the small opening.

Now the darkness seemed less intense, or perhaps her straining chest was about to burst. CeLa reached out to the edges of the crevice and pushed her head and arms through it even as she noted the narrowness. Then her legs were pushing, a swirl of water lifted her, a grooved rock was in front of her and her fingers caught at it. They touched air and she saw light filtering down. Then, with a strength she did not know she possessed, she held onto the rock and pulled herself from the water. She lay face down and drew long, gasping breaths, the sweetest she had ever taken.

When the pounding in her heart slowed and the brackish taste of fear receded from her mouth, CeLa rolled over and sat up, so thankful to be alive that her surroundings seemed to be of utter beauty. She saw a narrow cave with sloping walls hardly higher than a tall man's head. A fall of rock nearby partially obscured an opening that seemed to lead to another cave. In the top of this cave was a crack through which diffused light shone. After the terrifying blackness of the other cavern and the water, that was a blessing in itself.

CeLa murmured a quick thanks to Inanna, who, it seemed, still protected her, and looked about for Akl, but he was nowhere to be seen. Doubtless he had gone to check the opening yonder and would return shortly. But had he not promised to be waiting for her as she emerged from the water? She knew it had been long minutes since she had done so. Her call lifted in the beginnings of panic.

"Akl! Akl! Where are you?"

There was no response as she struggled unsteadily to her feet. Her arms and legs ached with strain, her hair dripped in her face and blood oozed from a slash on one arm. Where could Akl be? She stared down at the rushing water that abruptly went under the rocks again. Apparently it rose only in several places in the caverns, for these were primarily underground streams and seldom surfaced. Knowledge burst on her suddenly and she collapsed at the water's edge.

The crevice had been so narrow. Now that she thought about it, it had almost felt blocked. The sweep to the right had been a close thing; there would be no going back, for the relentless force of

the stream would push you on. Underground. Dead.
Drowned. CeLa clapped both hands over her eyes
but that could not shut out the picture of that smooth,
strong body, the proud profile, the loyal servitor going to his death for a vow. It could not be. He was
just yonder in the rocks. She cried out his name
until her throat was raw while the water swept on
at her feet.

CeLa got up leadenly as she thought that if there
were any chance of recovering his body, she would
willingly plunge into the water until she dropped.
But only a fool would do that. The rocks had probably already cut him to pieces. She wanted to cry
but savage rage tore at her as she stood by the underground grave and shouted aloud to the gods.

"Are we bright pebbles to play with? Dust in the
wind? Why? Why? It is all meaningless. A vagary of
the great ones. His life, our lives, ought to be worth
more than you who sport and frivol away our short
spans for your amusement. Be damned! Be cursed!
Did Gugal suffer those tortures for nothing? And
Kir dead while a madman lives?"

She did not know how long she sobbed and cursed
in the cave, but the light from above was dimming
when she looked up. She could not endure the
thought of spending a night in such a place. She must
go. Where, she did not know. She only knew that
she must leave this cave of horror. But it was the
place where a brave man had died; that death must
be honored lest his shade return.

CeLa looked down at herself. She had nothing to
give to the waters, for she was well nigh naked. The
dagger was a necessity and the little goddess a talisman from Gugal that would do Akl no good in the
netherworld. Her words must be enough. She knelt
and touched the rippling water as she saw once again
Akl's dark face in the sun as he waited for his mistress's commands. Tears roughened her voice as she

said, "May you fight with the goddess-priestess in the
fields of your heaven, whatever that may be. You
died in her cause as surely as if you were at her
side."

She turned away, rose and went toward the end
of the cavern without looking back. As she had done
in the past when it became too difficult to think,
CeLa forced her mind to remain in the present. She
must get out of these caves. Then she would seek
the village Akl had spoken of and present the little
image of the goddess as her proof. Perhaps she would
yet find a way back to Sumer. Now she scrambled
over rocks, out one cave and into a smaller one, up
over a great boulder and down into a small passage
that bore the feel of the earth's heat. The surface
could not be far away and suddenly CeLa felt a passionate longing to see the sky and breathe warm air
again.

The passage narrowed again and she was forced
to move more slowly, as some of the rocks were
jagged. In some places bushes grew from the sandy
sides and she was forced to duck around them. A
slit loomed up ahead when she jerked a branch of
a hardy desert plant away from her face. It took but
a moment to reach forward and thrust her body
through. She sank down on the sandy earth, let the
light pour around her and lifted her face to the sky
where one lone cloud hung poised. Her fingers dug
down as if to feel the land anew. She was still too
close to the senselessness of Akl's death to give thanks
for her own deliverance, but her very pleasure now
would have delighted the most jealous god.

CeLa finally stood up and surveyed the land
around her. She was standing on one of a series of
ridges dotted with rocks and a few bushes. Behind
her reared a range of mountains, the peaks of which
did not seem as high as they had on the other side.
Off to the left was a sheer wall of rock that seemed

polished in the late sun's rays. She looked back once and could not tell the place from which she had come. It was just as well. It was time to go on.

She slept that night in the open, sheltered on one side by a tall rock still warm from the heat of the day. Her turbulent emotions had taken their toll and her sleep was dreamless, even on the prickly sands and in the chill night. Hunger and thirst were her portion the next day as she headed toward the west and the sea. She was thankful that she had retained her sandals when preparing to go through the watery channel, for travel in this rock-strewn, hilly country was almost impossible without them. The length of cloth that served as her turban protected her head from the heat by day and served as partial cover at night, but her undergarment had been flimsy at best and now it was torn in places. Wryly, CeLa remembered the sheer, floating garments and rich jewels of Sirna's temple, the beauty she had first seen in her own face, the abundance of food and drink, and counted herself fortunate.

She topped a rise at midday and saw in the little valley below one sign of human habitation. Her strength was ebbing rapidly and her greatest need was for water. It struck her that she did not know what the language of this strange land might be or how the inhabitants might view a lone woman traveling and looking as she did. It took all her effort to reach the mud hut and approach it cautiously as she called out in Sumerian.

When no answer came, she moved toward the door, which was made of flimsily woven cloth. She pushed that aside and entered. Cooking utensils lay scattered about, a pallet took up one corner and several casks stood under a jutting ledge. A thick layer of sand covered everything in which footprints other than hers were still visible. Perhaps another wanderer such as herself, CeLa mused. She would take what she could find and go.

There was barley meal in a folded pouch near the casks. Age did not matter; she could live long on the cakes she would make. A terrible sour wine remained in one cask. She drank heartily, laughing a little at the tipsy feeling it immediately produced. There were even several dried dates wrapped in a cloth.

After she had made and stored the cakes, tipped the rest of the wine into her smallest cask and devoured the dates, CeLa felt her blood rise with challenge. She hated to strip everything from the hut, perhaps a kind of way station for travelers in these remote parts, but her need was great. She took the cloth down from the doorway and wrapped it around her body to make a combination robe and cloak. It was stiff with dirt and age but the protection it afforded was most necessary at the moment. She was sticky with sweat and sand but that did not matter; nothing mattered but that she still lived.

CeLa continued her journey through the burning days, sleeping at night wherever she could find shelter. It seemed that she was the only person in all the land, for there was no other sign of people. The character of the land changed as she came down from the hills. It grew flatter, less rocky, and there was more vegetation, an occasional palm tree or bedraggled bush, even hardy flowers.

When she came at last to a path that seemed wide enough for two to walk abreast and which pointed in the direction she was taking, CeLa felt such a surge of happiness that she was immediately overwhelmed with guilt. Wisdom told her that she had truly not been responsible for Akl's death or for Gugal's demands of him, but her heart still ruled at times. She knew she must accept the fact that noth-

ing could be done. She must go on and try to attain
some measure of security for herself.

She walked along the road that widened before her
and thought about the future. Her skills as a scribe
could help her and she was swift at learning. Akkadian had come easily to her and she knew enough to
get along reasonably well in it. Egyptian was another matter, but she had picked up some of the
rudiments. There were port cities on the sea to
which she journeyed, and if the cities of Sumer were
anything to go by, an honest reckoner was always
needed. This might provide an answer for now. All
Sumer was in ferment. Sargon would win his empire, that could not be doubted. Jagon would return
for that confrontation. She, CeLa, would be as nothing. The desert was wide and a new life might still
be had on the borders of a new sea.

CeLa swung briskly along, unable to keep snatches
of a song from rising to her lips. The most difficult
problem would be, as she knew, to find enough acceptance in whatever village she came to, to enable
her to live until she could put her plan into opera-
tion. She had ever been adaptable, she reflected. That
had been essential when living with Nandar. Now she
would truly put that quality to good use. Her life
was once again her own. She was free and that was
the most precious gift of all.

Her thoughts dwelt on the future and she did not
notice the abrupt downward turn of the path until
a stone caught her sandal, almost sending her sprawling. She threw her arms out to regain her balance,
looked up and saw the blue-green sea shimmering
ahead. She gasped in wonder and delight as it reflected against the rocks and lapped on the marshy
flats. The sky rose to meet it in the distance. There
was no sign of village or people.

Now that she had reached the sea, the first thought
in her mind was to bathe. She ran down to the edge,

stripping off her sticky, filthy clothes as she went. The water was faintly salty but wonderfully refreshing and only slightly warm from the sun. She swam out, floated first on her back and then on her stomach, plunging down and rising up, loving the feel of the water's silken touch on her body. Her hair floated behind her, a dark trail in the bubbling light. Her happiness lifted in a crown of pleasure.

She was so absorbed that she did not hear the shout at first. When it did reach her, she did not at first associate it with herself, and by the time she lifted her head and floated around to face the shore, the chance to swim away had passed. Three huge black men, entirely naked, stood by her clothes on the shore. She was near enough to see the size of their male organs as they touched themselves there, laughing and shouting. Only a fool could have doubted their intentions.

Her feet touched the sandy bottom and brought her upright. The water was clear enough so that they could see her body in outline. One of the men pushed his companions on the shoulders, laughed and rushed toward her. CeLa drew back and began to swim away with all her strength. She heard a splash as the others joined him, one on either side. They played a game to head her off as she struggled toward the open sea. It would end in rape. She knew that with one part of her mind; the other part told her that their size would likely rend her apart. Death by drowning would be easier.

31

He That Is the Desire of My Heart

CeLa felt her strength failing and she flailed helplessly at the water as the little waves lapped at her
face. The laughter was closer now and it would only
be a moment before they closed in on her. A hand
grazed her ankle as she kicked out; another ran down
her side. She saw the great dark face, split by white
teeth, bounded by yellow paint down one cheek, as its
owner called mockingly to her.

She drew in her breath and dived but it was too
late. He reached down and caught her easily, pulling
her up as he thrust the great organ toward her legs.
The others swam toward them, chattering in the
vaguely familiar language. With the last of her breath
CeLa screamed, the sound high and piercing on the
wind. The man holding her stopped grinning as he
pushed her face into the water. She gulped and saw
bubbles rise.

Suddenly she was jerked up, lifted into the big
arms and carried along through the water as though
she were a child. Her captor was calling out to someone on shore, his tone beguiling, explanatory. He
was answered by an angry voice that commanded.
CeLa drew her breath in; unable to think, she could
only shudder in the reprieve that might only last
until they could throw her down on shore.

She was placed on marshy grass at the edge. The
hands moved away from her and she was able to
dash the water from her eyes even as the sun shone

in them so that the figure of the man who was still giving angry orders was only a blur. The black men had moved back and stood in a respectful clump off to the left. CeLa pulled herself to a sitting position and tried to shield her nakedness with her hands even as she wondered why she cared. Rape had only been momentarily delayed. Likely the commander of these men had returned unexpectedly and now thought to have a tasty morsel before allowing them to have their way. Perhaps she could offer a willing and eager body in exchange for her life. Certainly it was worth a try.

She opened her mouth to speak. The man turned from her attackers and she heard the commanding voice address her in the strange language. It was a familiar voice to which her pulses leaped. She shook her head to clear it. The figure leaned closer and the world tilted. The man was Kir.

His hands were on her shoulders, the fingers she had never thought to feel in life were on her face, and the dark eyes were blazing into hers while his mouth worked convulsively.

CeLa stared at he who had haunted her dreams all these long nights and had walked beside her in the lonely days, he who had kept her sane during the agony of Jagon's tortures. Her lips moved stiffly over the words, "Kir? What land is this? You are dead, you know." That was it; they had drowned her and this was the netherworld.

"No, lady, I still live." He took her hands in his and squeezed them. "Are you all right?"

Did the blood still hammer in her body? Did her eyes still find the world fair? Was not life given back to her? She could only say, "Yes. How could I be otherwise?"

The hesitancy between them faded as she looked at his dark face, which was burned blacker than ever by the sun except for a seamed white scar on one cheek. His hand moved up her arm as he drew her to him gently. Then both arms went around her as hers joined together over his back. Their mouths locked in passionate eagerness and CeLa felt salt tears run down her face in this moment of restoration from death into life.

The desire that had always been present awoke within them both and CeLa felt her mouth answer his urgent one as the sweet, drowning warmth took them and the world faded. It was a feeling she had never thought to have again, one she had fought back both in sleep and waking. Her hand rubbed up and down the warm nape of his neck while her breath came in little sighs. Their bodies melted together as they trembled in longing.

With a swift sigh Kir set her from him and stripped off the short tunic he wore, leaving only the cloth about his loins. "Cover yourself, CeLa," he said. "There is much that we must discuss."

She looked at his almost nude brown body and shivered at the healed white scar that ran across his rib cage and into his stomach. The sun had not yet touched it sufficiently to make it fade into the rest of his flesh, which was so dark as to make him appear one of the dark men himself. Questions surged in her mind but for the moment it was enough that the man she loved still lived and that she had been spared for this. She pulled the tunic over her head, finding it of a soft, rich weave, and paused to wonder that she could think of cloth at such a time.

He called the men to him and spoke in swift, sharp words as he pointed to CeLa. By this time they had dressed in tunics of the same type he wore and their faces were impassive as they nodded to her in respect with no sign of servility on their broad features. She thought it foolish in the extreme to return the gesture; after all, they had meant to rape and kill her. But the command in Kir's eyes left her no choice.

He said now, "I am sorry for that; they are warriors who understand battle and the price that the
vanquished must pay. I command them and must
not lose face. Walk behind me and say nothing."

CeLa smiled at him. "Aye, my dear lord."

Desire flamed in his eyes and his mouth quirked
downward as he said, "I shall offer sacrifice to the
goddess this night in gratitude that you have come
through safely."

"I too have promised her much." CeLa remembered
with some trepidation her curses in the cavern. The
gods, who gave men such feelings and made all things
happen, must surely understand when their creations
acted upon the feelings and thoughts of the moment.

They walked single file over the rocks and marshy
land down to the shore, where a boat was beached.
It was a sturdy-looking craft with places for oarsmen
and a matting sail. Several men stood guard, and
one, taller than the others, watched before a small
shelter set off to one side of the boat's main area. Kir
spoke swiftly as he took CeLa aboard and directed
her into the shelter. The men immediately began
preparations for departure.

He bent to her as she pushed aside the curtain to
enter. "Make yourself comfortable. Food and drink
are there. Do not come out. I will come to you."

"I await your coming." She breathed the words
slowly and the little points in his eyes flickered. He
too remembered.

The boat swung free and danced on the waves as
the wind picked up in the sails. A low song rose
from the men grouped at the front. She heard Kir
speaking, and chills lifted on her flesh at the sound
she had thought never to hear again in this life.

A basket of sweetmeats lay near an elaborately
carved jug of wine. CeLa ate and drank sparingly,
for her vitals were knotted with passion. The rare
wine might have been rainwater for all that she

tasted it. She ran her fingers through her long, tumbling hair and loosened the tunic so that it lay lightly over her slender body. Then she lay down on the pallet, over which a linen coverlet had been tossed.

She could only wait but she whispered to all the gods, "Make him find me fair!" Her hand lifted one breast. Was it larger than when he had last seen her? Was she too slender? Too hard and drained from the rigors she had undergone? She frowned and her tongue pierced through her lips as she concentrated on the last time Kir had seen her as a woman and not as an embattled warrior.

His voice spoke from over her shoulder as she jerked around. She had not realized that the shelter had another side that was open for observation while the master lay at his ease.

"Lady, the time is ours." The wind ruffled his hair and the afternoon sun shone on his bronzed skin. The carved profile turned toward her and she saw the new lines that creased his forehead.

"Yes." Words failed CeLa as she flushed under his intense scrutiny.

Kir pulled the curtain closed behind him, then slid down on the pallet beside her. There was no need for words. He drew her to him and their arms went around each other as their mouths sought the honey sweetness again. He thrust savagely into her waiting thighs where the warm wetness dwelt. Her hips rose to meet his and they gyrated in an excess of passion that could not be satisfied. His mouth went to her neck, her ears, retreated and locked on her lips again. Then he lifted in a release so sharp that CeLa remained near the edge of completion.

Her breath caught as his withdrawal began. She seemed to feel each tiny movement of his shaft and could not restrain a sigh of longing. Kir touched the nipple on her right breast and watched it flare to exquisite life. His mouth encircled the rosy round-

ness, drawing hard, while his finger flicked back and
forth on the other nipple. He grew long and hard in
her, the length pressing her backward to make a
supple, yielding warmth of her flesh.

The fire burned in CeLa, stoked anew by the slowness of his movements. He did not seek her lips but
remained over her, rubbing and drawing, moving his
hands up and down her body in feather touches that
seared and ignited. Then he lowered his head and his
tongue slid slickly from the pulse at her throat to far
below her breasts. She cried out and lifted her hands
to him as he rose to withdraw himself almost to the tip.
Slowly, gently, he thrust so deep into her that she
felt her body clutch greedily. The dark eyes burned
into hers. Her mouth opened and she heard her own
voice far away begging for release.

Now the strokes came heavily and rapidly as she
rose to meet him with her legs spread wide and her
hands beneath her hips for balance. Their bodies
were dripping with sweat and CeLa's hair was wet
under her. Her breasts rose high and jutting as Kir
brushed his palm over them. Her flat belly was con-
cave, the rounded bones of her hips smoothed to
long, tapering legs that moved swiftly as the convulsive hammering began once more.

The lifting began as it seemed that she rose to a
great height, teetered there, drew back once, twice,
trembled and fell through air that was full of light
into incredible softness and exhaustion. Kir held her
against him for a timeless moment as she felt him
move in her again. Her own muscles held him as if
they could not bear to let go. Then sleep claimed
the lovers.

Sometime in the darkness of the night that was
burnished only faintly by the light of the slivered
moon, CeLa woke to see Kir lying on his back, his
arms thrown wide as if to embrace the world they
had so unexpectedly found. Shadows lay tangled in

the dark hair of his chest and down the hard stomach. The scar was discernible in the near night. The line of his muscular body was straight and pure, inviting her touch. His mouth was soft, his hair tangled, his nose arrogant still.

"Kir the Arrogant." She murmured the words under her breath as she touched the dormant stalk that had seeded the flowering of her delight.

"No. No. You cannot. She is too young! No!" Kir cried out the words in a shaking voice that was very unlike his normal assurance. He tossed in the rigors of a nightmare that twisted him double even as CeLa watched.

"Wake up! You ride the dreams. Kir!" She shook him, unwisely, for it was common knowledge that to wake one who struggled thus was to endanger both life and wits.

He shook all the more; she saw that he could not return from whatever place he had gone so she pressed herself against him and began to touch his face and body with warm fingers. She whispered words of love and passion in his ear, suggesting things they might do that she had read of in old chronicles and had wondered at the time how the scribes could have brought themselves to record such intimacies. Now she knew. They were the very breath of love, the expression of man for woman and they for each other, the transporting of joy, life itself.

Suddenly the writhing body stilled, then began to move in the rhythm of lovemaking as CeLa lifted his manhood to her waiting warmth. Her lips and tongue moved to his and clung. Kir pulled her hungrily to him as he whispered, "Little goddess of love, you delight me."

Her answer came from her heart. "Only you, Kir. Only you in my dreams and in my prayers."

His mouth closed over hers and she gave herself up to the rising heat of her loins.

They finally slept, wound together in each other's
arms. CeLa would stir and shift in a dream pleasant
or threatening, but Kir's hand moving on her body
soothed her. The ship sped smoothly on the rocking
waves as the men on watch sang softly with the oarsmen who took over when the wind faltered.

CeLa and Kir spent the next three days and nights
in the little shelter, emerging only in the cool of
the evening to rest and refresh themselves. They spoke
little to the others; Kir gave his orders and saw that
they were well received before drawing CeLa to him
again. For this little time they lived in and with
each other. Their bodies bent to each other in all
the nuances of love and passion. They went from
swift coupling to prolonged tenderness as mouths,
hands, tongues and flesh melted into one. Kir taught
CeLa with expertise and a warmth that often brought
her to the edge of tears. For his part, he welcomed
her eagerness and met it with all the fervor of life
restored. It seemed to them that this hunger could
not be satisfied; again and again they drank of each
other.

Kir said one morning as they lay in the first flush
of love taken, "You are my fountain, forever replen-
ished, my love in the desert."

CeLa ached to tell him of her love but she knew,
even then, that the language of poetry clothed a passion not fully matured. If he were to be truly hers,
she must go cautiously. There were depths in Kir
that she doubted any woman had plumbed. Thus,
her own words were light. "You are the beginning
and the end, my lord who lies in the sun god's brilliance." Her mouth touched his temple and he raised
his hand to her breast, to the sweet fire that dwelt
between them.

It was not until they lay satiated and sweating,
drinking sea-cooled wine in golden cups of a strange
make, that the time for serious conversation arrived.

The ship drifted slowly on the smooth sea and the chatter of the oarsmen came faintly to them. CeLa turned the cup in one hand idly, then lifted her eyes to meet those of Kir. He smiled but it was not the smile of passion; it was the look of a man totally in tune with his surroundings, a commander over many.

"CeLa, tell me how it has been with you and how you came to this place, which is surely one of the most deserted along the shoreline of the Red Sea. The last I remember, you were fighting alongside me as those tribesmen overwhelmed us. They took you captive?"

She remembered again the ripping of the sword as it entered Kir's body and how she had not wanted to live. Since then CeLa had learned how dear life was. The passion she felt for this man shook her very soul, but she knew that she must not spread out her very being for him. There must be restraint. Then she almost laughed to herself. Restraint was not what they had practiced in the past hours, but she knew that her instincts were right.

Kir leaned toward her and took her hand. "I know that Jagon was behind the attack and I have long known his reputation. CeLa, speak of it or it will fester in your soul."

So she spoke and the shadows grew long, but Kir listened and thus the poison was drawn.

32

Conspiracy's Leaven

When she was finally done with the tale, there was a lengthy silence in the cabin, then Kir rose and poured wine. His voice was carefully matter-of-fact as he said, "Your time has been bitter, CeLa, but you have shown courage worthy of a warrior. I honor you." He lifted the cup high and drank.

She felt tears burn her eyes. "Does it matter that Jagon did those things to me? I sometimes feel that I can never be clean again." Never could she confess to Kir that she had responded to Jagon's lure.

Kir said, "I think you are inviolate in yourself, CeLa, and that is all that truly matters."

He spoke firmly but she saw the shadow in his eyes and knew that she must be warned. How could she lie with Kir, joined in the flesh, and have him whisper love-made words into her ears, yet know that some part of him remained apart from her? Only the gods knew. Life with Nandar had taught her the folly of dwelling on that which was past; it could only lead to despair. Best to be content with the love she had thought dead in the desert with her ravisher.

"Tell me how it was with you, Kir, and how you came to command these men. Where are we and where do we go now?"

He stood and paced, then turned to her and his face was dark with memory. "The land to which we journey is called by some Yam and others Nubia. You will remember Raba, the dark woman of our caravan. It is her land and it was she who saved my life. The others were cut down. She herself fought as you did, as any man might, and was struck senseless. I felt the sword tearing me apart. It was strange; I have been wounded before, but this time it seemed that the netherworld waited and that my spirit rushed toward it.

"I woke to pain such I have never felt before and the sun blazing down in flames. I was consumed by them. I learned later, much later, that Raba and I alone of all our comrades survived. When she roused, it was dark and the scavengers were coming out, those robbers who haunt the oases and travel by night. When they came, she was ready. She is a prophetess and priestess in her land and the power went with her. A spell was laid, threats made, shelter given us in an oasis and a message sent to her people. They eventually came from the edges of the desert and moved us closer to the coast. A ship was sent in response to the message and we were taken to her homeland. During that time—it took moons— I recovered and regained my strength, a slow process."

CeLa groped backward in her mind, recalling the old horror of that battle and the destruction of her world it had wrought. Cusar, the vehement, determined priest. He of the long speeches and the tales of those who went against the will of the gods. Otu, wise old man of the desert, a lone man in truth. Idi and Zama, whose unborn child had been destroyed with them. Dear friends. Laz, who had journeyed far in a long life and who had loved to tell of it. All dead. She picked up the cup and tilted the remains of the wine onto the floor.

"To the brave ones." She looked up at Kir, whose eyes were haunted as he looked back into the past.

"Aye. They were truly that."

CeLa was puzzled. "Tell me, Kir, who are these

people of Raba's that are so powerful they can rescue at will? Why was she not taken back by them long since?"

"They trade with Egypt and are rulers of the great lands beyond the Nile River. They also fight with Egypt and others, for they are of warrior stock and there are many tribes. Some live along the shores of the Red Sea, though not openly, and ships make contact with them. They travel in the desert and know what happens through the caravans. Raba was stolen and sold into slavery, later rescued by Sargon, and she vowed to serve him. She was to be our link and guide to the mysterious lands of the Nile and beyond, for Sargon seeks knowledge of them all. She glimpsed the future in shadowy fashion; she could see that you were connected with doom and this was the reason for her warnings. She saw Jagon for what he was and he knew it."

CeLa heard the curious tenderness in his voice when he spoke of Raba and knew that Kir owed much to this woman who had saved his life; he was a man who paid his debts. She said, "Apparently she did not see Jagon as you say until it was too late."

Kir heard the tartness in her voice and his own sharpened as he answered, "The power did not always come instantly. It was fragmented. We know now that Jagon counts himself equal to and greater than Sargon, that he is a man of many disguises and schemes who has worked against our king from the start and was in the process of negotiating with Sirna and her forces."

CeLa drew in her breath with horror. "Evil joined with evil!"

"Even so. Knowledge of our mission went before us and there were those in Sargon's own camp who plotted against him. The girl, Pina, for one, she who was set to watch you. Utar, who taught you and hated you for what was being entrusted to you. And many others. All this came later to us by revelation, gossip and events past. After the battle Jagon's star was ascendant and retreat was the only course.

"We crossed this sea, passed through the mountains much as you did, I think, and came to her tribe, who welcomed us for her sake. I have eaten, drunk and warred with them. In time I was given command of this ship, which conducts trade missions, sometimes preys on the vessels of Egypt and others and surveys the coasts."

Kir stopped and wiped his forehead, which was wet with sweat. The telling seemed to have cost him much; it was as if the old scar were torn open again. CeLa guessed that he disliked owing his very life to Raba. His pride was monumental.

"Will you continue in this life, Kir? What of me?" She told him swiftly of the plans she had laid for working as a scribe and making a new life in one of the settlements on the coast. She did not believe he would let her leave him now that they had found each other, but her own fierce pride would not let her think that he must feel responsible for her. Her heart cried out that he would declare her his woman, his wife, dearer than all other things. Instinct told her that none of this would happen.

The dark brows drew together; his face seemed set in hard lines, the warmth fading. "There is still the mission, CeLa. I swore an oath to Sargon the king. Your duty is plain as well."

She was incredulous as she rose to face him. "Two people, one of whom serves another power? Emissaries to Egypt! We would not be believed. At any rate, the power in Sumer may have changed completely. Kir, we were but pawns. Let us live our own life, together; what have we to do with the rise and fall of empires?"

The words were a mistake. She saw that as soon

as they were out of her mouth. Kir's face did not change but she felt his withdrawal.

"I do not know how a woman holds an oath but I do know that my own was given to Sargon, and it binds me unto death. The mission shall be performed as best I can."

She held out her hands. "Kir, I did not mean . . ." She stopped, knowing how close she was to begging this man who had held her in his arms only hours before, who had made her blood sing of a deathless passion. Even now her hungry flesh called for him once more. Curse her foolish words! Would she ever learn to hold her tongue?

Kir was continuing in that same cold voice, "We carried priceless gems and treasures in our caravan to make sure we would be well received in Egypt as important emissaries of a great king. These were stolen by the raiders, but Raba has promised that the wealth of her people shall be presented and I am helping to further increase that wealth. She remembers her own debt. The time is rapidly approaching when it must be settled."

"You wish me to travel to Egypt with you then and record all that occurs, as was planned?" CeLa knew she wanted to be wherever Kir was. Sargon had more than enough to deal with and he was capable of anything. Kir served him and so would CeLa if thereby her love affair with Kir could progress.

Kir said, "You gave your oath to Sargon."

"I can see that I have no real choice." CeLa blinked the beginning of tears from her eyes. Why could he not say he wanted her with him? He was supposed to be wise in the ways of women.

"No, you do not. Forgive me, lady, but I must see to my crew, which has been neglected these past days while I sported with you." He bent his head and left her.

CeLa threw herself down on the pallet of their love and cried. What had been love for her was sport for him; was that not ever the way of men? She had let him see her love and he had retreated. Bitterness rose in her, payment for the happiness of the past time; so did the gods exact their dues.

When CeLa woke, it was to the movement of Kir's mouth on hers as he fitted her body expertly to his own. His tongue flickered in tantalizing touches and his fingers worked on her bare breasts. She could not speak, for their mouths were locked together and already the full, hard thrust of his manhood was deep within her. They moved together very slowly, then harder and harder. CeLa's hands cupped his buttocks as their bodies rose and fell together in the hot explosion of desire's satiation.

Later Kir whispered in her ear, "CeLa, let there be a pact between us. For this time that we are traveling, let us not speak of the past or the future but simply be a man and a maid who take delight in each other. Are you agreeable?"

Light from the waves reached through the curtain and dappled their bodies. The faint sea breeze lifted the curling hair from CeLa's brow and dried the sweat of passion. Kir's long fingers curled over the edge of a cushion while his warm eyes regarded her. She thought once again of her dreams of the boat lifting in the wind and the journey to another life. Was she to reject the gifts of the gods because reality had to intervene?

"We shall be a man and a maid in an enchanted world, Kir. Let it be as you say."

He settled back on the pallet and propped his head up with the cushion, stretching out his long body before her. He held out one hand. "Come to me, pretty one, my lady of the sea."

She stood above him, her hands holding both

breasts so that they cupped on brown fingers and
pink tips. The slight motion of the boat made her
sway gently with it and her hips rotated in a single
movement that seemed to come from her very womanhood. Lower and lower she came until she squatted
directly over his mouth and balanced herself on nim-
ble legs and hands while his avid mouth sought the
eager heart of her that his fingers had delighted earlier. CeLa felt as if a hot flame were consuming her,
a flame that she could not bear to release. She writhed
and twisted in his hands, which moved easily over
her sweat-supple warmth.

They turned so that his mouth continued as before, his tongue moving in and out of her orifice,
but so that her own mouth could take his stalk into
it and her hands could knead the flesh of his lean
stomach. Tantalizingly at first, then faster and faster
until the peak was almost scaled, then slower and
slower as the fire built and banked—that was the
movement of their passion. They drew out the moment of consummation until the tortured, hungry
flesh could take no more. He grew longer and harder
in her mouth as she sucked thirstily at him, writhing in the burning of her loins. Then the acrid,
salty taste of his seed came in her throat as his fingers
pushed deeply into her and they were joined in the
fire that did not go out for them.

The days that followed saw CeLa and Kir joined
in more than the flesh, though that occupied much
of their time and inventiveness. She learned to kneel
before him while his stalk explored not only the long
canal of her, but also the tight muscles of her lower
body and his hard hands on her buttocks held her
still. They sprawled on each other, turning and twisting as their tongues laved them from head to foot.
Standing, moving, balancing, they invoked the flames
of the goddess and were never disappointed. This

was the truest thing between them, CeLa thought, and wondered that she had ever thought to live without it.

In the early morning and the cool evenings they walked on the deck, their arms intertwined, talking of legends, the stars, the vastness of the desert, the old stories of wars and quests, of anything except themselves. They sat in the blistering noontime, trailing nets to catch the fish that were sometimes visible in the depths of the shimmering water. Sea birds cried overhead as they dipped and circled, then flew toward the sun. They slid off the edges of the boat and swam in lazy circles while several of the crew watched, spears at the ready in case some denizen of the water should attack. Kir pursued CeLa and she him in water games that might have drowned both of them since they dissolved into long passionate kisses under the hull of the boat or deeper in the water where it made a shadow. They ate fish and fruit, drank cool wine, quoted poetry and sang lilting songs while the boat ran on before the wind. And ever did they make love, passionately in heat, tenderly in warmth and in tears at the sweetness of it. So the days of their union passed and then purple mountains lifted on the horizon.

The motion of the boat slowed and the paddles of the oarsmen lifted as they began to chant in their rhythmical language. CeLa, still languid from a night of lovemaking, pushed back her tangled hair and drew Kir's tunic over her. They had seen the mountains the evening before but neither had mentioned the reality that lay ahead. CeLa did not know why she dreaded making landfall but something warned her to be ready. Now she sat up and debated whether or not to rise. Then the curtain was pushed back and Kir entered.

This was a different Kir than she had seen before. This was the leader, the chieftain. He wore a tunic

of purple with a golden band around his narrow
waist and another around his head. His sandals were
golden and a great dark stone set with flashing chips
of a paler hue was around his neck. An ebony-han-
dled dagger hung from his belt. His face was no
longer that of her lover and friend of the past days.
It was set and purposeful, his eyes hooded.

CeLa felt suddenly abashed but she would not
make the same mistake twice. She should have known
him well enough to know that nothing would come
between Kir and his king, his oath and his bond. She
said, "We have come to the end of our free time,
Kir. I know it well."

He put down the small bundle of material he held
and said, "We travel far. You must dress comfortably.
See to it. Then I will speak with you again."

She wanted to cry out that there was no need to
treat her as a stranger, but Kir would not tolerate
a woman's emotions. Anger swept her like a cleansing
wind. "Aye, my lord." The words were submissive
but the tone was not. She turned her back and heard
him leave.

The robe was of a soft weave and felt smooth on
her body. She knew its white and brown color en-
hanced her skin and made her hair more lustrous.
She lifted the long strands and bound them around
her head in braids so that her face shone like a pure
oval against the darkness. A cloak of a darker hue
was set over her shoulders.

CeLa did not wait for Kir to return to her but
went up on deck to see this new land for herself.
The boat was now almost beached on a strip of rocky
land that stretched flatly back for what seemed about
a mile before the mountains loomed up straight and
sheer. There were no trees or bushes, only rocks and
sand, a desolate land indeed. A small group stood on
the shore awaiting them. There was no mistaking
the commanding figure of Raba, for she wore purple

and golden garments similar to those Kir wore. They were close enough for CeLa to distinguish the proud smile on her carved features. The others, some twenty in all, seemed to be soldiers, though some might be priests or other officials. As CeLa watched, Raba lifted one arm in a gesture of welcome and called aloud in a voice that was half song and half words.

"You should have waited below as I instructed." It was Kir who had come up beside her. Now he stepped forward and gave the same greeting, his head high, his bearing proud.

CeLa opened her mouth to protest but was stopped by the intimacy in his public greeting to Raba. In all the time of their closeness there had not been such tenderness in his voice. The world fell away and it took all her courage to turn her unwilling eyes to him.

"Kir." She could say no more but all her feeling was in the sound of his name.

He turned to face her in all his golden arrogance and in that moment she hated him. "CeLa, I told you the days of reality would come. Raba is my wife."

CeLa was never more thankful for the pride that upheld her, for all the trials that had strengthened her since Nandar's death, for the endurance in adversity that had taught her the dearness of life. Her voice did not tremble or her face alter as she said, "I am ready to meet her again, Kir."

33

The Ib

The moments of debarkation and welcome passed in a dream for CeLa. Kir's words had hammered into her brain and rendered it numb. She bent her head before Raba, as was seemly, and tried to ignore Kir's impassive face as he stood behind his wife.

"Welcome to my people, CeLa of Lagash. Welcome to the land of the Ib." Raba spoke in accented but pure Sumerian, her voice silvery and clear. The men around her gave every attention; it was so silent that CeLa could hear the waves slapping on the shore and the call of a distant bird.

"I am grateful for your kind welcome and thank the gods for your deliverance." Her voice seemed to come from a great distance but she knew the words were correct and proper.

Raba extended a strong hand and CeLa took it, noticing how beautiful the woman was in her freedom. She was taller than any woman the girl had ever seen. Her breasts were full and proud, her hips lush, her waist incredibly small. Here was the very personification of the image Gugal had given her. Savagery lurked in her eyes still, but they were soft as they rested on Kir, and CeLa knew that she loved him. In the desert Raba had been older and more strange; here she conveyed the very essence of power.

"We journey now to the site of the ten springs. Walk with us, CeLa."

"You do me great honor." She bent her head again, this time to hide her tears.

They were joined now by groups of tribesmen and their women so that their procession was long as they crossed the little plain and headed into the mountains, which were as sun-baked and parched as the desert from which CeLa had come. This range seemed almost impassable but several men leading the procession moved rocks from certain narrow passages, guiding them down small trails and around ledges that fell away into nothingness and rose again to steep heights. For several days they moved carefully along, sparing little time for speech. CeLa was grateful for this time apart, for the rigors of the journey, that she might try to adjust to the fact that Kir was gone from her forever. The loss was bitter and she was forced to cloak her pain with impassivity.

One afternoon she was walking in the single file they had adopted for these narrow passages when she lifted her head to see a flat, barren land sloping below. Some hardy-blooming shrubs appeared in the distance with some stunted trees just beyond. A shadow on the horizon seemed to be a herd of running animals.

"It is Raba's land." The quiet voice spoke at her elbow and she whirled to look into Kir's face.

"And yours." She was thankful that her voice was as cool as his own. He must not know that her agony roiled close to the surface. Had she ever lain in this man's arms and cried aloud her joy? One would have thought them casual acquaintances to see them now, standing a little aside as the others went by. Raba had gone first, as befitted the queen-priestess of the tribe.

"You will be glad to know that I have sent a message to Sargon telling him that we three alone live and that the mission to Egypt will continue. I have sent warning about Jagon and his conspiracies." His

carved face was emotionless as he looked down at
her.

"But it has been many moons! How can you know
if Sargon even lives?"

Kir said soberly, "I cannot imagine a world in
which he does not. Other messengers have been sent; he
will know. My promise, our promise, will be kept."

CeLa drew in her breath sharply. "Raba will go?"

"She is my wife." The simple statement was far
more revealing than anything else he could have
said. "You too have sworn an oath to Sargon."

She looked into his dark face and knew that if he
willed it, she would go into the netherworld at his
side. "I know, Kir, and I will keep it."

He smiled then, making his face curiously young,
"The circumstances are difficult but how could you
understand?" He hesitated and the next words were
torn from him. "Sargon is both friend and king. We
were confidants even in the days before he saw the
bold way to power in Akkad and took it. There was
a time when I did not wish to live, seeing no reason
for life in any form. He gave me tasks to do, missions
to fulfill. He showed me great learning. Finally, he
taught me that the gods cannot be blamed for the
will of man. I owe him beyond the telling."

CeLa saw his hand shake, the vulnerability in his
face, and knew that even this revelation had cost
him much. Kir the reticent, who held everything inside himself, had spoken, at least partly, for her sake.
Or so she would believe, she told herself. She said,
"Thank you for telling me, Kir."

He turned abruptly and walked away, but CeLa's
heart was lighter within her. He was Raba's husband, but the deathless fire still burned between them,
that she knew.

They came fully into the land of the Ib one day's
march later. Here was a sheltered valley where the
plain was grassy beyond low hills and an under-

ground stream rose to supply water to a shimmering pool beside some palm trees. Crops were tended in the field beyond the tents of skin in which Raba's people dwelt. Raba's tent stood separate near a rock formation that was almost in the shape of a bench. There the water rose in spurts to form yet another pool before vanishing into the earth. A single large palm tree shaded the area and cast moving shadows on the tent walls, which were of finely woven red and blue cloth. A black banner striped with gold hung over the entrance. As she watched, Kir and Raba entered. CeLa felt her heart contract with pain but her face remained calm.

CeLa was given a tent of her own not far away with a calm woman of middle years to attend her. Here, for the first time, she was able to weep in the privacy for which she had longed. She knew that she must not give way to her feelings at any other time; one had only to watch Raba to know how much the Ib prided themselves on stoicism. This was to be her lot from now on, she told herself.

The next morning, after she had bathed in the pool and eaten, a young man approached her. "I am Teph, bidden by Raba to instruct you in the lore of Egypt when you feel that you are well rested. I am told that you already have much learning and I am eager to learn from you in return." He was tall and muscular, his black eyes serious. A young woman peered shyly around his shoulder. "This is my wife, Ara."

CeLa smiled and felt some of her heaviness lift. "I know little enough, Teph, and will be grateful for the opportunity to learn yet more." This would be her release; in hard work some peace would come.

Teph had traveled on Sumer's great rivers as well as into Egypt's border cities. He and CeLa worked well together under the soft smile of Ara as the days drifted into one another. CeLa's talents as a scribe met the challenge of the symbols and pictures of the written Egyptian language. The stories and lore of which Utar had spoken in the camp of Sargon took on new meaning as her knowledge expanded.

In the evenings Teph went away to talk and work with the men as they cleaned their weapons and spoke of days past or of a hunt to come. CeLa and Ara would walk far up the dry bed of the stream, exchanging halting words in Ibian and Sumerian, but for the most part simply enjoying the respite from the day's work and watching the stars appear as the herds of wild asses and sheep ran along the limitless horizon. Later CeLa would lie on her pallet and fight her hungry flesh that remembered Kir's arms. She woke in the long nights with her hands on her breasts in memory of his touch. It helped that she did not see him, although the sense of his presence in the camp was enough to awaken her to response though she knew she only dreamed.

One morning Raba and Kir, with a small party of tribesmen, summoned the three of them to view the treasure that was being gathered for Pharaoh. It was to be a ceremonial visit, for the priestess-queen and her husband wore tall head pieces and long cloaks made of gold and feathers. Kir was remote, his dark brows slanting over hooded eyes, his carved visage hard in the pouring light. Raba, however, was gracious and smiling as she pointed out the accumulated goods housed in a special tent and guarded by ten fierce warriors holding their spears at the ready.

CeLa's breath caught as she looked: ivory utensils and jewelry, beaten gold, ebony, sweet and pungent spices, skins of strange animals, horned masks of silver, robes spun so finely it seemed they floated in air, masses of the clear, flashing gems Raba often wore, rings, bracelets, earrings of turquoise and carnelian, even carved seats of intricate design. A treature worthy of being presented by one ruler to another.

She remembered Teph's soft voice saying, "Your journey will be overland to a place called the First Cataract. There messages will be sent to Pharaoh, and when his welcome arrives, you will go down the Nile to the city that is his own, called both White Walls and Memphis. The treasure will be given by Raba because of the debt she feels she owes to Sargon of Akkad and in thanks to the gods for her life and that of her husband."

CeLa had heard a note of discontent in his voice and noted the slight flaring of his nostrils but considered it of little significance. Now, as she looked at all this beauty and wealth, she wondered again. When their mission left the Zagros Mountains, Kir and Laz had carried, between them, enough jewels to ransom the greatest king. Kir had retained only a few after the betrayal in the desert. But Raba remembered her rescue from slavery. During his time with the Ib, Kir and his men plied the Red Sea, raiding and trading with those from other lands in the area. He led daring excursions into those lands beyond the usual sway of the Ib, returning with spoils and honor. Under Raba's encouragement their power reached out to the mountains and far down the coastline.

"Men have gone to bring more of this fine ivory, which our artisans will then carve." Raba waved a regal hand at the pieces lying on a thin cloth. The jewels flashed at her ears as she moved.

CeLa could not help it; she looked toward Kir and encountered the blazing eyes of one of the tribesmen, an older man with many decorative disks about his neck. His eyes dropped before hers but she did not miss the warning frown of his companion as their faces smoothed back into blandness. She saw

Kir and knew that he had seen the same thing. Uneasiness chilled her flesh. Then she forgot it as the pain lifted anew in her.

They were almost outside before the hand touched her arm in that motion she would know in the darkness or in a waking dream. "CeLa, is all well with you? You are thinner. Have you been working too hard with Teph?" His voice was kind and concerned but his eyes were those of her lover on board the ship.

CeLa wondered then at the absolute obtuseness of men. Was it possible he could not know of her hurt? She saw in him at this moment the shadow of that pain that had never left him in all the time of their knowing each other. "I am well, Kir, but I thank you for the query." The formal words left her lips and she saw the gentleness fade from his eyes. Good. Let him wonder for a change. Bitterness touched her mouth as she turned away and walked straight into Raba.

CeLa did not doubt that she had marked every moment of their exchange. This woman ruled absolutely here and her pride was unending; that she knew from the trials of the desert. Raba motioned to Kir and the others, her face very still as she did so. They moved away as CeLa lifted her head to confront this woman who might well be her death—Raba, wife of Kir. They stood just outside the treasure tent, the hot wind lifting their robes, CeLa's hair blowing back from her forehead as she waited for what must come.

"It is time you knew, CeLa." She spoke in faultless Sumerian, her voice low and even. "Walk with me." She stared straight at the girl, who bent her head.

"Raba's will is mine," she said, the proper words of a guest.

"Kir will be great in the annals of Sumer and Akkad; his life is touched by the gods. When he lay near death he raved constantly, crying out again and again for two women. Your name, CeLa of Lagash."

CeLa felt chills invade her body. In his pain and hurt, his heart had been at least partly hers. She hoped that the joy she felt was not mirrored in her eyes. "And yours, Raba. As was fitting."

The dark woman faced her then, and the words came swiftly. "Not so. I wanted him, I will not deny it. On the journey, even in the camp of Sargon, my heart reached out to him. Jagon knew of it. I saw the menace of him vaguely at first and then more clearly. By that time the plot threatening the life and power of Sargon, who rescued me from slavery and would help me return to my land, was known to me. It was too late. Jagon is shadowed in the future I cannot see, but he is dangerous to the rule of Sargon. I pretended for my own safety. He is devious, as you have reason to know."

CeLa could not dissemble before those compelling eyes. "Aye, he is a savage." All the humiliation she had suffered at Jagon's hands came back to her.

Raba said, "The priestess-queen of the Ib may have a husband but no lover lest she be branded dissolute. Kir was very weak and grateful, the marriage ceremony brief. The reality came slowly and by that time he understood the practicalities. We have loved well since that time and taken great pleasure in each other. But only a portion of him is mine."

It had not been wholly of his choosing then. He cared for her, at least a little. She must know more, much more. Heedlessly, she pressed on. "Whose name did he cry out in his delirium besides mine?" She caught Raba's hand and felt her draw back as she remembered that to touch the priestess without her consent was death. So had Teph told her.

Raba did not seem to notice. "Inta. A corruption of the name of your goddess, Inanna. A very young girl, most passionately loved, won with great strug-

gle and effort from her wealthy family by a mercenary only slightly older. It took many moons to get
her, three for her to die lingeringly and painfully,
a disease sent by the gods who sometimes despair of
the happiness of men. Her husband was Kir, CeLa.
He listened to her screams and pleas for death until
no more could be borne. He helped her from this
life with a potion that brought peace. Her family
and the priests called it murder and tried to have
him killed. He barely escaped, taking an obscure
vessel from the city of Uridu, to which he has never
returned. He knew he would be safe nowhere that
her family's power reached, so he went to Kish,
where he met Sargon, who was even then vying for
power. They became friends and the rest you know.
Kir vowed never to give his heart to a woman again
but to seek out those he could not love, for he felt
that his touch was death and destruction. He has
almost kept that vow."

CeLa's eyes were burning with tears. Kir's arrogance
and coldness toward her, his whispers to Inanna in
his dreams, his cries of hurt in the nightmares that
his touch was destruction, his devotion to the cause
of Sargon who had given him belief in life—much
was explained. She looked at Raba, all her heart in
her eyes. "I am grateful beyond the telling that you
have spoken so. But why?"

Raba drew up her tall body and all the dignity of
the priestess-queen was in her as she said, "We of
the Ib set much store by fruitfulness. In time I will
bear Kir's child, though as yet the seed has not quickened. You are both brave and fair; he cares for you.
It is permissible that the husband of the queen take
a lesser wife." She smiled at CeLa now and the girl
saw real warmth in the black eyes. "You will be
greatly honored among the Ib."

CeLa whispered, "And what has Kir to say to
this?"

"He will do my bidding. Such things are not unknown in Sumer, after all."

CeLa knew that Kir would indeed obey Raba, for he was intensely loyal. Her flesh clamored for his body even as her heart yearned for his love. She knew that Raba loved him but her passion was not yet the whole of her being. It was now CeLa herself who stood in question, the fusion of the woman beyond mind and body, her own sense of wholeness, her awareness of herself as a person. She thanked the deathless gods for the knowledge she had of Kir; suffering changed people drastically—just so had she been changed. Still, it was not easy to say, "Raba, I cannot. You honor me. Kir would honor me. I care for him, as you know, but it is not to be. I will seek the life of a scribe when the journey to Egypt is done and we stand once more beside Sargon."

It was no longer Raba but the priestess-queen of the Ib who spoke to her guest. "Then no more will be said. The choice was yours to make and it will not be offered again. Nothing more must pass between Kir and yourself. This is my will."

"It will be obeyed, lady." CeLa bent her head in obedience. There could have been no other choice for her, but longing for Kir would never leave her. Yet the knowledge that he did care for her eased the pain of her self-denial.

"Take this, CeLa of Lagash." Raba loosened a silver cord from around her neck. An intricately carved ivory lion with iridescent eyes, a thick mane and great wings folded at his sides was attached to one end of the cord. "It is Antatu, ruler of the desert and the river, he who is courage and pride and loyalty. Few may wear his likeness, for few are worthy. I, Raba, give you his protection." She settled the beautiful image around CeLa's slender neck and stepped back.

CeLa was conscious of the party waiting for Raba in the distance, of the clouds drifting across the face of the sun and the little whirl of sand at her feet that always made her think of the goddess Inanna. She looked into the strong, beautiful face of the Ibian queen and sank to her knees before her. The dark hand stretched out over her head and the rich voice lifted in a blessing.

34

The Challenge

Several mornings later CeLa was sitting with Teph and Ara translating word lists and sipping watered wine when a contingent of men marched by led by a tall man with commanding features. Their faces were grim. Teph paused in his explanations and frowned.

"What is it, Teph? Who are they?" CeLa had not seen him look so concerned before.

"It is Wanu, he who ruled in Raba's stead while she was captive in the far lands. He has just now returned from an expedition to the coast; the news does not appear to be good."

She thought no more of it until that night when the camp stirred with unrest, the noise penetrating to her tent. She rose and looked out to see fires burning high in the council area. Over and over she heard "Egyptian armies, provocation, tribute, invaders." When the shouts subsided, dull sounds of discontent continued.

When she went for her lesson the next day, Teph was not there. She started toward the center of the camp but was turned back by several guards who said only in Ibian, "Forbidden." She protested but one unsheathed his dagger and held it before her eyes in an eloquent gesture that left her no choice but to return to her tent. The next day was the same, and all her efforts to gain information from the servant and guards were to no avail.

That afternoon Kir came to her as she sat by the pool, ostensibly studying the picture writing of Egypt, but actually scanning the familiar terrain that had suddenly become so menacing. His skin had a pale hue under the swarthiness and the old scar throbbed on his face. Lines of weariness lay under his eyes. She looked up at him, all her questions in her face and body.

"Kir! What is happening?"

He stood well apart from her and CeLa remembered Raba's command. "Egypt is sometimes an enemy, always a rich trading source, both slaver and destroyer. The Ib, inflamed by Wanu, who has just returned from the Red Sea, fear the power of Pharaoh and do not wish the mission to proceed. Rumor has it that armies advance to the frontier and strange ships have been sighted. It is said that I have raided too far and stirred the lands against us, that I encourage Raba to endanger her people by our allegiance to a far-off king. No true priestess and daughter of the tribe would behave so. So they speak in the tents."

"Does this Wanu seek to abort the mission? The Ib were loyal to Raba before and sought long for her." She was amazed and fearful.

Kir laughed, the sound harsh in the still evening. "It is always the old argument, CeLa. The gods are angered. In truth, I think that the gods, if they exist, do not really care and abandoned us long ago."

She had never heard Kir speak in this defeatist manner, though she had often suspected his lack of belief and felt that Sargon supplied much of his faith in something outside himself. The boy of years ago had been truly marked. Now she said in her most rallying manner, "It does not matter what you believe, Kir. You have a promise to keep. What does Raba say?" Underneath her words was a fierce gladness that he had come to her in their mutual need.

"She has bidden me wait, for she rallies the people tonight. She will invoke the gods, point out that I, her husband, will this, and that you too were sent by the gods for this mission, which finds favor with them. We shall see." He hammered one fist into his palm as he paced up and down. "Perhaps I have been wrong."

"And if the people do not agree?"

He shrugged. "More is at stake than the mission, I think. When I pressed for it, I thought that Raba controlled her people. Now we are all in danger."

"Thank you for coming to me." CeLa smiled at him and for a moment the hunger for his body left her and she faced him in friendship.

Kir saw and his hand was warm over hers. "CeLa of Lagash, it was not an ill day that we met in the temple of Ninhursag."

He left her then, but the memory of their closeness went with her into the long hours of the day and comforted her.

As evening drew in and the air seemed breathlessly still, Ara came to CeLa with an armload of clothes and jewels. Her face was unsmiling but there was the scent of fear on her as she bade CeLa dress and join her outside as quickly as she might.

"What is it, Ara? What is going on?" Her questions only made the young woman retreat more swiftly to the door, where a guard stood with drawn dagger.

CeLa knew that once again danger waited for her; it was in the air and she knew that nothing could be more deadly for the hunted than to show dread of the hunter. She put on the fine leather sandals, the drifting robe with bands of alternating gold and silver rising from the hem to cross her breasts. A band of silver held back the flowing darkness of her hair. Another band spiraled up one arm and a rare scent was touched to her ears and throat. The robe

was cut high so that her long brown legs showed in
the shadows of it. She knew that she was fair and
prayed that it might not be her undoing.

CeLa walked between the guards as they moved toward the council area, which was lit with many
torches. It seemed that everyone in the tribe was
there, dressed in proud array of bright colors, dancing plumes and shining weapons. They were curiously quiet and the collective eyes followed CeLa's
progress as she was escorted up to the spot where Kir
stood in the light of six bunched torches. He wore
a short tunic that left his muscular legs bare, and a
sword of Sumerian make glittered at his belt. His
face was impassive but she saw the anger in his eyes.
She started to speak but a quick gesture of his hand
stopped her.

There was a sudden blare from the horn trumpets
that she had heard previously in welcome to them.
Raba came into the glare and walked slowly, proudly,
up to within a few feet of Kir and CeLa. Then she
turned and mounted a large rock that had been
placed there. As she looked at her assembled people,
she was truly a magnificent sight. Her ground-length
cape seemed to be made of golden feathers that flamed
into life when the light touched each one. A staff of
gold was held in one hand; the other rested on a
dagger that flashed with the clear jewels she alone
of the tribe seemed to possess. Her profile was clean
and pure, a perfect etching. A crown was set on her
high head. It too was made entirely of the clear gems
fastened to a slim golden band. CeLa thought that
she had never seen anyone more majestic.

Raba lifted one hand and nodded at Kir, who
stepped to CeLa's side. He said to her, "I am given
permission to translate these proceedings so that you
may know. It is your right, for you, as I am, are
deeply concerned in this."

Raba spoke in a voice that grew in intensity until it seemed to be part of the wild surroundings. The words might have come from the sky and the plains, a song and a promise. She held her symbols of authority high and her words became lulling as though they were of the sea. She stopped and the people muttered slowly at first and then on a rising note as they pushed closer.

Kir's whisper was rapid in CeLa's ear. "She speaks of the potential greatness of the tribe and of how it was lowly among the peoples of this land. Now the borders are extended and our ships strike out across the sea. The rest is about the need to expand and learn that trade, rather than war, is the means of prosperity now and in the future that their children will see."

There came a cry from the ranks of the people as they parted before the tall figure that came out from among them. It was Wanu. He wore only a loin-cloth and he carried a long, plain dagger that glittered in the red light of the torches. He walked to within a few feet of Raba and when he spoke his voice was low and clear. CeLa understood some of his precise Ibian and guessed he spoke so that there might be no misunderstanding among the outlanders.

"You have introduced the outlander and his ways to our sacred people and thus have endangered them. You would trade with the enemy that has carried our people and yourself into slavery. You have opened up the vastness of our land to the outlander. You, Raba, are no longer of us. You have incurred the wrath of the gods. You are no longer an inviolate priestess-goddess. I, Wanu, challenge you!"

Kir whispered the translations into CeLa's horrified ears but it took little understanding to grasp what Wanu had said. Raba stood very still as the silence stretched out. Then she lifted her voice in a cry that seemed to shake the very ground. Those around her drew back in alarm.

"My authority is grounded in the gods and cannot be shaken!"

"By the ancient law of our people, you must meet me in mortal combat. He who lives rules unchallenged!"

The people cried with one voice, "So be it! So says the ancient law that is older than our language itself! You must yield, Raba. There is no choice!"

Wanu cried, "You have heard. I challenge you, Raba, priestess-goddess of the Ib!"

Kir said to CeLa, "They will fight and if Raba dies in combat, they will kill us." He sounded almost matter-of-fact.

They could not be heard for all the shouting. CeLa bent to him as she said, "Surely it is not too late to give up on the mission to Egypt. That seems to be what has inflamed them."

Kir laughed and she was surprised to detect real amusement in his tone. "That is only an excuse, CeLa. Wanu has long coveted power and while Raba was gone, he had it. He but sought an agreeable reason to rid himself of her. Rumors have been carefully planted and fears stirred up. It is an old trick that works every time. Sargon uses it often."

"But how can Raba fight him? He is far stronger than she."

"There you will be surprised. Raba is a woman who surpasses all others in many things."

He looked at his wife and there was admiration in his eyes. CeLa thought that he loved her and bitter jealousy struck her heart, but she held her tongue.

Raba's deep-toned voice called out, "You have spoken against me before the gods and assembled people. You deserve to die! I accept your challenge!"

The people cried out in pride and acclaim at her courage. Wanu braced himself and stood erect. The

torches flamed off his muscular body. He might have
been an ebony statue of a long-forgotten god of the
desert. He lifted his dagger in striking position.

Raba lifted both arms and the cloak fell from her
to reveal her supple nude body, magnificent tilting
breasts and long, perfect legs. Light flashed from the
crown and the torches to reflect on her dark skin and
upheld weapons.

"To the death." Wanu cried the words aloud.

"To the death." Raba's voice rose over his and
fell into silence. Above them the cold moon glittered
on the plain of combat.

Raba and Wanu circled each other in the wide
space that had been cleared for them. The silence
was complete as they looked for the opening that
might be the beginning of victory. Sweat raised a
sheen on the beautiful, deadly bodies.

Kir stood slightly in front of CeLa, one hand poised
lightly on the sword at his belt, the other on her
arm. She did not need the pressure to warn her to
remain still. She could not have moved if she had
wanted to do so; fascination and fear rooted her to
the spot.

Raba reached out at Wanu suddenly and her dagger flashed down. First blood was drawn. Now they
closed in and withdrew to circle again. His foot
sought to trip her but she evaded it and pulled the
dagger across his gleaming chest. His rose and sliced
at her nipple, causing blood to pour out over her
flat stomach. They breathed heavily as the deadly
pacing began again.

CeLa loosed her breath in a long, shuddering sigh
that caused Kir to tighten his hold on her arm. Her
mouth was dry but the palms of her hands were
wet. This seemed a nightmare that might go on forever. It had seemed safe here, the journey to Egypt
planned and settled, a relationship of caution prepared with Kir and Raba. Now all was in jeopardy.

Wanu closed with Raba again and they grappled
as their daggers locked. Blood poured down from
them both and smeared their faces. Raba's dagger
went flying and Wanu grinned as he aimed for her
heart. She caught his wrist and twisted it so that he
fell heavily to the ground. Instantly she was on top
of him and her knee sought his groin. He threw her
back but she rolled with the movement and rose to
her feet, then sprang for him, long fingernails thrusting for his eyes. They connected and he screamed in
agony as her thumb followed with an audible pop.

He thrashed about on the sand as Raba rose in
all her bloody nakedness to stand erect while she
dashed the blood from her own eyes. That movement
was her undoing. Wanu still held his own dagger in
one hand; in his pain he had not let go of it. Now
he raised up and squinted through the curtain of
blood over his remaining eye. He pointed the dagger
upward and lunged after it with all his mighty
strength and fury. His bellow was that of the wounded lion at attack.

The sharply honed blade caught Raba in the extended pelvic area and ripped up to glance off bone
and splinter it, then into the softness of her stomach,
almost ripping it in two. Her entrails spilled out between her fingers as she gave one shriek that must
have reached to the mountains themselves. She fell
to the ground. Wanu bent over her and withdrew the
dagger. Then, in one incredibly savage gesture, he
sliced through her neck so that her head was separated from her body.

"Behold, the victor! I rule now!" His bellow shook
the people to life and they acclaimed him in voices
that spoke of blood lust not yet slaked. "Behold the
head of the vanquished one!" He lifted the bloody
thing high while gore dripped from his body and
empty eye socket and the people cried aloud again
and yet again.

Wanu turned round and round in the ecstasy of victory. CeLa felt vomit rise hot and vile in her throat. She must have made a noise, for Kir's fingers clamped tighter than ever on her arm, the nails digging in so that she thought the skin must be broken. She met his eyes and saw that the same sickness was in them, but they both must fight it.

"Death to the interlopers who have profaned our land!"

The cry came from the thickly massed people in one voice and was soon taken up so that the deafening roar rang in CeLa's ears and she began to shake with the fear of the crowd. Wanu looked straight at her and Kir. He had wiped some of the blood from his socket and the empty hole gaped in the light. He seemed impervious to the pain. The bloody head had been handed to one of the guards, who mounted it on a long pole and set it down in the clump of torches so that the death grimace was starkly illumined.

Wanu cried now, "So be it! Your will shall be satisfied!"

The crowd surged forward, faces hot and filled with the lust for revenge. It became one face and CeLa felt her senses swim as darkness neared.

"Men of the Ib! You have fought with me. Have you suffered from our venturing forth from the boundaries of your fathers? Have the borders of the land not been extended? Have our treasure chests not increased? You have slain my wife, the priestess-goddess of this tribe, in lawful combat. I weep for her. Her shade will wait for me in the netherworld. But this is the will of the gods. By what right do you claim the lives of the guest within this land and the mate of Raba? Where has it been stated that this must be done? I claim my life and that of the woman of Sumer!"

Kir had stepped forward to confront Wanu and

his bold words rang out against the madness that had been exhibited. CeLa felt her legs shake under her as she fought against nausea and persistent faintness. The silence was absolute. Even Wanu paused as he assessed the temper of the people he had inflamed.

Kir spoke again, this time directly to the people in front of him, so that their eyes shifted uneasily to Wanu, each other and back again. "The wrath of the gods will surely follow you if you do this thing. It will never leave you from this day on to beyond death. Think, men of Ib, on what you do!"

A man close to him flung one arm out in an eloquent gesture. "Give them their lives! He is right, the gods will not deal kindly with those who slay the guest in the land."

Another voice cried, "The mate of Raba is no guest. He lived among us and fought with us, imbued us with his ideas that now bring the hordes of Egypt near our lands. Kill them both!"

"Aye! Aye!" The crowd roared approval to both points of view.

CeLa caught her breath. Kir's audacity was compelling, even more so when she thought how the death of Raba must have agonized him. It was hard to imagine that matchless beauty and courage so savagely destroyed. She lifted her head proudly, hoping that if it came to death, she might perish with Kir.

Wanu burst into laughter and roared, "You shall have your lives! Let no man say that Wanu does not heed the warnings of the gods themselves. I grant you your lives. Most willingly!" He waved one hand and a rock crashed down on Kir's head so that he fell almost at the feet of the eager young guard who had been waiting for just such an opportunity.

CeLa screamed but the sound was lost in the roars of approval that went up from the people.

"Take the woman to her tent and guard her well.

I shall enjoy her in private and then she shall be yours!" Wanu spoke to his soldiers and they laughed loudly.

They put their hands on CeLa and she did not struggle, for it would have been useless. She could only hope that the blow had been meant to stun Kir only and not to kill him. She walked with her guards toward her captivity, cheers of approval for Wanu ringing in her ears.

35

The Capricious Ones

Four long days and endless nights passed while CeLa was held in the tent. She was not allowed out in all this time and saw no one except the mute old woman who brought her food and drink as well as water for washing. Questions were useless and she learned to save her breath.

On the fifth day, however, a guard entered with the woman and said, "Rise, woman of Sumer. You are summoned to Wanu. Come instantly."

CeLa had fought hard for calm in these past days; her tears for Raba, her fears for herself and Kir, the retreat before the panic that the thought of Wanu roused in her—all these had exhausted her. She could stand erect now and say, "I am ready," with a sense of unreality.

The brilliant sun made her blink as she emerged from the tent but the fresh air was wine sweet. As sweet as life itself, said her hammering brain. The tents of the Ib had been folded down and the camp area was almost bare. They were preparing to move, it appeared. Close by her own tent stood two cages made of wood and bound with sturdy strips of hide. The top slats were small and set apart so that the sun shone down inside. Food and water were arranged at all angles so that it could be seen but not reached. The cages looked just big enough for a large child. The guard halted her by them and his grin was savage.

"For you and the man Kir." He laughed at the expression of horror she was unable to control. "Our leader is wise. Your lives are to be spared, for none will place a hand on you. Those who have walked with the gods may not be slain."

CeLa fought down her sickness at the thought of such a cramped and lingering death. Sweat filmed her forehead and her hands clenched as she jerked her gaze away. She would not give him the pleasure of seeing her despair.

After a long moment he turned and led her in the direction of the tent that had been Raba's. It still stood, splendid as ever. The banner outside the entrance was now flaming red and CeLa thought the color suited Wanu well.

The guard pushed her through the opening and she stood dazed in the half darkness. "Enter! Enter!" Wanu stood in front of her then, his great height seeming even more so in the opulence that surrounded them. The treasures they had thought to take to Egypt were ranged round and costly draperies hung everywhere. Wanu himself wore a short scarlet skirt. His eye socket was covered with a leather patch and his smooth skin shone with recent oiling. He advanced toward her, extending a hand to touch her silken hair and the smooth skin of her face. She recoiled instinctively and waited for him to retaliate savagely.

He did not move and then she saw the sheen of sweat on his face and head and the grayish cast of his skin. His hands trembled and as she stared directly into his one eye, she saw that there was a milky haze over it and that his vision was obscured. His head turned and this time he saw her. He said in a flat voice, "The wise man tells me that this comes from the gods, that soon the world will be dark before me. He could not tell me why I have been so stricken since I have only done what is proper by our laws and custom. I have even withheld my hand from you and the other outlander these many days. Still, the malady worsens."

CeLa knew the sweetness of revenge. She relished the sound of his heavy breathing and the delight of seeing his pride go down before fear of the darkness. He struggled to retain his calm but sweat was rolling down his long body. Just so had she fought to survive. The gods were good, after all.

Wanu's voice deepened as he said, "I have commanded that the man Kir be brought before me so that you may feel my mercy." He turned his head at the sound of footsteps. A guard entered, Kir behind him.

CeLa saw that Kir's pride had not dimmed despite the dark bruises on his face and several welts on his bare back. His eyes met hers across the space between them and gladness leaped in them. She smiled and saw his lips curve in response. Just so had they faced danger together in the desert.

Wanu said, "Raba spoke often of your skills, Kir of Sumer. You are wise in the ways of the flesh and its afflictions. Cure my sight, restore it to me, and you, along with the woman, shall have food, water and weapons as well as freedom to journey toward the borders of Egypt. Fail me and you shall dwell in the cages."

"What assurance have we that you will keep your word?" Kir might have been lifting a casual cup of wine with friends, so easy was his tone.

"The word of Wanu is enough." He spoke firmly.

"Very well." Kir leaned close. "Let me look at your eye." Obediently, Wanu sank down on the pallet almost at his feet. The guards drew closer still, their spears at the ready. "Bring a torch."

CeLa looked with Kir at the cloudy section of Wanu's eye, seeing the yellow material that had begun to cover it, noting the puffed and swollen lid.

Kir lifted the flap of leather and peered at the hole
where the other eye had been. The same yellow, puru-
lent material was there in abundance along with inflamed skin and fragments of shattered bone. A
stench arose from the area.

Kir sat back on his heels with a sigh. "I have seen
many such wounds and must tell you truly that unless the gods intervene, you will lose the remainder
of your sight before the moon is out." He lifted his
eyes to CeLa as if to give her courage and continued,
"There are potions that must be prepared, incanta-
tions to be chanted. You yourself must rest and be
purged. In three days time I will be ready."

Wanu stood up carefully, maintaining his balance
before his men. All the force of the chieftain was in
his words. "All that you require shall be furnished.
Remember your fate if you fail. The woman will
belong to my men if you do."

"For now she remains with me, for she is the handmaiden of the goddess we serve. Her force is powerful,
all the more so because she bears the black goddess
of the south and the winged god, Antatu. We will
plead for Wanu." Kir stretched out a hand to CeLa
and she took it thankfully, feeling the iron hardness
of his grip and drawing courage from it.

"I too serve the gods of Ib. We do not recognize
strange gods here. Obey me!" Wanu waved to the
guards, who escorted them from the tent.

They were taken to CeLa's tent, where many guards
were posted, their weapons bare and sharp. Kir ignored them and gave rapid orders to one of them,
ending, "Leave these at the doorway. None must enter, for our work is sacred." The guard nodded respectfully and hurried away.

Once inside, Kir threw himself down on a pallet
and mopped his forehead. CeLa knelt beside him.
"Can you restore his sight, Kir?"

He spread his long fingers and looked reflectively at them. "I was trained as a physician at the court of Sargon and sent to those who practice that art in many ways that I might learn to cheat death. I saw the injuries inflicted in war, the harm men brought upon themselves, agonies of children, the senseless snuffing out of life, the horrors given out by the capricious gods." His voice slowed and CeLa knew that he remembered his young wife, who had died by his merciful hand that she might not suffer longer. "I grew sickened and vowed that I would not continue to fight against such ravages, although I once would have given my all to possess such knowledge. I returned to Sargon asking only to fight at his side and that was granted me."

CeLa expelled her breath softly. Kir touched her hand in one of the few spontaneous gestures he permitted himself. "I have indeed seen this before. Where one eye is destroyed or goes blind, often the other will follow, especially with an injury of this sort. Wanu believes he is cursed and this contributes to his loss of vision. I cannot help him."

"What are we to do?"

Kir turned his head from her. "Fight for our lives as best we can. I only regret that you are here. It is true, I destroy all I touch. Raba died because of me; you will also. I cannot fulfill my vow to my king . . ." His voice shook and trailed away.

CeLa had never thought to see Kir reveal himself so, and she was torn with the pity she must not show. She loved him all the more for this and longed to comfort him. She said instead, "I weep for Raba but she will not return from the netherworld. I have no wish to go there, nor should you, Kir the Arrogant. The commands of Sargon still lie heavily upon you. You have a plan. I know it. Use it."

There was the sound of materials being placed at

the door to the tent and footsteps moving hastily away. Kir stared at her for a moment. "You are right. While we live, we fight."

For the rest of that day and night Kir worked over the assortment of plants and powders that had been delivered. CeLa offered to help but the gaze he turned on her was distracted and dark. She watched for a time but her eyes soon began to burn as smoke rose in swirls and mingled with foul odors. Weariness stifled her fear and curiosity; turning her head into her mantle, she finally slept, Kir's chanting ringing in her dreams.

She woke to a loud voice crying, "Why have you started a fire? It is forbidden! We enter!" The tent flap swung back and several agitated faces looked in. She saw the agitation change to real horror as they backed away, almost falling over themselves to escape.

A hollow voice came as if from the depths of the grave. "This place is holy. He who profanes it will surely die!"

CeLa turned to look at Kir and drew back, her own fright clearly visible on her face. Smoke hung heavily in the tent, rasping her nostrils and almost making her gag. His long body was naked and shone with the gleam of silver, as did his hair. One eye was covered with what appeared to be blood and pus. Bone fragments glittered in the light of the guard's shaking torch. Red streaks were over the entire side of his face and the bones shone white on the other. One arm appeared to be eaten away with white blots and the hand of that same arm was turned under and twisted with deformity. He limped painfully into one coil of the smoke and they saw the beginning of the putrescence in the remaining eye. CeLa gave a low cry and put both hands over her mouth.

"Gods! What manner of magic is this?"

"Gods protect us!" The guards backed away still

more as Kir made to move toward them. "Look, the woman is terrified also."

"I take Wanu's agony upon me at the bidding of the gods. Go from this place for the allotted time or we will all die. Such is the command of the great ones. Go!" Kir's voice rose to a low howl as he staggered back before what seemed to be a rush of pain.

The guards cried, "Aye, lord, we go! We go!" The flap fell down and they heard the slap of running feet and cries of alarm. A mournful drumbeat began in the distance.

CeLa shook her hair back and stared at Kir, who stood in the smoke, his arms folded, a truly ghastly sight. Her voice quavered as she whispered, "It is true, then? You have dealt with the gods to save our lives? Kir, what folly is this?" What savage bargain had he struck? Did he think she would desert him? Right gladly would she die with him! She rose to go to him and was stopped by his savage whisper.

"Stay as you are. Do not move. Keep that look of fear on your face. Obey me, CeLa, if you would live to draw another breath!" His eye looked at her with all the power and determination of old as he lifted his voice in the demonic chant and the smells grew yet more foul. "Weep, wail. Do so loudly!"

CeLa's sympathy withered at his tone. Whatever his appearance, he was still Kir the Arrogant. She put all her frustration and fright into several painfully drawn wails and was gratified to see one corner of his mouth lift up as he nodded approval.

More smoke billowed up and Kir's body shone now white and yellow through it as his teeth flashed against the blood that seemed drawn from his mouth. There was a gasp of sheer terror from one side of the tent and they heard the clash of bodies outside. The tent flap waved slightly and then was still. Only the sound of the drum continued in the distance.

As far as CeLa could guess, she had seemed to

sleep for only a little time and it had been early
night then. Now the very air had the feeling of lateness as she and Kir kept up chanting and weeping.
Finally he gave a deep moan and sank to the ground.
Smoke was now coiling upward and outside, leaving
them a little space to breathe. Under its cover Kir
crawled to her side and put a hand on her shoulder.
CeLa looked at him, willing herself not to recoil, and
saw that his face was covered with paint and that
his body and muscles were skillfully twisted. Tears
flooded her eyes and she leaned against the sweaty,
dripping body, giving thanks to the deathless ones
that he was not so afflicted. His hand touched her
hair briefly, then drew back.

His breath tickled her ear as he spoke urgently.
"No questions. Just do as I say." She nodded, for
emotion rendered her incapable of speech. "Good.
Put on that tunic and robe. I think these sandals
will fit. Hurry."

As he spoke, he was stripping the paint from his
body and slipping into a thick robe and turban. A
sword and dagger hung from the belt around his
waist. CeLa obeyed him, her fingers trembling in her
haste as she wound her hair and adjusted the folds
of the turban. She took the slender dagger he handed
her and their eyes met for a brief second. What she
saw there shook her to the core, for there was camaraderie in them and flickers of remembered passion. Beyond that was Kir himself, a man faced again
with destruction. He made a quick gesture and was
again his shuttered self.

Smoke was even more dense in the tent now and
CeLa saw that part of the fabric was shredded in
the lower section. Kir parted it and looked out, then
motioned to her to follow him as he moved through
and flattened himself to the sand. The night was
moonless and cloudy but they could see the reflection
of the fires from Wanu's tent. The drum still sounded

hollowly but there was no sign of any guards around this area of the tent.

They lay quietly for long minutes, then crept stealthily along in a half crouch, half run until they reached the bend of the long, dry riverbed and the stubby palms partially hid them from the camp. Then they threw themselves flat once more and breathed heavily in sudden release. CeLa risked a quick glance and saw that smoke still rose above the palms. She shuddered with fear and tried to catch her breath.

"Lord Kir." The voice spoke from the side of the small dune and rocks just beyond them. Kir jerked up and his sword was instantly in his hand. "I mean you no harm."

Teph stepped into view, his empty hands held before him. His dark face was drawn with lines of grief that were clear even in the dark and he seemed somehow shrunken. CeLa felt a flood of relief but Kir did not relax his stance of watchfulness.

"We go, Teph. I do not want to kill you, but I will do so if I have to."

"I have watched these days for a chance to help. Raba was my queen-priestess. She gave us all opportunity to learn and grow, to be more than a wandering tribe of the desert. She urged me to travel. It was she who persuaded Ara's father to let us wed. She will be revenged, for even now a challenger rises to battle Wanu, should he recover. I have whispered to the man. He will know what to do." Teph smiled but there was no mirth in it, only implacable hatred.

Kir said, "She was my wife, my queen, the saver of my life."

"Take these." Teph pointed to two desert asses that stood in the shadow of the dune. "They are well trained and quick. Small bags of provisions are fastened to them as well as two bottles of water. Go up this dry river bed, swing to the right and follow this map I have drawn. It will take you, Antatu will—

ing, within sight of the borders of Egypt, some eight or ten days swift travel from here."

"How can we thank you?" CeLa whispered the words as Kir moved closer to Teph and clasped his hand.

He shook his head violently. "Do not. I loved Raba. Let that be between us. The gods keep you."

Kir said, "And may they bless you eternally." His tone changed as he mounted the animal and watched CeLa do the same. "They will pursue us when they learn of our escape."

"Of course. But you will have a good day and more start. The winds will blow over your tracks and in the meantime they will consult me, as a teacher of wisdom and languages, about the meaning of the smoke and your appearance. I heard them speak of it at the council fire and knew that your plans had been made. I will talk long. You will have your chance, you and the woman who has your heart."

CeLa gasped. Did Teph see more truly than she? Kir's mouth pulled into a straight line and she saw his hawk profile as he said, "We will remember you always, Teph."

Teph lifted his hand and said no more. They touched the reins of the asses and the hardy animals began to move as they had been taught by generations of Ibians. CeLa's heart lifted in gladness, for Kir had not said that he loved Raba or herself, but he risked much for them both. Teph honored Raba even in her horrible death and would keep her name alive among the Ib. CeLa's eyes burned with ready tears of relief that they still lived and that Kir surely cared for her.

Thus they rounded the last curve of the dry river and headed toward the far line of dunes that would lead them to the borders of Egypt.

36

Keeper of the Doorway

They rode rapidly through the remainder of the night, the burning day and into night again without pausing. The sun blazed on the rocky, sandy plain that was occasionally broken by grassy expanses and scrubby bushes. At times they moved through drifting sands that were much as those of the great desert between Sumer and the Red Sea had been. But their mounts were larger and sturdier than those of Sumer, for they were bred to this land.

Talk was difficult with the vigilance they kept and with the jouncing of their pace, but CeLa was able to ask, "By what miracle did you save our lives, Kir?"

It was late afternoon and they had ridden far without a word. He had seemed remote from her, his back straight and tall as he continually scanned the horizon. Now he grinned at her, his teeth a white flash in the sun, his grim, inward look momentarily gone. "When I studied with the learned physicians at the command of Sargon, I learned much about potions and powders from one of the oldest of them who was reputed to be something of a magician. I thought such study womanish and rebelled, but he chided me and led me into the revelation of some of his secrets. I knew we must trick Wanu and so the concoctions brought to me produced the smoke which was of a type often used in temples to invoke the arrival of the god. One of the powders mixes well with others and causes slow burning effects without actual flame on any surface touched. This enabled the tent material to shred and tear. The paint was also produced by a combination of the plants and a dye that I carried with me. They did not remove my pouch during my imprisonment. Now you know my secrets."

CeLa smiled with him. "Aye, we will be traveling magicians." She could not add, if we live. Her courage must match his. She blessed the fate that had led Kir to that training as a physician and wondered again at the strange ordering of the lives of people. Had she never gone to the marketplace that day so long ago to work as a scribe, she might never have met Sirna, loved Kir or started the chain of events that had led to this place and time.

She and Kir did not speak again for a long time but the knowledge of their shared danger and goals lay warm between them. She did not feel the anguished passion for him now; it was enough to meet his gaze, to smile with him, to see his strong body move with the gait of his mount. When they were forced from exhaustion to stop, rest and refresh themselves, he drew her into the circle of his arms, holding her there while she slept and he watched. Then she did the same for him, studying the vulnerability of his face as he rested.

On the afternoon of the seventh day, they saw riders on the horizon, dim at first, then more distinct in the clear air. This was the first sign of anyone else in this land, which had begun to seem even more desolate as the great rocks and barren ground increased.

"Do you think they are the Ib?" CeLa had to voice her fears.

Kir shrugged. "Who can know? We must go faster."

The asses were already exhausted with the speed of their pace but Kir and CeLa were forced to kick and prod them yet again. Kir drew his dagger and inspected it, then kept his hand close to it as they rode. The hills rose more steeply and the rocks were more jagged. They were forced to slow their pace and the riders drew closer. When they topped a little rise and paused to give the animals time to breathe, Kir looked back once more. His muttered curse caused CeLa to turn as well. The horizon was filled with a horde of warriors and riders. She knew that the Ib had arrived.

They pressed on, trying to get as far into the rocky area as they could. There was no time for talk or fear, for it seemed that certain death was upon them. Kir rode first past an overhang with CeLa several lengths behind him. Sudden instinct made her look up and her blood chilled. A man stood poised on the rock just above Kir, a spear in his hand, ready to drive it down into Kir's back. She did not hesitate but jerked the dagger from her belt, took aim and threw it upward all in one movement. It struck him in the throat, causing him to gag and call out as he clapped both hands to it and fell.

Kir whirled around, his sword seeming to leap into his hand. There was not a sound anywhere as they waited. CeLa sat very still, knowing that she should retrieve her dagger, but unable to bring herself to pull it from the throat of the man who lay sprawled at their feet. Kir dismounted, bent and pulled it loose, wiping the blade on his tunic.

"You have saved my life with your quick action. I am grateful."

The words were stilted and formal. She felt tears sting her eyes. "Is he of the Ib?"

Kir looked into the dead face and his own was cold. "Yes. I have lifted many a cup with him. He was a good warrior when he sailed with me."

CeLa could not be sorry the man was dead. "He would have killed you. What was I to do?"

Kir shook her gently. "It is war between the Ib

and ourselves, CeLa. Do not regret what you have done." He tilted her chin to his and his eyes softened. "I will need to thank you properly if ever the day comes when we are safe."

"What can we do, Kir?"

He shrugged. "Ride on as swiftly as we may."

They gathered up their belongings and went toward the asses. Suddenly arrows swished by them and buried themselves in the sides of the animals. CeLa looked up to see a party of Ibians rushing at them across the little plain between the great spans of rock. No more arrows were shot and CeLa knew that this meant they were to be taken alive. There was no time for fear. She pulled a second dagger from the pack and held them both in her hands. The loose robe was tossed aside; she would fight in her tunic. Kir drew sword and dagger, then placed himself in front of her. Just so had they fought in the battle that had left him for dead all those moons ago. He looked at her and in their gaze was all the passion and caring that could not be said. CeLa felt her heart lift inexplicably as she braced herself for the moment when the fight would begin.

The first wave hit them and Kir's sword sliced across two throats, then up at a raised arm. A dark face loomed over CeLa and she thrust at it with the dagger; the man withdrew in a howl of pain. Others were behind these, however; it was only a matter of time.

CeLa was only dimly conscious of yet more men appearing to join the fray from the side. There were howls and curses, the clash of swords and spears, the outpouring of blood into the sand. She and Kir stood in the crevice, partly protected by several bodies piled up in front of them. Suddenly a leather shield appeared on the edge of her vision and the slash of her dagger was blunted on it. She tried the other but it was turned aside and the soldier grabbed her.

Kir turned to protect her but was stopped by a spear held at his chest, another at his throat.

Other soldiers appeared close at hand and now CeLa saw that the remainder of the Ib were fleeing before them. She had thought all these were the Ib. Now there were new captors. Something in her decided that was funny and she began to shake with laughter.

One of the soldiers swung her up in his arms despite her struggles and another urged Kir forward. A part of her mind that was still free noticed that this contingent seemed well disciplined, far too much so to be another desert tribe. The men wore brown tunics and sturdy sandals; their weapons were polished and sharp. The hands that held her were not harsh, only firm. Hope began to move in her. Death had been certain with the Ib; here there was doubt.

They walked for a short way only, then rounded a great rock and came onto what was most certainly a road in this desolate land. Other soldiers waited in orderly ranks beside a chariot of gold decorated with plumes and drawn by a team of the sturdy asses of the region. A tall, bronzed man in his middle years stood alertly in front of it. His clothes were of simple brown cloth, his sandals the same as the soldiers wore, but around his neck was a golden necklace and on it were the combined symbols of Upper and Lower Egypt, the vulture and the cobra, with the lotus twined underneath. Whoever he was, this commanding man was the shadow of Pharaoh in the land. The emissaries of Sargon of Akkad and Sumer had arrived in the outermost boundaries of Egypt.

"What is going on here and who are these people? Put that woman down. You look ridiculous."

CeLa was glad to know that she could understand most of what he said as well as the explanations of the soldiers, two of whom spoke quickly and to the point. Her legs wobbled when he set her down and she realized that the battle had taken a great deal out of her.

The man held up his hand for silence and was instantly obeyed. Then he looked at them with compelling dark eyes full of authority as he said in careful Egyptian, "Why did the Ib try to kill you here at the very boundaries of power? Who are you?"

Kir stepped forward and executed such a bow as he might have produced at a full court of Sargon. His voice rang with pride as he said in faultless Egyptian, "I am Kir of Akkad, ambassador from Sargon the Mighty, King of Sumer and Akkad, Ruler of the Valley of the Rivers, Lord of the North and South, whose name is exalted in the lands, and who sends greetings to the Lord of Upper and Lower Egypt, Pharaoh, Lord of the Two Lands, Son of Re, Great Horus."

The tall man returned the bow saying, "You have named him whose unworthy servant I am. My name is Herkhuf, Keeper of the Doorway to the South, Overseer of Upper Egypt, Sole Companion, Ritual Priest. You are welcome to this land in Pharaoh's name."

Kir turned to CeLa and drew her forward. "This is CeLa of Sumer and Lagash, personal envoy and recorder of the king, whose voice is equal with mine."

Herkhuf nodded with no sign of surprise on his face. CeLa wondered at Kir, who had elevated her to status when he might so easily have dismissed her as friend or mistress. Then she thought that, had he done so, she would have fought for her position and he would naturally wish to avoid a confrontation.

Herkhuf was saying now, "I realize that you have encountered many difficulties and trials. You must tell me the tale in entirety when you have rested. But you will understand that I must have some proof that you are indeed the personages you say you are.

Few in our land have heard of Sumer. We prosper by being watchful."

CeLa spread her hands. "My authority is in these. I carry no badges."

Kir reached inside the pouch that had seldom left his body and drew out a square of cloth and a small medal. He handed the medal to Herkhuf, who took it and looked down at the fierce, bearded face of Sargon, the jutting chin and firm mouth. He turned it over and saw, in smaller relief, the face of Kir and the title, "Friend to the King."

"Few bear that title in our land. I am so privileged." Kir unwrapped the cloth and let the sun strike the clear stone in his hand as it reflected a thousand sparkles. "This is for Pharaoh, a valuable jewel in our land, a small thing retained by us in our troubles, a mere shadow of the presents we thought to bring."

CeLa thought then of the little goddess and the invaluable gifts of life she had brought. She drew the ebony figure out and gave it to Herkhuf. "She is from the lands beyond Yam and near to the Land of Ghosts. For Pharaoh, in Sargon's name."

Herkhuf waved a hand at the chariot. "Thrice welcome to this land. Pharaoh will greatly treasure these gifts when he receives them from your hands. Already he honors your king. Ride with me to the city of Elephantine, which is just beyond the rise here. You shall rest in safety in my own house."

CeLa's mind was numbed by all that had happened on this momentous day but she would remember their journey into another world all her days. The road ran down a cleft, through a rocky section, into curving dunes, past a mighty rock with many inscriptions and toward a wide expanse of water, red-brown and shading to blue. Little islands and rocks, polished smooth by the ages, dotted the surface. A larger island held a city where buildings gleamed and a port with docks bustled almost at the feet of the travelers. In the distance CeLa could see great rocks rising up out of the water that flowed so smoothly here, and she guessed that this was one of the natural barriers that protected Egypt, the First Cataract, as Utar had explained so long ago.

Herkhuf saw her delight and his eyes sparkled. "That is the Nile, mother of us all. Yonder on the island is my house where you and the Lord Kir shall be made comfortable."

The city was bustling and lively with a degree of noise that made CeLa uncomfortable at first, accustomed as she was to the silence of the desert. Strings of asses, loaded with every conceivable kind of goods, passed around them. Officials bawled orders and were answered with indignant cries. Processions moved by in stately array. Pens of goats and sheep were set up and taken down as servants from the temples came to choose the best sacrifices. Exotic materials were loaded and unloaded from ships and docks. Soldiers were everywhere, for this was the garrison town, the bastion of the frontier.

Herkhuf's house was large and spacious, made of sun-baked brick and whitewashed walls with airy rooms filled to capacity with all the treasures acquired by the mightiest man in Elephantine. CeLa was given over to a bevy of servant girls and led away to a room that had a garden and a pool at one end. A raised dais at the other was hung with gauzy curtains and piled with cushions.

CeLa soaked in warm water, drank strong wine and ate cooked meats that were brought to her. Her hair was washed and polished, then left to float silken to her buttocks. Her skin was oiled and smoothed, lotions applied to her face, the calluses on her feet deplored. The wine rang in her head. Her body seemed not her own. The soft notes of a lyre dropped gently into the room.

CeLa could not believe that only this morning she had fought for her life, not really believing that she or Kir would live. She put out a hand to raise the jeweled goblet to her lips and encountered another hand. She turned her head and saw Kir kneeling beside her. Her lips were slow to respond.

"How long have you been here?" The maids had vanished and she lay nude on the cushions at the pool's edge. The sun drifted through the open roof and shading gauze to dapple her long legs and lifting breasts. It did not seem at all strange that Kir should be here or that he should be looking at her with desire in his eyes. "Should you not be conferring with Herkhuf?" she asked.

He traced the line of her hip with one finger, feeling the little rise at his touch. He too was naked and his body was long and lithe under the dark skin. His broad shoulders and wide chest tapered to a narrow waist and firm legs where the muscles stood out as if on a statue. His lips curved in a smile and the old scar flashed.

"He wished, he said, to deal with the urgent business of the day. We are bidden to rest and will dine with him tonight. This time is ours, CeLa."

He took her mouth then, folding her lips into his, turning and cherishing them, while his hands moved slowly over her oiled flesh to caress and burn. She moaned under the pressure of his mouth and her body opened to him as she cupped his head with both hands. His slowness was agonizing. She burned with a fire that could not be satisfied. The earth swung and there was a roaring in her ears.

He rose above her and she saw his organ, large and pulsating as it touched her cleft and rubbed softly, touched her chest and swung toward her mouth. She opened it to take him and the length thrust deeply into her throat. He balanced there for endless minutes while she sucked and drew on him, then he

withdrew to cup her buttocks to his own mouth while
his tongue licked and moved slowly over the mound
of her pleasure.

"Please, Kir, hurry!" CeLa heard her own voice as
it sounded from far off. Her hands beat a tattoo on
the pillows and her hips rose and fell with the rhythm
of unslaked passion. He finally entered her, seeming
to split her body with the force of his thrusting as
he grew larger and longer in the convulsive grip of
her loins. Then he withdrew for a moment to place
her legs on her stomach and entered her from an
angle that drew out the sharpest sword edge of passion. Her hands were on his shoulders. He hammered
her into a jelly of submission and then was trans-
ported himself so that their fall into the abyss was
simultaneous and savage. They rose and fell together
as sweat streamed from their bodies and their cries
merged into incoherence.

Later they sat in the shallow pool, drinking wine
and rubbing each other in an ecstasy of touch. CeLa
kissed the rising stalk, feeling it soft at first, then
blooming in her mouth. Kir rubbed her gently as
his hands made soft plops in the water and her hips
moved slowly in answer to his urgent hands.

In the deeper water he turned her so that she
rose on her knees, then he entered her again, moving slowly at first so that she should feel no pain.
She whimpered at first but he held her firmly and
began to stroke in a smooth fashion. The water
swirled about them and they rose and fell in it until
she at last began to throb with the same fire that
burned in him and they collapsed, he still strongly
in her, his hands on her breasts, thumbing the nipples so that they rose and contracted.

Then Kir lay on his back while she drew her
tongue over his stomach and slowly downward. He
let her work with him, moving the skin back and
forth over the head of his organ, kissing and blowing

on it. Then she lay down, positioning herself so that he could slide smoothly inside her while her feet rested on his shoulders and they could watch the excitement on each other's faces. Kir's nostrils flared wide and his hands caught at her ankles. CeLa threw her head back as the consuming flames seared them yet again in the sweetest pain of all.

This time they settled into exhausted sleep on the cushions by the pool while the early evening light drifted into night and the smell of incense trickled down. The watcher behind the painted curtains on one wall sat on for a time, then rose and moved slowly away.

37

Down the Sacred River

When CeLa woke, the moon was a faint sliver in the sky and there was a sense of lateness about the room. A slave slept across the far doorway and a torch burned low. Her body felt cramped but it had the delicious lassitude of love satiated. She stretched and yawned, wondering what had happened to the meal they had been bidden to with Herkhuf. Hunger gnawed at her stomach. Her mouth was parched and dry. She decided to try to find the anteroom where she knew there were wine and cakes. If she moved about now, she might be able to sleep again and dream of Kir, as she had been doing.

She wrapped herself in one of the loose linen robes that had been brought for her inspection earlier in the day. This one was of the very green of the river itself. Her hair was left loose down her back. CeLa tiptoed cautiously out the side door and in the general direction of the place where she thought the anteroom to be. She realized almost at once that this was a mistake, for there were so many passages that she was instantly lost and could not even find her own door to return. There was no hope for it; she must wander on until she found a servant who could redirect her.

She went down some steps, along a corridor and around some huge storage jars of beautiful design, then was stopped short by a small balcony that looked out over an elegant room with walls painted to re-

semble a marshland where the nobles hunted. The
remains of a meal were spread out before Kir and
Herkhuf, who lounged now in wooden chairs inlaid
with gold and silver. Both wore loose robes of white
linen. The chain of his authority was around Herkhuf's neck and a band of gold stamped with a lotus
seal encircled Kir's head. CeLa felt annoyed that
they had not included her in an obviously festive
occasion and started down the little incline to join
them when Kir's voice stopped her.

"Your price is paid, my lord. I am surprised that
one so powerful as yourself has chosen to exact it."
His voice was bitter and his dark face looked baffled.

Herkhuf laughed and for the first time CeLa saw
the looseness of his mouth. "Neither you nor the
lady was harmed and I have not had so entrancing
an afternoon for a long time." His hand moved to
Kir's arm, lingered and was withdrawn. "Your countryman was far more agreeable, but there were men
at his back and lies on his lips. I used him and
sent him away."

CeLa sank down in a small shuddering heap. She
remembered that, in one of the delightful excesses
of the afternoon, she had flung her head back and
seemed to see something moving behind one of the
curtains. She had thought nothing of it at the time
but now her flesh crawled. He had watched everything—and with Kir's consent!

"Jagon." The word was flat but Herkhuf heard
the blaze of hatred underneath.

"I guard this land. He too said he came from Sargon of Akkad. I know men and there was madness
in him."

CeLa could bear no more. She stumbled out of the
alcove, away from the balcony and into the passage.
Two slaves stood talking at one end of it and she
was able to make them understand her needs. In a

few moments she was back in her quiet chamber with food and drink before her; but now she could not eat and her mind roiled with anger.

She woke to the excited cries of the slave, who demanded that she bathe and dress with all speed. A ship from Memphis had come with special instructions for the ruler of Elephantine. The presence of the ambassadors from the court of Sumer and Akkad was commanded. CeLa was ready with hot words for Kir and did not care how she looked, but she was woman enough to be delighted with the gauzy green-blue gown, the coronet of jewels and shells that was woven into her high-piled hair and the slender sandals that whispered on the polished floors as she moved.

Kir was waiting in the anteroom of the council chamber when she approached. He too was elegant in dark linen with chains of gold. He gave a half smile and said, "You slept so soundly that I did not wish to wake you. I told my lord of our trials and he has promised to send personal messages to Pharaoh, who, by the way, is a young child. His ministers rule and it is they to whom we must address ourselves. When a ship returns to Memphis, and that is frequent, we travel with her."

CeLa lost her fatal temper and her voice was that of the peasants in the fields of Lagash. "I heard you last night! What kind of man watches the lovemaking of others? You sought me for that purpose, did you not? Not because you cared? He is a man of power, you an honorable ambassador. Why? What sort of man have you become, Kir?"

He came to her side in one stride and clamped his hand over her mouth so hard that her lips broke over her teeth. "Cease that caterwauling or I will slap you! The alternative to that was you, my dear. The Keeper of the Doorway to the South is a brave man but his tastes are bizarre and I did not think you would care for them." His eyes blazed down into hers.

CeLa felt shame flood her as she stood still in his grip. It was the truth; his fury told her that.

He was going on, nailing her heart to the wall with his words. "I would not have sought you out but for his insisting on it. Raba remains with me, as you know. It was necessary and now I will hear no more of this. Herkhuf is all-powerful here and he is capricious."

Pride came to her rescue and she wrenched free. "You shall hear no more, my lord Kir. It is well that you have explained yourself."

A hesitant servant murmured from the open door, "His Excellency will see you now."

Herkhuf was alone in a room that contained long tables over which maps were spread in both tablet and papyrus. There was an air of urgency about him that contrasted with the individual of the night before. He looked up and his voice was laden with authority; his was the voice of Imperial Egypt.

"I am commanded by Pharaoh to take armies and men into the far lands from which you have just come, there to penetrate to the treasures and peoples and open up the way for trade and relations with them. I am to send such of their representatives as will come to the court. This is to begin immediately. The ship has been sent with my orders. These are the commands of great Horus, Piopi II."

CeLa looked at Kir but his eyes were riveted on Herkhuf. She would not again betray herself, she vowed. Had he truly loved Raba? So immersed was she in her musings that she did not hear Herkhuf until his voice lifted sharply.

"The ship shall take you with all speed to Pharaoh, who will be pleased with your accounts of these lands into which I go. The girl shall record that

account for his library as a present from me. You
leave at dawn. These are my own commands."

Kir said, "We are honored by your hospitality and
will do as you wish."

He said, "Your confident countryman, Jagon, went
into the desert with his men when I forbade him to
return here. You need not fear that he will carry
false tales to Memphis."

"He is all that is evil and despicable." CeLa felt
the words rip from her and then stood abashed, for
she did not know how much Kir had told this strange
man.

Herkhuf faced them. The audience was over and
his next interview was approaching. "The gods of
Egypt are powerful. Walk carefully here in all that
you do."

The ship of Pharaoh sat solidly in the water at
earliest dawn. It was large, with private shelters for
the noble passengers and separate places to walk.
The sails were wide but oarsmen were still used if
need be. The symbols of Upper and Lower Egypt
were carved on a plate of ebony and set aloft. Men
stood ready to cast off at first notice. CeLa and Kir,
dressed in the garments of the night before, waited
as Herkhuf spoke the ritual words of farewell.

"The gods give you good and safe journey. May
Pharaoh look upon you with favor."

Kir's words were sparing. "The great one of Egypt
shall know of all that has transpired between us,
my lord of Elephantine. The gods watch over you
in the lands beyond the cataracts."

Herkhuf's eyes narrowed as he perceived the warning behind the fair words and his hands were warm
as he clasped CeLa's. She remembered that she had
been spared his touch and shame lifted in her again
as she smiled in farewell.

The woven sails lifted in the wind and Pharaoh's

ship moved out into the mainstream of the river, threaded its way through the rocks that were such an effective barrier to any invader and then floated free on the surface of the verdant Nile, gift of the gods of Egypt to their children and servants.

CeLa stood long on the private section of the deck and watched the river that was the veritable bringer of life. Birds followed them. People stood on the cliffs above and pointed to the tall ship that was so unlike the trading ships and freighters they usually saw. Other vessels moved aside for them. The wind was warm and sweet in her face. Below, a fish jumped high and fell back, and the sails moved majestically above her head. Happiness lifted in her suddenly and she spread her arms wide to welcome it.

In the next days CeLa came as close to her dream of drifting down the river in her own ship bound for adventure as she had ever thought she might. In the mornings she rose very early to watch the river unfold itself with an ever-changing pattern that she never tired of watching. After many moons in the desert, it was bliss to be so close to water and the rocking sway of a ship. Later, after the morning meal of barley cakes, dates and beer, a scribe called Eron, sent by Herkhuf, wrote down all that she told him of their adventures on a papyrus roll that was carefully stowed away afterward. Then, on scraps that were cut from these, he taught her to inscribe the pictorially precise signs that were the written language of Egypt. It was a complicated process and CeLa thought it would take years for her to become proficient at it, but she enjoyed the learning, especially in so beautiful a setting.

After the noon meal she and Kir would listen to Eron as he told them tales of Egyptian history. These went on at length, for he had been instructed to teach the foreigners thoroughly and Eron was not one to shirk his duty. After this CeLa would return

to her own section of the ship and watch the river.
Kir, immersed in his own thoughts, spoke little to
her.

CeLa tried to apologize to him one day but her
words were awkward and she stumbled over them,
feeling herself a fool.

Kir looked at and beyond her, then lifted one corner of his mouth in a half smile. "It took me a moment to remember what you meant. I have more
important things on my mind that must be considered. The wandering of a woman's mind is not one
of them."

CeLa snapped, "Did you think so when I stood
beside you in battle or faced Wanu?"

He shrugged and walked away, leaving her to
seethe.

The Nile carried them now into fertile lands that
shone green against the aridity of the desert that
pressed close. CeLa saw trees and crops with peasants
tilling the fields, settlements built close to the life-
giving water, boats and fishermen moving in the
marshlands, women fetching the day's supply of water and laden ships plowing toward Lower Egypt.

CeLa was never to forget her first sight of a pyra-
mid, several of which were visible as they moved
slowly along. She, who had seen the ziggurats of Sumer and worshiped in Nippur, was still surprised by
the mighty shapes rising out of the fading day on
the flat land. The gods themselves might have dwelt
in such, she thought, wondering how such structures
could have been cut and fitted from the living rock.

"We will visit the greatest of them all, the one
at Gizeh that belongs to Khufu, then those close by
that are the wonder of this land, and the Sphinx
of which you have been told."

It was Kir, lounging beside her, friendly as though
they had not parted in anger days ago. CeLa was
too excited by this exotic land to hold a grudge. She

smiled up at him and said, "I am eager to learn all that I can, Kir. Such knowledge will be useful when we return to Sumer."

"Return." His voice was wistful. "If we return, I mean never to leave again."

In this peaceful setting, drifting by the tombs of the god-kings, she could say the fearful word. "What of Jagon? Why do you think he sought to follow us into Egypt? What could he have accomplished here?"

Kir sighed. "He is a genius, as I have told you. The gods alone know his mind. Sargon likely drove him out of Sumer and he seeks a sanctuary. There are other ways to enter Egypt. We can only be grateful that Herkhuf turned him back."

CeLa felt the ever-present desire rise in her. She could not control the way she felt toward this man and she felt that he knew it. His long fingers rose to adjust the amulet at his throat and she thought of them on her flesh, shivering with the pleasure of it. In an effort to hide her feelings, she turned away and was obscurely glad to hear him bid her good rest.

They entered the city of Memphis, seat of government for all Egypt and the dwelling place of the divine Pharaoh, in the burning noon of the next day. The ship entered a canal and moved slowly up to the harbor. CeLa was conscious of a welter of impressions: massive white buildings that appeared to form a fortress, a jumble of mud brick houses, a few spacious gardens just visible from their heights, the white shimmer that could only be a temple, the hammer and pound of workmen busy in the great shipyards and hordes of people in every type of dress as they gathered to watch Pharaoh's own ship make for her berth.

CeLa and Kir had worn casual tunics and gone barefoot on board ship, but now they were dressed in the elegant costumes worn on their departure from

Elephantine. Eron, the scribe, stood with them. He was, he had revealed to CeLa, whom he liked for her love of knowledge, a personal friend and companion to Herkhuf. All that happened in Memphis would be reported to him.

The ship was being unloaded now and the soldiers as well as the crew were leaving. CeLa and Kir looked about for someone to greet them, but the dock was quiet except for those who watched. They knew that a small, swift boat had left the larger one in the early hours of the evening to speed ahead with messages. Surely the arrival of ambassadors from a far country, coupled with the fact that they had intimate knowledge of the country into which Herkhuf was being sent, merited special attention.

Several men wearing white tunics and rich jewels now approached and looked upward. One, taller than the rest, stepped apart and spoke briefly. Then he came aboard, followed by two soldiers.

"I am Heto, one of the councillors to Pharaoh. Your tale has gone before you." His voice was unpleasant and grating, his eyes insinuating.

CeLa felt a pang of misgiving as Kir answered with all courtesy, giving their names and the titles of Sargon of Akkad and Sumer. "We request the high honor of audience with the divine one as may be convenient so that we may apprise him of this information and our honor. "

Heto began to laugh. "Such a tale is rubbish, of course. The only safe way to arrive in Egypt from such a far land is by sea and that is perilous indeed. The messenger gave the bare highlights of your claims and I must say that you would do well as a street player. Herkhuf believed you, I know, but this is a wiser city, as you will discover."

CeLa intervened as she said, "But this is in the personal interest of Pharaoh. Surely he will want to know."

Heto said, "He is very young and grows daily in wisdom. We who must help him are honored indeed; we do not weight his mind uselessly."

Kir stepped in front of Heto and showed him the medal of Sargon. "This is deadly insult from one land to another."

Heto's olive face turned dark and he waved the soldiers forward. "These people are deluded. Remove them but do not harm them. One must be kind to the mad." He leaned forward. "I would advise you not to make trouble. You have had a free voyage down the Nile. Go to one of the inns nearby and rest for a time. But this tale must not be told abroad. Pharaoh's health is not the best."

The little eyes glared into theirs and suddenly CeLa was afraid. She put one hand on Kir's arm and said, "My head swims from the sun. He is right. I wish to rest. You know that you have had the same trouble."

"You are wise," Heto said coldly, but his eyes watched her every move.

Danger walked with them again, this time in the land of Egypt.

38

In the Street of the Hawk

Screams and curses rose in the air as CeLa turned over to try for another bit of sleep. The customers and hangers-on had roistered long the night before. Now good fellowship had given way to anger. She sat up and pushed the hair out of her face, shuddering at the grimy surroundings, yet knowing she should be grateful for this shelter.

They had been in Memphis for almost a moon now. Several attempts to approach even the low officials of Pharaoh's courts had proved hopeless. Ambassadors traveled in pomp and splendor, laden with many gifts, followed by trains of servants; they did not approach on foot talking of strange misfortunes and in disarray. She and Kir were laughed at the first few times and then driven away harshly. Kir tried several men whose names he had learned in the course of conversations with others, but it was useless. Petitioners thronged every day to the palace; Kir and CeLa were only two and they had no gifts with which to bribe the guards. While pursuing their attempts, they had eaten and drunk of the food and beer that was distributed daily by the priests at the many temples, but soon Kir accepted the fact of their defeat, at least for the moment, and they began to look for shelter other than that provided by the temple walls.

CeLa rose now and dipped her hands in the dirty water left from the night before. It was not far to the river. She would need to fetch more water later. In exchange for this small bit of space behind a tattered curtain, she worked in the kitchen of the inn, drawing beer, baking cakes, scrubbing and washing, sometimes assisting in the cooking of meat. Kir did heavier work in the day, helping in the endless construction of mud brick houses, butchering animals, removing some of the more obvious debris from the streets and calling out the wares of merchants who wished to lure more customers. His beard had grown again and his hair was longer. In that thicket his black eyes flamed. No customer of the inn gave CeLa more than a passing glance. It had been given out that they were from a village far down the Nile and had come to the capital to seek a better life.

CeLa remembered her question of the first few days. "Do you think that Jagon managed to penetrate Egypt and has a hand in this? It seems we are cursed and doomed to failure," she had asked Kir.

He had laughed with the bitterness that never left him these days. "No, CeLa, I do not. Mad, he is, but not to the point of foolishness. I doubt not that he would slay us on sight if he could, but I think he believes we perished in the desert; I in that battle, you in the storm. I firmly believe now that we cannot reach Pharaoh without bribes, and if he did see us, what good would it do? He is young and not likely to believe our tales."

She had tried to question him further but he had gone out and returned raging drunk on the cheap, bad beer. He had tried to take her as one might a whore, out of hungry need, but he could not. Cursing at his failure and refusing to allow her to touch him, he had vanished for the remainder of the night and into the day. He was sober on his return but spoke only in monosyllables. So it had been between them ever since.

CeLa put her head in her hands as the hopelessness of their situation weighed her down. She was penniless in a strange land where she did not know the language well, loving a man who lay with her because there was no other space but did not touch her. She had no prospects for the future, only a life of grinding servitude in exchange for enough bread to keep starvation away, the only relief a festival of the gods when the poor were allowed to celebrate. Her inner cursing rose to an even greater height and something in CeLa snapped.

She jerked the curtain aside and ran into the dark, ill-smelling room that was the life of the inn. Two fat men sat over their beer, listening while a third called down all the furies of the Land of the Dead on his wife, who had dared to remark on his propensities for drink. What was the world coming to when a woman dared speak so to her master?

"And you, I suppose, are such a paragon of virtue, you fat pig, as you sit here and swill? What good is the language when you use the same words over and over at the top of your voice so that decent people cannot rest before beginning the day's toil to clean up the vomit you leave?"

CeLa's Egyptian deserted her but she continued in Sumerian with bits of Ibian and Akkadian thrown in. The dumbfounded drinkers gaped at the slender woman with the dirty face and tattered dress who excoriated them so savagely. CeLa lost all restraint as she recited the litany of their ancestors and the physical attributes of each. Release was sweet and she felt her anger melting away.

Behind her the landlord howled in agony and the bedlam rose higher. Kir saw them as he stood in the doorway. It was too much. He burst into laughter such as had not touched his lips in many long and weary moons. CeLa whirled and saw him. The foolishness of the situation caught her and she sank down on the dirty floor and laughed until the tears ran. The drinkers jumped up and ran from this place of madness, the landlord in pursuit, for they had forgotten to settle the bill.

Kir came to CeLa and they clung together while laughter continued to shake them. Then he held her away while they giggled and their sides ached.

"Madwoman! You have lost us our livelihood. But listen, I have helped a man repair his boat. He takes pilgrims to the great pyramids at Gizeh, and he will take us there today if we hurry. That was my price. You must come now!"

"Kir, what a perfect time to come. Let us run before he comes back." She darted into the alcove and snatched up the little parcel of their belongings, took his hand and they ran into the street, laughing as they went.

That day was a gift of the gods themselves: the rich, watery smell of the Nile where the sun glittered, the cries of the boatmen as they went back and forth, the ripe green of the fields and trees, arguments and devotions of the pilgrims, Kir's laughing comments in her ears.

"This time will be ours, CeLa. Think of nothing serious."

She smiled up at him and he put his arm around her. So did the gods sometimes reward their servants. "You have spoken, master," she answered. They laughed together.

The vastness of the desert stretched in front of them and high above rose the mighty tombs of the Pharaohs, the greatest of all, Khufu's. The smooth blocks fit together as beads on a necklace and light poured over and down them to be reflected back. These houses of eternity were well named, CeLa thought. The Sphinx crouched in the land as though it meant to leap forward in the next breath, yet it was immeasurably old. They stood near the mighty paws and gazed up with a sense of their own smallness on the earth.

"Do you think it is a monster or a god, rendered immobile forever, or until dusk?" CeLa spoke half in fancy and half in fear. "Sumer has never seen such as these." She waved her arm at the wonders around them.

"That is why we must join together, the best of each land." Kir's face went somber for a passing moment, then he passed her the bread and meat they had brought from the boat.

The lion's body and the human face fascinated CeLa even more than the rearing pyramids. She lingered long as the sun moved in the sky. Kir went off on an excursion of his own while she stared at it in wonder. A strange and contradictory land, this Egypt, its people enjoying and loving this life, preparing for the eternal journey to the next. Kir had told her that many Egyptians believed only Pharaoh himself and the great ones around him were privileged for such a life but this belief was not held universally. To look at such monuments made her believe in the godhood of such mighty ones.

A little wind sprang up and whirled the sand at her feet. The nail of the paw would be enough to kill a strong man if it were flicked. A hand came down on her shoulder and she screamed in terror. Kir stood laughing at her.

She jumped at him in the pleasure that was part of this day. He caught her and tilted her face up to his. Her arms went around him and drew him swiftly closer. They kissed long and hungrily, their bodies fitting together in a passion that had not arisen for many days. He drew close to the side of the great beast and his fingers found her erect nipples.

"Kir! We cannot. There are people all around."

"Where?" He looked at the empty plain and the distant village.

"The boat will leave us."

"There will be another. Cease this chatter." He pushed her up against the rough stone, thrust aside her brief clothes and entered her, moving long and deeply in her. The passion caught CeLa and she opened her mouth to his seeking tongue as they stood erect, joined in their hunger for each other.

The shadow of the god-beast was long as, later, they ran swiftly toward the distant river, the pyramids glittering in the reflected light of the sun. The boat they had arrived on had long since departed, but it would be simple enough to catch one of the many returning to Memphis before dark. By helping with the fishing nets, they would pay for the ride.

"Hurry!" Kir pulled at CeLa's arm as they started down the last rise.

CeLa turned back to look at the massive head and slowly darkening body of the Sphinx. She remembered the little image of the winged lion Raba had given her; here too was the lion rampant, her own symbol of battle and faith. Was it only chance that the idea came to her as she gazed at this wonder of the land of Egypt? In her heart she offered up thanks to whatever gods watched over them that day.

Later they sat on the bank of the Nile and talked. It was very late, for the owner of the fishing boat had exacted full services, including beaching his craft and cleaning the catch. The thin moon lifted and faded in the sky while the noises of the city slowed. CeLa dabbled her feet in the slowly moving water, dried them and slipped on her battered sandals.

"Kir, it was meant to be. Did not Heto himself say that you should be telling the tale in the streets? Does not everyone like a good tale properly told? We do not look the same way the people of this land do; our skins are slightly browner, I am shorter than the women. My voice is sometimes passable, and you have the look of the great soldier you are. Few people have been to Yam and the Land of Ghosts. Those who have are not on the waterfront or in the Street of the Hawk."

He smiled slowly and she knew that his fancy was caught. "You would have us be storytellers, CeLa?"

"Not exactly. We can return to the landlord of that terrible inn and offer him a proposal. Food, drink, clothes and better quarters in exchange for the custom we bring in. Those who come will listen to our tales and drink more. If they give tribute, we will keep some and divide the rest with the landlord. If we are good enough, and I think we will be, word of those who talk of the strange lands to the north will reach the palace."

"By the gods, it is a bold scheme. If nothing else comes of it, we will at least eat better."

CeLa thought afterward that had she suggested this on another day, Kir would have glared at her sullenly and departed. But would she have thought of it had they not been so close on a rare day? The great god-lion had given her courage, she thought.

When approached, Lar, the landlord, saw no great loss so long as CeLa worked as she had done in the past and did not insult the customers. Kir would help with repairs around the inn as well. Lar was sleepy and half drunk but he knew a bargain when he saw it.

Then CeLa and Kir lay together on the grimy pallet and created their own world of light. His hands were tender on the length of her body and his lips kindled the familiar flames. She answered his eagerness with her own and they were welded into one. She lay on him, running her fingers through his hair and over his face, down his sides and up again. He lifted her and slid into her with one movement that

sent shivers of delight as he penetrated yet more
deeply. Then they rolled and twisted in a rhythm
that seemed born of the day and the passion they
felt for each other. Their mouths locked together
even as their bodies and their breath rose as one.
The explosion lifted them silently and together in
the final sweetness that was like no other thing.

Several nights later drinkers at the Hawk were
startled to find the place even darker than usual with
only one torch flaming in a corner where a woman,
dark hair flowing about her and melting into her
tunic, sat with a lyre in her hand. A golden bracelet
curved up one arm and her profile was carved in
pale ebony. A dark man stood behind her, a bare
sword at the ready.

They voiced their displeasure, for there was no
ceremony at the Hawk. "Serve the beer!" "What is
this, a player from the temple?" "We came to drink,
not to watch!" "Away with this!"

Lar looked at his angry customers and waved toward CeLa and Kir. They did not move and the din
rose. "I am leaving. No one has brought my beer.
The Falcon down the street knows what I like." The
speaker pushed his bulk up and swayed there.

Kir snatched up the torch and lifted it so that
the radiance illuminated the dark cavern of the Hawk
and the very young girls who stood ready with casks
of beer. He cried, "Hold, masters, or you miss a
mighty tale of passion, deceit and death in the fabled
land of Yam whence we have recently come."

"Why are you here at the Hawk then and not in
the palace?" The man who bawled this fancied himself a wit.

Kir's voice dropped. "The gods have their ways
and we were lucky to escape with our lives. Will you
hear the tale and judge?" He lowered the torch so
that it shone on CeLa's face, highlighting her huge

eyes outlined with kohl and lingering on her shimmering hair.

She looked straight out at the assemblage and raised
one arm as if in command as she rose to her feet.
Her voice took on the deep, compelling note of Sirna
as she said, "It is a far journey to the fabled land
of Yam where the Ib live, they who even now would
take our lives in blood sacrifice if the boundaries of
Egypt could be penetrated."

Kir replaced the torch and struck a note on the
lyre that was repeated at every pause CeLa made. The
girls circulated among the benches, pouring the beer
freely. The tale this night was short and deadly, taken
freely from his imagination and that of CeLa, combining as it did strange gods and mysterious natives
and a curse.

CeLa let her voice go low so that they had to
strain to hear. "And after the sacrifice was freely
accepted and the gods propitiated, we took leave of
those people, not knowing that they would pursue us
after their fear had left them. The journey before us
was long and the adventures that occurred are for
another telling."

The torch blazed up and she lowered her head. Silence held for a few moments, then one of the drinkers pounded the table. "There is a tale for you!"
"Aye!" Trinkets of gold and shells fell at CeLa's
feet as the applause began.

39

The Passion of Oth

In the days that followed, the inn of the Hawk prospered and Lar, the landlord, had reason to be pleased with CeLa and Kir. They did not perform every night, for he was shrewd and knew that demand would cause his business to rise. He would ascertain the mood of the crowd, delay as long as possible and then produce "the travelers from Punt." Names and lands varied but it did not matter. The people came eagerly and their fame spread.

CeLa and Kir were given new quarters in a house several doors away from the inn. They had half of it; a blind man and his old wife lived in the other half. Each had more clothes now and sandals as well as some cheap jewelry. Moreover, they had each other and their love grew daily.

They slept late each day, walked by the river and in the city, returned and made love into the afternoon, then went to the Hawk. They lived in the present with little talk of the future. Kir taught CeLa more Egyptian and they practiced together on the writing that was said to take years to perfect. They visited the many temples of Memphis and wondered again at the proliferation of gods, some very similar to those of Sumer. CeLa wondered at times if Inanna's hand could reach this far and prayed to her in the event that it did.

Kir smiled often now and his hands were gentle where they had been heavy many times in the past.

Often their lovemaking was rendered so tenderly that
CeLa would feel close to tears. But it was not in
the honey of passion that she found evidence of Kir's
growing caring for her, but in the everyday things
they shared, in the laughter and the grumbling, the
shared jokes and annoyances. He helped her carry
the wash to the river, much to the surprise of the
women washing there. Later he helped to wring it
out and hang it up. When she cooked meat and
made barley cakes in the tiny cooking area of the
house, he was always ready to help. In the cool evenings when they went to the roof, he taught her the
songs of Egypt with their mingling of death and life.
Never did they speak of love, but it was there in the
fabric of their daily life and both of them knew it.

They had been at the Hawk for two moons when
CeLa began to feel watched each night. She did not
tell Kir, but her eyes swept the drinkers carefully
and finally isolated the tall man whose face was like
a hatchet and whose hair had touches of gray in it.
Wrinkles radiated out from his eyes and spoke of
long exposure to the elements. Under the thin tunic
his body was straight and firm. Authority sat on his
shoulders and rang in the voice, which he raised to
demand beer and praise the performance. He always
sat in the same place, on a bench near enough for
the one torch to illumine his features. His hard eyes
would fix themselves on CeLa's face and never leave
it until she was done.

She told Kir, who teased her about her admirer
and returned the stare on the next night. The man
was oblivious; Kir might not have existed. Gold
brooches, silver pins, delicate necklaces, choice wines
and fresh meats were delivered to CeLa. He never
spoke to her or approached her in any way, but the
obsessive watching began to wear on her nerves and
on several nights she faltered in the telling of the
tale.

She told Kir later, "That man frightens me. Should you perhaps not speak to him?"

He looked up at her with rare irritation. "What can I say? That he should not look at you who are a paid performer? That he should not offer payment as he does? You are being foolish."

"Who is he? Perhaps he is from the court and will spread tales of our fame there." CeLa could not shake off a feeling of danger.

"Unfortunately not. Would that he were. Little is known of him. Lar is proud of the custom of so obvious a wealthy gentleman and tells me that he was a general in the armies of the previous Pharaoh and sustained a severe wound in one of the border battles. Since that time he has lived apart and is reputed to be working on a history of the reign, although this is not really certain."

Kir put his arm around CeLa and lifted her face to his. The yearning began in them and they melted together in passion suddenly so sharp and longing that they yielded to it even before they could remove their scanty clothes. Later it was prolonged and tender between them as they lay on their sides, he deep in her, his tongue moving over her face, her hands hard on his hips as they rotated together in pursuit of consummation yet again. When it came, it was both sweet and savage, a passion that shook them to the very core and caused them to cling to each other in the aftermath.

Kir's voice trembled in CeLa's ear as he cupped her head in his arm. "Gods, lady, you have fastened yourself to my heart and made it yours."

So tender did he sound that she made bold to say, "It has always been so with me, Kir."

As his voice trailed into sleep, she heard him reply, "And for me, CeLa. And for me."

Several days later Kir left CeLa for the day, saying he would join her at the Hawk in the evening; one of

the customers there had had a run of extremely bad
luck and was wondering if an investment in one of the
trade expeditions to Punt might not both placate
the gods and be of help to him in this life, for he
had a new wife who was very demanding. Left alone,
CeLa decided to go and watch the Nile, since this
was one of her favorite pastimes and one in which
she found great pleasure. Not even the seat of power,
Memphis itself, was so luring to her as this great
river that was the very soul of Egypt.

She sat on one of the rock embankments, her tunic
folded about her knees, her hair tossing in the wind
as it rose and fell. She dreamed not of the past, but
of the abundant present and of the last night with
Kir. It had been one of his masterful times and her
flesh had quivered as he made her his willing instrument, silencing her mouth with kisses and thrusting
in her until she wept with eagerness. He seemed content here in Pharaoh's city and had not mentioned
Sargon in days. CeLa knew that with the happiness
she now had, she would be perfectly willing to spend
the rest of her days here with Kir, leaving the affairs
of the great to others.

"Alms for the servants of Ptah, lady. The god will
bless you for it if you give." The beggar's whining
voice intruded on her fantasies of what she and Kir
might do in the warm dark after their work at the
tavern was done.

"I have nothing with me and I do not know your
god." Her reply was more brusque than she intended.

The beggar was bent and grotesque with a hump
on one shoulder and his head twisted at an angle so
that it seemed to lie in his armpit. His voice was
surprisingly deep and cultured as the whine faded
and he said, "CeLa of the Hawk inn, I am bidden
by one very high in the estimation of many to ask
if you would look with favor on the face of Oth,
servant of Egypt."

She looked at him in surprise and growing horror,
for she knew that this was the servant of the man
who watched her each night. Kir had not told her
his name but it could be no other. She answered,
"The man Kir and I are plighted. I have no interest
in any other."

"My master wishes you to spend a moon with him
at his house on the Nile. He will reward you richly
and see that a suitable husband is found for you
later, since, of course, no former woman of his could
work now as you do in the public inn." The beggar
seemed not to have heard her previous words.

CeLa began to laugh. "No! I will not repeat this
again. I am no wench and will entertain no such
offers."

The beggar snapped, "Your lover would sell you
easily enough for an introduction into the court and
to have the ear of Pharaoh. You would do well to
heed my master."

"Tell him to enjoy the performances!" CeLa felt
her horror fade and life-giving laughter pervade her
being. She thought once again that it was Kir who
had taught her to laugh and take joy in the moment,
grim though he could be.

Because she loved him, she was free to be her own
self. She rose and ran lightly past the beggar, not
noticing that he began to straighten up even as she
went by, his eyes terrible in their dark anger.

CeLa planned to tell Kir but the night went swiftly
and the trade was the best yet. She added embellish-
ments of her own to the tales, as she often did, and
her audience trembled with her before the lion people and their cruelties. Some of the tales were by
rote now and the audience relished these even as
they did the new ones. Afterwards she and Kir shared
with Lar a new wine slightly less bad than those
offered the customers. It went to their heads and they
reeled as they made their way to the house. Kir

turned to her and they kissed deeply, then fell asleep in each other's arms.

The next few days were uneventful. There was no sign of Oth at the Hawk and CeLa gradually relaxed. Kir seemed somewhat remote but she put it down to the fact that he had been speaking of the other lands with some of the drinkers who frequented the Hawk regularly and was remembering Raba or his vow to Sargon. It was enough that life flowed smoothly; she felt as if she had known upheavals enough for a time.

One night after their performance, Kir sat down with some of the men, as was his custom, and was soon deep in conversation. CeLa went toward the back of the inn where she would take a private moment for a cooling drink. She ducked behind the curtain and reached for the wine, grateful for a moment to herself, for the inn was crowded this night.

There was a rustle of movement and then a deep voice said, "You refused my offer, CeLa, and were rude in the doing. Now I am forced to take other measures." Oth emerged from the corner where he had stood. He was smiling but his eyes were savage. "You will come with me now. Willingly and in full sight of the man, your lover."

CeLa laughed, she could not help it. "You have overindulged in drink. Surely my answer to your messenger was clear enough."

A tiny dagger appeared in Oth's hand and he was at her side in several quick steps. "One outcry and this will mar your face in a most interesting fashion. Now listen, I know that you love this Kir. You value his life and well-being. Is it not so?"

She saw the fury in his face then and her fear rose sharply. This was a dangerous man. She nodded silently.

"Many have served with me and honor my name. I have followers in all sections of the city. Some are

here tonight; several sit drinking with Kir now. By
all the gods of Egypt, if you do not come willingly
with me, smiling at him as you go, he dies now in
a brawl and none will think more about it." He jerked
her close to the curtain and she saw the circle of men
around Kir. Two were watching alertly. "I want you
and I shall have you. Your lover's life is in your
hands."

"Why me? Why do you do this?" She could yet
hope to turn him from her.

"Amusement. Death as well as life amuses me.
Well, your choice? We can maim him so that he suf-
fers long, you know."

CeLa looked at this man and knew that he meant
what he said. She must obey for now and watch her
chances. "Yes."

It was a nightmare to feel the point of the dagger
in her side, Oth's arm familiarly around her, his
fingertips at her breast as they walked slowly through
the Hawk under the suddenly sharpened eyes of the
drinkers. Oth bent his mouth to her ear and nipped
at it tenderly as he whispered, "Smile, seem happy.
I warn you, these men are mine."

CeLa could not doubt that he spoke truly for two
men stood directly behind Kir, their hands on their
daggers, their eyes looking straight into those of Oth.
Kir stared at her for a long moment, the smile of
welcome fading from his face as Oth touched her
nipples through the thin tunic she wore. CeLa saw
anger lift in his face as it grew rock hard and his
hands clenched on the table top. She longed to throw
herself on him and weep, but she forced a smile to
her lips as she felt them stick drily to her teeth.

"Do you leave us, lady, with yet another performance to be done?" His tone was light and cool but
she knew it concealed his fury.

Oth's dagger pricked her once more as she said
softly, "Aye, Kir. I do."

His face darkened. "And the company you keep? Have you not protested to me in the past? Of a certainty your mind is swiftly changed." He beckoned to Lar, the host, who was standing nearby watching Oth with worshipful eyes. "Fetch your good wine for us that my tongue may be smooth with the tales I tell!" He turned away from CeLa then and engaged in animated conversation with the man next to him.

Oth's low laugh sounded as they walked out into the street. CeLa felt the pain growing in her heart. Did Kir know her so little or hold her so lightly in spite of all that they had shared? Had it all been a mockery?

"He suffered you to go easily enough. I doubt that he will miss you."

Blind fury caused CeLa to lift her hand to Oth's mocking face. He squeezed the side of her neck with hard, experienced fingers and welcome darkness came upon her.

When CeLa woke, she was in total darkness that did not lift even as her eyes became accustomed to it. She felt that she was somewhere deep underground. Had Oth abandoned her to die or was he watching her with avid eyes. Time passed endlessly as she tormented herself with possibilities and remembered the way Kir had dismissed her. Tears ran into her mouth but she would not let herself weep aloud as she longed to do. Bitterness faded before hunger and thirst, and the chill of her prison penetrated her bones. She thought longingly of the great river and its peace but her physical discomfort was too great.

A sound in the wall made her look up though she could see nothing in the blackness. Then a light shone behind the figure there, illuminating it, glinting off the pointed, raised ears and the slender, clawed hands. A long snout raised as if to scent the wind. A man's silver-shod feet thrust out from the stiff, jeweled skirt.

CeLa knew little of the gods of Egypt; Sumer had more than enough deities. This one she recognized, however: Anubis, jackal-headed god of the tombs and the dead. Had he come to seal her in this tomb? One claw reached out to touch her shoulder and she fell to her knees. "Lord Anubis, what am I that you have deigned to come before me? If I have sinned against you, it was all unknowingly." Her palms were slick against her face.

The god touched her bent head but she dared not look up. She felt chills rise along her spine as the claw drifted down her neck and around under her hair. Chills rose on her arms as well as laughter began, harsh and muted at the same time. Human fingers gripped her chin and forced it up. The clawed hand pushed the jackal mask up as the glittering eyes shone down into hers.

40

Princes of the Far Lands

"Many think that the jackal-headed one walks here and speaks with me; I am held with great reverence by Egypt." Oth lowered the mask and looked at CeLa, who leaned against the slimy wall as she tried to quiet her hammering heart.

"What do you want of me?" She forced herself to speak quietly.

"Come. I take it that you will not require more of the darkness?" Without waiting for her answer, he jerked her along the dimly lit corridor that stretched from her prison. She did not struggle even though she knew that he led her to a fate that might well be unbearable.

Finally they came to a long, cool hall with polished floors and blowing draperies that curtained off a small area where couches and cushions rested. The fresh air was more heady than wine. Oars slapped just outside and a soft cry arose from a boatman as a party of merrymakers drifted by. The Nile must be nearby. Platters of delicate cakes and ripe fruit stood close at hand, and a finely made pitcher held chilled wine.

"Kneel before me." It was a command.

"You are not worthy, for all that you hold yourself so high," she said, unable to resist the angry taunt.

Oth said, "Do not be predictable. That bores me. I thought one so exotic, coming from a far land, working as you did, would interest me. So far, however, you act as the others have. Will it disturb you to know that your lover still seeks Pharaoh's ear and sports with the women Lar offers him?"

CeLa forced herself to stare at him, her face unmoving. Oth shrugged and removed his robe, letting the ornamental skirt fall to the floor. His body was tall and straight but his sexual organs were tiny and shrunken between the long legs. He touched himself and his hands writhed.

"Kneel before me. You shall pleasure me with mouth and tongue. Then the blessed Nile just yonder will lull us into sleep."

CeLa shook her head numbly. He would not allow her to live knowing this about him and she could submit no longer. His hand barely seemed to move but she sprawled on the floor, her head ringing with pain.

"Henceforth, for you there is no will but mine. They savaged me, those brutes against whom I led the armies of Egypt, and yet my name is legend. When one has been in command of life and death, one cannot cease so swiftly. I was not judged able to fight due to my injuries but I am still a man! They marvel at the women I take. No one knows the extent of my wound for no one lives who can speak of it." His voice rose to a cry as he jerked her up by her hair.

CeLa saw spittle ring the edge of his mouth and the way his tongue darted back and forth in anticipation. He thrust his leg between hers and began to massage her breasts with rough hands while he muttered under his breath. Just then a large boat drifted by, lights and laughter mingling with the rush of water and the sound of oars held up. A particularly shrill laugh caused Oth to glance up, distracted. In that instant CeLa rammed up her knee with all her desert-bred strength as her fingers with their sharp nails clawed for his eyes. He fell heavily, his head cracking sharply against the edge of the marble table.

"Swine, how do you like the taste of pain?" CeLa jumped over him, ran out between the tall pillars, down the stone steps and plunged headfirst into the waters of the Nile.

The water was cold and swift as she was carried along. Her burst of strength was waning so that she went under several times, rising only to gasp and choke. Her breath came in sobs and her arms felt leaden. The next downward plunge might be her last. Sounds of music came to her and then several waves pulled her against the side of a drifting boat as another boat moved rapidly by. She clawed at the wood and cried out but her voice faded as she sank again. Fury rose in her that she should die this way.

Suddenly a torch illuminated the water around her. There was a splash and firm hands held her up until a rope ladder was tossed overboard. Then her rescuer hauled her up until willing hands could grasp her body. Moments later she lay on the deck, her ribs lifting and heaving with the effort and blessing of breath. A cup was put to her mouth. She gulped and the tart wine burned in her throat. Almost instantly the faces around her resolved into those of men and several women whose skins were much lighter than hers and whose hair was black and brown with several shades like new gold. A man leaned close and spoke in a strange, spiky-sounding language. She drew back a little and they saw her confusion.

"Take her to our sleeping room and make her comfortable. I will sit with her." The speaker's Egyptian was soft and accented as she sat down beside CeLa, who saw that the girl was dark and slender with very white skin and deep green eyes. "We will speak together when you are rested. Do not fear."

One of the men scooped her up into his arms and

carried her down a slight incline into an airy, cool chamber where she was settled on soft mats. Her exhausted senses could take no more even if she died for it. Her last thought was of the young woman adjusting smooth linens over her body and calling for water that the bruises might be washed clean.

When CeLa woke, the sun was already high and hot. The ship was moving slowly and sounds of laughter came from the deck. She turned her head on the pallet and looked at the same young woman, who sat fanning her.

"How do you feel? It was a near thing for you. What happened? Oh, I am Beca, wife to Xay, friend to Minos of Crete and commander of this trade expedition to Egypt. What is your name?" All her words ran together in her eagerness and her eyes sparkled with warmth.

"Forgive my wife. Her tongue runs before her." The tall, black-haired man who entered had gray eyes that seemed to pierce CeLa. He put his hand on Beca's shoulder and smiled down at her in a way that made the girl's heart twist. So, not long ago, had it been with Kir and herself. Now . . . but she could not face that just yet.

"I am CeLa of Sumer." She wondered just how much of herself to reveal to these kind people. "A traveler recently come to this land."

Xay said, "We are emissaries from Crete, an island far away from Egypt, and have come to establish a definite trade relationship here. We will have audience with Pharaoh in ten days and have been furnished with a great palace on the Nile. Rest and refresh yourself as our guest." He smiled at her again as he and Beca left the sleeping room.

CeLa lay very still, thinking that truly Inanna had been merciful. Strange indeed were the ways of the gods. These people were to meet directly with Pharaoh and were accepted as ambassadors, whereas she and Kir had tried for moons and been turned away. Crete must be a prosperous land, for the people were richly attired, the area where she rested well appointed and comfortable, the ship well settled in the water and her sails spread and carefully tended. She sighed, surprised that she remembered so much from the night before. She was safe now. Oth's power could not reach out to sacrosanct ambassadors.

In the next two days CeLa regained much of her strength and courage. She was given a separate room in the glittering Nile-side palace, one of those whose white beauty had earned Memphis the name of "White Walls." She had a wide view of the river and the sloping area to it that was covered with green plants and palms. The area itself was furnished with inlaid gold and ebony chairs and tables, hung with blue and crimson curtains fluttering between wide white columns. Scrolls and tablets as well as a variety of musical instruments awaited her touch, and servants were always in readiness for the slightest command.

CeLa and Beca talked at first of impersonal things. CeLa recalled Sumer and her heart longed for her own land even as she remembered that where Kir was, there also was her world. The island of Crete rose before CeLa as Beca spoke of it with pride and love. The rulers there were called Minos even as Pharaoh was called Pharaoh down the generations. The Cretans were a proud race, moving into the far seas, seeking trade and expansion, pursuing the arts and beauty. She said little of the religion and practices of Crete, and CeLa wondered at the pride that could speak so arrogantly of accomplishments without giving the gods due credit. One did not speak thus in Sumer lest they be angered; it seemed that Egypt was much the same.

CeLa had told Beca little at first and the other woman did not pry. But as they walked in the garden early one morning, Beca said, "The maidservant tells me that you cry aloud in the night and weep. A name. Kir. Kir. You may speak freely with me, you know." The soft wind ruffled Beca's hair and the palm fronds made shadows on her cheeks.

CeLa felt her guard go down and she was able to tell the tale more easily than she had at first thought possible. Her throat clogged with tears as she spoke of Oth and Kir's rejection of her that night. Pain came sharply to her and she felt the gauzy sense of detachment fade as life was restored. Beca put her arm around CeLa and murmured soothingly. CeLa had never had a true woman friend and she experienced a great warmth for this woman from a far land.

Beca said, "It took me long to win Xay, for my father wished me to wed another with more prospects in the court. Xay's fancy turned elsewhere once and I felt as you do now. I made sacrifice to the Mother and she was merciful." She talked on then in her artless way about the Mother Goddess who was called simply the Mother in Crete. CeLa thought, as she often did, that in Sumer Ninhursag was but another manifestation, as perhaps even Inanna might be. She showed Beca the little ebony goddess that was always with her. Beca smiled her slow smile. "The gods understand the ways of love and suffering, CeLa. I will invoke the Mother for you and your Kir. May I tell Xay of all that you have endured?"

CeLa smiled at her friend and felt the warmth between them. "I am truly in your debt, Beca. Do as you wish."

Once again time flowed for them as tranquilly as the great river. Beca and CeLa exchanged secrets, told tales of the men they loved and spoke often of Crete and Sumer. CeLa found that Kir's name came easily to her lips and she woke less often in the nights. Calmness came to CeLa and she was herself again, a proud woman with her way to make, a person of value in her own right.

Beca and CeLa were sitting on a bench beside the Nile one burning afternoon when Xay came to them, his face grim. He spoke to Beca but CeLa felt his words burn her. "I have done as you asked, lady mine. For love's sake I can refuse you nothing, but I cannot jeopardize our mission. Remember that." Beca's face went whiter still as he lifted her palm to his lips. CeLa rose to him, her head tilted. "The one called Kir waits yonder," he said. "Be prepared."

She felt as if a hammer blow had struck her when she looked in the direction where he pointed. They moved away swiftly as Kir approached. CeLa could only watch numbly, for she knew by the manner of his walk that he was angry. His long, tapering body, muscular shoulders, well-set head and bold stance were the same. Kir the Arrogant. He wore a simple tunic of white linen with a short sword at his side and the medal of Sargon at his throat. His hawk face was remote, his eyes cold.

Kir said, "I see that you are well. Your new friends are influential. Was Oth not enough for you?"

CeLa looked at this man with whom she had shared so much and loved so greatly, whose body had joined with hers in the heights of passion and with whom she had faced death. She burst out, "Oth told me they would kill you as you sat in the Hawk. His men surrounded you. I escaped at the risk of my life, which the Cretans saved. How could you believe such a thing of me, Kir? Have I shown myself so faithless?"

His lip quirked up in a gesture of disdain. "You are a woman, that is enough. What does it matter? All Memphis knows that Oth died of a head wound ten days after the girl storyteller vanished from the Hawk. His strange ways were well known, but he was greatly honored because of his generalship in the past. Some have vowed vengeance. I left the Hawk soon after you did and have earned my way working at the Nile docks. It was there that Xay's men found me. What do you want now?"

CeLa felt faint. She had not meant to kill Oth but she could not regret his death, only the consequences of it. She said, "Did you even search for me, Kir?"

A flush mounted to his bronzed cheekbones. "You had made your choice. By what right would I have interfered? Your life is your own. Mine is bound to Sargon of Akkad and I shall not rest until I have presented his name to Pharaoh."

CeLa's hurt burned in her that he had cared so little. She wanted only to wound him as she cried, "Always Kir the Arrogant! You worship Sargon and have given him your life! You are not capable of true caring! You are a tool to be used, a thing broken inside, a destroyer. Do you think that you will ever gain recognition from Pharaoh? You, a worker on the docks! Your king will have forgotten that you live." She laughed harshly, glad to see pain and hurt mingle in his dark face. Then a murderous anger blazed in his eyes. She could not stop her tongue now. It was blessed relief to let the words spew forth. "Destroyer, I said! Your first wife, Inta. Then Raba. Myself not least! Aye, you are admirable indeed. Bull-headed brute!"

His hands closed around her throat. His reserve had always hidden a violent temper, but this was the anger of battle. The world shifted and grew red. Then she was at his feet where he tossed her and his voice was breaking as he whispered, "Curse you! I could have killed you. How dare you try me so? How dare you link yourself with those I have loved, you who are as the dust beneath their feet!" He turned away and she saw his shoulders shake with emotion.

CeLa felt cold pervade her being. It had come as she had known it would. She was truly alone; if she did not live for herself she would not live at all. She rose and stood straight; though her body trembled her voice did not. It was, she thought later, as if Inanna filled her and told her what to say.

"We have said the unforgivable here this afternoon, Kir. Let it be forever done between us. The Cretans will help me and I shall seek another city in this land of Egypt where I may know peace. I owe nothing to Sargon, but for the sake of my promise and yours, I vow that you shall stand before Pharaoh in Sargon's name. After that I hope never to see you again."

Kir turned and looked at her; his eyes were flat, his voice as cold as hers had been. The violence was gone from him and now there was only a deep weariness. "Do that if you can, though I greatly doubt it, and I will erase the memory of this day. How can you understand the meaning of loyalty? In one thing, at least, we agree. Would that I had never met you, CeLa of Lagash."

He walked rapidly away toward the palace and CeLa watched him out of sight. Then she sat down on the bench and gave herself up to the bitter sobs that seemed to wrench her apart. Death might be more welcome than this anguish.

Gentle hands touched her shoulders and Beca's soft voice said, "Weep and wail as you must, CeLa. You will be the better for it. Just so deep is my love for Xay. I understand."

CeLa wept all the harder, hating herself for what she now planned, but knowing she could do nothing else. Because of Kir, she would betray her only friend.

41

Divine Horus, Ever-Living

Twelve days later, on the date chosen especially by the soothsayers and priests, the delegation from Minoan Crete was honored by the attention of the vizier, blood relative of Pharaoh himself. They were informed that the mighty one had agreed to see them so that gifts might be presented and fruitful discussion entered upon. This meeting took place in the anteroom of the ornate and beautiful palace, a palace so rich and rare that beside it the dwelling given to the Cretans was as nothing.

A rare gift was to be presented to Pharaoh and this required the services of certain slaves brought by the Cretans, who alone knew how to handle so delicate a rarity. Pharaoh, of course, would know since he was above all. So spoke Xay in the lengthy, convoluted language of the court. The vizier nodded gravely, looked at the ten assembled Cretans, one of whom was Beca, and at the hooded, bowed slaves of which there were four. Two of them were Kir and CeLa, smuggled in by Beca, who had finally given way before CeLa's pleas and anguish. Then the vizier gave the signal to begin.

They went through a succession of halls gilded and inlaid with gold, precious stones and woods. Everywhere men and women bowed before those fortunate enough to go before the face of the great one. CeLa kept her head bent as she had been instructed, noting that even the floor was polished and shimmering.

Finally they entered a wide room that was absolutely silent. CeLa risked a peep upward and saw magnificent walls covered with drawings of brilliantly colored scenes from wars, deserts, marshland, the netherworld and the immortal gods themselves at meat and drink. Pillars rose up to the high ceiling where they were banded in gold and circled in blue. In one place the floor was painted blue with tiny fronds of green seeming to drift on it. One might have been walking in the very Nile, for so it seemed to flow. Their garments whispered over the smoothness as the procession came to a halt and a voice boomed into the stillness, giving them pause.

"Lord of the Two Lands, Guardian of the Nile, Great One of Egypt, Divine Horus, Ever-Living, Pharaoh Piopi, welcomes the delegation of Minoan Crete."

CeLa barely heard Xay's voice as he went into the ceremonial oration proper at such times. She was intent on peering out from under the hood in order to see as much as possible. Kir stood behind her. She could sense his frustration and leashed expectations. The voice of her friend ceased and the rich, rolling tones of the vizier lifted. CeLa saw the crowd banked around the throne of pure white material, a stone she had never seen before. It seemed to create its own light and reflect it into the face of the divine being who sat there holding the symbols of Upper and Lower Egypt and whose head was crowned with the double crown, the vulture rising above it and mingling with the cobra. A restless, divine being no more than seven or eight years of age with a merry eye and tapping foot, a boy seeing a present and waiting impatiently for it.

They seemed to stand there for hours while the ceremony of greeting and compliments continued. CeLa's back ached and she wanted to sneeze, but they must not move. She still had no idea how she and Kir might introduce themselves without destroying Xay's mission. At this rate they would soon bow themselves out and all would be lost. She risked another glance at Pharaoh and saw the muscles of the small face struggle to suppress a yawn. So far he had not said one word or made a gesture except to smile benignly down at his servants.

CeLa slipped a finger down the length of cloth covering the Minoan gift and waited. She wondered if she dared; they could all lose their lives if displeasure resulted. Then she thought of the streets of Lagash and how the boys there loved a new toy. Was Egypt so different? She jabbed her fingernail hard into the soft flesh of the creature there and a furious bellow rose up in the very midst of the mellow tones of one of the court officials who was recounting the delight of Pharaoh in the gifts of the Cretans. Another bellow followed that one and then the sound of kicking came from the cage.

"Uncover that at once!" It was the voice of Pharaoh himself as he sat forward on the throne, his eyes dancing with interest, his voice that of unquestioned authority despite his youth.

CeLa jumped forward, Kir with her, and they whipped the covering off the cage, at the same time pushing back their hoods so that the differences in their coloring showed. CeLa spoke in Sumerian to the animal in the cage, which was in no mood for a language it did not understand and bellowed yet again. Xay turned horror-stricken eyes on the two of them and the Egyptians looked furious.

"Are they alive?" Pharaoh stood up and then moved down the steps of his throne, an unprecedented event and a great honor. He looked with a boy's enchantment at the miniature bull, which would come to midleg on a man but which had a full reddish coat and cruel horns with a temper to match. About

the same size was the small person who sat in another part of the cage. He was small boned, both
deaf and dumb, but with alert eyes and darting gestures. Kir loosed the top and he emerged to stand
lightly out on the floor in front of Pharaoh, where
he executed a perfect bow.

Xay stepped forward then and said in a voice that
did not shake, "These are the gifts of Minos of Crete
to Pharaoh of Egypt. The bull is one of those rari-
ties of our land, a thing that happens so seldom that
it is a gift of the gods when it does. The man is his
keeper, born of normal-sized parents in our mountains and given to Minos by them."

Pharaoh circled them with awe and delight, ex-
claiming, "These shall be the wonders of our court.
I am greatly pleased."

The onlookers sighed as if they were reeds in the
wind and relieved smiles touched the anxious faces
of the Cretans. Xay said, "Divine Horus, in our land
there is a ceremony that is performed between bull
and man in honor of the gods who made all things.
May we have your leave to show you?" At the en-
raptured boy's nod, he spoke swiftly in pantomime
to the boy-man, who lifted a hand in understanding.
"Now, great one, behold the bull dance of Crete."

All was still as the contest began, for it was that;
the bull trying to gore the dancer and he now fleeing, now turning to vault over the horns, leaping to
the back of the animal and poising there as it stood
still to look for him, seeming to slide, then rising
almost in front to bow and retreat. It was agility
and poetry and homage, the mingled beauty of man
and beast. At last the dancer caught the horns and
somersaulted over the bull's head, coming to land at
the side of it. The animal stopped, winded and blowing. The dancer bent before Pharaoh.

The boy stood bemused, a look of delight on his
expressive features. Kir looked at CeLa and she at

him. He nodded and went forward with her at his side. They knelt and held out the medal of Sargon and the little ebony goddess. Xay came to stand at their sides and CeLa breathed a sigh of thankfulness, for she knew that he had come to ally himself with them. She had not missed the glance of anger he had previously given Beca or the pain in the girl's face.

"Who are these people?" It was the voice of a Pharaoh, not a boy.

Xay said, "Ambassadors from a far land, Divine Horus, from a land of two rivers, ruled by a mighty king who extends all honor to you. They have a mighty tale to tell, full of trials and struggles. These things they offer you are all that is left of the load of offerings that were to be laid before you."

The vizier chose that inopportune moment to intrude by saying, "They were not registered as of your party, Lord Xay. I must protest."

Pharaoh rounded on him. "Silence, I will hear. these people. Further, I will receive them and the Cretans in private. Out!"

Private meant a gathering of about ten or so lords, CeLa noticed, but this must have been unprecedented because the faces of those around them were dark with surprise. She thought of Sargon, who walked among his people easily. This boy was hedged round with ceremony and she felt a stab of pity for the Lord of the Two Lands, then wanted to laugh at her own temerity.

Pharaoh was saying, "You have pleased me greatly, Xay, and have given me honor with your imagination. You shall ask what you will of me and it is yours." Then he said to CeLa and Kir, "Tell me of your king and of your land."

It seemed to CeLa that this was a dream indeed, for in the next few hours they ate and drank and talked in a setting that would have done the very gods themselves no shame. Kir told most of the tale,

embellishing it in the battle scenes, for one could
easily tell that that was where Pharaoh's fancy lay.
He was most fascinated by the stories of the land to
the south of Egypt, called Yam, Land of Ghosts and
Punt in the lore. He demanded more knowledge of
the lands of Sumer and Akkad and swore that he
would send messages to Sargon in his struggle for
consolidation. "Of course," he said loftily, "this was
done in Egypt long ago, but we are the center of the
world, after all."

Kir said gravely, "Our king will be greatly honored by the advice of Pharaoh."

The boy said, "The small man, do you think there
are such in these lands? How I should like to know!"
His face was suddenly autocratic.

CeLa said, "Doubtless there are, Great One." Her
comment was idle and she sipped at her wine, surely
the best in Egypt.

Pharaoh stood up suddenly and called for the vizier. The company dared not rise, for his face was
dark and they did not know what this portended.
The man came hurrying in, his bearing agitated,
for he was not used to being exiled from the presence of his ruler. This was reserved for underlings.

"Fetch the scribes at once. An expedition must be
sent to Punt. No, two expeditions. I want a dwarf
like this one. Send word to Herkhuf who travels there
now. Send it by land. Tell him my wishes. He will
know how to satisfy them." He turned to Kir and
motioned him closer. "I can only ask you to grant
my request. Take my ship down the great water into
Punt, find me a dwarf, extend my boundaries. You
shall know the gratitude of Pharaoh, for I will enter
into such trade agreements with your king as will
make him the wonder of his lands, and your own
cause will be greatly advanced with him."

Kir smiled and CeLa sensed the joy within him.
"Right willingly will I do as Pharaoh asks."

CeLa felt her blood chill. She was not deluded into thinking that the Cretans would help her again. Xay's contempt was obvious as his eyes rested on her. Pharaoh could as easily have expelled them all from the land or imprisoned them for misbehavior before his godhood. Kir was lost to her; indeed, she wanted no more of him. She must leave Memphis by stealth and make her way to another city where she might be able to work as a scribe and earn her own way. She lifted her head, for Pharaoh was speaking once more.

His dark eyes met hers calmly but there was laughter in them. She knew he understood who had loosed the bull so that it would bellow. "You too will go on this expedition, CeLa of Sumer and Lagash. I treasure your gift of the dark goddess to me. Her hand is clearly over you."

Kir cried, "I will not have this woman on the ship. She cannot go!"

The others gasped in horror but CeLa felt a swift rush of gladness and exultation sweep over her like a great wind. She remembered that Kir was wont to speak his mind before Sargon, who tolerated it. Not so here.

Pharaoh's voice was as soft as the wind on the Nile but all the mighty power of this land of Egypt was behind it. "You do not speak so to the Lord of the Two Lands. I have commanded that the woman go and so she does. All here have heard my voice and will obey. You have accepted my request, Kir of Sumer and Akkad. If you disavow it, even so will I renounce my promises to you for your king."

Kir bowed his head but his stance was rebellious. The words jerked from him and CeLa alone knew the effort they cost him. "Forgive me, Great One. I will do as I have promised." As he lifted his eyes, they caught those of CeLa and she saw the baffled anger that boded ill for her. She gave him look for look.

Pharaoh said, "Go now. This has been a most in-teresting day." His boy's laughter rose once more in his court.

It did not take long to ready the ship, *Triumph*, but the selection of the crew was another matter. The men must have stout hearts in order to venture into the dangerous far lands; still, it was a great op-portunity and they flocked to Kir and his Egyptian co-commander, Entet. Kir spent much time at the docks and in council with mapmakers and scholars. CeLa seldom saw him but when she did, he was un-failingly cold and polite. She herself was already pre-pared, for the young Egyptian maid who was to attend her arranged simple tunics and sandals, thin robes and hair ornaments into chests of wood and hide within the first few days, leaving nothing else to be done. She spoke little to CeLa and the girl was conscious of dislike but it did not seem to mat-ter. Time hung heavily for CeLa now, for though they still remained in the palace of the Cretans, she saw Beca no more.

Beca's sad message had read, "I am forbidden by Xay to resume our friendship because I placed our mission in jeopardy. He feels that I was tricked by your passion for Kir and believes that you would do anything for him, that you used me. I love and obey him in all things. He serves his Minos as Kir his Sargon. We are women and understand the ways of the heart. I will petition the Mother Goddess un-ceasingly for you, that your Kir may come to learn that he loves you as you love him. Dear CeLa, let the bearer of this message teach you of our art, the bull dance of Crete. We do it in honor of the Mother, who will watch over you and your Kir because you too honor her. I can accept no reply to this message."

CeLa wept bitter tears at first but she knew it was no more than she deserved, and she was grateful for Beca's kind understanding. Had it been Xay, she knew Beca would have done the same. This did not ease her sense of loss but she now knew that she and Kir were welded together in a bond that would last as long as she, CeLa, lived. For a time she had deluded herself into thinking otherwise. With this new realization she felt some peace.

The little maidservant spoke no Egyptian and CeLa no Cretan but they progressed swiftly as CeLa closed her mind to all else and renewed her body's agility by learning the bull dance. She fell so many times on her back and buttocks that they seemed permanently bruised. Her ankles, legs and arms ached so much at night that she could hardly sleep. Ia, her teacher, could turn easily over the likeness of a bull that they had erected of reeds and palms and float downward to land on her feet, moving gracefully with her hands uplifted in the free gesture that their gods loved. CeLa knew that she could never attain such skill. She knew further that much of this dance was religious ritual. But as the days passed, her determination and her body matched each other until finally two bull images had been beaten down by her falls and twists. She learned to abstain from self-pity and her wound of the mind was healing. By the time she had grown adept enough to leap, twist and throw herself over the horns, then roll and slide free to stand erect, two moons had passed and the time of sailing was at hand.

CeLa would long remember that early dawn when they boarded the *Triumph* as mists rose from the Nile. The tall ship moved gently, her sails curving in the wind, stamped as they were with the lotus and the hawk. Officials and priests stood close by as they called on the gods to bless this expedition. The sun gleamed brilliantly on an ornate closed litter surrounded by guards and all present knew that Divine Horus, Ever-Living, was among them, though no word was said. A final hymn of blessing and praise

to Amun-Ra, chief among the great ones, and to
Pharaoh, god himself, was sung by a chorus of beautiful women. Then the wind came strongly, setting
the waves to dancing and belling out the sails of the
ship. CeLa thought of Inanna, for this was her own
omen. Kir's brooding gaze met her eyes and she
averted them hastily. Then all thought faded as the
great ship of Pharaoh spread her sails, drifted out
into the life-giving Nile, turned and set forth on the
long journey to unknown lands.

42

Destroyers of the Flesh

CeLa lost track of the days as the river gave onto the sea and they moved out of the sight of land and voyaged on the seemingly endless waters. She gained her own measure of peace from the rolling surfaces that varied with each glance. The Egyptian girl who was to have been her maidservant had not come and CeLa was glad of the solitude of her existence now. She was familiar with those legends that stated that a woman on board a ship was ill luck; thus, she walked the decks in the early morning only. Much of her time was spent in the enclosed area prepared for her privacy. Here she studied Egyptian, perused the scrolls they carried, looked at the maps that excited her imagination and practiced the movements of the bull dance. Sometimes she lay just outside the door for coolness and watched the stars wheel overhead, seeming to move with the gentle motion of the *Triumph*. Kir did not come near her; if they happened to meet in the dawn walks, he spoke her name civilly and passed on. They might have been strangers to each other.

The *Triumph* docked several times in the next turn of the moon and expeditions were sent out into the barren lands, returning empty-handed. She now heard some of the men grumbling that the ship had somehow incurred the anger of the gods, who withdrew the riches of the lands from them in retaliation. Sailors often talked this way and she was not disquieted by it now. She was, however, aware of being watched during the few times that she walked about. It reminded her of the manner in which Oth had marked her movements and trickles of fear chilled her in spite of the growing heat.

One morning she woke to see that the ship was drawn up to another strange shore from which mountains rose in the distance and slopes lifted in gentle green waves. The shore was rocky and barren with little hills of sand here and there. The oarsmen idled at their posts; soon enough they would have to work. A small contingent of armed men patrolled the deck and another waited on the shore. A man was working on a strip of sail nearby and CeLa went up to him, knowing that the sailors would know, possibly to the last action, what had been planned.

He turned an uncomprehending face to her questions, however, and CeLa did not feel that she could pursue the issue, although she knew that her Egyptian was certainly good enough for comprehension.

"He is both deaf and dumb but a good worker for all that." A tall man polishing a spear handle stood nearby and watched her with shadowed eyes.

CeLa held her anger back; he had let her struggle with a mute and only now volunteered information. "What has happened? Why are we stopped? What land is this?" She remembered that in all the maps and tales of Punt, the Red Sea widened and would narrow later on when one might then pass out into an unknown sea. At the narrowing place was one of the fabled places where treasure and goods might be obtained. Here too was the place where the expedition might be mounted to go inland. If they were indeed at such a place, she intended to go with them. These thoughts passed swiftly through her mind as her eyes snapped.

"Very early this morning we saw natives floating

ahead of us in a strange make of ship decorated with what appeared to be feathers; they glittered with some sort of shining stones that they say are favored at the court of Pharaoh. We gave the sign of peace but they fled before us and we followed to their landing place; a group went after them inland."

"Do not distract the men from their work. A woman is annoying enough on board as it is. Return to your sleeping area."

CeLa swung round to see Kir standing behind her, his hawk face impassive, his eyes flashing. His skin was even darker in the sunlight and his lean body sent shivers over her arms. He saw her reaction and his nostrils spread. She blurted, "I too am part of this expedition, Kir, as by Pharaoh's wish. I record the journey as a scribe. Do not think to order me so."

The sailor was listening avidly and several others had drawn near at the sound of her clear voice. Kir caught her arm and jerked her into the comparative privacy of one of the areas housing their weapons.

"Be silent, foolish one. The men are restive enough as it is. They talk and mutter among themselves and grow still when I approach." His warm breath fanned her cheek and his voice was curiously gentle.

CeLa felt her senses swim at his nearness. Sweat beaded her forehead as her nipples rose under the sturdy brown tunic she wore. "I did not think. I will be cautious in the future."

"See that you are." He lifted one hand as if to touch her face and then stepped back sharply. He strode away rapidly, calling to several men to work more swiftly for there was much to do.

He did not hate her, that much was evident. CeLa felt gladness permeate her very being until she wanted to sing with it. She forced herself to study the papyrus scrolls over and over for calmness; nothing must jeopardize her with Kir now. His dark face rose up over the descriptions of trade expeditions, goods taken and bartered, battles fought.

The cry came late the next morning. It was a shriek of pain and fear that shook CeLa to the bones. The cabin had been very peaceful as the *Triumph* rocked slightly on the water and reflections from it flickered on the ceiling. She jumped up as the cry came again and now she could distinguish some of the words, which were almost incoherent.

"Betrayal, death, betrayal! All taken! We are lost!" A low sobbing lifted on the last words.

She heard Kir's voice questioning and calming then rising in horror as well.

She slipped outside and went to the rail. Several of the soldiers who had been on the expedition stood around Kir and those who had remained on the ship. She saw that they were shaking and pale under their dark skins, the ravages of battle on them; some were bleeding from unstanched wounds. Wine was brought and people came to tend them while Kir conferred with the others. CeLa stayed hidden as well as she could, but no one was paying any attention to her and she could understand nothing of what had happened. She could only assume that they had gone into some sort of combat and lives had been lost, but it seemed strange that experienced soldiers should so completely lose their nerve. She went back to her papyrus scrolls but the tales had lost any savor they might have had and she puzzled over the problem, glad enough to have something to divert her mind.

The youngest of the guards brought food and wine to her much later, saying as he did so, "The commander does not feel that you should go out among the men, lady. He asks that you remain here." His eyes were sympathetic and she wondered if he thought they had had a lover's quarrel.

"What happened earlier? I saw some of the men

return in a battered condition. Have we been attacked?"

The young man's face grew pale. "We came farther
down the sea than many have come and did not
stop at several of the usual places for trade, since
Pharaoh's express command was for new and different lore and folk. We thought that those encountered yesterday, those who fled from us, might either
be such or give us some idea of what lay ahead."

He paused for breath and CeLa saw the shine of
fear in his eyes. Her own flesh had begun to creep
as if she knew what might follow. She knew that he
talked as much to bolster his own waning courage as
to answer her questions. Her own courage might falter in the face of the unknown.

"The expedition that was sent out was captured
and taken away by these natives, who were very tall
and cadaverous, yet decorated with those jewels the
court loves that are so rare. The five who escaped
say that they eat human flesh and that our comrades
were regarded as not being weighty enough. They
are brave men and well known to me. I cannot believe
they would show such fear under a normal condition
of battle or raid." His face flushed and he shut his
mouth abruptly; he knew that he had spoken too
much already but the quick gulp of wine had been
heartening. Now the glow was fading.

CeLa stared at him in horror and her throat grew
dry. He turned quickly and left. She guessed that
no more information would be coming from that
quarter for a time. Hurriedly she lifted the wine to
her lips and drank, but it did not warm her, for she
was suddenly very much afraid.

A contingent of soldiers, Kir at their head, left
in the late afternoon, armed and ready. There were
few left to guard the ship but they were placed so
that any approach could be easily covered. CeLa wondered that Kir would take soldiers away at such a

time but it was possible that those who had escaped
could lead them directly back to rescue the others.
There was no longer a guard at her door and no
one paid any attention to her as she walked the deck
around her cabin.

The night air was fresh and cool now. A great fire
burned below on the rocks, raising a smoky, wet scent
to her nostrils. The sail hung limp but she saw that
some of the oarsmen were ready at their posts. She
had put on a belt that held two sharp daggers, and
a short sword curved through it as well. A short cloak
billowed back from her shoulders and her hair was
securely wound around her head.

CeLa had no idea how long she stood there watching and waiting. It seemed that she could not go
back inside; all her instincts told her that something
was about to happen. So it proved. The moon was
low in the sky when the first sounds of approaching
feet caused the men on the ship to ready their weapons. CeLa's own hand was on her dagger. She was
as ready as she could be in the circumstances. The
column came into view, the fifteen or so men who
had gone with Kir and Kir himself. Even at a distance they looked worn and exhausted; she guessed
that the search had been hard and long. Lines
grooved Kir's face, which was hard and set in the
harsh light of the fire.

They came on board and Kir lifted his hand for
silence. His voice was flat with exhaustion as he said,
"I grieve to report that our comrades could not be
found. Those who escaped could not rechart the way
and we dare not venture too far inland lest we be
divided and become good targets for those who may
have that very aim. In the morning scouts will be
sent out by threes to investigate the interior and report back. Once their camp is located, we will invade."

They dispersed in silence; there was nothing more
to be said. Kir leaned over the rail and looked into
the dark distance, his face haunted. CeLa felt her
heart quicken. For all that had passed between them,
she knew that she would never be wholly free of
him, nor he of her. Wordless sympathy rose in her
and she felt it flow outward. Almost as if he felt
it, Kir looked upward and saw her. His expression
did not change nor did he make any move, but CeLa
knew that he sensed her feelings and something of
the hard core of her relaxed. In this danger there
was no room for personal confrontation.

CeLa sank down where she was, for she could not
bear to go back into the cabin. It was fairly certain
that no one would sleep this night, for tension mounted high. She must have dozed, for when she lifted
her eyelids again it was faintly light in the eeriness
of near dawn and the fire had burned down. The
water lapped at the sides of the ship and shone gray.
The hills on one side seemed to rise to the sky, the
fading green a smudge only.

She looked up and her scream split the dawn sky.
Instantly the ship was pandemonium as soldiers and
others alike rushed to their places. On the rocky sand
at the edge of where the actual heights began stood
a party of men who were very tall and so slender that
she could see their ribs. Their dark hair was dressed
high and wound around bones that also hung in
necklaces and were bound around their waists. They
were heavily armed—all except for two younger men
who bore a reed basket between them as they advanced cautiously toward the ship. In the water behind them and to the side of the *Triumph* were several small boats filled with warriors.

Kir called for the men to assemble beside him and
they rushed to obey. The oarsmen were commanded
to be ready in case the ship needed to be moved.

CeLa felt her heart hammer within her chest but she jerked out her short sword and prepared herself for battle.

"Men of Egypt!" The voice was heavily accented and the syllables thick, the words emphasized wrongly, but the sense of them was easily understood in the silence. "You seek your friends. Do so no longer, for here they are."

The young natives advanced and poured out the contents of the basket in the sand, then retreated. It was a pile of bones, some remnants of hair, leather gear, a broken sword or two and some sandals. What horrified CeLa, whose vision was very keen, was the sight of some six skulls shining picked and white in the light. Kir's upheld hand held the men back and he motioned for silence as the native continued:

"Word of your coming went before you in the ways of our people. Let other lands do as they will, we will have none of you amongst us. Look not for your commander; he was a brave man and I have partaken of that bravery. You will find his skull there. Take your ship and those who remain and go toward the great sea. You shall not pass here. There are enough of us to destroy you. Tell others."

"There are other ships with us who will destroy you. You cannot think to escape the justice of Egypt." Kir tried to keep his voice expressionless but horror rang in it.

The rays of the rising sun touched the speaker, who was the tallest and gauntest of those assembled, and turned him to a sheet of living flame. He wore the glittering stones that Raba had favored, the most precious of those at the court of Pharaoh. He called out, "You live by our wish. If you turn back, you will be taken and killed. This way there is a chance of life. Your men are dead; if you return, give Egypt our message. The choice is yours. When the sun is high, if you are still here, you will be ours. We watched as you led your men out in the search. Do you think we are fools?"

Behind the ship the small boats loaded with warriors increased. A low chanting began and rose in volume. The men began to mutter and move about even as the group of natives and their chieftain turned and went back into the rocks.

"Let us go and take them. Egyptians can match natives any day!"

"Murderers. Cannibals. They should be killed slowly and lingeringly."

"Death to them!"

"Take them!"

Kir lifted his hands. "The final decision is mine and I have made it. We sail for the great sea within the hour."

The men cried out in fury, some brandishing their weapons at him, others actually threatening. He waited until the first surge of anger was done and they stood shuffling their feet and muttering. They would never have dared behave so before their own captain. Egyptian law was strict on this point.

"Those in the small boats alone could easily overwhelm us and destroy the ship. Once in captivity we would share the fate of our comrades. My decision holds. Hoist the sail!"

Some of the muttering rose up to CeLa as she heard the anger rise again, but this time they dared not voice it openly, for Kir looked savage indeed as he stood there, sword in hand.

One soldier, bolder than the rest, cried out, "But we are of Egypt and mightier than any native horde. I say fight lest we shame our dead fellows."

His mates roared agreement. One said under his breath, "The commander is not of ours and a coward to match."

"Obey me! This instant!" It was the voice of the commander of the armies of Sargon who called out.

The men responded and the sail rose majestically in the freshening air. The oarsmen plied themselves diligently and the *Triumph* moved in defeat toward the great gulf of the unknown.

43

Revenge of the Dead

The ship was filled with tension as they continued the journey. They were in the gulf now, having passed the narrow straits and rocks that signaled the last known land. The maps and tales were silent after this point, although they hinted at a paradise world beyond the sea. The men were openly sullen and even rebellious. Kir watched constantly as he walked among them with the four or five who were loyal to him. Only the Egyptian obedience to authority held them in check. For many days after they left the glittering cannibals, fires burned on the horizon and at the shoreline when the ship passed. Well-armed natives stood waiting as they cried defiance.

CeLa watched Kir grow gaunt and weary from his vigils but there was nothing she could do and she dared not risk his anger at such a time. Sometimes she wept in the night for all that they had shared in Egypt, but she did not try to tell herself that she no longer loved Kir. Now she prayed for his happiness and safety before her own, hoping that Inanna, the goddess of all love, would be merciful.

CeLa woke the next night with a start of fear. A bearded man was bending over her with ropes in his hand. Before she could cry out, he had thrust a gag in her mouth, bound it tightly and secured her arms behind her back. Then he gave a low whistle and two others entered her sleeping area, which was lit by the sliver of the fading moon. Her captor thrust

her aside savagely and she fell to her knees before
the tallest man, one she knew only as Soh, for he had
been mentioned in the papers of the voyage as an excellent navigator. He was black-bearded and savage
in appearance, with a huge scar that ran the length
of his face and almost split his nose.

He spoke now in a whisper. "Ah, we are well met,
bitch woman. Oth was our friend and general, worth
forty of any woman who ever lived. You slew him
and then curried the favor of Pharaoh, who is too
young to honor those of the past. We vowed to kill
you, for you would never have been properly punished in Egypt." The battered face twisted with hatred. "We shall be honored for this deed among the
soldiers who fought with Oth."

CeLa was already numbed by the tight bonds and
could not struggle as he swung her up in his arms
and carried her outside, his men following down a
ramp, along a narrow passageway and yet another
until a small open door was reached. They were near
the water line and she saw that a little boat bobbed
there with another silent watcher beside it. CeLa
was sick with fear; it seemed that life would end here,
all her battles and trials for nothing. She wanted to
live so fiercely that she shook.

Soh laughed softly. "You are afraid. That is good.
So did Oth long for more years that were denied him.
You go bound into this boat, which will drift on the
sea for many days before you die of hunger and thirst
Water and food will tantalize you as you die."

"Stand aside from the woman or you die this instant." The cold voice paralyzed them all. Kir stood,
sword at the ready, in the narrow way just behind
Soh.

"Commander! Leave us and all this is forgotten.
We are four to your one." The man who had bound
CeLa spoke quietly, reasonably. "Even now the men
cry against you. You cannot battle everyone."

"Obey me." Kir stabbed the point of the sword at Soh and blood trickled down his chest. "The woman is mine."

"Then die with her!" Soh ducked and hit Kir with all the force of a thrown rock so that he fell heavily. Then they were upon him, binding him and holding him erect as he gasped for breath.

CeLa forgot their terrible circumstances. Kir had fought for her; she would die with that knowledge against her heart. Their eyes met in communication of the warmth that had returned to them and she felt her courage rise.

Kir said, "Let her go. Use me to vent your anger. Oth was a degenerate, all know it. You are fools."

The black-bearded man whispered, "This is the grace of the gods. We are rid of them both and can return to Egypt with tales of a great battle in which many were lost. We will attack those natives too."

Kir strained at his bonds and CeLa could see the dark harshness of his face in the pale light. "Let the woman live, I pray you." Soh slammed his heavy hand against Kir's face and he fell backward, stunned.

They picked CeLa up and threw her into the little boat that was used for rowing into land from ships anchored out at sea. Her body hit heavily and she shuddered with pain. Death by drowning would be preferable to dying by inches in the burning sun while bound, she thought dazedly. Then Kir landed on top of her, almost knocking the breath out of her chest. He had yielded up his pride to ask for her life, Kir the Arrogant who had hated her.

Soh kicked the boat into the water and called in a low voice, "The shade of Oth will be at rest, for he is avenged!" Low laughter followed them as the oarsmen moved the *Triumph* away in the dawn light.

The sun rose and blasted them with its heat. CeLa fought her bonds but it did no good. The gag was choking in her dry mouth and feeling had long since left her arms. Thirst was a raging beast within her. She saw the flesh rise red and hot on Kir's arms and wondered if they had killed him. How long would it take her to die? She cursed the plotters in her mind.

A husky voice made her jump. "Turn yourself so that your hands are near my mouth. Praise to Inanna that they did not gag me."

Tears of delight sprang to her eyes as she looked at Kir's bruised face with the shadows under his eyes. They still lived! Surely there was hope now!

It was full dark by the time they were both free and had drunk from the little water so mockingly provided. They were exhausted from the effort and their skins were parched, their lips swollen. Already CeLa had begun to feel light-headed and foolish. She said, "Kir, I thank you for your attempt to save my life. I know the effort it cost you. Will you let me tell you what happened with Oth before we descend into the dark world?"

He said softly, "I will listen."

She spoke slowly, for she was already drained but the accounts must be settled. When the tale was done, she sighed and lay back. Kir touched her hand and she felt the power of it.

"CeLa, nothing has been of value in this life except my service to Sargon. We are as we are. I believe you but it does not matter. We must make our peace with the gods, for I think we will die soon. We shared much and I do not regret it."

Even with her body parched dry and her brain reeling, CeLa could think of their passion and mourn its loss. He smiled at her and it was as though they had just met, a man and a maiden, the passionate, fearful, loving, hating past yet to come. "Well met, CeLa of Lagash."

For what seemed the last time, she smiled at the man she loved. "Well met, Kir of Sumer and Akkad."

* * *

CeLa seemed to float up from the depths of a blue green sea into a warm, blowing world filled with soft voices. Her limbs moved in fragrant oil and liquid trickled into lips that were normal size again. Kir was there too, his eyes filled with warmth and concern, his dark skin drawn tight over the high cheekbones. She drifted in coolness and rose again to the surface. He was still there.

"CeLa, how are you? Do you know me?" Never had he spoken so gently to her.

CeLa heard her own voice rise thin and shaky. "Is this the netherworld? Death is no fearsome thing then, and you are with me still."

"Aye, CeLa. We have been rescued by this ship from a mighty city near the Indus River, Mohenjodaro. I am with you still and we live." He leaned over her and touched her face.

"We live." She smiled mistily up at him as the hammer of sleep smote her.

Her strength came back rapidly in the days that followed and her skin regained its normal smooth sheen. She had had a fever of the sun, Kir told her, that raged for two days before they were rescued, and he himself had been slightly afflicted. They had been placed in a quiet, sheltered area on the ship that gave them privacy and yet allowed them to watch the general activity. Kir knew that the language was close to that of Sumer; Sumerian ships had once traded with Mohenjo-daro in the days when the ships of both lands ventured out on long voyages. The captain of the ship was a dark, slender man in his early thirties called Ndar. It was he who spoke most often with Kir in the combination of languages that they managed to work out.

Kir told her, "They call their city Daro and regularly send out ships to ply the coasts. This one was blown far out in the sea by a storm and was forced to put in at an island for repairs. Disease broke out and decimated the crew, forcing them to remain there until it ceased. They have been gone for many moons and are now returning slowly because of the damages."

CeLa was thankful for this quiet time when Kir was friendly toward her and they breasted the blue waters of the great sea toward a city only vaguely recorded in the annals she had studied. Kir taught her some of the rudiments of the language of Daro and she had never been so grateful for her own aptitude for languages as now. She wandered freely over the ship, which was much like those of Sumer with its curved front and back and exterior of reeds that made it skim across the water as the sail spread wide. The crewmen smiled at her and spoke too rapidly for her understanding, but she knew their words were complimentary. Kir had told her that the men of Daro were taller than the average Sumerian, swarthy and clean-shaven in the city, but bearded here. Kir spent much of his own time working in the riggings of the ship or taking turns at the oars. It was a comfortable time and they spoke little of the past.

Their peace was shattered one afternoon when Kir came up behind CeLa as she stood watching the wide, changing expanse of sea. Her hair had regained its blue-black brilliance and streamed behind her in the freshening wind while her scant tunic was molded to her body. She turned at his step and saw that his dark eyes were hooded, his face hard, all friendliness gone.

"What is it, Kir?" Her voice shook though she fought to control it.

"Will you be my wife?" The words seemed forced from him in jerks.

Had Kir asked such a question in Egypt, there would have been only one answer and that given in joy and gladness. Now she must be wary. "Why do you ask it? Kir, what is the matter?"

He blew out his breath in a sigh of relief. "Neither of us wishes such a bond, of course. I am glad that you feel as I do. When I spoke with Ndar yesterday, he gave me warning. When he left Daro moons ago, a new ruler had taken the throne by right of combat. This ruler had risen from the ranks of the armies and had spoken of conquering the lands around Daro. This was in marked contrast to the policy of other rulers who had preferred to remain in their city and render it fair by peaceable trade."

CeLa did not trust her voice. "What does all this have to do with us?" She was surprised that she sounded quite normal to herself even as she ached with hurt. Why could he not have meant it and wanted her in love? Had they not shared much together?

The coldness had left his eyes and she saw that he was greatly relieved. "Simply this: there is no way of knowing how foreigners will be dealt with. There might be a royal welcome; there might be imprisonment. It may be fortunate or unfortunate to be from Sumer. One thing is certain, Ndar says. It is that marriage is respected in Daro, but a woman has not even the smallest vestige of the rights she takes as a matter of course in Sumer. You might be made a slave. We cannot know. He is my friend now and has suggested that he wed us, as is his right, for he is also a priest of the Mother, the great goddess of Mohenjo-daro. We are also invited to remain at his house as his guests for as long as we will until it can be determined how matters will go."

"Where are we to be from if not Sumer?" So great was her stress that she could say nothing else.

Kir said, "From an obscure tribe on one of the islands to which the ship was blown. We were fishing and were swept away. Our rescuers naturally had to return to Daro as swiftly as possible."

CeLa knew that marrying Kir was the wise course.

"We must be thankful that the captain has saved us," she said.

"When we return to Sumer, you will be set free to pursue your own life. Marriage in the eyes of the gods of Sumer is not valid unless by their ceremonies."

"On such terms I will accept your offer. For both our sakes."

Kir said, "I knew you would be sensible. I do not like this either, but there is really no choice. You will understand that we must behave as though we were truly man and wife."

"Of course." CeLa was proud of her calm and knew that she must hold on to it. They could still be friends and she would put the love that could not be quenched safely aside, knowing that some things are not decreed by the gods. With that thought, peace came to her and she was able to nod quietly at Kir's next words.

"We are but a few days from Daro. The captain awaits us even now. I felt sure that you would be agreeable."

"I am ever concerned for my life, Kir, even as you."

CeLa went to the little shelter of reeds where the only other tunic she had, one taken from the smallest of the crew members but still too large for her, was hung. She put it on, washed her face and confined her hair in one long braid that she coiled around her head. Thus she went to her wedding that was no wedding.

CeLa and Kir, both unsmiling, stood before Ndar, who now wore a circlet of gold around his head and a flowing white robe emblazoned with embroidered eyes. He was both impressive and a little frightening as he stood there, intoning words that had little meaning for either Kir or CeLa, for this was the ceremonial language of the servants of the goddess of Daro.

Ndar said in Sumerian, "We are all emissaries and
servants of the great goddess while on this earth. I
am privileged to serve her in the world of men. By
her power and that of your own gods, by the gods
without number, I join you in this life and beyond.
Serve her well."

"I swear it." Kir's words were firm as he turned to
CeLa.

"I swear it."

"Her hand be ever over you. Her power be yours
and your lives hers."

Kir and CeLa crossed their hands over their chests
and bent gravely before him as the goddess's representative. He lifted his arms wide and spoke long
in his own ceremonial ritual. CeLa felt a chill run
across her shoulders and down her back. Just so had
Sirna stood while seeking the goddess before the actual sacrifice in the pits of Lagash so long ago. Memory pulled at her and she told herself she was being
foolish.

"Go now." Ndar was again the captain, Kir's
friend. His eyes were laughing and warm. "This marriage is our secret, my friends. We will guard it well.
Others shall believe you long wed."

That night CeLa and Kir lay together in the little
shelter as they had not done since the days of her
illness.

Kir reached for CeLa but she drew back and said,
"There is no quiet. All the others will know. I do
not want to."

She could sense him gritting his teeth in the semi-
darkness. "Do not be foolish. We must behave as
though we are truly wed and have been for some
time. You are not normally so reticent."

How could she say that she wanted some kind and
gentle words, no more talk of self-preservation? That,
whether the words were true or false, tonight was
the first night she would be a wedded wife and

surely this was a time to remember. Why could he
not pretend with her? His hand moved as he pulled
her hips toward him and this time she yielded.

He spread her legs apart and mounted her without
preliminaries. His hands found her breasts and
rubbed awkwardly across their erectness, but he did
not pursue that past sweetness, nor did he kiss her.
There was no waiting for her wet readiness. He
thrust deeply into her and pumped hard, bruising
her flesh and seeming to tear her with the speed of
his action. He held her shoulders firmly as he rode
her and she could not relax to move with him. It
was the taking of any woman, the action a man does
to relieve his lust, especially when he has been without a woman for a time.

Kir twisted in a brief spasm and rolled away from
her. He was almost instantly asleep. CeLa fumed by
his side, her own passion rising now that he was
done. She raised her hand to touch him and then
drew back. If he would come to her, it must be at
his own volition and at his own time. She would not
beg his favors. Her flesh crawled at the idea of simply being the receptacle of his release, especially when
she remembered the honey passion of times past. Then
she lay back. He was still Kir the Arrogant.

A half moon and more passed. Kir took her several
more times, always coldly and quickly, but she did
not protest. He must exorcise his own demons. He
was cool to her by day and left her alone much of
the time, for now they were well into the mouth of
the river called the Indus. Far mud banks, waves of
green reeds and distant hills came into view as they
moved along. They had passed several ships flying
the sickle insignia that their own ship bore and CeLa
deduced that they must not be far from the city itself.

One morning she woke to the reduced speed of the
ship. When she went outside, she saw a clump of
brown and white buildings on the horizon. Marshes

stretched around them on every side. The crew, Kir among them, was working to guide the ship through the treacherous river currents. Ndar stood watching them and spoke to CeLa as she came near.

"Soon you will see that jewel of the Indus, Mohen-jo-daro, that peerless city. I have been long from my family—my three daughters and my wife, Utis. It may be that she has given me up for dead." His warm eyes smiled into hers. "I pray nightly for you and your husband, that your marriage may be fruit-ful and both of you happy."

CeLa felt a faint chill in spite of the hot sun, a sensation that always warned her of danger. She pushed the thought back and returned his smile. "You were truly sent by the gods, Ndar. I know that the great goddess is graced by such a servant."

The brilliant light seemed to darken as if great wings had been momentarily spread over them. Then one of the crew called, "Captain Ndar! Can you come now?" He moved away and CeLa rubbed her arms with numb fingers. The shadow drifted away and Mohenjo-daro rose on the horizon.

44

Until the Knell Has Struck

Daro was a red-brown city that seemed part of the plain and the river at the lower levels. Great buildings near the water rose white and sparkling to reflect the sunlight. The docks swarmed with people and goods. Ships bearing the sickle emblem moved slowly on the river. Palm trees and flowering shrubs were everywhere in the hot light. Ndar's ship docked at a special place in the harbor and they saw that ramps were placed for the easy unloading of goods, materials and other cargo.

A contingent of soldiers, all wearing the sickle device, surrounded the men and Ndar as they came ashore. CeLa and Kir, well muffled in large cloaks, stood well in the rear. The captain spoke heatedly with the leader of the soldiers, who smiled and gestured in what appeared to be sympathy. CeLa could catch only scattered words for they spoke too rapidly but one was repeated over and over; "Dahrata." She looked at Kir, who stood impassively, and followed his pattern. They must not call attention to themselves. Ndar gave a final roar and beckoned to his men. The soldiers parted before him as the leader saluted Ndar and stood back.

There were public carriages for hire, ox-drawn vehicles that moved at a steady rate. Ndar urged Kir and CeLa into one and put his finger to his lips when they would have spoken. The driver yawned and moved out into the open streets that led away from the several great buildings that housed palaces, temples and harbor. Many soldiers thronged in the streets, marching with intent faces, hands ready at their weapons. Citizens paused to watch them, pride on their faces. The straight, clean streets gave onto a wide section with houses set well back, blank walls to the street itself. They paused before one such two-story, imposing dwelling and knew from Ndar's joyful face that this was home.

The tall, dark-haired woman who stood in the anteroom to which they were taken by the smiling servant showed traces of recent tears, and CeLa guessed that she had barely received the news of her husband's safety before his arrival. Now she said softly, "The gods have been kind, my husband."

Ndar came close and looked down into her brilliant eyes. "Utis, in my dreams and waking thoughts you were ever with me."

CeLa felt her eyes burn at the tenderness in his voice. These were people of great pride who did not readily reveal themselves to others. There was such intimacy between these two that she wanted to turn away. But she felt envy as well. Would it ever be so for herself and Kir?

Utis spoke words of welcome, then said, "The servants will help you remove the ravages of the journey."

CeLa and Kir followed the maidservant, as they were bidden. CeLa turned back for a moment and saw Ndar sweep the placid woman into his arms as the storm of weeping began. He spoke urgently in her ear as her arms went around his neck. CeLa felt a trickle of fear once more and hastened to catch up with Kir.

They were given one wide room in the upper section of the house where steps led to the roof. A window looked down on an interior courtyard where plants grew and a small ornamental pool shone blue as the sky. A clay statue of a woman, crudely shaped with huge breasts and a wide headdress, dominated the area. As CeLa watched, several servants bent low before the statue before going on their way.

When they were alone, Kir said, "We must be circumspect, CeLa. Ndar was challenged on his return, for it was recorded that his ship was lost. The crew and records will be checked in the event that spies came with him. The ships on the river are those of Daro only; no others are permitted. Strangers in the city are few and they are closely watched. The king, Dahrata, suspects rebellion and plans for expansion at the same time. He is known to be harsh."

CeLa thought of her warning fear and knew it justified. "But Ndar is priest to one of their gods as well as to the Mother Goddess herself, is he not? Surely they cannot suspect him?"

"She bids hospitality to the stranger. We will be safe enough but the sea routes are closed and any attempt to reach Sumer by land would be a fearful journey through hostile tribes and wild terrain. For the time being, we do nothing. Ndar will assess the mood of the king."

The maidservants came to CeLa then and bathed her, washed her hair in scented water and oils, then dressed it high and placed a golden circlet about her forehead. She was given a long, loose robe of thin material that left one shoulder bare. Her golden body and pink nipples shimmered through it and her slender legs showed to the thigh when she moved. Costly scent was touched to her palms and neck. She was a woman waiting for her lover. Excitement held her stiff as they left her.

She waited in vain all through the long night while the moon slid down the sky. Kir did not return and he was not on the roof when she went to seek him. Anger gave way to tears; finally she slept uneasily, for she had strange, dark dreams and the floor seemed to move and tilt when she woke. She knew that her face was pale and sticky from her restlessness but she did not alter her appearance when the little maid announced Utis's summons. What did anything matter if Kir deserted her?

The gracious woman met CeLa at the bottom of the stairs and held out her hand in greeting. Her winged brows were lifted; there was a smile on her lips. CeLa could guess the delights of the night past. Now Utis said, "Your lord confers long with my husband. They rose very early. Will you let me show you our city? I understand too that you need clothes." Her smile was artless and CeLa took the outstretched hand in gratitude for her understanding.

In the days that followed CeLa gave herself up to shopping and seeing the sights of Daro. Ndar had made a medium of exchange available and would not let his hospitality be refused. So CeLa now had trinkets of bronze and gold, bead necklaces in many colors and several of the wide headdresses favored by ladies for great occasions. There were skirts and tunics, sandals and big belts to be worn low on the hips. She and Utis also went to the huge public bath near the city granary and CeLa marveled at the complexity of both. The high citadel, complete with walks and towers, offered a commanding view of the plain and the river. One large court was occupied by the king when he ritually came to honor the city and they him; here too the priests came and went in the panoply of their calling. The cities of Sumer that CeLa had seen were not as grand. She was continually awed at the ornate woodwork of these buildings, the beauty of the hangings, and the clothes and jewels of those who walked there. They often went down the precisely planned streets that were on a regular, straight pattern with public wells and benches at intervals and watchmen for every certain number of blocks. The houses were always well kept and nearly every one of them had a freshwater system for bathing and the disposition of wastes.

CeLa met the three young daughters of Utis and Ndar. All were under ten and each had a maid to look after her and entertain her. They were brought in the evenings to greet their parents and were then taken away. Tutors taught them in the garden in the mornings and often CeLa would go there to listen and learn more of the language of Daro.

Other than the great hall of the king at the citadel, there was a curious dearth of temples and signs of the gods in this well-organized and efficient city, where everything seemed to operate for the benefit of the citizens. When she asked Utis, the reply was generally vague and spoken in terms of the Mother Goddess whose image was present in the house. For all her kindness to them, Utis yet held herself apart and CeLa would not press her. But the mystery grew on her in the lengthening days.

She and Kir occupied the same room but he never touched her and often spent the night on the roof. He spoke politely to her but she had the feeling that, for him, she was not there. Pride forbade her to press the issue. If her senses clamored for his touch, wisdom told her that she would lose any gains she had made. CeLa threw herelf into learning as much as she could about Daro, both past and present, even as she had done in Egypt. It occupied her mind and gave her thought for the long, hungry nights.

One such night CeLa was still tossing when she heard the sound of sobbing coming from one of the family rooms on the other side of the garden. The sound grew in intensity until it could not be ignored. When she looked out, she saw the youngest daughter of the house, Ti, being held in the arms of her distraught maid, who was weeping herself while Utis

tried to take her and Ndar paced nearby. CeLa knew
that she should not interfere at such a time but the
din was such that anyone would have inquired.

One of the maids hovering on the edge of the circle whispered, "She has been fretful all day and now
she is so hot that her skin almost burns you. The
demons are lodged in her and the priests have been
called."

The little hands beat her mother's chest in frenzy
and the cries rose higher. CeLa met Ndar's anxious
gaze as he watched Utis's face contort. The children
were treasured for themselves and for the deep love
their parents bore each other. CeLa wondered what
Kir's actions would be if they had a child in such
anguish as this one seemed to be. Would he be tender? She doubted it.

The voice was so high and strained that CeLa had
to look up to recognize Utis. Her calm had deserted
her and she cried, "She twisted and went limp. Now
there is nothing!"

Ndar and CeLa were instantly at her side. It was
true. The pale lips were parched and the skin burned
but the child lay as though sleeping. Her breath
came in labored rasps. The fingers were turned like
talons.

"She will die." Ndar's voice was harsh. He whirled
on the weeping maids. "Send the guard, command
the priests to hasten. Promise anything but get them
here. Go!"

"What is it?" The departing girl had almost over-
turned Kir as he came through the door. A babble
of voices answered him but he could see for himself
as they placed the child down on one of the nearest
mats. He touched her face and murmured to himself,
"She burns from within. I have seen this often."

Utis cried, "What is it then, this thing that takes
my daughter from me and leads her into the netherworld?"

Kir went to her and placed his hand on her shoulder. The warmth in his voice was comforting and the authority evident as he said, "Will you let me see if I can help her?"

Ndar was uneasy. "The priests are coming, Kir. They will know what to do."

CeLa looked at the child's pale face and heard the breathing that was slowing more with each passing moment. She could not hold herself back. "He is a physician, trained in the temples and the armies of Sargon, our king. If any can help, it will be he."

Kir glared at her but the pain rose in Utis as she cried out, "Help her! Only help her!" Ndar crossed to her and took her hands in his as he nodded at Kir.

The child was taken to another room where Kir took one of the powders that he had managed to protect through all their trials, dissolved it in warm water and fed it to her in tiny driblets. At his request the parents remained outside. CeLa and two of the maids worked with him to sponge the little girl and give her the effusion, which she could sometimes swallow and which sometimes ran out of the sides of her mouth. When she began to show some response, Kir directed one of the maids to hold her head and massage her gently about the temples. Finally the child slid into a natural sleep and color began to return to her cheeks.

Kir looked at CeLa and smiled the old smile of friendship. "She will live. It was one of those quick, burning, malignant plagues that I have seen kill strong men between dawn and dusk. You were right to tell our friends of my old skill. It has been long since I used it."

It was full day now and light slanted into the room as Ndar pulled the curtain back and looked in. His face was drawn, the dark brows strongly marked. Utis was trembling as she held his arm. Behind them walked several men clad in the long white robes and high headdresses that identified them as priests from the citadel where CeLa had seen such in procession.

One of them advanced to the pallet and looked down. "She sleeps. You held us back and angered the goddess because of a charlatan's remedies? Your daughter will pay for that, I fear, in death." He folded his hands together and looked gravely at them.

"Nonsense. The fire has left her body and she will only be weak when she wakes." Kir stepped forward and nodded at Utis, who ran to feel Ti's cool body and burst into tears.

"What trickery is this? We alone can heal." The priest was angry now.

"Trickery, indeed, and affront to the goddess as well," said a cold voice from the doorway. "This matter must be thoroughly investigated." The speaker came fully into the light. It was Jagon.

45

Dahrata of Mohenjo-daro

CeLa sat on the roof in the burning noon that she did not feel, for her senses were whirling with fear and anger. Below, Ndar and Utis slept with their little daughter, thoroughly exhausted. A guard stood by the entranceway to the house, posted by the priests and Jagon as they left. Kir was checking the others in the house to see if the burning illness had taken any of them. She wondered that he could behave normally after seeing the monster who had tried to take their lives and sanity, but he had spoken no word to her at all.

She wondered again what devious game Jagon played. He had given no sign of recognition but had repeated his ominous declaration, eyed them for long moments, announced that a delegation would return later and left. Surely he had recognized them; the intense force of her hate alone must have touched him. The passing moons had not changed him, for he still had the enigmatic look that had once fascinated her, and the polished smoothness of his face remained the same. The tall, conical headdress he wore hid the dark hair, but his eyebrows still lifted with his frown and cruelty still lurked in his dark eyes.

Kir climbed the steps and sank exhausted onto a mat placed on one of the benches. He held a flagon of cool wine from which he drank liberally. "Thanks be to the gods, or to me, that the others are well. I do not think the illness will spread."

CeLa whirled on him and cried, "Kir, I think you are mad! Does it not trouble you at all that Jagon has a position of authority here? You do recall that he tried to kill you and abused me shamefully? Those matters have not fled your mind, have they? Shall I refresh it for you or does the scar on your chest not remind you?"

"Stop acting like a foolish woman. For his own reasons Jagon did not wish to recognize us. Had it been to his advantage to do so, he would have demanded that we be taken prisoner. He spoke of an investigation, no more. Ndar did summon the priests and in the meantime I took over. Priests are all alike, jealous and sensitive. It is likely no more than that."

Fury rang in her voice. "I will kill the fiend if you are not man enough to do so. Have you forgotten that he plotted against your blessed ruler? Surely that is an unpardonable sin!"

Kir lost his patience then and caught her arm that was uplifted to strike. "To challenge him without knowing his game would be to destroy ourselves. You will obey me in this; you will be cold and polite until we know more. Jagon will be punished in due time. I do not forget all that has gone before. He had to flee Sumer and Akkad. Egypt was closed to him, and this was a natural place to come. He will not willingly jeopardize a position of safety."

CeLa jerked free and rubbed her arm as she looked fiercely into the dark eyes so close to hers. "You are making the mistake of thinking that Jagon is a reasonable person, Kir. He is not. He is mad with cruelty —I should know. You will regret this day."

Kir snatched up the wine and stalked down the steps, not deigning to answer her. CeLa put both arms around her body and began to shiver with fear. "Grant that I may one day destroy Jagon! Grant it,

gods!" A faint cloud drifted across the blue expanse
of sky and she shivered.

Ti continued to improve and soon Kir pronounced
her safe from a return of the malady. Jagon's guards
remained at the door but did not interfere with the
comings and goings of the family. Ndar had been
informed that it was for their protection, lest the
people learn that a powerful new healer was within.
Kir and CeLa warned him and Utis about Jagon,
holding little back. CeLa could not bring herself to
tell much of her captivity at his hands but they understood.

Kir ended, "You risk much in this involvement,
my friends. Perhaps it would be well to let us make
contact with some travelers. Surely there are some
who cross the wasteland to Elam and beyond." His
eyes met CeLa's and she nodded.

Ndar paced up and down in the little courtyard
where they had gathered as the cool dusk came on.
One of the servants was singing a lilting song to
lull the children to sleep. Ndar clasped Kir's arm
in sudden warmth. "By now the king knows of you
and doubtless of your origins. He likely would not
have believed that you were simple island folk in
any case. I will send a messenger to him this day
requesting audience. I have ever been loyal to Daro's
rulers."

CeLa was looking at Utis and saw the hard look
she gave Ndar, who came instantly to her side. In
the next instant her face was soft and smooth. Dis-
quiet touched CeLa again and she was grateful when
Kir suggested they retire.

That night he took her as he had on the ship, in
duty and determination. There was no tenderness
or waiting for her to join in pleasure. He jammed
his erect stalk between her legs, rubbed her breasts
perfunctorily, then rested on his elbows and hammered into her so that his seed spilled in a matter of

moments. Then he rolled over and prepared for sleep.

CeLa's denied body began to tremble as she sat up and addressed the large back that faced her. Her blood was running hot and clamored for his warmth. "Am I your chattel that you thrust yourself into me, take your release and settle to snore? By the gods, have you forgotten the sharing we once had?"

He did not turn but the words came sharply. "Was that your word for it?"

She did not stop to think of the consequences of her next action. Her hand rose involuntarily and the blow landed stingingly on his ear. He turned and grabbed for her, catching her arm as she tried to pull back. His face was furious but she was equally angry. They tumbled together, wrestling and twisting, their bodies now together, now apart. Neither knew when the fury became passion. Kir leaned over her, savoring her, before thrusting his hard manhood deep into her, moving it tantalizingly as his hands tormented her nipples into glowing pools of fire that spread to her loins and heated them both into near frenzy. Her hands were as swift as his as she gripped his buttocks to her, seeking to hold him in her flesh as their mouths locked and their tongues twisted together. They came apart and moved into each other as he held her placed so that her back was toward him and he slid smoothly, lengthily, into her and she leaned over so that he might go more deeply. Then she was standing above him, moving her slender body so that he groaned with lust for her, and then she knelt to take him into her mouth that she might draw and feed on the flames that they kindled together. Then they had held back as long as they could and flesh could endure no more. They toppled into the sweet honey abyss and the light drifted, faded and was no more.

Kir was gone when CeLa awoke and she did not see him until late that night when he went to the

roof. No words were spoken between them and she
wondered that such passion could arise and they so
pleasure each other yet not meet in simple friendship.

Utis woke her in the heat of the next day. The
night had been sleepless and CeLa's rest had been
hard and broken. Her eyes felt matted and her body
stiff. "You must hurry, CeLa. The message has only
just come. We are commanded to the presence of the
king within the hour. A guard waits to escort us."

In less than the appointed time they stood in the
anteroom of the king's chamber, waiting the command to enter. CeLa was conscious that the flowing
white tunic, the simple band of white over her coiled
hair, the necklace of shells combined with jewels and
the simple sandals gave her an air of purity and
clearness that might mislead one who did not know
her into thinking her artless. The others were simi-
larly clad without ostentation. She caught Ndar's
eye and he smiled to give her courage. Kir saw the
look and his face darkened but he said nothing.

"Come into the presence!" The call seemed to
come from somewhere above them and it rang around
the small room. A curtain was drawn aside and si-
multaneously a door opened. A gorgeously clad slave
was backing away even as another led them forward
into a huge chamber that seemed filled with stone
sculpture and beautifully inlaid woods mounted on
stone. A lifelike scene of a king or god receiving the
homage of the people as he stepped from a boat was
painted on the long wall behind the high throne
chair, where a man sat alone. Other people lined
the sides of the chamber, men and women alike, but
they were silent and far from the throne. Only their
eyes were watchful as the party was led up to the
very steps of the throne, where they knelt at the
barest gesture from the slave.

"Rise." The voice was hard and guttural, the words

slow paced but filled with unquestioned authority. "I have granted you audience, Ndar, because of the strange and conflicting tales I have heard about you and these people, but also because of the faithful service you have given our city. Yet you have brought strangers from a foreign power here at such a time when I am seeking to mold our solidarity. Explain yourself!"

Ndar stood and began to speak, telling the tale that CeLa and Kir had told him but slightly altering it so that it appeared that they were indeed from Sumer and Akkad but had left it long ago, sojourned for a time in Egypt, where they had run afoul of a man of power and fled from that land to be shipwrecked on the Red Sea, captured by natives from whom they escaped by raft and drifted into the gulf where they were found by Ndar. They asked sanctuary of the mercy of Mohenjo-daro.

Dahrata of Mohenjo-daro was short and heavily built but he had strong muscles in his arms and a bull neck. His eyes were piercing and they never left Ndar's face. He was very simply dressed in a short brown tunic and sandals, with a dagger at his side. A single jewel of ebony and red shone on his chest. CeLa began to understand Ndar's strategy; this man must hold the very center of the world and none must distract from it. Thus Ndar had cast them on the mercy of the ruler who would never have understood or allowed emissaries from another power to walk unmolested in Daro.

Dahrata was saying now, "It is a goodly tale. You did well, Ndar, to be truthful with me. Woe unto you had you not."

"How could you have thought that I would not? You who see all things clearly." The flattery sounded sincere and CeLa felt her stomach contract at Ndar's expression.

"How indeed?" The grin on the king's face was

not pleasant to see. CeLa could well understand how
he seemed to hold Daro in a firm grip. "Let us say
that the priests are zealous in the welfare of our
city. Very zealous. I alone rule here!" The last words
were a shout and those nearest the throne, Ndar and
Utis, moved back a few paces.

"None doubt it." Ndar spoke so softly that it
seemed Dahrata could not hear, but he did and
leaned forward to look into his eyes.

"You understand that. Others do not." The king
snapped his fingers at Kir, who approached, his face
impassive, his bearing erect. "You and your woman
wish to remain in our city, is that it?"

"Aye, great one. We have wandered long and would
settle now."

CeLa knew that Kir and Ndar had agreed upon
this course of action, which they hoped would appeal
to the sense of power in Dahrata. She thought of
Sargon, that ruler of humble origins who embodied
empire in his every gesture and did not demand false
humility from others. For a moment she understood
something of the friendship and destiny that welded
Kir to him.

The hard voice was saying, "And what have you
to give our city, to Mohenjo-daro that will one day
rule the valley of the Indus and beyond to your own
land and Egypt?" His eyes searched Kir's as he said
these inflammatory words.

"What do you ask?" She heard her own voice rise
and saw the dark eyes swing to impale her.

"There is no need for the woman to address me.
She is ignorant of our ways. Keep her silent."

"Aye, lord. It shall be done." Kir glared at CeLa
and she bent her head. She too could play this game,
which was for their lives and safety.

The king shifted on his throne and lifted a hand.
A servant hastily knelt with wine and he refreshed
himself with a single gulp, followed by a loud belch

as he arranged himself more comfortably on the cushions. "I asked you what credit you would be to this city. I do not grant charity."

Kir's tone was respectful but not servile. Ndar looked at him with alarm, one eye on the king. "I am a physician trained in the use of herbs and potions, with special knowledge of those burning diseases that come to those who live, as we do, by the great rivers of the world. I know of the ways of battle wounds and the cures that can be effected; it will be an honor to utilize this knowledge and skill in the service of so munificent a ruler as yourself."

"Do you speak with the gods on these matters as the priests do? What god revealed to you the way to heal Ndar's daughter so swiftly? I put it to you that you are in communication with other gods than those of Daro!"

CeLa felt a moment of panic, then knew that Kir was equal to the trap into which the wily king sought to lead him. Other gods might challenge those of Daro and a battle might ensue. Only the priests might speak with the great ones of the heavens; for a wanderer to claim such benefits for himself was dangerous temerity. She saw the grin on the heavy, jowled face as he waited for the trap to spring.

Kir said, "I know nothing of such matters, King Dahrata. I was taught this lore in my youth and practiced it in the armies of my homeland. As to the gods, that I will leave to the priests whose duty it is to instruct us. I will serve the gods of Daro as diligently as I serve her king."

The grin faded and Dahrata sat a little straighter on his throne. CeLa knew who had put that into his mind; the hand of Jagon was evident. Once again she wondered what power their enemy held in Daro and what form that hatred would take.

The king said, "In time you will learn of the worship of our gods. The woman, your wife, will she

be fruitful, do you think? That is a necessity among
our women." He ran an expert eye up and down
CeLa, who burned with rage even as she bent her
head in modesty. "It is well that you are wed, for
one so fair might well grace my own bed."

CeLa's head snapped up and she looked angrily
into the dark face of the man who held their lives
in his hand. He looked back and she saw lechery
there. Kir moved to her side and put one hand on
her shoulder.

"We have traveled much and there has been little
time for the gods to bless us with children. We pray
for fruitfulness now. You are kind, great king, to
remark on her beauty, for I have always found her
so." Kir looked at CeLa as he said this and she knew
he spoke the truth, that these were no idle words,
that they spoke of caring—more than he knew in the
saying of them.

"It is well that you are wed." Dahrata repeated
himself almost absently. He brushed a hand over his
head and gulped more wine. Then he laughed aloud
and the sound was not pleasant in the great hall. "I
shall test you, Kir the Wanderer. There is a man
among my guards who lies as though dead and has
done so for almost a moon. He breathes and swallows
thin soup. The flesh does not melt from his bones,
but he cannot move or speak. The priests have tried
to heal him but the gods do not hear. Heal him and
you and your wife may remain in Mohenjo-daro, honored and respected, for as long as you will, and you
both shall be under my personal protection. Fail, and
you go forth as you came. I will keep the woman for
my bed. Refuse, and you both descend into the depths
of my prisons, there to be treated as spies. Well?" He
roared with laughter and the sound slammed against
their ears unbearably.

46

The Test

Kir did not flinch. He waited until the laughter had died down, then advanced a few paces, not looking at any of his own party. Quietly he said, "You have left me no choice."

"Then you accept?" The king was almost gleeful.

"I do. But I must know how the man came to be injured, and what has been done in the time he has lain as he has. And I must have time and space to work. My wife will help me."

CeLa felt her pride in him rise up. It did not matter that this might be an impossible task against impossible odds. They would be together in the attempt to solve it and for the moment that was all that mattered. She met Kir's eyes and they exchanged looks. Ndar and Utis looked terrified at the turn the audience had taken, but for this instant in time CeLa and Kir saw only each other. Dahrata stood up, looking vaguely disappointed, and CeLa thought once again that she knew who had contrived this test.

"You will be conducted to him at once. Ndar, you and your wife may go to your home. You will know soon enough how matters go." He snapped his fingers and several slaves appeared. "Take them to Yoc immediately and say that he is to obey the man in all things."

CeLa and Kir were taken through what seemed miles of corridors, up stairs and around bends, until they reached a series of small rooms with curtains over the doors. A larger alcove opened out and here a tall, slender man in middle life sat perusing a stone tablet, oblivious to anything else. One of the slaves advanced toward him hesitantly, clearly fearful of the responsibility set out. The man looked up then and Kir saw the intelligence in his eyes.

"I am Yoc. Who are you?"

Kir stepped forward as the slave started to speak. In a few swift sentences he explained matters and saw a flush darken the other's face.

"I am the keeper of the servants of the king and treat them as best I can when the priests are not summoned. The man of whom you speak will die soon and a mercy it will be."

There was a trumpet call in the distance and the sound of tramping feet. They looked up to see a guard entering. He said, "We are instructed by the king to watch this place until either you cure the sick man or show that it is hopeless. We remain here."

Kir ignored them and said to Yoc, "Will you help us?"

"If I can, but I am no believer in all this mummery." He gave a snort of disgust and led the way into one of the rooms where a young man lay as if sleeping. His face was pale and sallow. His chest barely moved with the slowness of his breath.

Kir moved toward him and ran gentle fingers over his body and head as he tested the movements of the muscles and looked under his lids for responses. "How did this come to be?"

"He marched in the escort for the king at one of the sacred functions. As they went through one of the narrower streets, a mud brick dropped from the roof of one of the houses and glanced against his head. Nothing was thought about it until he suddenly fell down while standing watch at the banquet that evening. He has been that way ever since, just as you see him now."

Kir beckoned CeLa closer and directed her fingers toward a curiously depressed section at the upper part of the skull under the curling black hair. He said, "I have seen these before. Sometimes they are accompanied by a kind of palsy and shaking. Sometimes the speech is almost lost. There is pressure here and when it is removed there is more chance of recovery. These things happen in battle or in hand-to-hand combat."

She spoke in Akkadian. "Can you cure him, do you think?"

He answered in the same language. "If I had been able to reach him within a few hours or days of the accident and had I been able to perform the technique described in the chronicles, the chances would have been better. As it is, we must try. There is no choice. Can you help and not show fear?"

She nodded, unable to speak for the apprehension that flooded her whole being. Yoc watched them and smiled a sour smile as if grateful for the diversion in an otherwise boring day. There was a clatter at the door and they looked up to see Dahrata standing there with a cluster of people.

"Well, now that you have seen him, what do you think? Is my bargain not a just one?"

Kir snapped, "I must have quiet. The room must be cleared and the man prepared. There must be no distractions and none shall watch."

One of the councillors around the king made as if to protest but Dahrata silenced him with a gesture. "Very well, it shall be as you say. But we wait here."

Kir shrugged, then sent slaves running in all directions to carry out his commands for wood, sharp-pointed instruments of bronze and stone, the sculptor's tools, a basin and water for shaving as well as a knife for the same purpose. Several slaves were commanded to keep an endless supply of water hot and ready. Cloth for bandages was ordered and soothing ointments prepared.

The sick man was placed on a wide bench covered with a white cloth. His legs were bound to it and his hands secured at his sides. Yoc watched with eyes full of pity. During the binding he made as if to intervene, but one glance at Kir's stony face made him stop and retreat to the watching place by the door. Bags of sand hastily made from the supplies brought held the guard's head firmly in place so that he could not move it.

Kir set CeLa to shaving one side of his head with the sharpest of the knives. That done, she touched the depression from which the darkness of a bruise had faded to leave only a faint shadow. A small fragment of bone had worked its way up through the flesh and her finger brushed it as she washed off the area with the hot water a frightened slave had brought to the door.

"Are you afraid, CeLa?" He smiled at her as he worked with the crude tool he had fashioned from the sculptor's instruments, a brace and a twisted, curving bit that was used to bore holes in the wood. She had seen such things in Sumer and wondered at the patience the woodworkers and sculptors needed for such painstaking work in the precious wood, since any trees were so far away that legends grew up around them.

"Terrified." The word moved past her dry lips.

"I am too." He put the instrument down and bent to inspect the area. "It is time to begin. Yoc, stand at the door and let no one pass. You shall remain as our witness to what transpires."

Time stood still for CeLa as she watched Kir take the sharpest of the knives and cut the skin around the area that bent so oddly inward. He had commanded that wine be brought and now he sponged away the mild bleeding with a cloth dipped in it.

The flesh was pushed away now and she saw a glimmer of bone. Her senses rocked.

"Kir, what if it is a demon there?"

He put the knife aside and took up the borelike tool, which he examined thoroughly before turning to her. "When I work this way I am convinced that demons are of our own making. Who can know, CeLa. We must do as best we can in this life and hope that they who gave us life for the short span will not judge us too harshly in the netherworld."

It was too close to what she had often thought herself for her to doubt the sincerity of his words. She spoke softly. "I will pray to Inanna that she be with us even in this land that knows her not."

Kir turned back to the guard and she saw that he had forgotten her completely. Thoughts of their plight faded as she watched him work, he who had barely acknowledged his training in this art, and had once forsaken it. Much depended on him now, she knew, and yet every move was as delicate and precise as though they had all the time in the world.

He set the bore upon the depression, which he had lifted slightly with the point of the knife. Then he spun the tool slowly and CeLa heard it grate on the bone. He lifted it and did the same procedure three more times. He set it aside and took up the knife once more to lift the bone up.

There was a clatter at the door and then a roar of command as Yoc resisted only a moment and then was pushed aside. King Dahrata stood in the entrance. Behind him were several men who looked like councillors, while beyond them were three white-clad priests. One of them was Jagon. His face was impassive, but CeLa recognized the glitter in his eyes. It mean that a new type of torment had been devised.

"Enough time has passed, charlatan! Half the day is gone. Do you think to delay your fate?" Dahrata started to come closer, then saw the exposed flesh of the bare head, the gaping holes and the oozing blood. He coughed and turned his head away.

Kir did not look up from his delicate task but his tone was bitter and cold. "King or no, get away from me while I work. Three lives are in the balance here and I will take the chance to save them. Get away!"

Dahrata's face turned red and his neck cords pulsed with fury. CeLa lifted her eyes to Jagon and saw the satisfaction in his. She saw too that the king would not be put down in front of his advisers and that he was fully capable of ordering the work to cease and them to prison.

She said absently, "Something passed from the wound. I vow it went by me only a moment ago."

The others, already fearful in the presence of what few understood, moved away in a body, tumbling over each other in their attempt to reach the door. Dahrata stood his ground but the flush was ebbing from him and he looked crafty. Kir had not looked up; he might have been alone, heedless of interruption.

Blood, dark and old, was now seeping slowly up through the holes of the wound. Kir took the thinnest of the blades and made several gentle movements with it at one of the larger holes. A clot came through on the end of the metal, then another and another.

"Demons!" The whisper rose in the little room. "Get the guards!"

There was an almost unintelligible moan, then another. CeLa stared as the others murmured. She caught up a white cloth, soaked it again in wine and pressed it to the edges of the wound, which was no longer depressed. The bleeding was increasing in intensity now. Kir took up the bore again and set it to one of the holes. Some of the watchers groaned but none came closer. Dark clots spurted, then the pumping of fresh red blood behind them that dwindled almost instantly. The guard moaned and gave a convulsive shudder as all his limbs writhed for a few moments. Then he was still.

Kir took the cloth from CeLa and bound it around his head, then moved the heavy bags and ordered him loosed from the bonds. The guard opened his eyes and gave a feeble whisper, then another. It sounded like a woman's name, so CeLa bent to him and said, "She will be brought to you? Your wife?" The whisper was softer but the unmistakable agreement was there. She looked up at Kir and their eyes blazed together in the triumph that was theirs alone.

It was her voice that rose in the room now as she cried, "He moves and asks for his wife. He that was near death lives again because of the genius of Kir the Wanderer."

Kir said, "He is strong of build and seems healthy. Barring any complications, he will live."

Dahrata, his voice now simply questioning, asked, "What made him lie so still? Did a demon truly oppress him? If so, what fault was his? Or do the demons seek to strike at me?"

Kir was not foolish enough to enter into debate with this despot while the priests stood ready to claim all they could. He said, "I cannot speak about what I do not know. His skull was bruised by a blow and pressed inward, causing the blood to stop up and render him unable to move. I have seen such battle wounds. The treatment is written in the chronicles of my city and so I was taught by the masters. I have been their instrument."

Dahrata said, "I keep my bargains. You and your wife are free and under my protection. Further, you are welcome to become citizens of Mohenjo-daro, for you have proved that you have skills in abundance. I would ask that you join the ranks of my court physicians with special emphasis on such problems as these."

CeLa knew that he commanded them but Kir's reply was gracious. "We are pleased to accept your noble offer, my lord Dahrata."

"But, my king, these people have dealt in affairs that must only concern the gods. Did not the woman herself say that she felt something fly by her? Who knows what strange gods have been brought here and what they will do if our gods object to them. Remember that I have traveled and understand such matters." Jagon's voice was high and angry.

Dahrata whirled on him and roared, "You forget that I rule in Daro! You were given sanctuary even as they and have risen high. Take care, Jagon, for my memory is long!"

The wounded guard murmured something that might have been a call for water and Kir held some to his lips. Then he said, "This man must be watched night and day for some time since he is still likely to move about too easily. Yoc, will you set someone to this task?"

"Right willingly." He was subservient now where he had been doubtful before. "All caution shall be taken."

Kir and CeLa took their leave then and went through the palace halls, out into the street, where they were joined by a very deferential escort that took them to Ndar's house. There the entire experience was told and sorted out once again while they drank wine and made merry. They drank to the past, the future and all the time in between. CeLa felt her head reel with weariness, for it was now far into the night.

Kir slid a smooth hand down her arm and his compelling dark eyes looked into hers. "Come, wife, the day has been long, has it not?"

"Aye, long." She felt little flames begin to burn and her nipples hardened at his fingers on her body.

Her mouth was suddenly dry with hunger too long unslaked.

In the room they shared, CeLa and Kir came together first in an explosion of desire that left them battered and greedy for more. He put his hands in her hair, lay atop her with his stalk deep and moving in her and kissed her deeply, their tongues twining together and probing in unison. CeLa was drowning in honey, her arms wrapped around his neck and shoulders, her pelvis moving in slow rhythmic contraction as he plowed more deeply into her. They rose and fell toegther, turned and melted into each other as they drank of their one flesh and joined it yet again.

CeLa lay at one point on her side, Kir between her legs. They joined and moved slowly together in the enjoyment of passion held back to grow yet more sweet. He touched one breast, then leaned forward to suck deeply on it as she cupped his head to her. Then he looked at her and she saw that the bitterness was gone from his dark eyes and the slight wariness had departed from his manner. There had always been something of him held back. But now there was a difference.

"Why do you look at me that way, CeLa? Can I not hold your entire attention or must I work more heartily?" He reached out for her waist and began to rotate his own hips more so that she gasped with the delight of the thrusting. One hand cupped her chin and he kissed her open mouth lingeringly, as if he could never let it go.

"Tell me or pay a forfeit." He laughed and released her mouth that he had traced with his fingers.

"What is the forfeit, lord husband?"

"More of this if I like your answer. More of this if I do not."

"How can I lose such a bargain? I see that I must answer you. I thought, Kir, that you seem happy for the first time in many moons and I took joy in that."

He put both hands on her face and spoke as seriously as she had ever heard him. "I have only just begun to realize what manner of woman you are, CeLa. Proud, brave, a good comrade and excellent lover, a fair woman."

It was more of an honor than he had ever paid her and from Kir it was tantamount to paeans from another. She melted close to him and they took each other fervently in passion and tenderness that was the sweetest they had ever known.

47

A Promise Shall Be Given and Kept

Kir was often absent in the next few days, for he was in attendance of King Dahrata, who had forsaken his earlier hostility and distrust and now treated Kir like a true friend. When Kir had free time, he and CeLa ranged over the city, walking in the street of the sculptors, of the furniture makers and of the jewelers, going along the docks and watching the high-prowed ships sail the Indus. As they walked they talked, gaining more knowledge and insight of each other than ever before.

Kir said once, "The king is indeed building an army and preparing ships for war. I am to look after his men's bodies and the priests will deal with their spirits. There will be no conflicts, he says, and I am almost inclined to believe him. I wonder where he will strike first."

CeLa answered, "It will not be our battle, wherever it takes place."

"This could, in time, threaten Sumer and Akkad. We have traded with Daro in the past but it fell off when our own internal struggles increased." He turned her mouth up to his and took a quick kiss, Kir who had never touched her in front of others and never showed affection.

CeLa felt the quick response that he never failed to kindle in her and thought of the glory their nights had been lately. How could such happiness last? The thought of Jagon did not fail to terrify her. Kir had told her that he had come overland to Daro with several natives of the desert who had subsequently died. Jagon had said he was an outcast from Egypt, that he had served many gods but now wished to give thanks to Dahpur, principal god of Daro in the male line, and serve in his temple. His request had been granted and he had risen rapidly. CeLa knew that as long as Jagon lived he was a threat to them. The time of their trial had proved that.

Now that they were free and had time to be happy, CeLa began to experience chills and bouts of nausea that left her weak and shaking at odd intervals of the day. Kir would usually finish with his business at the court and return in the burning afternoon when many slept. It was one of their favorite times for wandering. He came one day when she lay weak and exhausted on the pallet in their room; she had sent Utis and the slaves away when they made inquiries. She had dozed until a jerk on her arm woke her.

Kir was leaning over her, his eyes anxious. "What is the matter with you? They tell me that you do this daily, that you seem to guard your strength for the times we are together. What did you think to conceal from me, foolish woman?"

CeLa put her head in her hands and began to cry. The devilish weakness had such possession of her that she could not even rise to defend herself. "We have been too happy these last days. The gods are jealous and will take me for it." She could barely voice the thought that had haunted all the nights after they had taken their pleasure and lay in the soft dark, their limbs intertwined in love's lassitude.

"CeLa, CeLa. Whatever it is, we can deal with it together. Will you trust me enough for that?" He raised her tear-wet face to his and caressed it with his lips.

There was a movement in the doorway and then the soft voice of Utis said, "Forgive my intrusion,

Kir. I did not see you come in. I heard CeLa crying
and knew how it was with her, so I came to see if
there was anything I could do."

"How it was with her?" Kir repeated the words,
then rose to face her. "What do you mean, Utis? What
is it that I do not know?"

Utis stared at CeLa's uncomprehending face and
Kir's worried one. His anxiety was real and palpable
as his eyes searched hers. "Gods of Daro, can you not
know? But why should you? It was so with Ndar
and our firstborn. But you, Kir, are the king's first
physician. I think it is well there is no queen at this
time." She began to laugh as Kir turned to stare at
CeLa.

CeLa felt nausea swing upward and she was past
controlling it as she reached for the ready basin. Kir
caught her and held her head, then eased her back
down and applied a cool cloth hastily brought by
Utis.

He said gently, "Lady mine, you will soon fulfill
the commands of the king that you be fruitful. You
are with child, CeLa."

She stared in wonder. The world swung and then
she said, "Do you mind, Kir?"

"Mind? I am honored. We are wed, are we not?"
He held her to him and then began to shake with
laughter. "I, the physician to the ruler of Mohenjo-
daro, did not know that my wife was with child."

Her nausea over and the terrible fear behind her
for the moment, CeLa could see the humor in it and
she began to laugh as well. They held onto each
other and rocked with shared laughter. Neither saw
Utis go as she slipped silently from the room.

"And by my reckoning, Utis, it was that night on
the ship when Ndar wed us that Kir took me in duty
and our child was conceived." CeLa and Utis had
talked long about children and the having of them,

the pain and the joy and the longing for sons. Utis had asked several pointed questions as to possible conception times and, in her pleasure at having a confidante, CeLa had answered readily, giving more details of her intimate life with Kir than she might at one time have deemed prudent.

"But he loves you now, CeLa. None could look at him and doubt it."

They were sitting on the roof under a shade of woven palms in the cool of the morning. CeLa had bathed earlier, as they all did, and her dark hair floated behind in the little winds that sprang up sometimes at this hour. Happiness had given a new sheen to her skin and a radiance to her face. The changeable nausea shifted patterns and she never knew when it would come, but the exhaustion and irritability were passing, thanks in part to an effusion Kir prepared for her every day, but mostly due to the security she now felt and the concern he took for her welfare.

"I have ever loved him, I think, but the quality of that love has grown in all the time we have been together." CeLa was reflective and Utis seemed fascinated by her every word. "We began as comrades, turned to anger and misunderstandings, delight in each other's bodies, to all that and caring for what is in our minds and hearts." Not even to this sympathetic ear would she speak of the bitterness that had ruled Kir for so long and blighted his life so that his friendship with Sargon and their mutual cause was all that had kept him from seeking the land of the shades. So might her own life have been blighted had Nandar not been the man he was or had she not met Kir.

Utis was smiling at her and the dark eyes were warm with sharing. "The child is most welcome, I see. That is good. Ndar and I loved each other more when ours came and we grew in love after the marriage was made. So is it with us in Daro."

"And in Sumer. But you know that story." CeLa stretched and drank more of the bitter brew that Kir insisted she take daily.

"You are fortunate, CeLa. Children of passionate love are the best."

CeLa looked up from her drinking cup, a little startled by the intensity with which the words were spoken. Her friend was looking, not at her, but beyond, and the soft mouth was curved into a hard line. She wanted to ask what the matter was but the languid peace of the moment was such that she did not want it to end. She murmured something noncommittal and stretched out even as her mind whispered, Inanna, love goddess of Sumer, if you can hear me in this far land, know that I thank you with all my heart and all that is in me. The erratic wind lifted her hair again and CeLa smiled, hoping that it was an omen.

The days seemed spun together after that and CeLa found that her body was adjusting to being with child, for she was no longer plagued with nausea and the lassitude had given way to a feeling of well-being. She and Kir spent much of the afternoon together, either lying on the roof or in the cool of their room making slow, tender love. Sometimes they wandered in the city or walked up by the river or watched processions move about the great citadel. But it was their times of talk that CeLa cherished most, for in this manner she came to know Kir and to love him more deeply.

One night when the moon was a curved sickle in the sky and the winds blew soft against their naked bodies as they lay on the roof, Kir told CeLa about his young wife, Inta. She knew the tale from Raba, but Kir's halting words made it more real. The

depths of his pain even after these long years made
her know how much Sargon of Akkad had truly saved
Kir's life and mind.

"She was my youth's love, the personification of
the goddess. She cried out to me in her body's pain
that only death could alleviate. The potion I gave
her brought death and I could not be sorry. Our
time together was so very short. Bitterness was my
daily leaven. She died with my name on her lips.
When I escaped from Uridu with her family seeking
my life, I vowed never to love again and I sought
only those women I thought I could not love. Raba
was brave and beautiful; I cared for her." His voice
faltered and faded as he shifted so that CeLa's head
lay in his lap. His hands touched her hair. "Sokar
was my friend in the camp of Sargon. He hates me
now. How could I say that his fair young sister whom
he idolized was one who lay with all men? Better
that he hate me than destroy her memory."

CeLa lifted her hand to caress the brooding face
above her and he pressed a kiss into the palm. She
longed to have him speak of their relationship but
knew that she must not ask it. Time must be their
leaven. She said now, "You have endured much, Kir,
and been silent for too long."

"You are like no other woman I have ever known.
I hope that our child will be as you are."

He could not speak the words of love; instead, his
deeds were the proof of it. Happiness ran golden in
CeLa as they melted together in the lifting passion
that had been between them from the first.

One day Utis came to CeLa at midmorning, saying,
"Do you feel like going with me to one of our
shrines?"

CeLa was intrigued. Religion was everywhere in
Sumer and governed everyone's lives. Here it was
strictly relegated and the temples of the gods re-

mained apart. The gods did not govern in Daro, she
thought; the king did. The gods were given proper
service, as must be done, but the priests were cautious. CeLa said now, "What sort of shrine, Utis? I
must confess that I am ready to move about more;
I grow restless."

Little flickers shone in Utis's eyes and there was
a strange intensity about her that belied her normal
passivity. "The goddess herself, CeLa, to her whose
blessing is on those who truly serve her."

CeLa knew that the primary deity of Daro was the
goddess whom all called the Great One or the Mother
and that there were other female goddesses as well.
But there was no ornate temple or place of worship
such as every god or goddess had in Sumer's cities.
Religion in Daro was a small mystery and learning
about it would help pass the time until Kir came,
she thought now, as she rose to make ready.

In Daro the ritual bath was of great significance
and was performed before every occasion of import,
this in addition to the regular daily ablutions. Certainly CeLa had not been so clean in Lagash, that
city on the very tributary of the great waters of the
region. Bathed, perfumed, combed and carrying gifts
of jewels and food, she and Utis set forth to the
shrine. A young maid went with them to carry their
offerings.

They walked through the bustle of the main city
streets, along a quieter street where the houses backed
up to form an almost unbroken wall, through a less
prosperous section and then toward one house that
had an ornamental wall with strange signs and symbols down the length of it. When they entered, there
was the tinkle of bells and the smell of incense. A
courtyard was laid out with the same signs that were
on the wall and a passive-faced goddess, wide-hipped
and narrow waisted, sat benignly on her pedestal.

Utis seemed to know the way as she walked quickly into the cool hall, down some stairs and into a wide chamber that was curtained off. She turned to CeLa and her voice was urgent. "Do as I do, CeLa. Do not risk offending her, for she is all-powerful here. She is Mohenjo-daro; she is all."

CeLa could only nod. The strangeness of the moment caught at her. One must, of course, be reverent, but should one be so fearful before one's own gods? The silence of the place, the absence of people, the darkness lit only by an occasional torch—all these things were combining to make her jumpy. Suddenly she wanted very much to be out in the hot sunlight, to feel the grittiness of the streets under her sandals.

Utis began to chant in some ceremonial language that sounded very much like the one Ndar had used when he wed them. She pulled the curtain aside to reveal a long narrow room at the end of which was an image like none CeLa had ever seen before. The goddess was standing with one hand on a bull that had very long horns and was humped with its neck gathered in folds of skin. The goddess herself was tall with wide hips, a narrow waist, very full breasts, long fingers and an elaborate headdress. She wore long necklaces and a girdle spanned her hips. But it was the face that caught CeLa's attention. It was both benign and malevolent, with an arched nose, round, curving forehead and half-lifted eyelids with jewels set in them for glitter. The mouth had a sinister expression. CeLa felt a chill run down her back and knew she could not approach with reverence.

Utis spoke long and urgently as she bowed before the goddess. CeLa knelt too, out of respect, but she was conscious of a growing unease. Suddenly Utis reached out and caught her arm, pulling closer as she chanted. What could she want so much, CeLa wondered? What did she herself want? To live with Kir, have his child and be happy? CeLa pondered for a

moment, lost in the rising incense and the hum of
the chant. There must be more. Then in a flood of
insight, she saw the obvious. To be herself, CeLa of
Lagash, a separate individual, working toward a goal
that would give her satisfaction. In her case her
goal was to be a scribe, a scholar, a searcher in the
old lore so that today might be improved. She knew
too that Mohenjo-daro was not the place she wanted
to live, even with Kir. In Sumer women were persons
in their own right, far more so than in Egypt or
here. She wanted to be part of Sumer and Akkad, of
the bright, expanding future there; she did not doubt
that Sargon now ruled the land between the rivers.
Had he not said it?

Happiness flooded her being and she lifted a bright
face to the image of the goddess. Utis saw and caught
her breath with barely suppressed excitement.

"She has heard me, CeLa. Look there!"

The mist of incense rose thick in the room now
and CeLa saw, or thought she saw, the head of the
goddess lift and the piercing eyes look straight into
hers. There was a pull in them, a call to give and
to be immersed, to be one with the infinite and to
know all. The bright, ordinary, human things of the
world faded for a moment and CeLa took a slight
step forward. Behind her Utis laughed softly and
chanted.

The hawk face of Kir rose in CeLa's mind then so
clearly that she saw the curving brows that lifted
when he laughed, the pulse that often beat in his
temple and the carved lips that fit so expertly on
her own. She saw the hair that clustered in curls at
his temples when he was hot and she saw the sheen
of sweat on his skin. She wanted to feel his arms
around her and hear him inquire about herself and
the child. Reality rose up and she pulled back, coughing as she did so.

Utis saw and knew that the moment was lost. She

made a swift sign that reminded CeLa of the sickle-shaped designs on the temple. Then she put her arm around CeLa as if to support her but her hand went lower and touched her flat belly, where it lingered. The incense rose again in puffs and she chanted.

CeLa cried, "Enough, Utis, I cannot breathe. I will wait for you outside!"

Utis turned to her then and in the dusky room her eyes seemed twice their normal size. "You are of the outlands, that is made clear, but your child is accepted! Know that, CeLa! The promise is made and the seal set!"

48

The Hunt Begins

CeLa ran for the street with all her strength that had
seemed to ebb while they had been in the temple.
She gained the safety of sunlight and heat, then sank
down just as she was, put her head in her hands and
breathed deeply until her heart ceased to hammer
and her wavering senses restored themselves. Her oppressive fear was gone but now she must try to make
sense of what had happened. She lifted her head and
saw Utis coming toward her.

"What came over you, CeLa? Why did you flee
that way? The goddess is doubtless offended and must
be propitiated with offerings."

Her answer was pure instinct. "The illness rose up
so suddenly that I could only leave lest I profane the
sacred place. I think the incense must have overcome
me."

Utis peered at her and for the first time CeLa was
conscious of the calculation in her face. She wanted
to ask questions and dared not, for danger was around
her; she knew that as clearly as she had ever known
anything. If anyone had been their friends in Daro,
it had been Ndar and Utis. Others about the king
had sought Kir's advice and he had spoken casually
with them, but he and CeLa had remained in their
own world, in the closeness that they had with Ndar
and his family. Now that rock was shaking.

CeLa said, "What did you mean 'the seal is set

and my child accepted.' Is the great one truly angry,
do you think?"

They walked along as Utis answered, "The Mother
rules in Daro and all live by her will. Your child
needed her blessing and it was freely given. You
must do homage. We will return to the shrine on
the days when you are better."

CeLa bowed her head in apparent assent but she
vowed to herself that she would not return to that
stifling place with the strange lure of the senses. Tonight she would tell Kir all that had happened and
she would ask that they find a place of their own
against the time when the child came. She would
have her own household and, in time, they would
find some way to return to Sumer. She had made
that vow in the shrine and would keep it. Her heart
lifted; Utis had her peculiarities as anyone did. Doubtless most of the women in Daro worshiped as she did.

What did it matter? She smiled to herself once
more at the thought of Kir and the new freedom she
felt with him, then lifted her eyes to meet those of
Utis, which seemed to hold some unfathomable secret.

It was late afternoon when they reached the house,
and CeLa was thankful to go to the coolness of her
room with only a quick farewell to Utis. She washed
her face, loosened the mass of her hair and wound
a thin robe about her breasts and lower body, then
went to the roof to watch for Kir. A palm fan swung
in her fingers as she idly watched the passers on the
street. Far in the distance the Indus glittered in the
sun and CeLa's memory swung back to all those
moons ago when she watched for Nandar from a roof
in Lagash. Disaster had come shortly after, beginning
a journey that had not yet ended.

Terror smote CeLa then and she knew beyond any
doubt that she and Kir stood in mortal danger. Instinct had told her this when she was with Utis; now

she knew it for truth. She stood shivering in the heat, one hand across her stomach as she remembered that Utis had touched her there.

"Inanna, goddess, protect us. Protect my child." The words were heavy on her lips and she knew that they were not heard. She ran to the stairs in a blind panic, for she knew that she must get to Kir even if she had to go to the palace itself. What could she say to him? It would be put down to the fancies of a breeding woman who is sensitive to every change in the wind. She stumbled and almost fell but managed to save herself by catching at the corner of the roof.

"Mistress, be careful. You will hurt yourself. I have brought wine for your refreshment. There is a message for you from the lord Kir. He is delayed in the service of King Dahrata and will return late this night. He bids you care for yourself and rest."

It was the same maid who had accompanied them to the temple, and CeLa saw that her eyes were watchful; they held their own caution. Now she would go back and report to Utis that CeLa was dashing about as if she were crazed. She forced herself to speak calmly. "My sandal was loose and I did not tighten it enough. Foolish to be so careless. I will sit here for a time. You may go."

"Aye, lady. Mistress Utis can come to you if you wish it." The small face tilted up to hers and a tiny smile moved in the corners of her mouth.

CeLa did not doubt the instinct that told her every hand was against her. She must dissemble until she could speak to Kir. Suspicions must be allayed at all costs. "No, I am very weary from the day. I will just rest quietly here. I may even sleep through the lord Kir's coming."

The maid left and CeLa drank some of the wine to compose herself, knowing she would have a long wait. She began to rehearse what she would say to Kir while the sun sank, the shadows faded and the night melted down.

She woke to the first faint light of day to see Kir standing by the door as if he were in the act of leaving. Her senses were still sluggish from her exhausted sleep and her body felt heavy. She tried to call his name but could only utter a faint groan. He turned back to look at her and she saw for the first time that he wore only a short skirt belted at the waist and sandals. He carried a short sword on one side, a dagger on the other. His hair was wet from the water he had dashed through it and his usual composure was gone from his face, leaving it alive and mobile.

"CeLa, are you ill? I did not want to wake you. It seemed that you slept so heavily. Utis told me she gave you a potion." He sat down beside her and took one hand in his. "These first moons are very hard sometimes, especially in one so active as yourself. It will pass."

At his touch she seemed to revive, though it took every effort to bend her tongue around the words. "I waited for you. I wanted to talk to you about something very serious."

Kir smiled and she was reminded of the expression on the faces of the young boys in Lagash when there was a feast day or a procession. "We will speak together when I return. Several great tigers have been reported on the edges of the valley in that jungle area and the king has decreed that a hunt shall take place this day, night and tomorrow, longer if need be. He has commanded that I ride in his personal chariot with him and be the bearer of his weapons. Many from the court will go; it is a relief from the continual drilling and planning. The tigers have ravaged several of the villages, so it is not only sport that we will perform."

CeLa saw only that she was to be separated from Kir when she needed him most and she heard the wail in her voice as she said, "Wait, Kir, this is urgent. I must tell you about the danger that is in this place for us."

He twisted away impatiently. "The messenger of Dahrata waits below. I must go now. I promise you that we will talk long when I return." He rose and looked about for the short cloak that would later shield him from the heat of the day.

She sat up in a burst of energy that left her shaken as her anger flared. "Let him wait! Must I have an appointment to speak with the great lordling that you have become? I tell you, Kir, I am very much afraid!"

He went to the door and stood looking at her, his face annoyed. "In the manner of many women, you are experiencing the discomforts and fears of becoming with child. You are no different than they, CeLa. You of all people should know that I dare not run the risk of offending Dahrata. He is touchy about his royal dignity since he was not born a king and has to fight for all he has. I must go."

She sat back on her heels and looked at him. Her dark hair fell about her shoulders and between the already fuller breasts. Her face shone white and strained and it seemed that her heart would tear out of her chest with the force of its hammering. That strain of fatalism that ran deep in her told her now that what would be could not be fought against any longer. She lifted her hands in resignation.

"Then I wish you good hunting, my lord. May Inanna's hand be over us all."

Kir hesitated at the strange use of the benediction used by Sargon of Akkad as he went into battle. His face grew troubled. "CeLa, I—" Then a trumpet sounded below, the call high and urgent. He said again, "I must go."

She must say it once more or die; if she never looked on his face again or felt the warmth of his flesh moving against hers, the words she had said so often in her mind must be made real and voiced. "I have ever loved you, Kir, remember that."

As the trumpet called again, this time more urgently than before, he turned to her. His face was unreadable but she knew it would do no good to try to make him stay. She had done all she could and it was not enough. He thought her fears were only the vagaries of a breeding woman.

Kir snapped his cloak around his shoulders with one swift gesture and darkness closed over his face. The words were wrenched from him. "If I were capable of loving any woman again, it would be you." Then his feet clattered on the stairs and she heard him hail the messenger in a loud voice that did not sound quite steady.

It was the closest that Kir had ever come to saying that he cared for her. CeLa let the tears scald her eyes. They had come so close to mutual love and sharing; was it now to be lost? She could not bear it. She dropped to the pallet and let the sobs come as she wept for love that might be lost, the fear that would not leave her and her own memories of her mother, who had died in childbirth.

She did not hear the footsteps until they were in the room. Then Utis was saying with real concern, "What is this? You must not weep so. It is bad for the child."

CeLa raised her tear-drenched face and saw again the look of calculation on the face of the woman she had counted her friend. All her instincts warned her to dissemble and play the shrinking, fearful maiden who longed for her husband and was plagued by all the terrors of her condition. She had learned well the lessons of her time at the inn of the Hawk

in Memphis; now they would stand her in good
stead.

"He went to the hunt when I wanted him with
me. Callous! And I not yet unsightly!" Her hair
fell about her face as she lowered her eyes and let
the tears run down her face. They, at least, were real.

Utis put a hand on hers and murmured sympa-
thetically about the ways of men and how one must
strive to understand. "Women are the carriers and
breeders of the race, CeLa. They are the truly important persons. The male is a tool. The Mother
Goddess takes lovers but they are only that." Her
words throbbed with intensity.

CeLa whispered, "You give me comfort, Utis. I
have great need of that."

"The Mother protects you."

"And my child?" She raised her tear-wet eyes and
shook her hair back from her face. "What of the
child?" It was not as yet real to CeLa, this child
that seemed already to demand so much of her, but
she thought that such a question might tempt Utis
into some revelation of what mysterious fate lay in
store.

The other woman smiled. "When you are well
rested and have recovered from this quarrel with Kir,
we will go again to the temple. I think you will be
more receptive to what you will learn there. You
need not fear for the child, that much I can tell you."

CeLa forgot that she must appear placid and agreeable. "What does all this puzzle mean? What are you
planning?"

"The Mother is far-reaching. You were chosen. Let
that be enough for now." Her light manner had vanished and she spoke in earnest, her eyes glittering
much as those of the goddess in the temple from
which CeLa had fled.

The girl took refuge in pretended exhaustion. "I

am so weary. It must have been the potion Kir said you gave me. I know you meant well but it did make me vomit. He says such things loosen the child."

Utis sniffed in disdain. "My potions are ages old but you are not of this land. It may be that you react so because of this. We shall see."

"You are kind, you and Ndar."

Utis again smiled that same glittering smile as she said, "He too serves the Mother, CeLa, and these things were ordained. It is well to remember that."

When she was alone, CeLa knew that there was no safety in this house. She had been warned that not even Ndar was her friend. There was nothing to be expected from Kir; if the hunts of Daro were anything like those of the cities of Sumer, it would be many days before he returned. She could only rely on herself. Once again CeLa was grateful for the way her body had responded in the past days. She felt strong and resilient since the effects of the potion were leaving her. The easy tears faded but deadly fear remained; it was the spur that drove her on.

She waited until it was very late and the house lay sleeping. Then she crept about the room assembling her oldest and plainest tunics, several jewels that Kir had taken in trade, some pieces of barley cakes left from an earlier meal and a small pouch containing several packets of powders that Kir used to mix others. She had no idea what they were but they might prove useful.

CeLa crept down the outside stairs, her bare feet making no sound on the bricks. Her sandals were in the bundle bound to her back. Her hair was wrapped around her head and a turban was firmly in place. She might have been any early rising servant on her way to shop at the marketplace. She was the prey, going to ground, out of sight of the tiger. The side entrance, used mainly by the family, had a trick catch that she manipulated easily. A sleepy guard sat in the courtyard and did not notice her as she sidled by and moved into the shadow of a palm tree near the wall. He yawned, stretched, looked about as if trying to be alert in the remote possibility that anyone was watching, then settled his chin on his chest and began to snore.

The darkness was lessening now and CeLa knew that she must take the chance of flight. The problems of survival would confront her shortly, she knew, and she must be ready. Her knowledge of the language had improved but she could not understand rapid speech or speak it. Once in Lagash she had pretended to have fits; this time she would be mute, dirty and unkempt, a creature of the docks, scavenging for her barley cakes. Just so would she hide until Dahrata and Kir returned and she could approach them in safety.

Her course established, she slipped smoothly along the wall, reached around the brick and loosed the cord, then stepped into the street and walked briskly on her way. Her heart thundered and her palms were wet with the sweat of fear but she went on. At the turn in the street she risked a cautious look back and the blood stood still in her body.

Two men in white robes stood at the entrance she had just left. They spoke together in low voices, as if trying to settle some point before waking the guard. CeLa knew the taller of them; there was no mistaking that bearing and the set of that head. It was Jagon.

Her own tiger had begun to walk.

wife!" she said and they could only hold each

49

To Stand Alone

CeLa slipped quickly into her role as a beggar, confused and muddled, far from the docks and trying to reach them. She pulled her head down into her shoulders, jerked the folds of the turban over her face and scuttled along the street as fast as she could go without attracting undue attention. There were no others abroad and she knew that if she could reach the inner city and the main area of business, she would have a chance. It was a relief to be doing something definite, not awaiting her fate in a supine manner. Hatred for Jagon illumined her world; she could very easily imagine driving her dagger into his sneering face.

The straight streets of Daro made it almost impossible to become lost but CeLa found there was a great difference in strolling casually along and running for her life. The latter tended to make her confused and she took several wrong turns that brought her face to face with the blank walls of the houses of the wealthy. One such turn made her almost collide with an official out for his morning walk. He was old and portly but his voice was not impaired as he shouted at her. She could not understand the gist of the words but she took that opportunity to run as fast as she could until safely away from him.

The morning was cool but sweat stained her tunic and dripped inside the folds of the turban. Her teeth chattered with fear as she crossed the wide area that led toward the citadel and thence to the market where she could see crowds of people already engaged in raucous bargaining as they moved purposefully back and forth. Their very numbers made her feel safer and she drew a deep breath of relief as her vigilance relaxed a little. She melted among the throngs, a bent brown figure moving as they did, every step bringing her closer to the area that would eventually give onto the docks.

Suddenly an arm closed on hers and a well-remembered voice spoke in her ear. "Did you really think to outwit me, CeLa?"

She gasped and looked up at Jagon, who now wore a brown cloak over his finely woven white robes of priesthood. His face was partially concealed by a draped hood, but she saw the satisfied glitter of his eyes and the sardonic curve of his cruel mouth. Her reaction was swift; she jerked back with all her might even as her sandaled foot struck out at his ankle. She spared an instant to be grateful that she had paused to put on her shoes after her flight from Ndar's house. Jagon winced in pain and his grip relaxed. CeLa jerked away with what seemed strength given of the gods and ran toward the nearest street.

"That woman has taken my pouch! After her!" His voice rose over the babble of those nearest and they turned to stare. He stripped off his cloak and stood revealed as a priest of Dahpur. "Take her!"

CeLa saw this out of the corner of her eye as she tried to dodge those who rushed to apprehend her. It was no use. A wiry young man and a paunchy older one seized her at the same time, then called to Jagon with eager voices. He strode over to them and she saw that several others, apparently lesser priests or followers, came in his wake. A grin split his dark face but she saw the anger burning behind it.

"Here is the thief, lord priest. Pray for us in the

shrine of the great one of Daro." The fat man was obsequious and earnest.

CeLa straightened up as well as she could in her captors' grasp and tossed her head so that the hood fell back and the massed hair fell from its bindings. The movement from beggar woman to fair young girl, dirty though she was, caused all eyes to shift to her. She took the moment for her own and cried, "Thief I am not. He wanted to lie with me and promised me food. I agreed but he is no man who seeks women! He, a priest, sought to use me as an animal might. I fled and he followed. He is not a man! Release me, I pray you, or I am condemned to his revenge."

Her very passion stirred the people around them, for it seemed that no one could utter such words against a priest if they were not true. She saw their hesitation and took advantage of it. "Search me! There is no pouch, I swear it."

The young man ran quick hands over her, enjoying the motions, while another took her pack and looked at its meager contents. There was nothing, and the people muttered angrily. The followers of Jagon, some five in all, massed protectively beside him.

Jagon spoke directly to CeLa and it was as if none of the others on that crowded street existed. "You shall pay triple over for what you have sought to bring upon me by this insolence. That which you thought you suffered before will now be purest pleasure. I owe you much and it is a debt I will be delighted to pay."

"What is the truth of this?" The fat man came closer to CeLa as his eyes rested on the swell of her bosom. She gave him a dazzling smile and was rewarded by his angry look at Jagon.

Jagon's temper broke as he raised his arms. "She

is Dahpur's! Who challenges him challenges all and I am his priest!"

The others backed away before this invocation of authority. CeLa's hand went to her dagger. Jagon laughed and her arm went numb from his blow. His other hand rose toward her head and the world faded as she fell.

CeLa's head rocked from side to side with the little blows on her cheeks. They were irritating and then painful. Her eyes felt matted and heavy; her head hammered. She tried to move her body but could not. She heard soft laughter and recognized it instantly. Her lids lifted and she looked into the amused face of Jagon. He stopped slapping her long enough to enjoy her dismay. She saw that she was lying on a pallet in a small underground chamber with dark walls where one torch blazed high above their heads. Her hands were bound tightly behind her back and now she was conscious of the tightness of the cords and her own nudity. She tried to speak but Jagon's hand slammed against her teeth and blood spurted out. Then he twisted the nipples of her breasts, driving his nails into the tenderness, causing her to whimper.

"Not a sound, bitch. Not a sound." His eyes glittered with rising fury.

CeLa obeyed him; only a fool would not fear Jagon. Suddenly he flipped her over, spread her buttocks wide, and thrust his swollen member deeply into her again and again as he drew himself out so that the very tip was barely inside her and then hammered it full length into her tenderness. Tears ran down her face and she bit the insides of her cheeks but she dared not cry out. He was capable of anything.

When she thought he would tear her apart, he groaned and rolled from her. In a manner of seconds

he began to take her from the front in the savage
way of a street bully. She watched his contorted face,
his eyes pinpoints of fire, and forced her body to go
limp so that the pain was not so strong. Kir's face
rose before her and she drew courage from that as
well as from her hatred of this man.

He finished, shook her lolling head savagely and
dug his nails into her chin. "Enjoyable, is it not?
There will be many such times. Not a man, I think
you said? On what evidence do you base that, I wonder? You are with child. How amusing it will be to
make you lose it!" He laughed again on the high
keening note that frightened her even more than
his rapes.

"Kir will find me!" She found that her voice was
strong in her fear for their child. "You will be punished."

Again that laughter. "Do not bore me, CeLa. I am
dangerous when I am bored. I have plans for you,
Kir and that fool who calls himself a king. You will
not see the light of day again but you will live to
plead for death. I remember all that passed between
us. Oh, I remember well." He clapped his hands
together and two dark men emerged from the shadows. "Clean her up and feed her. If she speaks, gag
her."

Time faded for CeLa after that. Jagon did not
touch her again but he had her bound and gagged
naked before him, then he told her of all the practices and cruelties that would be done to her in time
to come. She fought him only once. That time one
of the slaves hit her lightly in the stomach and the
nausea made her certain that she would lose the child.
Her sleep was disturbed at night by Jagon coming
to whisper lewdly and run his fingers over her slender body. She dared not flinch away or speak lest he
savage her again. The men bathed and perfumed her
daily, polished and combed her hair, made certain

that she ate and drank properly. She fought against fear and invoked the goddess constantly, but the only thing that was real was her hatred of Jagon and the need to preserve her child.

Jagon came to her one day—there was no way to measure time in this hell—and she saw that he was smiling with no hint of his usual cruelty. There was an air of suppressed excitement about him as he leaned close to her. The fresh scent of outside came to her nostrils and she thought with sudden agony that she would die in this darkness. His mouth took hers and his tongue thrust deeply into it. She drew back before she could think of how resistance enraged him. He jerked her head back so that her eyes looked straight into his.

"I would have you willing. Nay, eager. I shall be obeyed."

CeLa forced herself to remain still as she looked at this handsome man who had raped and pillaged her body, tortured her mind and heart, tried to kill her child and her husband and would now destroy her utterly. She must play his game and live as long as she could. Hunger for life rose in her and she smiled tremblingly at Jagon. "Aye, Jagon. I obey."

He rubbed her breasts as his knee parted her legs. They slipped down to the pallet and his tongue entered her mouth again. She twined her own with it and felt his stalk begin to rise. One hand went to her mound of warmth and moved slowly up and down. Her body was beginning to respond. Jagon's hands were hard but not cruel and she sensed that in some strange way he wanted her willing. She forced her arms to encircle him as he lifted his face to stare down at her. The planes of his face were elongated in the flickering light of the torch and his tongue moved over the curve of his lips. His hand rubbed her again and she felt the pleasure begin. He saw and smiled.

All CeLa's hatred and revulsion for this man rose

up as she spat full into his eager face. She almost welcomed the blow that stopped her own triumphant laughter and sent her into blessed oblivion.

She was left alone for what seemed a long time in almost total darkness. Any hope of life depended on her own wits and resourcefulness. She knew herself incapable of subterfuge. It was not likely that she could outwit Jagon again, but she must be ready. So CeLa brought Kir's face before her inner vision and waited.

When Jagon finally came, it was with a sinister old man whose smile showed snaggled teeth as he fingered a small sack. One guard was posted at the door. Jagon was smiling, his eyes brilliant with cruelty. "I have decided to relieve you of the burden you carry, CeLa. Soon you will grow heavy with the child and I do not find the prospect pleasing." He urged the old man forward. "He has removed many unwanted children in his time. He works very rapidly."

CeLa clutched her stomach and cried out, "No, you cannot do this thing."

"Beg me." Jagon put both hands on his hips and laughed. "Kneel and do it."

She fell to her knees before him, wondering at her loss of pride, then knowing that life went beyond all else. She babbled to Jagon and knew that her words made no sense even to herself. He yawned and called to the guard. Even as she crouched there, CeLa felt her anger come upward until she forgot fear and hope in her all-consuming hatred for this man who was less than a beast. A snarl came from her lips as she launched herself at him, fingernails raking the air, then curving down his face to draw blood. He aimed a blow at her stomach but she twisted aside just in time.

Suddenly a dagger sang through the air, pinning his upraised arm in its long white sleeve to the wooden section of the door. A voice spoke in tones of command, a voice CeLa knew, whose owner she had once counted friend. Utis said, "Another such move and the mate to that dagger will find your heart. You have abrogated your bargain, Jagon."

CeLa sat up and saw that a number of men armed with short swords and spears had entered and come to stand beside Utis, who looked taller and older in a white tunic with the sickle emblem.

Jagon said coldly, "You knew I wanted this woman. It was understood between the priestess and myself."

Utis said, "For two days and nights only, with no bodily harm done. It has been ten and she looks ill with marks of torture. And you meant to destroy the child. We have further—"

CeLa screamed, "I do not know what either of you is talking about but you have no rights to me or my child! Give me that dagger. I will kill that beast where he stands."

One of the guards stepped close and barred her way. She clawed at him in vain. Utis snapped a command and he moved away. She came to CeLa and put a hand on the girl's shoulder. CeLa jerked back. "You are my enemy too."

Utis smiled. "You and your child still live. He would have killed you a few minutes ago. You are safe now, CeLa, and under the protection of the Mother."

"If that is so, then take me to Kir." Dark eyes challenged dark eyes.

Jagon laughed explosively. "That would be hard to do. By all rights he is dead now and that rabble of Dahrata's with him."

CeLa's cry was wordless, an animal in pain. She was more torn than she had been during Jagon's torture. "What is this all about? Tell me? If Kir were dead I would know it."

Utis said, "There was an uprising in the city while many were gone on the tiger hunt. Dahrata's followers were scattered but some managed to flee to him. It is known that many are dead but the fate of Dahrata we do not know. Kir was with him, of course. There is fighting in the streets but we expect victory."

Jagon said savagely, "Then why are you here and not in the temple praying for all that we have struggled for?"

"Because this woman was promised, she and her child. You asked the priestess for her for a time and your request was granted, but you misused her. Surely you recognize the forces with which you tamper?"

CeLa saw that they tossed her back and forth as young children play with stone balls. Jagon's will meant certain death with incredible slowness. Utis's goddess might be safer but, of the two, she thought she feared Jagon less. Because she was less than human to these people, CeLa knew that she could not appeal to any sense of rightness they might have. She must bide her time and wait.

Jagon stared at Utis as she stood there calmly with the guards behind her. Then rage came over him like a storm in the desert. He began to sweat, the whites of his eyes showed as they rolled, his voice rose to a bellow and sank to a whisper, and the cords in his neck stood out like ropes. His curses were monumental, coming as they did in languages CeLa had never heard and many that she had. "This accursed society where the will of a woman prevails will never survive! I have marched with Sargon of Akkad and greater generals than he. I am poet, soldier, musician, artist, servant of greater gods than all these and worthy to walk with them. I, Jagon, should have ruled in Sumer and might have done so had it not been for that girl there and her lover! Of course I want revenge. I am power. I alone hold the secrets!"

He raved on and on. The old Jagon had never given way so completely to wrath; CeLa saw the deterioration even as she knew that this man was a threat even to those he might count as friends. She knew also that he was mad.

Utis said, "The goddess must have what is her due if we are to rule in Daro. I could do no less than obey. I am sent to bring her to the priestess. It is time for our forces to unite. Do you come?"

Jagon's anger ceased as it had begun and he gave CeLa a malevolent glance. "I do; this woman is unworthy and I shall tell the priestess so."

Utis shrugged and the guards moved around CeLa. Others moved behind Jagon and they began to march out of the little room where she had endured so much. They walked through underground passages lit with scattered torches and lined with guards who gave instant salute. The air was still and hot; once CeLa tripped and almost fell. Instantly Utis was at her shoulder with a cup of wine and fresh dates as she urged the girl to rest and eat.

"It would choke me. Utis, what is all this? I thought you were my friend as well as Kir's. How could you so betray us?"

Opaque eyes met hers and did not falter. "I serve the Mother. All else is dross."

It was the same kind of fanaticism that CeLa had met in Sumer and among the Ib, when people forgot their human origins and sought to be the very gods they served. Hatred for that kind of thinking blazed up in her and the contempt she felt showed in her eyes and words.

"What will happen to us? What kind of plot is this? You are mad, the lot of you!"

"There will be no more insulting words from you, CeLa, even if I have to gag you. You will obey. I think you should remember the fate you might even now be suffering had I not arrived!"

CeLa was silent then, for she knew she must be wary. She ate and drank as she was bidden, finding that the sustenance restored her in part. She had need of it, for the way grew hard as they toiled through passages that were partly fallen in with debris, went up and down steps cut in the mud of centuries ago, and finally climbed down what seemed a sheer wall, so narrow were the foot and hand holds. CeLa was wet with sweat and her hair hung in wet tendrils as her breath came heavily. The period of inactivity had weakened her but she was slightly comforted to see that the others panted as well. Only Jagon was cool and smiling, although hatred flared in his eyes when they met hers.

"I hardly think the goddess will think she has the best of this bargain, Utis. Why not take a suitable virgin and let me have this woman?"

She did not turn her head as she said, "Go and refresh yourself, Jagon. Then wait upon the priestess. I speak no more with you on this matter."

CeLa saw Jagon's hand start toward his belt, then move as quickly away when he saw the instinctive movement of the guards.

They came out now on a wide, smooth floor that was silken to the touch of bare feet. Torches blazed in wall sconces every few feet and there were woven hangings and sculpture depicting the Mother Goddess in various poses. In many of them she stood with a hand touching a bull-like creature or one-horned beast. In others she writhed in the positions of passion but always remained in the dominant position. There was incense in the air and the sound of singing rose softly. CeLa thought that they must be very far underground and wondered if she would ever again see the light of day or the sun on a river. Surely if Kir were dead, she would know it. Then she knew again that if he were, she would yet live for herself and the child.

"Inanna, goddess, let me live!" She waited but there was no sign of an answer. Beyond, in the far passageway, a gong sounded melodiously and she knew that her time was fast approaching.

CeLa was taken to a little anteroom where a silent maidservant bathed her in scented water and polished her hair with a cloth, then combed it until the black strands leaped with a life of their own. Golden ornaments fit over her hips and were belted with flashing jewels. Breastplates of gold clasped over her full breasts and a short, thin coat of gauzy material was draped over her bare shoulders. Necklaces dripped over her bosom and a headdress of gold with flashing stones crowned her hair.

"You are worthy to go to the goddess, CeLa. She whose service is all will be honored by your beauty." Utis spoke from the doorway. "Jagon will pay for treating you so."

CeLa swung round to face her. "You made a bargain with your goddess, did you not? Myself and my child in return for what, I wonder? You are slaves here. In Sumer we do not make our gods mirrors of ourselves."

The gong came insistently several times and Utis said, "It is time."

CeLa knew that she must play this out; thus, she offered no protest as they walked along another ornate hall, up some stairs and into a wide room furnished with carved and inlaid chairs. A carved scene of the great goddess took up nearly all one wall. She sat at judgment, arms on her knees, sickle headdress in place, eyes stern, expression both taunting and sad. Sinners and the faithless knelt before her gaze. Beside her was the branch of life and the skull of death.

A curtain moved aside and those with CeLa fell to their knees. She remained standing, rooted to the spot, knowing that this was the supreme jest of the cruel gods. The priestess of the Mother Goddess of Mohenjo-daro was Sirna, once high priestess of Ninhursag of Lagash and Sumer.

50

For the Sacred Life

Sirna walked to a seat set artfully in the wall and arranged herself there. She looked the very duplicate of the carved scene on the opposite wall. CeLa could see that she had changed little in all the time since Lagash. Her beautiful face was still arrogant and willful, the body still tall and supple under the revealing tunic she wore. The phrase "daughter of the gods" sprang to mind and CeLa remembered the power this woman had wielded in Lagash. Did she possess it here as well?

"You alone do not kneel to me, CeLa of Lagash. Do you not know that your life was forfeit to the goddess long ago and that she will have her due?" The voice was powerful and resonant with a thread of curiosity turning in it.

"Life is a gift of the gods, Sirna, itself a precious thing. I do not think that they capriciously drink of human blood." Oddly enough, CeLa thought, she believed what she was saying. Human love had taught her much of what she hoped the gods to be.

Sirna laughed and the sound was rich in the room. She waved a commanding hand and the others moved back out of earshot. "I am powerful here. My will is the law and I promised the goddess long ago that she should have you for her own. I keep my promises and she keeps hers."

"Why me?"

Sirna said, "You have qualities of courage and wit

and beauty that must be returned to She who gave them. Those who are sacrificed have such qualities. I assume you noticed that?"

CeLa found that she had reached the point where she moved in a dream. Nothing seemed real; she could not be standing here discussing her own death with this woman who chose her for sacrifice much as one might choose a bird or an animal for the temple. Out of that feeling of unreality, she sought to satisfy her curiosity, for she had heard the boastfulness in the rich voice of Sirna.

"How came you to such power in Daro? Does Ninhursag rule here?"

Sirna's brows drew together in a frown and her voice was edged with venom as she said, "Cursed be the name of Sargon! Word was spread of my rituals in Lagash and my followers were infiltrated by his agents. We who were a secret society with faithful in many places were suddenly scorned and labeled. The city of Lagash was torn from the inside and fell to him. A price was set on my head—I, the foremost servant of the Mother—and I was forced to flee with some of the bravest of my followers overland toward the sea."

"Sargon rules Sumer and Akkad as he said he would?" CeLa could only be glad that the powerful man had triumphed, that he had used the information they had managed to get to him. Would Kir ever know that his friend had won?

"Much good it will do him," snapped Sirna. "The goddess rules here in many forms, as you will have seen. There is an old prophecy about a woman coming from afar to rule here and how the city will rise in might because of her."

"Are you she?" The question was asked almost lightly but CeLa was not surprised by the fanatic light in the great eyes.

"It is the destiny promised me by the goddess who

was with me in the misfortunes of Sumer, even though her sacrifice was profaned by your escape. You shall not escape again; that I vow!" Her voice rang through the chamber and the kneeling servants murmured softly.

CeLa looked her full in the face. She would not cringe before this woman. "You will kill me." It was not a question.

Sirna's voice hammered at her. "I have worked here to build my followers. It was easy, for they always preferred the goddess in her sternness. Dahrata would have none of me even before he took the throne. He will pay. We went into hiding but every day saw us stronger. Gossip and rumor fermented; his rule was harsh and the discontented have flocked to us. Jagon helped in his way, but he is blinded by you. Now the great ceremonial is upon us and the battles are being won. The great one will have her due. I, even I, have done this thing!"

There was silence in the chamber as her voice faded. The beautiful face was distorted, the great eyes staring. CeLa knew again that this woman was mad.

"Surely you want to live?" The worry in Sirna's next words made CeLa tense. The priestess was frowning, all elation vanished.

CeLa whispered, "If Kir is dead, then I do not care what you do." She would catch at any hope. A sacrifice is doubly precious if the desire for life is strong and the victim yet chooses to die. Might there not be some vestige of a chance if they thought her passive and willing? She would never give up, not while she lived. She made that vow silently even as tears came to her eyes at the thought of Kir.

"Jagon told me of your passion for this man. Did you truly love him?" Sirna was all interest; they might have been two girls gossiping at the well. "Men are but tools. The goddess teaches us this."

CeLa saw Kir again as they walked in the streets of Daro, his hand touching hers, his eyes saying what

his voice could not yet venture. She thought of his
tenderness and his passion, of their long road together, his loyalty and of the pain they had endured.
She would not profane his memory by discussing him
with this woman. "Do what you will, Sirna. He was
the sunlight for me. It is ended. My dying prayer
to Inanna shall be for the eternal destruction of you
and Jagon."

Sirna's voice rose in a scream. "Take her away!
Guard her well!"

CeLa was taken to another dark chamber and
locked in. She felt that she had acquitted herself
well. Now the waiting would begin.

There was no way to know how time passed in
these dark caverns. It was two sleeps later when they
came for her. She had expected the servants at any
time and had tried to gird up her waning courage.
She was once more gorgeously arrayed as she had
been when conducted into Sirna's presence. This time,
however, breastplate and girdle shimmered with encrusted jewels and she wore bracelets ornamented
with the image of the goddess in her life-giving aspect. Her hair was bound high and fastened with
jewels. A wide headdress held it down. She saw her
image in a shimmering pool of underground water;
she was both barbaric and beautiful. The long golden
robe was draped over her near nudity, then the women
did obeisance before her.

"It is time, lady." One held out an arm for her.

CeLa put her hand on it and summoned her most
miserable expression. "I am well ready to quit this
world." They paced along slowly and she pretended
not to notice that one of the slaves had detached herself and disappeared into one of the corridors.

They seemed to walk in a circle that went slightly
uphill, but CeLa knew that her sense of direction
was off and there was no way of telling for sure. The
change in the attitude of the women did not puzzle

her. She was sure that this was the interim time before her death and that her death would take fearful form. There might be nothing she could do to
avoid the final outcome, but if she practiced her current docility and seeming uncaring, it was possible
that she might be allowed close to Sirna before the
end. Then all her desperate fury would be unleashed
with teeth, fingers and body. She would not go to
her death tamely; Sirna would bear her marks.

After walking what seemed a very long way down
narrow corridors, CeLa was dazzled when they came
out into a vast, brilliantly lit area that seemed capable of holding an army. Seats were cut into one
side of the high wall and in the center of these was
a thronelike structure richly ornamented and inlaid
and hung with rich fabrics that were themselves jeweled.

The major part of the area was flat and hard, covered with a fine sprinkling of sand, and stacks of
mud bricks stood at intervals in the space. Its use
was not immediately apparent and CeLa turned her
eyes to an immense statue of the goddess that loomed
diagonally across. This time she stood erect, breasts
out, wide hips indicative of fecundity, face stern,
hands bearing the united symbols of life and death,
eyes glittering in the flares of light given off by the
numerous torches. Behind her was an enormous stone
sword, its edge toward the open area. At her side
was the great bull that CeLa had seen so graphically
reproduced earlier.

The hand on her arm suddenly squeezed and they
paused in the doorway. She looked questioningly at
her escort and the woman said, "We wait now until
we are summoned. You are blessed indeed, lady, for
it is said that the goddess accepts you."

CeLa said, "Nothing matters except that this be
swiftly ended and I join my husband in the dark
world."

The woman said intensely, "You must not feel so. There is not one among us here who would not willingly take on your fate. We were not so honored."

In a wild moment CeLa thought of screaming at her to take it then, but that was not the best strategy. The woman's face was resentful and the wide eyes looked at her with envy. CeLa realized that others of her escort looked the same. Was this something she could use? Hesitantly she said, "The priestess commanded, did she not? She is herself an outlander, even as I. Does the goddess speak with her tongue?"

"Blasphemy!" The whisper was sibilant but another answered, "Is it so? How can we know?"

There was a sudden trumpet blast that lifted and rose oddly in the caverns. CeLa took time to wonder if they were indeed underneath Daro or far from it in this network of what might be a forgotten civilization or yet a city built on a city. People were entering from the various doors around the walls and taking their seats. They seemed ordinary men and women dressed in simple tunics and skirts with the many necklaces that the inhabitants of Daro favored. There seemed to be more than a hundred but they mixed and mingled so that it was hard to tell.

The trumpet blew again and several white-robed priests entered to take their seats by the side of the throne. An equal number of priestesses came with the next blast. Silence stretched out until a low thumping began, rising higher and higher until broken by the music of one superb voice lifted in an invocation to the goddess. Drum and voice matched each other, then a low sound moved over the crowd and Sirna entered. Her voice rose to spiral from the roof of the cavern and down again.

She stood in the center of the area and lifted both arms to the goddess. Her superb body shone through the thinnest of white robes. Gold shone on her arms and legs and in her high-piled hair, which bore a headdress similar to that of the statue. She bowed and turned to the people, her matchless voice a lyre.

"Followers of the Mother Goddess of Mohenjo-daro, her time and yours has come. You welcomed me, an outlander to your shores who has served her all my life, and made me your priestess, for her hand was on me. Word has lately come to me that our forces are winning in the street battle for the city and the next sunrise, if the goddess smiles on our efforts, will see the rule of Daro firmly in her hands and those of her servants.

"We are come here to honor the goddess in cere-monial rite and to give her that which is her due, a sacrifice long promised and others which are newly come. Glory to the goddess!"

The people stood as one and their voices hymned both Sirna and the goddess. CeLa felt a chill go down her back as she looked toward the priests and saw Jagon rise. Under the priestly robe his body was firmly muscled and hard, shimmering with light oil in the blazing light. His voice was that of the poet, rich and strong, the voice that had given them heart in the desert.

"I too have been greatly blessed by the welcome of this city and by the goddess, for I follow her male counterpart while acknowledging her awesome power. It is in deference to her that I now speak. The sac-rifice to her should be pure and undefiled; the woman offered is not! She has lain with many and the child she bears might be that of a common slave. I say that she is unworthy. I speak thus only because of my great faith in the goddess. I can give three virgins from my own household in place of this defiled one."

The people muttered among themselves, bending forward to stare and then looking uneasily at Sirna, who stood tall and proud before them. A signal must have passed between her and CeLa's escort, for the hand on her arm pulled and they went out into the circular area. Jagon stood as he was while they moved away from CeLa and left her standing a few yards from Sirna. A little wind blew the golden robe about and lights shone on the richness of her attire. The long silence drew out.

CeLa knew that Jagon gambled much, for the controlling power here was undoubtedly Sirna's. He desperately wanted his revenge and was willing to risk much for it. If it came to a conflict of power before the assembled throng, it might truly be that Sirna would give her over. There was not much to choose from as far as CeLa was concerned, but then the choice was not hers to make.

Sirna spoke slowly and deliberately. "Jagon, you suggest that the sacrifice offered to the goddess is unworthy? You speak of your wonted devotion to her whose power has raised you high. Come then, take part in the sacred rites. Your participation will raise you even more in her esteem and afterward we will accept the three virgins offered." She stepped forward and held her hands out to him. "Come, in the name of the Mother Goddess of Mohenjo-daro, be one with us in this most sacred of rites, that of life and death."

He hesitated and CeLa saw him draw back from the incandescence that was Sirna. The crowd called as one, "Obey the priestess! The goddess calls! Obey!"

A little smile curved Sirna's lips. She was well pleased. The noise built up until Jagon held his hands up in surrender.

"I am grateful to the priestess and will join in the rites as she asks, conscious always of my own unworthiness."

CeLa felt chills go up and down her spine at the look on Sirna's face. Just so had she smiled in the last moments before the death-pits of Lagash.

51

I Will Lift You Up

Silence came again to the vast area as Jagon came down to stand beside Sirna, and together they went to the statue of the goddess, where he stood several steps below Sirna. A slave came to light a torch between them and in the light it gave, CeLa saw a stone bench, as long again as a person, which another slave covered with a fresh white cloth.

"Bring the two!" Sirna's order rolled out. The crowd breathed a sigh of anticipation.

A very young girl and a young man were brought out. Both were beautiful in the perfection of youth that would not have the chance to wither. They clasped hands and smiled mistily at each other and the world, then knelt before Sirna. She spoke briefly to them as they embraced.

"Is this of your free will and choice then, that you go to the goddess?"

"It is." The clear voices rang with assurance.

"With her blessing!" Sirna caught the hair of the girl and slit her throat with a swift gesture that left CeLa gasping. Barely had the blood poured over the slaying hand before she did the same to the boy. So precise had she been that no blood stained the purity of her gown.

CeLa began to get some inkling of her own fate when the next sacrifice was brought out. He was a young man in his twenties, tall and powerfully built with fearful, rolling eyes. He was tightly bound and gagged but he struggled against those who held him even as he was placed on the altar.

Jagon approached and even at a distance CeLa could sense his excitement. He lifted the knife high, brought it back to test the sharpness, then put it down to run his hands over the terrified victim's body and caress the manhood there. He caught up the knife again and plunged it deeply into the broad chest. Blood pumped out in a steady stream and Jagon dipped both arms in it as he raised them to the goddess in silent tribute.

The world swung before CeLa and she put her hand to her face. She no longer had any sort of plan. All conscious thought had left her, and she stared at what followed in a kind of shock that held her rigid. The crowd cried approbation to the zealous servants of the goddess as yet another sacrifice was made, this one a blooming woman in her twenties who embraced the knife as a lover. A frightened, screaming boy of about twelve followed, held to the altar by Jagon as the knife was driven home again and again. He and Sirna took joy and pleasure in their task and the crowd knew it. Finally it was done. The bodies were taken away and the cloth replaced.

Sirna cried, "Bring the woman forward. So shall the dual nature of the goddess be celebrated, for as she is life so is she death, as she is mother so is she father, and in the end she is all. In blood and death do we rise to life and return. Glory to the goddess!"

The excited cries of the people rang in CeLa's ears as she was brought to the altar. There her robe was stripped from her as well as the breastplates and girdle so that she stood naked before them all. She could not struggle, for the slaves held her tightly. Her arms were bound behind her back with cords and then the headdress was removed so that her hair tumbled down her shoulders. Beyond fear and anger, CeLa felt as if she walked in a dream and might wake at any moment in Kir's arms. Perhaps it might be so; their enemies triumphed in this world but the netherworld would be devoid of them. Kir had once told her that all sensible men feared battle and had their terrors, but once there, they usually fought well. No chance was to be given CeLa of Lagash or her child.

The drum thumped and thundered in ever-increasing rolls as CeLa was placed on the altar. Sirna loomed over her, her eyes dark with triumph, her mouth wet. Jagon took off his robe and she saw that his stalk thrust out in front of him, quivering with his every move; he ran his hands, still red with the blood of the slain, up and down her body.

"I will purify the sacrifice with my seed!" He faced the crowd and heard their blood lust. Sirna nodded and waved him toward CeLa.

She fought as best she could but it was no use. His smooth, slick body pressed down on her and the mad eyes flamed into hers as he hammered deeply into her flesh.

He looked long at her. Jagon the powerful, handsome and ruthless, the light flaming on the planes of his face. He had won; his pride was avenged.

Sirna was suddenly beside him, her hands eager on his body, her eyes flaming with lust as she cupped his manhood. Jagon laughed, a low, hungry sound, and caught her to him. CeLa saw the stalk of his manhood lift, ripe and hard. She swung herself off the altar just as Jagon pulled Sirna down toward him and thrust upward so that he penetrated into the lush mat just above him. Sirna came down on him and rose again so that the very tip of his stalk touched her. Slowly, slowly, she pushed down on him and his groan of delight was clearly audible to all.

Then, at the moment when culmination seemed to approach, she pulled back slightly, raised the dagger that had been hidden in her hand, and drove it into his chest with all the considerable strength in her hand. Blood and seed roared forth as she pulled it out and hit his chest again with the same powerful blow. Her laughter rose and encircled the area while the drum thundered out the triumph of the goddess and a great bellow shook the cavern again and again. She rose and stood before them all, her arms high, blood and seed dripping from her as she cried, "Death to all who would oppose the goddess! Death! Death!" They took up her cry and the noise was deafening over the continuous bellows.

CeLa rose to her feet and stared down at the body of Jagon. Her hated enemy was dead at the moment of his pleasure and triumph. His chest was a red mass but his face still mirrored that pleasure. Delight and hatred came together in her and she cried to the dead body, "For Kir! For CeLa! As you would have done to us and more, has it been done to you!"

The bellow came again and she looked up to see the largest bull she had ever seen standing in the center of the sanded area. Four slaves were holding him. The great horns swung back and forth with the movement of the head and the folds of flesh at the neck seemed to drop from the hump. The body was long and sinewy.

Sirna gave an order and slaves gathered up the body of Jagon. They took it out into the vicinity of the bull and dropped it there. Those holding him let go and ran for safety. He gave one enraged bellow and began to trample it. Shards of bloody flesh rose in the air and bone crunched on the floor as flesh mixed with sand and became a soggy mess. Then the cruel horns lifted and tossed the remains until they merged and were no more. The people shouted now and then but mostly they watched, their lust seemingly sated by all the bloodshed that had gone before. Finally the bull finished and stood still, blowing a bit, swinging his massive head back and forth.

Sirna stepped out again in all her beautiful nudity and the cries of the crowd were idolatrous. CeLa had strained against the bonds that held her hands but she could not loose them. Now Sirna's full attention would come to rest on her. Sirna cried, "He who would have poisoned your minds is dead! The woman and her unborn child still live but the goddess shall have her due, for this woman was promised to her long ago and yet fled. For this perfidy she shall be bound and ripped open, the bare seed of the child taken from her and all burned while yet alive before the goddess. Such is her decree and by this shall we win victory in Mohenjo-daro!"

CeLa heard her fate and shivered with paralyzing fear as she shrank back from the roar that rose up. She had been wrong; the crowd yet hungered for satiation. Sirna turned to face her and she saw the blood lust on the arrogant face and knew that this woman found passionate pleasure in what she did. Anger woke in CeLa and killed her fear as it poured over her in waves of such hatred as she had felt for no one except Jagon. She remembered the desert and the challenge that Raba had been forced to honor. She looked at the great bull and saw him paw the floor as his nostrils spread wide. Knowledge suddenly came together in her mind and the boldness of her plan fed her anger.

Sirna was walking closer now, her very movement like that of a lioness stalking her prey. Behind her the people were silent in anticipation and CeLa knew that they waited for the spilling of her blood. Sirna was twisting the handle of the heavy knife in her hand, one blow of which could disembowel and yet not totally kill.

CeLa jumped up on the altar itself, her bearing as confident as though she were safe, and lifted her voice, projecting it as she had learned from Sirna herself. It rang fully and did not shake. Sirna, caught by surprise, stopped and stared at the helpless victim who had rallied to defend herself.

"Let the goddess decide this! She loves a willing victim. That she shall have and more also, for as the mother, so the child. She spared my life in Lagash and in the land of Egypt. She gave me the child of my lover, who was a mighty warrior."

She paused for a moment as the bull stamped, and in that time she caught a movement by the door and her mouth went dry. In the faint light that shone against the brilliance, she saw figures with bull horns and beards standing there. More of Sirna's ritual, she thought, and opened her mouth to speak again.

Sirna cried, "Let the sacrifice begin! We have waited long enough!"

CeLa shouted, "Hold in the name of the Mother Goddess! I invoke her and let her stand as my witness. I challenge you, Sirna, to combat to the death. The loser will go willingly to her death before the goddess here and before the people. Combat to the death!"

Sirna laughed and advanced on her. "You will die, you fool, as I decree! Challenge, indeed. I could kill you with my bare hands and you know it."

CeLa did indeed know it and now she took her last chance into consideration. Her voice rose on a high, keening note that was almost song and whine combined. "Let the goddess decide. If she wills this contest, let her speak through her sacred beast. I appeal to it!"

The bull, tormented by the sound, lifted his head and flung it back and forth while his eyes rolled. He loosed bellow after bellow and the people in the nearest seats covered their ears. CeLa took advantage of that reaction to lift her voice again in the high whine that she had learned to use in mischief as a child when she wanted to scatter animals or make a nuisance of herself. The bull bellowed again and took a few running steps as if he could not decide where to go.

CeLa shouted, "She has spoken, Sirna! It is her will!"

Sirna stood still, a black and hunted look on her face. In the silence, the crowd roared, "Combat! Combat! Hear the will of the goddess!"

Still Sirna said nothing and CeLa taunted, "Do you fear that she will leave you? Has she perhaps departed from you even before this?" The crowd rumbled its displeasure in the fickle nature of the moment.

In a sudden jump, Sirna was at CeLa's side and the heavy knife slashed through the bonds so that her hands were free. Sweat trickled through Sirna's black hair and fell onto her chest, where the superb breasts jutted. "You think in vain to escape me, bitch!"

CeLa moved rapidly away from her and rubbed the circulation back into her aching hands. The two women circled each other warily as silence fell on the crowd at this new excitement. Sirna turned to them and all her knowledge of the ways of people came to the fore as she spoke.

"I accept the challenge for the greater glory of the goddess who commands us all. Since I am the challenged, by ancient law it is my right to choose the manner of combat. I am stronger by far than this foolish woman who seeks to avoid the fate ordained for her; therefore I will not insist on hand-to-hand battle."

"Inanna, Inanna, it was you who placed this scheme in my mind. Lady of Sumer, lead her into it. She is all that is evil and cruel. Be with me." So CeLa prayed to the faraway goddess she had taken for her own in the days when choice was still possible.

Sirna flung a triumphant look at CeLa and added, "She chose to invoke the sacred beast of the goddess. Very well, he shall be the deciding factor. We will enter the area with knives. He will remain, and whoever inflicts the first severe wound on the other without being trampled or gored wins the battle. He is fierce and untamed, unknown to me or any other, kept as the symbol of the goddess. This will be fair combat in truth!"

The crowd burst into wild applause and cried her name again and again. The bull pawed the ground and watched the movement around him. CeLa drew in her breath shakily as she offered up a prayer of thanks to Inanna.

52

The Bull Dance

They faced each other in a world that narrowed down
to the sanded area, the great bull and the knives in
their hands. The people were silent, drunk with the
excitement of the hour. CeLa's breath came in short,
shallow gasps as she hefted the sharp, heavy-handled
knife. Sweat shone on her naked body and savagery
shone from her eyes. Sirna was tall and grim, determined to dismiss this upstart and return to the pattern of ritual she had already chosen. They hastened
to kill each other.

Sirna kept a low-voiced description going of exactly
what would happen to CeLa and how it would feel,
but CeLa ignored that and shut her mind to everything else but the bull and the movements of the
other woman. She did not waste her breath by reply-
ing to the taunts. Sirna edged close to her and the
knife rushed down, missing only by a stroke. CeLa
whirled away in a swift motion that set the bull to
pawing again. She approached Sirna from the side
and thrust at her with the blade, but Sirna sidestepped
and came at CeLa with deadly intent and a force that
threatened to overpower her rival. She was swifter
than CeLa and one hand closed on the girl's upper
arm. CeLa brought the dagger up and Sirna caught
that arm, bearing her to the sand. The furious face
of her enemy bent over her in triumph and the blade
blade bore down toward her eyes.

There was a furious bellow and the bull charged,

head down. Sirna cursed and let CeLa go as she
dodged back. CeLa rolled over and over as she removed herself from his path. She pulled her feet under her and rose to a crouch. The bull thundered
past and came to a halt some distance away from
them. He shook his great head, pawed the ground,
bellowed and waited. Sirna came at CeLa, who
dodged, and once again they moved in their own
deadly circle. CeLa ran at her once, the knife held
low as she sought to cripple her enemy in the fleshy
section of her body. Sirna pulled aside with ease
and laughed.

"You are already growing tired to try so foolish
an attempt."

"Save your foul breath. You will need it later."

The bull charged several times, once directly at
Sirna, his sharp hooves barely missing her as he
whirled and came again. In the moment that she
jerked back from his rush, CeLa drove the knife at
her chest. CeLa's foot slipped and she missed. The knife
clattered to the sand and the bull went past so close
that she could have touched his slick hide. She tried
to rise but there was blood on the area from Jagon's
demise and her own sweat caused her to flounder.
Sirna bent and snatched up the knife, then launched
herself at CeLa with a howl of triumph, an evil grin
pulling her lips back from her teeth.

The bull bellowed and lowered his head as he
charged directly at the fallen woman. Sirna cursed
and drew back from the onslaught. CeLa saw her
action and readied herself in the short time that stood
between her and death by goring. She drew her body
into a ball, ran her hands through her hair to dry
them, held her breath and then he was upon her.
Dimly she heard Sirna's laughter and saw her standing, both daggers in hand, waiting her turn to wreak
vengeance.

The deadly curved horns were only inches from

CeLa when she reached out for them with hands
that suddenly did not tremble. She caught them at
the exact moment they would have tossed her. Her
slender, wiry body moved with the animal's own force
and she twisted it as she arched up over horns and
hump to land on his back. The force of the landing
jarred her and he stopped when the victim was no
longer in sight. CeLa slid down the smooth body
onto the floor and danced backward from him on
legs that shook.

The crowd rose as one and cried approval for the
"outlander" as Sirna had called her. Their calls were
heartfelt and warming to CeLa, although she knew
they wanted only blood. Sirna, taken aback, gaped
at them and CeLa felt waves of hatred pour toward
her from the priestess. She screamed savagely at CeLa
but the girl could not understand the words, for they
were in the ceremonial language of Daro. Some people in the crowd heard, and the call for the outlander
and her courage lifted again. Sirna ran at CeLa, deadly purpose in every step. The bull caught the movement out of the corner of his eye. CeLa was still behind him so he ran at the nearest target, his pace
faster, his bulk silent and determined.

The horn caught Sirna in the side and penetrated
all the way through her body. She screamed in agony
and fury as he tossed her high and brought her to
earth again, slamming her into the ground that was
suddenly red with her blood. He tossed her again
and this time, when she came down, his hooves tore
at her and she came loose from his horn while still
alive, screaming in mortal agony. CeLa saw the
hooves land in the once beautiful face and heard the
thud as her eyes melted in a rush of blood. The mad-
dened animal savaged her as he had done Jagon and
then he was suddenly quiet.

CeLa stood very still and stared at the followers
of Sirna and the savage goddess, who stared back in

amazement at the fate of their priestess. Then elation took her, for she lived on and her enemies lay dead, victims of the horror that they had planned for her. She lifted both arms in Sirna's own gesture and cried in Sumerian, "Inanna! Inanna! The cursed ones are destroyed and your servant lives!" She felt tears on her cheeks and heard voices as the crowd began to mutter its bewilderment.

There was a sudden clatter of arms, and marching men entered from the various side doors. The first twenty or so wore the strange masks CeLa had noticed earlier, that of the bull horns, bearded face and slanting eyes. Their tunics were black. The remainder of the gathering army wore the ordinary clothes of Daro and their weapons were at the ready. They moved to block off the exits lest the people try to flee. A slave ran forward to fetch the bull away.

CeLa caught up one of the daggers from the bloody pulp that was Sirna even as she rejoiced that her enemy had met so appropriate an end. She held the dagger in front of her and raised her head, ready once more to fight for her life. She had no fear and no thought of her naked body; only survival mattered now and her lips parted in a faint smile as she faced this new challenge.

A tall man in a bull mask approached her, sheathing his sword. He put out one hand to her as he pushed the mask back on his head. "CeLa, CeLa." The anguish in his voice made it break and his face emerged twisted with pain.

CeLa looked upon he whom she had not thought to see again this side of the netherworld. "Kir? But you are dead?"

"Obviously not, foolish woman." He threw the mask to the ground and caught her in his arms, straining her to him. She put her head on his shoulder and this time the tears poured down. "CeLa, my wife!" His voice broke and they could only hold each other in this time when words had no meaning and life was restored to them both.

Time faded for Kir and CeLa then and they had no idea how long they stood in the midst of the place of death, on the blood-smeared sand, and murmured to each other words of love and survival. Noise rose and faded as the soldiers surrounded the followers of Sirna and removed their weapons, then marched them away. A few resisted and were quickly dealt with, but the majority yielded to the superior forces.

There was a cough at Kirs' elbow and they looked up to see the chunky figure of Dahrata standing there. He, like Kir, was battle begrimed, and his face bore the marks of sleepless nights. Several of his men stood behind him and from their smiles there was no doubt as to how the battle had gone.

Dahrata said, "Lady CeLa, we thank all the gods that you live. Are you grievously battered?" His ugly face was full of sincere concern and his eyes were warm. He who had been an enemy was also a good friend.

CeLa looked down at herself, wrapped as she was in the dirty short cloak that Kir had removed from his own shoulders; she was bloody and sandy, with numerous small cuts and a slash on her arm where Sirna's knife had glanced off it. Her whole body ached from the strain it had undergone in the turn over the bull. She leaned against Kir, who clasped her warmly as she answered, "I still live, King Dahrata."

Kir said, "And the city? How stands it?"

Dahrata's eyes burned with momentary anger as he said, "The plotters have been taken and will pay the penalty. Those who joined our forces in the field and as we entered the city will be set free to pursue their own lives. Those who think to continue this rebellion will be wiped out."

CeLa heard him through a fog of exhaustion. Her breath came slowly and she longed for fresh air. Dahrata saw the movement and ceased his speech.

"Kir, my friend, take your wife and go with these men to the palace. Both of you have endured much and I shall not be ungrateful."

They went through the corridors that CeLa had not thought to see again and with every step the darkness seemed to dissipate. Bodies littered several levels and the crudely cut steps were sticky with blood. The followers of Sirna and her cruel goddess had not given up their ambition easily. Finally they climbed a steep incline and emerged some distance beyond the citadel into the light of day. The exit was so small and well concealed behind a thatch of palms and bricks that one could easily have passed and not known what horror lay below.

It was a bright, hot morning with a small breeze blowing and the sky shining blue over them. CeLa drew in deep breaths of the freshness and spread her arms wide. Kir looked down at her and said gently, "What of the child? Do you hold him still?"

CeLa was to remember that he thought of her first and then the child next. The hawk face was drained and tired but his eyes held no shadow. "I hold our child securely, Kir, be it male or female."

Then before the men of the army and several of the interested passing citizens of Daro, Kir took her in his arms and said to her yielding mouth, "I love you and I think some part of me has always done so."

Her body said what her mouth and words had already said so long ago. They were one, bound together in passion and adversity, won at last to love beyond the body, to the eternal force between them both.

Kir and CeLa were given royal rooms in the palace of Dahrata and their every need was anticipated. Servants brought food, wine, fruit, fresh clothes and scent for the baths that they took together. Two others stood constantly at the door lest anything else be required.

In the first healing it was enough for them to be together to caress and touch and kiss as they sat long in the laving waters of the bath that was a fundamental part of every house in Daro. The soreness and pain ebbed from CeLa's body and mind as the fearful image of the savage goddess faded from her dreams with Kir's clasping of her in his arms. They were young and had come to each other through fearful odds. For the moment it was enough.

When they came at last to speak of what they had endured, Kir told CeLa that the tiger hunt had progressed for a day and a night before the rebel forces attacked them by surprise. The defenders of the city had been lured forth with news that the king had been defeated in battle with a jungle tribe and needed them. Then those remaining in Daro had been attacked by Sirna's followers, who had carried the day.

"All this was going on while I was a prisoner of Jagon." CeLa mused again at the enormity of what she had escaped.

"Yes, Sirna meant to rule from the time she arrived here. So powerful was her will that she almost succeeded. Worship of the Mother has always been carried on here in a very intense manner and she took advantage of that. Jagon sought to use her, to his own undoing. Ambition made them join forces here as in Sumer." He kissed the upturned face so close to his and saw desire kindle there.

CeLa said, "How did you know where I was and even that I still lived?"

"I did not. Many of the citizens who thought they disliked the rule of Dahrata thought again when knowledge of Sirna's ways was made public. They escaped the city and came to join us. Many had known of the underground paths near the citadel—it is very old—and some of the hardiest of us put on the ceremonial masks and went to the sacrificial area. I saw you, CeLa, in that battle with the bull. You were braver than I could ever have been. Where did you learn that skill? Apparently none know it here, although the bull has been part of the worship of the goddess here in Daro for generations."

She turned in his arms and her bare breasts brushed against his chest. His manhood rose, hard and strong to her hand. "It was the gift of the Cretans. Beca stood a true friend to me."

They were silent for a few moments, remembering those who had not been true to them. Although Ndar had rescued them in kindness, he had yet been the tool of Sirna, who had ever looked for ways to prove her right to power. Utis had told her of the woman from across the seas and that had signed CeLa's death. Now Utis was dead by her own hand and Ndar in battle.

Kir said, "It is done, CeLa. The future is ours. Come, wife, I would taste your sweetness." They melted together then in the eagerness of passion become love as their mouths clung and parted and his hardness explored the reaches of her body. There was a depth and intensity to their lovemaking that had been there only slightly before; now it would grow to enrich the rest of their lives. They whispered together of their love and of the child to come until passion claimed them again.

Two days later, Dahrata, King of Mohenjo-daro, received them in private audience and made his gratitude known for the part they had played in making his throne secure. Jewels, fabrics, statuary, slaves, a rich house—all was theirs for the asking.

Kir said, "You are more than generous, Lord King, but I am first and always the servant of Sargon of Akkad and Sumer. It was he who sent us on a mission and that charge will not be completed until we stand before him with duty done."

"It is so also with me, Lord King," answered CeLa as the piercing eyes turned to her.

Dahrata rose, suddenly majestic in spite of his battered face and fleshy body. "I envy your king such servants as well as the skill of his physician. My swiftest ship shall return you to the land of the two rivers and my councillors shall discuss trade relations with his. When Daro reaches beyond her boundaries with ship and sword and trade to grow powerful, Sumer and Akkad shall know her friendship. The Mother Goddess is honored here, always, as in your own land, but this time we laud life and not death."

Kir and CeLa bent before him, grateful for his generosity and understanding. Then Kir said, "In the name of Sargon, I thank you."

"I would you both were citizens of Daro," was the simple answer.

The sickle ship rode high in the river and the sails flapped in the fresh wind of early morning as they left the city of Mohenjo-daro some fourteen days later. The ship was loaded with items for trade and gifts to the ruler of Sumer. There were councillors and an escort for Kir and CeLa, gifts to the gods of Sumer and special ones for the goddess of love, Inanna, who was Sargon's own, as she had come to be for Kir and CeLa.

CeLa stood high on the prow as she had often dreamed in moments of adversity. Her hair streamed behind her and her tunic clung to her slender body. Kir was with her, his dark face alight as they waved their farewells to the king and his party at the vanishing wharf beside the great citadel. The rich smell of mud and lapping water came to their nostrils and several sea birds circled overhead. Their escort ship moved slowly ahead of them, the sickle emblem of Daro flashing on her sail. They seemed one with the richness of the world present and to come.

CeLa lifted her face into the wind and turned to Kir, "It is fair sailing now, my husband."

He turned her body to his and clasped her about the waist. His voice was soft as he answered, "Now and evermore, CeLa of my heart."

Epilogue

Trade relationships were established between Sargon of Akkad and Sumer and Dahrata of Mohenjo-daro, and proved vastly profitable for both. Sargon founded a great dynasty in the united land between the two rivers and his power increased with the years. Kir remained his honored friend, councillor and physician, and CeLa became his friend as well. Sargon held ceremonies of thanksgiving for their safe return at the great ziggurat in Nippur, holy city of Enlil, where he had first celebrated his victory over the ruler of Lagash and Umma. CeLa and Kir's first child was indeed a strong son, named Sar-Ina in honor of the king and the goddess, Inanna. Their names were great in the chronicles of the united lands.

Bestsellers